KU-498-482

PRINCE OF HAZEL AND OAK

JOHN LENAHAN

FRIDAY
FICTION

The Friday Project
An imprint of HarperCollins*Publishers*
77–85 Fulham Palace Road,
Hammersmith, London W6 8JB

www.thefridayproject.co.uk
www.harpercollins.co.uk

This edition published by The Friday Project 2011
1

Copyright © John Lenahan 2011

John Lenahan asserts the moral right to be
identified as the author of this work

A catalogue record for this book is
available from the British Library

ISBN: 978-0-00-742559-4

Typeset in Adobe Garamond by
G&M Designs Limited, Raunds, Northamptonshire

Printed and bound in Great Britain by Clays Ltd, St Ives plc

Mixed Sources
Product group from well-managed
forests and other controlled sources
www.fsc.org Cert no. SW-COC-001806
© 1996 Forest Stewardship Council

FSC is a non-profit international organisation established to promote the
responsible management of the world's forests. Products carrying the FSC
label are independently certified to assure customers that they come
from forests that are managed to meet the social, economic and
ecological needs of present and future generations.

Find out more about HarperCollins and the environment at
www.harpercollins.co.uk/green

This novel is entirely a work of fiction. The names, characters and incidents
portrayed in it are the work of the author's imagination. Any resemblance to
actual persons, living or dead, events or localities is entirely coincidental.

All rights reserved. No part of this publication may be reproduced,
stored in a retrieval system, or transmitted, in any form or by any means,
electronic, mechanical, photocopying, recording or otherwise,
without the prior permission of the publishers.

This book is sold subject to the condition that it shall not, by way of trade
or otherwise, be lent, re-sold, hired out or otherwise circulated without the
publisher's prior consent in any form of binding or cover other than that
in which it is published and without a similar condition including
this condition being imposed on the subsequent purchaser.

For the oh so achingly beautiful Nadene

Chapter One
Detective Fallon

Detective Fallon seemed to have given up on shouting.

'I've seen people get off by claiming insanity,' he said, sitting back in his chair. 'Conor, you ain't doing it right.'

'So you don't think I'm crazy then?' I asked.

'Oh, I think you're plenty crazy but not insane.'

'Aren't they synonyms?'

'Not in my thesaurus. If you want to get off by reason of insanity you have to be a nutcase all the time, you know, with the drooling and the swatting at imaginary bats. You, on the other hand, kill your father and then act completely normal – except for claiming that Daddy was attacked by Imps and Pixies from Faerieland.'

'Tir na Nog,' I corrected.

'Sorry, from Tir na Nog.'

'And there are no Pixies in Tir na Nog.'

'Look, O'Neil' – Detective Fallon leaned in and I could see he was inches away from returning to shouting mode – 'you've been arrested for murder. They've got a death penalty in this state.'

'I didn't kill my father – honest. If I killed him where's the body? If there is no body there can't be a murder.'

'You've been watching too much TV, O'Neil. You can fry without out a body – trust me.'

1

'So what do you suggest I do?'

Fallon softened back into his good-cop mode. 'Tell the truth.'

'Oh that. I was kinda hoping you had a better suggestion.'

The truth – telling the truth is how I had gotten into this mess in the first place. As soon as I returned to what the Tir na Nogians call 'the Real World', all of the Real World problems crashed in on me like a tidal wave. I've never been very good at lying but what else could I do? Dad's boss had reported him missing and the cops were waiting for me when I returned. They had lots of questions after finding the front door wide open and the living room trashed. I made up a lame excuse about a boisterous party and told them that Dad was on a spontaneous trip with old fishing buddies. The cops accepted that explanation, but as I later found out, they didn't believe it.

Sally was really mad at me. She went on and on about how worried she had been and how thoughtless I was for not getting in touch. The sad thing was I didn't care – not only about Sally but about pretty much everything. What's that old saying? Home is where the heart is. Well, I had left my heart back in The Land.

Even though I missed the actual ceremony, apparently I had graduated high school. I forced myself to show up for enrolment at the University of Scranton but after just one day I knew I couldn't face it. What could a college professor teach me? What did they really know?

All food tasted like cardboard and, even worse, when I slept – I didn't dream. I remembered once telling Fergal that some of the Real World was like The Land but covered in a grey film. Now all of it seemed like that.

And then there was Essa. I knew it was unfair but I couldn't help comparing her with Sally – and Sally didn't match up – how could she? It didn't take a soothsayer to notice my thoughts were elsewhere. Sally finally had enough. She said I had changed, and she was right – we broke up.

I suppose I should have gotten a job but that seemed even more trivial than university, so I spent my time staring at the walls. I couldn't even stomach watching television.

The trouble really started when the electric company turned off the power. I hadn't opened any mail, let alone paid bills, but darkness forced me to do something about it. I had the PIN numbers to Dad's bank accounts (well, he didn't need money any more, with him living on top of a gold mine). I can remember standing in front of the cash machine as Dad's words swirled around in my head, 'There is nothing back there for you.' I hated it when he was right. I punched the buttons and withdrew a wad of cash. I didn't think I could feel any lower – I was wrong.

The police showed up at the house that evening with a search warrant. They had been monitoring Dad's bank accounts, waiting for me to do exactly what I did. Forensic specialists in plastic jumpsuits took samples of the carpet, confiscated my clothes and all of the weird weapons in the house. When they finished, a policeman told me not to leave town, like he was in some old TV cops show.

Word of the police raid spread through the neighbourhood like wildfire. The authorities, it seems, weren't the only ones who thought I had committed patricide. I didn't know what to do. Sally showed up as I was packing in preparation for making a run for it. I decided to tell her the truth. I sat her down and told her everything (playing down the Essa stuff) and amazingly she took it in her stride. She told me that she believed me and wished me luck. Two minutes after leaving the house, she called the cops and told them I was crazy. The only crazy thing I had done was to come back for her.

A uniformed officer and a badge-brandishing Detective Fallon were standing on my front porch when I opened the door with a bag over my shoulder. It was Halloween. The first thing I said to Detective Fallon was, 'Don't you have a policeman's costume?' The first thing he said to me was, 'Conor O'Neil, I have a warrant for your arrest.'

'Here's how I see it, Conor,' Detective Fallon said as he paced around the interrogation room. 'Your father – the mad one-handed ancient language professor – was a strange man. I'm not saying that to make you angry, but I've done some research and you have to admit he was, at least, unusual.'

'You won't get any arguments from me on that one,' I said. 'Pop was the weirdest guy in town.'

'I also heard that he used to make you sword-fight with him just to get your spending money.'

'Strange but true.'

'So one day you just had enough, in the heat of one of your fencing practices—'

'Broadswords,' I interrupted, 'Dad hates fencing.'

'OK, in the heat of one of your broadsword bouts you flipped out and accidentally killed him – then you panicked and buried the body.'

I laughed, 'You don't know how many times I came close to doing just that, but no, that's not what happened.'

'Conor, we found your father's blood on the carpet.'

'He was injured when we were attacked. I didn't do it.'

'And we found traces of blood in a splatter pattern on a leather shirt.'

'That's not Dad's blood.'

'The pathologist disagrees. She said the shirt and the carpet had one of the most unusual DNA patterns that she had ever seen.'

'That's 'cause the blood on the shirt came from one of his relatives.'

'I thought your father was an orphan?'

'So did I!' I said, throwing my hands in the air. 'Look, I've explained all of this. Haven't you been listening?'

Fallon sat down and sighed, 'To be honest with you, no I haven't. As soon as you start going on about hobgoblins and dragons I just glaze over. I figured if I let you ramble on with this cock and bull story you would get it out of your system and we could get down to the facts.'

'Sorry to disappoint you, Detective Fallon …'

'Call me Brendan.'

'Sorry to disappoint you, Detective Fallon,' I repeated, 'but those are the facts.'

'OK, Conor, I'll humour you. Tell me this thing from the top and I promise I'll pay attention.'

So I told him the truth. What else could I do? I knew it wasn't going to help but lying wasn't working either. I told him the whole tale about how Dad and I were abducted and taken to The Land of Eternal Youth – Tir na Nog – where I found out that Dad was the heir to the throne. Unfortunately, because of an ancient prediction saying that *The son of the one-handed prince would be the ruin of all The Land,*' everybody wanted me dead, especially the unlawful king – Dad's nasty piece of work brother, Cialtie. With the help of a mother I never knew I had, we escaped Cialtie's dungeon and hooked up with an army that was preparing to forcefully oust my slimy uncle. They had scary information suggesting that Uncle Cialtie had hidden a magical bomb that was threatening to destroy everything. Dad and I and a couple of others snuck into the castle before the attack and disarmed the bomb. Cialtie was dethroned but he got away.

'So,' Fallon said with a quizzical look on his face, 'you saved the world?'

'I had help.'

'And when in all of this did you cut your uncle's hand off?'

'Just after Dad reattached his.'

'I take it all back, Conor, you are insane after all.'

After listening to myself I wondered if he was right. It wasn't the first time, since my return, that I had grappled with my sanity. The only thing that had kept me from going over the edge was the stuff I had brought back with me: my clothes, Fergal's Banshee blade and Mom's present. Many a night I sat and just touched them, wishing they could somehow transport me to The Land. But they weren't with me now, and at that moment I wondered if I had imagined them, too.

I think I would have lost it right then and there if Fallon hadn't unknowingly thrown me a lifeline. He reached into an evidence folder and placed in front of me a paperback book-sized sheet of gold in a wooden frame. 'What is this?' he asked.

I picked it up. 'It's called an *emain* slate,' I said, feeling my throat tighten. 'My mother gave it to me.'

'It's solid gold.'

'I know.'

'We found faint writing on it. What's it for?'

'Anything written on this slate appears on its twin.' I picked up a pen from the table and clicked the ball point back into the chamber, with the blunt end I wrote the contents of my heart. I wrote, '*HELP!*'

'And you are saying your mother has the other one in this land of yours.'

'Yes.'

'So how is she?'

My anger erupted. How dare he be so flippant about this! If I had had a *banta* stick I would have clocked him in the head for that. But anger gave way to understanding. Firstly, he was trying to get me mad and I wasn't going to play his game, and secondly, he didn't take this seriously, he didn't understand how deep his quip cut.

After spending one day back in the Real World and waking from a dreamless sleep, I realised how much of a mistake returning had been. I had found a mother – my mother – something I had wished for with all of my heart, for all of my life, and as soon as I found her – I left her. How stupid is that? I wrote her every day for a month and spent countless hours wiping the tears out of my eyes just so I could see that the emain slate gave me no reply.

I looked Fallon in the eyes and admitted, 'It doesn't work here.'

'Are you sure? Maybe your mother sent you little notes on this thing and told you to kill your father?'

'No. I told you it doesn't work!'

'Look, Conor, I'm just trying to help you. The story about the Leprechauns didn't convince me that you were insane, but getting letters from an imaginary mother just might save you from the chop.'

I thought about that. Maybe he was right, maybe he was my friend and this was good advice. I looked into his kind countenance and almost bought it, but then his eyes gave away the truth.

'You're not trying to help me,' I said. 'I know what you are doing. You are trying to get me to say I did it, so you can get a tick in your little score sheet and go home to your wife and kids and tell them that, "Daddy got a bad guy today", but I am not going to oblige. I did *not* kill my father!' I screamed. 'I love him and I miss him and I … I hate myself …' I broke down and wept.

'Why do you hate yourself, Conor?' Fallon said in a calm voice, like a psychiatrist getting to the crux of a problem. 'You hate yourself because you loved him and you hurt him?'

I picked my head up off my damp arms and looked at him through the blur of my tears. 'No,' I said, 'I hate myself for being so stupid. I hate myself – for leaving him.'

Fallon picked up his notepad and stood up. 'Let's take a break,' he said. 'Maybe you should just sit and think for a while.' I could tell he was disappointed. I'm sure he thought I was about to confess. He unlocked the door, but before he went through he stopped and said, 'Just one thing.'

I looked at him confused.

'I don't have kids. I just got one – a girl. And I promise I won't tell her you're a bad guy. You're not a bad guy, Conor, you're troubled and *in* trouble – but you're not a bad guy.'

That was it. I had hit rock bottom. I dropped my head onto the emain slate and closed my eyes not caring if I slept or not. Sleeping brought me no relief; I couldn't even escape into a dream.

I felt the message before I saw it. My cheek was resting on the emain slate and a tickling sensation stirred me enough to lift my head and take a look. There underneath my cry for help was a sentence, 'Are you in trouble?'

'Yes!' I screamed. I don't think I had ever been happier in my life. Like a bawling child lost in a shopping mall, I was found, and my mother was going to clutch me to her breast and wipe away my tears. I reached for the pen and realised that Fallon had taken it with him. I frantically searched around the room trying to find something I could etch a reply with but the only thing in the room was me, two chairs and a table. I tried to use my fingernails but I had bitten them down to nothing. I hammered on the door and shouted. After what seemed like ages it opened. Standing there was Detective Fallon and a uniformed cop holding a club.

'Gimme your pen!' I shouted as I jumped up and down.

'Back off, Conor,' he demanded.

'OK, OK,' I said, putting my hands up and doing as I was told, 'just give me a pen.'

The two policemen cautiously entered the room. 'Why do you want a pen?' Fallon asked.

'I just do! Give me your damn pen!'

'I'm not going to give you my pen,' the detective said in pacifying tones, 'until you tell me what you want it for.'

'OK, I did it. I want to confess. Give me your notepad and pen and I'll write a confession.'

'What did you do?'

'What you said I did. Give me your pen and I'll write it all down for you – everything.'

The two policemen looked at each other in amazement. Fallon gave me a sceptical look but he offered out his notepad and pen. I snatched the ballpoint, ran over to the table and turned the slate around to write on it. Fallon grabbed the pen back before I could etch a mark and tried to read the Gaelic sentence aloud. 'Did you write this?' he said.

'Yes, yes I did. See I'm crazy. I'm writing letters to myself in made-up languages. Here I'll show you.' I reached for the slate but he pulled it out of my reach.

We stared at each other, his eyes narrowed with an effort to figure out what was going on. I gazed back wide-eyed and pleading. 'Please,' I said. 'Trust me, this is important.'

He handed me the slate and I wrote on it, 'YES!!!'

I dropped the slate on the table and stared at it. So did Fallon. Just when I thought my eyes were going to burn a hole in the gold surface, letters appeared one by one. 'I WILL BE RIGHT THERE,' it said.

Fallon's eyes shot up to look at me. They were a lot wider than before. 'What just happened here?'

'I got a magic email.'

'What … what does it say?'

'It says, "I will be right there."'

'And what does that mean?'

'It means – my mom's gonna bail me out.'

Chapter Two
Jail Break

'Conor,' Detective Fallon said, 'no one is going to bail you out.' It was just the two of us again. I had finally calmed down enough for him to dismiss the guard. 'You saw what was written on the slate.'

'I did. How did you do that, some sort of conjuring trick?'

That made me laugh. 'Not a conjuring trick, it's a magic trick – real magic.'

Fallon picked up the emain slate and turned it in his hands. 'So what, is there some sort of electric gadget in here?'

'Look at it. It's just a sheet of gold. Come on, you're a detective. What did Sherlock Holmes say? "When you have eliminated the impossible, whatever remains, however improbable, must be the truth." I've been telling you the truth all along. My father is fine and my mother is coming to take me to him.'

'So you imagine she is going to show up and you and she are just to walk out of here.'

'Ride out of here,' I corrected, 'she'll be on a horse.'

'OK, that's it,' Fallon said, slapping his palms on the table, 'you win, I'll get you the psychologist.'

He stood to leave but I grabbed his wrist. He instinctively balled his other hand into a fist but then relaxed when he saw I wasn't going to attack him – I had something important to say.

'When she comes, Brendan, don't fight her. She is … well, she's not a normal mom.'

Fallon threw off my grip and said, 'Bah!' Just then there was a knock at the door. A young officer poked his head in looking excited. 'What?' Fallon barked.

'There are two women outside on horses,' the officer stuttered. 'You have to see them, they're gorgeous. They want to see the prisoner.'

Fallon whipped his head around and stared at me, the colour draining from his face.

I shrugged. 'That will be my ride.'

I paced around the room for what seemed like an eternity. I don't think I had ever been so excited, it took all of my willpower to stop from jumping up and down shouting, 'Mommy, Mommy, Mommy!' I tried to relax. 'Right, what should I do?' I said, talking to myself. 'Pack.' I looked around the room and laughed, the only thing there was the emain slate. I picked it up. I paced some more. 'Come on, come on,' I said out loud.

The door flew open and Fallon came storming in. 'What the hell is going on here?'

'Where is she? What's happening?'

'There are two women outside on huge horses wearing trick-or-treat outfits. The one who spoke said her name was Deirdre and that the other was called Nieve.'

'Nieve! Nieve's here? She's my aunt.'

Fallon was angry. He grabbed my shirt with both hands and pulled me close to his face. 'What are you playing at?'

I tried to be as calm as I could. 'What did you tell them?'

'I told them they had to wait.'

'You didn't …?'

'I did.'

'That probably wasn't a good idea.'

'Why?'

'Well, I don't know my aunt all that well but waiting isn't Mom's strong suit.'

As if on cue a huge explosion shook the room. Fallon let go of me and said, 'Stay here!'

As the door swung behind him I dived across the room and painfully trapped my arm in the doorjamb before it could lock.

The hallway was filled with dust and smoke. Cops were lying unconscious everywhere. In the distance I could hear screams of 'My eyes!' Nieve was casually riding towards me. She had blown out all of the door archways so she didn't even have to duck. Her right hand was held out to her side and two marble-sized balls of gold were orbiting it like atoms around a nucleus. Two policemen appeared out of a room to her left. Without even looking at them, she flicked her wrist and the gold marbles hit them in the chest. They were thrown back into the room with an explosion of light.

She spotted me. 'Conor, are you harmed?'

'No, I'm OK,' I shouted. 'Where's Mom?'

'She is outside preparing a portal. Catch,' she said, throwing me an oak banta stick.

I examined it. 'I prefer hazel.'

She gave me a dirty look but then smiled. 'Come,' she said, holding out her hand.

I started to reach for it when I heard a voice from behind me say, 'Freeze!'

I turned to see Detective Fallon pointing a gun at Nieve. He was obviously freaked.

'Nobody move. Put your hands in the air and get off the horse, lady.'

'Conor,' Nieve said, 'what is that in his hand?'

'It's a weapon, Aunt Nieve.' She went to reach under her cloak.

'I said freeze!'

'Hold on, Nieve,' I said, 'let me talk to him.'

Fallon kept the gun pointed at Nieve but flicked a glance in my direction. He was real edgy.

'Brendan,' I said in my calmest voice, 'this is my Aunt Nieve, my father's sister. She's from Tir na Nog, that's why she is riding a horse. Remember, I told you about that?'

The muscle in Fallon's jaw twitched. I wasn't sure if I was getting through to him.

'I'm going to go with her. Put your gun down and no one will get hurt.'

'What, I'm just supposed to let you walk out of here?' His gun shook as he spoke. 'She killed all of my officers.'

'Conor, why are we talking? What is he saying that is so important?'

'He is upset 'cause you killed his men.'

'They will live,' Nieve said. I could hear the impatience in her voice. 'Conor, we do not have time for this.'

She was right. The longer we stood here the more likely it was that more cops would show up and I was desperate to see my mother. I decided to take Fallon out of the equation.

Unfortunately I was holding my banta stick upside-down so I had to flick the gun out of his hand with the heavy end and then use the light end on his neck. Dahy wouldn't have been very impressed with the blow but it did the job and the detective went down. I grabbed Nieve's hand and she lifted me onto the back of the saddle as if I weighed nothing.

'I never got your Christmas card,' she said as she manoeuvred the horse into the opposite direction.

'Christmas isn't for two months.'

'Well, that explains it.' I wasn't sure if that was a joke or not.

We rode back through what used to be a police station. No one stopped us. The only sounds were a few moans. Daylight poured through what used to be the front door. I shaded my eyes and was

rewarded with the sight of my mother. My heart leapt and I invol-
untarily kicked the back of the horse, the mount lurched and I
almost fell off.

'Be careful, Conor!' Nieve said. 'I would prefer not to fall.'

'Of course, sorry.'

Nieve walked her horse next to Mom's. I hugged Mom and she
returned it. 'Conor, are you all right?'

'I am now,' I said.

'Deirdre,' Nieve said, 'I do not like this place.'

'How's Dad?' I asked, still holding my mother. I never wanted
to let go.

Mom pushed me back. 'Nieve is right. We must get out of here
– we can talk when we get home.'

Mom took some sap and a gold disc out of her saddlebag and
began to chant as she rubbed them both between her hands.
Amber light shot from her fingertips and created a spider web that
eventually filled in to produce a large glowing disc.

'Are you ready?' Mom asked.

'Born ready.'

'Everybody stay right where you are!' It was Fallon – with one
hand he held his neck, in the other he held a gun.

Nieve and Mom stepped their horses sideways for a look. 'Who
is this?' Mom demanded.

'Mom, this is Detective Fallon – Detective Fallon, this is my
mother.'

Fallon pointed the gun menacingly. 'Everybody get down, we're
all going back inside.'

Mom and Nieve started to reach inside their cloaks. I raised my
hand and stopped them. 'No we're not, Brendan, we don't belong
here – I don't belong here.'

'I said get down!'

'They can't, Brendan, it would kill them. You see that glowing
disc over there, that's a door into another world – The Land. We

are going to enter it and we will be gone. If we are not, then you can shoot me.'

'I'm warning you, O'Neil.'

'Brendan, I didn't kill my father, he is right on the other side of that door, you have the wrong man. You said it yourself – I'm not a bad guy. Please – you have to trust me.'

I could almost hear his brain cells working; he lowered his gun and we walked towards the disc. I didn't look back.

We arrived in the Hall of Spells. I expected the journey to be painful (most of this Shadowmagic stuff is) but other than a few spots in front of my vision and an annoying ringing in my ears, I was fine.

I jumped down and gave Mom a proper hug. She returned it quickly but then said, 'I have to go, I will talk to you later.' I didn't like the way she looked; she was still undisputedly the most beautiful woman in the world, but in her eyes I saw a haggard look. She dashed out of the room.

I was a bit taken aback. I turned to Nieve and said, 'Is she all right?'

'She is fine, Conor.'

I let out a sigh of relief and then took in a lungful of air and it hit me, I could feel the vitality seep into every cell. A smile took over my face and I said to myself, 'I'm back.' Then I threw my hands out to my sides and shouted to the roof, 'I'm back!' I startled a stable boy who quickly led the horses away – that's when I saw him. Detective Fallon with dishevelled clothes and hair shooting out in all directions was crouched in the corner and he had a wild glint in his eyes. He looked like one of those girls in a slasher movie that had just witnessed her entire sorority get killed.

'Oh my gods,' I said.

Our eyes locked, it scared me, I had seen that look before. He was wearing the same face that Fergal wore when he went mad and tried to kill Cialtie.

'Brendan?'

At the sound of his name he pulled the gun from between his knees and levelled it at me.

I dropped my banta stick and said, 'Hey, calm down, Brendan, no one is going to hurt you.' I walked slowly towards him, palms up. He aimed the gun at my face, his arm shaking. I wondered if he even knew who he was. 'It's OK, you're safe. Your name is Brendan Fallon, you have a wife and a daughter, it's OK we'll sort this out.'

At the mention of his family a spark of sanity fluttered in his eyes. He dipped the gun a bit, but then both of us were startled by a voice to the left shouting my name.

'Conor – catch!'

A banta came sailing through the air. As I caught it, time slowed like it always does when I'm in mortal peril. I saw the lights go out in Fallon's eyes and I could actually see the muscles in his fingers as they tightened on the trigger, I could almost hear them. I suspected that guns didn't work in The Land but I didn't want to take that chance. I performed the same manoeuvre as before, except this time I hit the gun with the light end of the stick and rounded on Fallon's head with the heavy end. I hit him way harder than I wanted to – that wasn't my fault, the stick had been thrown by Araf and his stick is filled with lead. The gun clicked at some point during the fracas but it didn't fire. I was right, they don't work here. Fallon went down like a ton of concrete and I instantly felt real guilty.

I rushed to him – he was out cold. Nieve strolled over and placed her hands on both sides of his head. 'Did I kill him?' I asked.

'He'll live,' she replied and unceremoniously dropped his head back onto the floor.

Two guards arrived and I instructed them to carry him to the infirmary and keep a guard. 'Be nice to him,' I called after them, 'and make sure he gets some of that willow tea when he wakes up, he's going to need it.'

'Can I have my stick back?'

'Araf!' I shouted as I turned. I had almost forgotten he was there. I ran to the Imp and wrapped my arms around him. It was like hugging a refrigerator and I could tell he didn't like it.

'Are you injured?' he asked.

'No, I'm fine.'

He nodded. 'I have to get back to work now,' he said and turned to leave.

'Well, it's great to see you again too,' I called after him. I laughed – this was the strangest of homecomings.

Well, it was just me and Nieve. Not my favourite relative but I didn't care. She stood in the middle of the room wringing her hands; the look on her face wiped the smile off my own.

'Where's Dad?' I asked.

'Conor,' she said, looking down at her hands and then directly into my eyes, 'Oisin is dying.'

Chapter Three
Dad

I followed Nieve through the winding corridors of the west wing. Dad was in The Lord's Chamber, the same one that Cialtie had used and where we had found Dad's runehand.

'Prepare yourself,' Nieve warned, 'he does not look good.'

My stomach churned as I opened the door. Mom, Fand and an Imp-healer were standing around a bed wearing expressions ranging from puzzlement to grief. I had to cover my mouth to hide the gasp – he looked awful. My father's skin was ashen grey, paper-like, and his face was dotted with sores. Most of his hair had fallen out and what was left was pure white. My first thought was that he was dead already, that's how bad he looked. I knelt down next to the bed and held his hand.

'Dad, Dad, it's me, Conor.'

I didn't think he could hear me but then his eyes flickered and opened. An almost Duir smile lit his face. 'Conor? Conor, are you all right?' His voice was faint and raspy. 'Deirdre said you were in trouble.'

'I'm fine, Dad.' I didn't know what to say, his famous dark eyes had lost their shine. I could hardly stand it.

'Good,' he said, 'I was worried about you. So how was your trip home?'

I laughed, one of those painful laughs that are half a chuckle and half crying. 'It was awful.'

'What happened when you got back?'

'The police arrested me for your murder.'

This brought a huge grin to his face. 'No!'

'Yes,' I laughed through tears.

Dad started to laugh too but his laughter was replaced by a spasm of coughs. He had to close his eyes for a half a minute. When he opened them he squeezed my hand and said, 'I'm glad you're here.'

'Me too.' I held his hand for a while and then said, 'Thanks, Dad.'

'For what?'

'I never realised until I went back, just how much you gave up for me. I don't know how you stood it.'

'Well, when it got really bad, I used to go to your room and watch you sleep, that gave me strength.'

I dropped my head on his chest and wept openly. He stroked my hair. 'I have to rest now,' he said, 'we'll talk later.'

Mom put her hands on my shoulders and guided me out. In the hallway we held onto each other; then she led me into an adjacent room.

A Leprechaun brought in a tray of tea. Mom thanked her and sent her away. As she handed me a cup, I asked, 'What's the matter with him?'

'We're not sure,' she said as she poured herself a cup, 'but we think it is his hand.'

'His runehand? The one he reattached in the Choosing?'

'Yes. The Land has a life force that binds us to it; your father gave that all up when he escaped to the Real World. I thought getting his hand back would restore his immortality – I was wrong, it has done just the opposite. Our best guess is that The Land is confused, it sees your father as two things, a young hand that belongs here and an older man that does not. The Land is choosing his hand.'

'Like a heart transplant patient rejecting a donor organ?'

'I don't know what you mean but *rejecting* is a good word. Oisin's hand is rejecting the rest of him. It is killing him.'

'Isn't there anything you can do?'

'We have tried everything, to no avail, but there is one desperate measure left to us. Just before you arrived Fand and I decided it is our only hope.'

'What?'

We are going to use Shadowmagic to encase all of Oisin in tree sap, just as I did with his hand. It will not cure him but it may give us time.'

'Are you sure it'll work?'

Mom took a long time before answering. 'No,' she said, 'I am not.'

I stood on the ramparts of the east wall. The stones under my feet were new and whiter than the rest of the castle. This was the wall that was blown out when Cialtie's golden circle misfired. Lorcan had done a fine job rebuilding it.

I looked out and took a deep breath, savouring the pollution-free smell of summer's end. At a first glance I thought the forest in front of me was on fire. The oaks were incandescent with the colours of fall. Leaves the size of notepad paper had transformed themselves into reds and yellows and golds that looked as if they were lit from within, like Christmas decorations. I remembered the first time I had seen this vista when it was green, I remembered the strength and joy that it had given me. I felt the strength returning, but the joy was denied to me now.

Below I saw the top of the dolman that Fergal was buried under. 'Oh Fergal,' I said to myself, 'how I could use a friend right now.'

'I'm sorry, Conor,' said a voice from behind me – it was Araf. 'I'm sorry about your father and I'm sorry I was so short with you before. It wasn't my place to be the first to tell you and I'm not very good at hiding my emotions.'

'You surprise me, Araf, I didn't know you had any emotions,' I chided, trying to lighten the mood.

'I have them, Conor, although right now I wish I did not.'

I put my arm over his shoulder and together we looked down at Fergal's grave. 'I still miss him terribly,' he said. 'He was truly my brother – I never had the chance to tell him that.'

'He knew, my friend, he knew.'

A guard showed up and said my mother wanted to see me in The Lord's Chamber. Araf led me down to Dad's room but he didn't come in. When we got to the door he didn't say anything, he simply nodded. I think he must have used up all of his allotted words for the day. Mom, Nieve, Fand and the Imp-healer were standing around Dad's bed; a Shadowfire flickered on a table. I didn't think it was possible but he looked worse than he did only a couple of hours earlier.

'We are almost ready,' Mom said. 'He wants to speak to you.'

I knelt down next to him; he turned to me and I could see the effort it took. 'Conor,' he whispered, 'you must take the Choosing. The Land needs a Lord of Duir.'

'You're the Lord of Duir, Pop.'

'Promise me.'

'I promise.'

He straightened his head and took a deep breath. 'Deirdre,' he said, trying to raise his voice above a whisper, 'I'm ready.'

Mom placed a small gold disc on Dad's tongue. He received it like a Catholic at church, then Mom and Fand each picked up a waxy fist-sized ball of amber sap. They cupped their hands and held it over the Shadowfire; the sap melted leaving them both holding a pool of glowing amber, as if they had scooped water from a stream. Dad's sheets were removed and I gasped to see that the sores on his face covered his entire body. The only part of him that looked healthy was his runehand. Its heath and vitality only highlighted just how deathly the rest of him looked.

Mom and Fand stood at the foot of the bed incanting in Ogham – the oldest of tongues. As they chanted they let the sap drip onto Dad's toes. It covered his feet, then his ankles and then his legs, like it had a mind of its own. I watched in horror as the amber travelled up his chest. When it reached his neck he closed his eyes, took one last gasp of breath and was completely engulfed.

Mom carried away the remaining sap and let it drip into a bowl. It left no residue on her hands. Then she slowly examined the Shadowmagic shell. When she rolled Dad onto his side to have a look at his back, it shocked me to see him pop up like a marble statue. Fand covered him with a sheet as Mom placed her hands on both sides of his head. After a few minutes she let him go and wiped her nose on her forearm; she looked drained.

'Did it work?' I asked.

'We will know tomorrow,' she said.

I wanted to keep watch over Dad all night but Mom wouldn't let me. Since she missed my rebellious teenage years, I toyed with the idea of making this my first defiant stand against her, but she was right, I was exhausted.

She led me to a room two doors along. 'This is The Prince's Chamber,' she said, 'it once belonged to your father. It is your room now.'

It was huge. A massive bay window and an equally large four-poster bed were draped in purple fabric. *When I get some time*, I thought to myself, *I'm going to have to do some redecorating*. The walls were panelled in hand-carved oak depicting all of the major trees of The Land. I noticed one of the panels was full of chips and holes.

Mom followed my gaze. 'Oisin told me that is where he used to practise throwing Dahy's knives. He got in trouble for that.'

'I promise I won't throw any knives in here, Mom,' I said, but I knew I would.

She wrapped her arms around me. 'I have missed you. I wrote you every day.'

'Me too. How did you finally get the slates to work?'

'It was Samhain.'

'Samhain, I remember that word,' I said. 'When Dad wouldn't let me go out trick-or-treating at Halloween he used to say, "There is no way I am going to let you wander around alone during Samhain." What does that have to do with the emain slates?'

'Samhain is when The Land and the Real World are closest. The slate must have started to work simply because it was in range.'

'Well, I'm glad it did. I'm here now, Mom, and I'm not going anywhere.'

She squeezed me tighter then kissed me on the cheek. 'Get some rest.'

'You too, you look like you need it.'

'I will try,' she said and left me alone in my new bedroom.

A chambermaid came in and placed a pitcher of water next to a bowl on the dresser. When she turned I recognised her. It was the Leprechaun who helped Dad and me sneak into Cialtie's room. 'Aein!' I said, calling her by name.

I surprised her when I hugged her but then she returned it, her arms only making it to my sides.

'How is Lord Oisin?'

'Not good.'

'If he—' She stopped and placed her hand over her mouth as if to push back the words.

'What is it, Aein? You can say anything to me.'

23

'If … If Lord Oisin should die …' she said and made a little gesture like she was warding off evil spirits, 'will Cialtie come back?'

'Over my dead body.'

Her worried eyes went steely. 'Mine too.' We shared a determined smile. 'If you need anything, you pull that cord.'

'Thank you, Aein.'

'Welcome home, Young Prince.'

My head hit the pillow like I had been hit with Araf's banta stick. In that twilight moment between wakefulness and sleep I felt the impatience of a dream desperate to begin, like a troupe of actors waiting for the opening curtain. 'Here we go!' I mumbled aloud.

I was a bit disappointed with my first dream back. Deep down I had hoped that I would be able to have a conversation with my father, but my dream was a collage of fleeting images. Trees, salmon, horses, knives, castles, bears, mermaids, archers and a myriad of other images zoomed in and out of my sleep. I only had one vision that stayed with me. It was of a young girl I didn't recognise; she was crying, and an older woman that I somehow knew was her grandmother was comforting her.

I had slept later than I meant to. I dressed quickly and jogged to my father's room. Fand was sitting at his feet, cross-legged with her hands folded in her lap, Buddha-like. She turned to me when I entered. 'There is no change, Conor. We will know more after nightfall.' I leaned over and kissed Dad on the forehead; it was like kissing a cue ball, cold and hard. 'Hang in there, Pop,' I whispered.

'Go get something to eat,' Fand said, 'we will find you if there is any change.'

I found the breakfast room all by myself (well, after getting lost for a half an hour). Everywhere I went people pointed at me and whispered to their companions, or, even worse, bowed. No one dared to sit with me at breakfast but that didn't stop them from staring at me. I'm not sure if it was 'cause I was their prince or 'cause the food was so awesome that I moaned while I ate.

A guard approached as I was finishing. I was surprised to see he was a Banshee. I was glad that Dad had chosen not to banish all of the guards that worked for Cialtie.

'Prince Conor,' the guard said, bowing. He was young and I could see he was nervous. I smiled at him. 'The prisoner is getting – difficult.'

'Prisoner? What prisoner?'

'The one who shouts with the strange tongue.'

'Oh my gods,' I said, 'Detective Fallon, I forgot all about him. You'd better take me to him.'

Chapter Four
Prisoner Fallon

I heard him before I even rounded the corner. When I reached the door two guards, a Banshee and an Imp, snapped to attention.

'Take it easy, guys,' I said. They relaxed but not much.

I jumped when I heard the volume of the shouts on the other side of the door.

'DO YOU KNOW WHO I AM?' Brendan bellowed with a voice that was going hoarse. 'YOU ARE ALL IN BIG TROUBLE! DO YOU HEAR ME?'

I motioned for the door to be opened. The Banshee reached for the handle and the Imp stepped in front of me gripping his banta stick.

'Hold on,' I said, putting my hand on his shoulder. 'That won't be necessary.'

'Are you sure you want to go in there alone?' the Imp asked.

'I'm sure.' Just then a thunderous crash shook the door from the inside. 'Well, maybe you could lend me your stick.'

The Imp stared at me with an *It's your funeral* look and handed me his banta stick. 'Brendan,' I called through the door, 'I'm coming in, don't attack me. OK?'

There was no answer so I braced myself and stuck my nose around the jamb. Detective Fallon was standing in the middle of the room. His shirt tail was half out, his hair stuck out at a wacky forty-five-degree angle. He was panting and covered with sweat. His eyes weren't as crazy as the last time I saw him, but I wasn't about to shake his hand. I closed the door behind me. 'I see you have been busy turning our furniture into toothpicks.'

'Kidnapping is a very serious crime.'

'You can add it to the murder charge if you like, but I didn't do either of them.'

'Where am I?' he said, taking a menacing step towards me.

'Easy, fella,' I said, positioning my stick, 'I don't want to hit you with one of these a third time.'

'A third time?'

'Yes, I hit you once in the neck at the police station and once in the head upstairs.'

'That was you?' he said, rubbing the side of his head where I am sure it hurt.

'Yeah, sorry, I got a little carried away.'

'I don't remember much about the second time,' he said calming down a bit, 'I was …'

'Freaked out,' I finished for him. 'Don't worry about it, The Land can do that to you – I know. Hey, let's sit down and talk about this nicely.' I looked around the room but there wasn't any place to sit. Not one piece of furniture was any bigger than my forearm. Keeping one eye on Brendan I backed up to the door and opened it a crack. 'Could you get us a couple of chairs?' I glanced back at the devastation of the room. 'Cheap ones.'

Brendan glared at me while I kicked pieces of smashed furnishings into the corner. A guard came in carrying two simple chairs. 'Are these cheap enough for you, Your Highness?'

'They'll be fine,' I said, indicating with a tilt of my head for him to leave.

Brendan examined his chair before he sat in it. I wasn't sure if he didn't trust me or if he was studying it to see how easy it would be to smash. 'What language are you are speaking?'

'Ancient Gaelic. It's the lingo around here.'

'And where is *here*?'

'You're in *The Land*, Brendan. I wasn't lying.'

'You're telling me that I'm in that Never-Never Land you babbled on about?'

'Tir na Nog actually, but now that I think about it, the concept is the same.'

'And who are you – Tinkerbell?'

'Well, I would prefer to think of myself as more of a Peter-like person but we are getting off the subject. You're here now. I don't know how you got here.'

'The last thing I clearly remember is grabbing onto a horse's tail.'

'Ah,' I said. 'That explains it. You were pulled through when my mother opened a door to another world, this world, The Land.'

'I don't believe you.'

'I don't blame you, it even sounds crazy to me and I've done it a couple of times before, but that's the truth of it. It would be easier if you accepted it.'

Brendan rubbed his head in the place where I had clocked him.

'Head hurting?'

He nodded.

'Have you eaten?'

In response he pointed to his left. A tray lay at the foot of a wall surrounded by broken crockery. Above it dripped the remains of a breakfast.

'I'll take that as a *no* then.'

I stood and opened the door a crack and spoke to the guards. 'Could you get me a couple of apples and some willow tea?'

'OK,' Brendan said when I sat down again, 'for the sake of argument, let's say I believe you. When are you going to let me go?'

'I'll talk to my mother about sending you back as soon as things calm down around here.'

'I want to see her now!'

A knock came at the door. I was glad for the excuse to stand up and put a bit of space between us. He was getting agitated again. The guard handed me a tray with two apples, a teapot and a couple of mugs. I placed it on the floor between us and offered Brendan an apple. He stared at it but he didn't take it.

'I'm not trying to poison you, Brendan. Look.' I took a bite out of the apple. It was gorgeous, as good, if not better than I remembered. 'You have got to try this,' I garbled as I wiped juice off my chin. 'It will change your whole outlook.'

Brendan took the already bitten apple from my hand, stared at it for a moment then took a bite. The look on his face made me laugh and almost spit out the chewed apple bits in my mouth. Now I know how I looked like the first time I ate an apple in The Land.

I watched as Brendan, while making the mandatory moans of delight, demolished the piece of fruit. When he finished he threw the core over his shoulder and then slapped himself in the face – hard.

'What are you doing?' I asked.

'I'm waking myself up. I get it now. This is a dream.'

'A dream?'

'Of course. Why didn't I see it before? Two beautiful young women single-handedly demolish a police station, I get kidnapped by extras in a King Arthur movie and I just had an apple that tasted like a five-course meal at the Ritz; of course it's a dream.' He slapped himself again.

'OK, Brendan, if that's what makes you happy then, fine, you believe it. Now, are you going to behave in this dream?'

'Sure, why not? I might as well enjoy myself before I wake up. The shame of it is that I probably won't remember it. I never remember my dreams.' He stood up and stretched and actually looked like he was having fun. 'Can I have the other apple?'

'Sure. Look, if you promise not to turn any furniture into kindling and generally settle down I'll get you a bath and a new room.'

'And more apples?'

'And more apples. Just behave. Oh, and try that willow tea, I think you'll enjoy that too.'

I instructed the guards to get Brendan a bath and a change of clothes and a new room. I told them he shouldn't give them any more trouble but they should keep a close eye on him. They looked sceptical but agreed.

I went back to Dad's room and kept vigil with Mom, Nieve, Fand and the Imp-healer, who I learned was named Bree. Minutes felt like hours, and as every one crawled by I wanted to ask how he was doing, but I knew they didn't know, so I didn't ask. I hate waiting, I always have, but that was the worst. I felt so helpless. Fand recited a healing mantra in Ogham and I asked her to teach it to me. I could feel the healing magic in the words but wondered if it was getting through Dad's amber shell. As the afternoon moved on, we all five chanted it together.

The curtains were drawn so I couldn't tell if night had fallen but Mom and Fand both looked up at each other at the same time, as if they were alerted by some soundless alarm.

Fand removed Dad's sheet as Mom placed a small dollop of amber sap in her palm and held it over the Shadowfire that was burning on a table at the foot of the bed. She dripped the molten sap onto Dad's foot. It was a darker shade of amber than his shell and I watched as it passed through the shell like water in a bowl of oil. The darker sap began to entwine and elongate, wrapping around the leg like a serpent and then continued to thin, until it wrapped his entire body with a fine line just under the surface of his glass-like sarcophagus. Fand placed her hands on either side of Dad's head and incanted in Ogham. The dark latticework spiralled and pulsed darker. Mom held Dad by his legs and swung them to the left so his right foot hung out of the bed. Even though I had seen it before, it shocked me to see Dad's whole body move as if he were made of marble. Fand released Dad's head and Mom cupped her hands under the foot. The dark spiral retraced its path and when Mom pulled her hands back, in her palm was the dark sap.

Mom held the sap over the Shadowfire and Fand, on the other side of the table, placed her hands under hers. Together they chanted words that sounded so strange I wondered how their tongues could make them. The sap dripped through their fingers and onto the Shadowfire. An image formed as they withdrew and as the vision cleared I saw it was my father, standing before me, upright, naked. His body was whole except for his right hand – it was in its proper place but detached from him by a few inches. The two Shadowwitches placed their hands into the vision and caressed Dad's shadow-form. Mom had her back to me but I could see Fand's face. Tears formed in her eyes – I didn't know what that meant. A cry escaped from Mom's throat and the two women reached for each other, breaking the vision, and embraced, both openly weeping.

'What?' I said, not knowing if I should speak but I couldn't take it any longer.

Mom turned and wiped the tears from her eyes but kept her hands over her mouth as she tried to compose herself. Finally she dropped her hands and crossed them on her chest. 'It worked,' she said.

It wasn't until it was all over that Mom allowed her fatigue and strain to show. Nieve and I had to help her walk to her chamber where she permitted herself to truly rest for the first time in a long while. I went back to check on Dad. Fand was still there, clearing up.

'Does he dream?'

'I do not know,' she replied.

'What happens now?'

'Now we have time to find a cure.'

'How long can he stay like this?'

Her answer should have comforted me but instead it sent a chill down my spine. 'For ever,' she said.

I checked on Dad before I went down to breakfast. The sound of Fand saying 'For ever' echoed in my brain and I wondered if this was the way I would start my day for the rest of my life. I was shocked by a transformed Brendan when I arrived at the food hall. He was smiling, cleaned up and wearing a leather shirt and trousers that surprisingly suited him. He was trying to communicate with an attractive red-headed woman who, when I arrived, stood, bowed and quickly departed.

'Aw, you scared her away,' Brendan said. 'I was doing quite well there. I already found out her name was Faggy Two.'

When he said that, I started to laugh.

'What's so funny?'

I then laughed so hard I had to sit down and cover my face until I could get some semblance of composure. It wasn't just what he had said that made me laugh, it was the tension of the last couple of days bubbling to the surface. 'I'm sorry, Brendan,' I said, wiping my eyes, 'I don't think you were doing as well as you thought, fágfaidh tú is Gaelic for *Go away*.'

'Oh.'

'And what are you doing trying to pick up women? You're a married man.'

'First of all, this is my dream, remember? A man can't get into trouble for having an affair when he's asleep, and secondly, I'm not a married man.'

'You told me you had a wife and a daughter.'

'No, *you* said I have a wife and a daughter. I only said I have a daughter.' His mood dropped a bit. 'I'm a widower.'

'Oh, I'm sorry.'

'Me too. Hey, what do you think of my new threads?' he asked quickly, obviously trying to change the subject.

'You look like a native,' I said and meant it. 'You're even growing a beard I see.'

'No, Frick wouldn't let me have a razor.'

'Frick?'

Brendan pointed to the Imp and the Banshee guards that I had assigned to keep an eye on him. 'I call them Frick and Frack.'

I waved to the guards who were standing by the entrance of the room; they gave me an official nod. I could tell this was not their favourite detail. 'Which one is Frick?'

'I don't know. I keep getting them mixed up.'

Breakfast arrived and Brendan ate like there was no tomorrow. Except for the chopping and moans neither of us spoke until our plates were clean. When we had finished Brendan said, 'The food in this dream is just fantastic, half the time I can't wait to wake up but for the other half I hope it will continue until the next meal.'

'Brendan, you have to stop thinking like that. I know it makes you feel better, but this is real.'

Nieve entered the dining hall. Brendan jumped to his feet and backed off. She sat down across from me and said, 'How is our guest?'

Warily, Brendan sat next to me, as if for protection, and pointed to Nieve. 'That's the witch that trashed my police station!'

'What did he say?' Nieve asked.

'Oh, he said good morning, it's nice to see you again,' I lied.

Nieve gave me a sceptical look.

'This is my dream and I don't want her in it!' he shouted, pointing his finger inches from her face.

'Careful, Brendan,' I warned.

'What is he saying?' Nieve asked again, but then said, 'Oh, this is ridiculous. Tell him to place his head on the table.'

It took a lot of convincing, but I finally got Brendan to place the side of his face flat down on the table. Nieve took a small piece of gold out of her satchel and rubbed it between her hands while incanting.

Brendan looked up with a wild panicky expression in his uppermost eye. 'Is this going to hurt?'

'He wants to know if this is going to hurt,' I translated.

'Yes, I suspect it will,' Nieve said calmly.

'No,' I told Brendan, 'you'll be fine.'

Nieve opened her palms and dripped the molten gold into Brendan's ear. He shot up, grabbed his ear, overturning the bench he was sitting on, and danced around the room howling in pain. I was glad no one other than me spoke English. The curse words coming out of his mouth would have made a prison inmate blush. He picked up a silver tray, sending half a dozen wine glasses crashing to the floor, and tried to use it as a mirror to view his ear. At his insistence I inspected the lughole and assured him that it looked OK – which it did – and finally got him sitting down again.

'What the hell did she do to me?'

'Now stick out your tongue,' Nieve demanded.

'No way, lady! I'm not letting you near me ever again.'

I looked at Nieve and she smiled at me. 'Brendan,' I said in Gaelic, 'can you understand me?'

'Of course I can understand you. You keep that crazy woman away from me.'

'Brendan, I'm talking to you in ancient Gaelic. Are you sure you can understand me?'

34

'Huh?'

'It seems that Nieve has given you a two-second lesson in the common tongue. You just learned a new language.'

'That's impossible.'

'Impossible things happen here every day.'

'Now, Brendan,' Nieve said, 'stick out your tongue and I will complete the process, then we will no longer need to speak through Conor. Personally I don't trust him as a reliable interpreter.'

Brendan clenched his mouth shut and shook his head no, like a baby that won't eat his dinner. It took even more of an effort to convince him the second time. I tried everything, including agreeing with him that it didn't matter 'cause it was all really a dream. It wasn't until I threatened to never feed him again that he gave in.

'Come on,' I said, 'stop being such a baby.'

'It hurt, damn it. You do it.'

I rolled my eyes at him but to be honest it wasn't something I wanted to experience.

'Ask her if it will hurt as much as the last time – ask her exactly that.'

I translated and Nieve said, 'No.'

Brendan watched with crossed eyes as the molten gold hit his tongue. He not only flipped over the chair but the table as well. He hopped around the dining hall screaming bloody murder and this time everyone in the room heard exactly what he was saying. Most of them left in order to get some distance between them and the madman.

'God almighty!' Brendan screamed from behind his hand in perfect Gaelic. 'You said it wouldn't hurt as much!'

'No,' Nieve replied in her usual calm manner. 'You asked if it would hurt as much as the last time and I said, *no*. I knew it would hurt more.'

Nieve gave me a rueful smile; I was starting to realise she had a wickedly subversive sense of humour.

'Now that I can converse with you,' Nieve said, 'I realise I do not want to. If you will excuse me.'

Nieve left. I asked a servant to bring Brendan a glass of Gerard's finest wine. It was a bit early but I figured he would appreciate it. He did. After one sip he downed the glass in one.

'Are you OK?' I asked.

'To be honest, Conor, I'm not sure. This dream is way too real for my liking.'

'I keep telling you – it's not a dream.'

'All right then, as much as I don't relish meeting another member of your family, how about that introduction to your father you promised me.'

'I don't think I ever promised you that.'

'As good as – well?'

'OK,' I said, 'come with me.'

Chapter Five
Fand

The closer we got to Dad's room the more worried Frick and Frack looked. They obviously thought Brendan was a nutcase and that letting him loose in the west wing was a bad idea. They were shocked when I told them that Brendan could enter Dad's room without them.

The first thing we noticed was that the curtains in The Lord's Chamber were closed but the room was bright with the light of about thirty candles.

'You must have a hell of a candle bill,' Brendan quipped.

'These are Leprechaun candles. They last for years.'

'Of course they do, silly me.'

As we entered the room we saw a woman sitting cross-legged on a stool at the foot of the bed. Her head was covered with an intricate gold-flecked veil that played weird tricks with the candlelight. Her arms were outstretched at her sides and she was chanting in Ogham. I couldn't see her face but I knew from the voice who it was. She stopped chanting when we entered the room.

'I'm sorry, I didn't mean to disturb you.'

'I am a difficult woman to disturb, Prince Conor,' Fand said without moving, 'it is I who will be disturbing you. Shall I leave?'

'No, please go on; Dad can use all the help he can get.'

Fand continued her chanting in a voice so low we could hardly hear. I motioned for Brendan to come closer to the bed and I pulled the sheet back from Dad's chest revealing his right arm and his attached runehand.

'What did you do to him?' Brendan said in an accusing tone.

'Oh give it up, Brendan, I didn't do anything to him,' I said, trying to whisper. I explained about Dad's hand being reattached during the Choosing ceremony in the Chamber of Runes and how Mom and Fand sealed him in this amber shell to stop his hand from killing him.

'So he's in some kind of magical suspended animation?'

'That's about right,' I said as quietly as I could, hoping Brendan would follow suit.

He didn't; he started to chuckle and then laugh out loud. 'Oh boy!' he said with no intention of being remotely quiet. 'I'm going to quit the police force when I wake up. I think I'm going to write science fiction movies.'

'Brendan, could you keep your voice down.'

'Why? I'm proud of myself. Who'd have thought I had such a vivid imagination? Or maybe I should write detective novels. I'll call my first one, *The Strange Case of the Father Who Was Turned into a Paperweight*.' He rapped his knuckles on Dad's solid forehead.

I grabbed his wrist and said, 'Don't do that.'

'Don't do what – this?' He thumped on Dad's forehead again like he was knocking on a door.

That's when I hit him. It was more of a forceful push than a punch but I knew it hurt. Brendan staggered back and held his chest.

'You want a piece of me, O'Neil?' he shouted. 'All right then, let's do it. Can you fight without a stick? Come on, man-to-man.'

I know I shouldn't have done it, there in my father's sick room, but I raised my dukes and squared up to him. I was sick and tired of his *I can do anything in a dream* attitude.

We were about a nanosecond away from going for each other's throats when Fand broke the atmosphere of blood lust. 'I stated before that I was a difficult woman to disturb,' she said in a voice that reminded us that she was a queen, 'but you two have succeeded.'

Brendan and I both turned and pretty much stood at attention as she lifted the veil from her head. Brendan let loose a gasp, and said, 'Oh my God.'

Fand stood and walked towards him. 'You are the traveller from the Real World?'

'Yes, ma'am,' he replied respectfully.

'You look as though you have seen a ghost.'

'Not a ghost, ma'am; for a moment I thought you were my mother.'

'Your mother?'

'Yes, you look remarkably like her, here I'll show you.' Brendan reached for his back pocket then remembered he was wearing new clothes and rummaged around in the pouch of his tunic until he produced an old leather wallet. 'I have a picture of her with my daughter.' Brendan pulled bits of paper out of his wallet looking increasingly confused. He went through everything a second time and then held a blank piece of paper in his hands repeatedly looking at its front and back. 'I don't understand it.'

'What's the matter?' I asked.

'Well, this is the photograph. Look, I wrote the date on the back, but the picture is – gone.'

I took the photo from him and it was indeed blank, not even the ghost of an image remained. 'I think I know what happened,' I said. 'Real World technology often doesn't work here. Electric watches and guns don't work, so I imagine photography doesn't either.'

'You mean I'm stuck in this dream without a picture of my own daughter?'

'Dream?' Fand said.

'Brendan here thinks this is all a long dream and that any second he is going to wake up in his bed.'

'I see. Well, maybe you are right, Brendan. Who can tell what is real and what is illusion? This may be a realm inside a dream but that is not what you think, is it? You think you are still back in the Real World and soon you shall awake – is that not so?'

Brendan nodded but I could see his resolve weakening.

'I am sorry, Brendan, as seductive as that thought must seem – it is not so. It is true you are in a different world but there is only one reality. What was your vocation in the Real World?'

'I was … I am … a detective.'

Fand looked confused. Brendan tried a couple of times to describe his job using words like 'perpetrator' and 'arrest'. Finally he changed his wording to 'I find evildoers and punish them.'

Fand nodded. 'You seek the truth?'

Brendan thought for a bit and then smiled. 'I suppose I do.'

'Like a Druid.'

'Now you not only look like my mother but you sound like her.'

'Oh, how so?'

'That's just the kind of voodoo crap my mother used to spout.'

'Conor has taught me the meaning of "crap" but what is voodoo?'

'OK, not voodoo, but she was always brewing herbs into potions to ward off colds or a rash or evil spirits, and when she wasn't doing that she was dancing naked around a fire or hugging a tree.'

'It sounds as if I would like her,' Fand said.

'Maybe you would. I don't get along with her very well.'

Fand answered that statement with a knowing smile – she had experience with a difficult mother; her mother had been responsible for the near extinction of her entire race.

'Let me see the … What did you call it – photo?'

Brendan handed her the blank piece of paper that once held the image of his daughter and mother. Fand took a glop of tree sap out of a silk bag that was hanging around her waist and walked over to the dresser at the far side of the room. She closed her hand over the sap, placed her fist into the bowl of Shadowfire and chanted under her breath. She then removed her hand and dripped sap onto the front of the paper, where the photo had been. Immediately the sap hardened into a thin film, not unlike the emulsion on a glossy photo. Then Fand dropped it into the Shadowfire.

'Hey,' Brendan shouted as he reached to retrieve his photo.

Fand grabbed his wrist and said, 'Wait.'

It was obvious from Brandon's face that her strength had surprised him.

When nothing happened, Fand asked, 'Has your daughter or mother ever touched this – photo?'

Brendan thought for a moment and replied, 'I don't think so.'

Fand retrieved the blank photo and held it in her palm above the Shadowfire. 'May I touch you?' she asked.

Brendan looked to me for advice. I shrugged; I had no idea what was going on.

'I guess,' he said.

Fand laid her palm across the side of Brandon's face and the Shadowfire jumped to life. An image appeared in the flame. It sent a chill down my spine. The last time I saw anything like this was when my mother performed a Shadowcasting for Fergal – not the most pleasant of memories. This image was of a woman in her late sixties. She was handsome with a strong face and long grey hair tied back in a braided ponytail. She cradled a weeping child of around six in her arms. Brendan pulled away from Fand's hand and the image vanished.

'That's not the photo. The photo is of my mother and daughter when my daughter was an infant.'

'Interesting,' Fand said, smiling. 'Strange things can happen during Samhain. I think, Brandon, what we have just seen is your mother and daughter as they are in the Real World now.'

'I have to get back.' The colour dropped out of Brendan's face like a water cooler emptying. The realisation of his predicament hit him – this was real. 'I have to get home – now!' He walked to the door and then realised he didn't know where to go. 'How do I get back?' His voice was panicky.

'You must speak to Deirdre,' Fand said. 'I know not how you came.'

Chapter Six
Mom

Getting Brendan an audience with my mother wasn't easy. Once Dad had stabilised, Fand had ordered Mom to rest. She agreed and slept but as soon as she woke up she threw herself into the task of queening Castle Duir. It took me a couple of days to get the cop in to see her.

Mom stared hard at the detective when he walked into the room. 'I remember you,' she said with narrowing eyes. 'You are the man that imprisoned my son. You pointed a weapon at me. Conor, what is he doing here?'

'I need to get back,' Brendan said.

Mom shot him a spectacularly dirty look and said, 'You will speak when spoken to.'

Wow, even I took an involuntary step back. I had forgotten how menacing Mom can be when she is in her bear cub guarding mode. She turned her back on Brendan and took a step towards me. 'Now, Conor, what is he doing here?'

Brendan said, 'You don't understand,' and then did that really foolish thing. He grabbed her wrist.

I guess I should have warned Brendan about touching a woman in The Land when she doesn't want or expect it. I had learned that lesson the hard way with Essa but it didn't even come close to how hard Brandon's lesson was with my mother. In a matter of nanoseconds she turned her wrist, broke the detective's grasp, grabbed his arm, placed her foot in his stomach, and then vaulted him clear over her head. Brendan sailed a good seven feet in the air before luckily hitting the back of a sofa. If the manoeuvre had been in any other direction he would have hit a wall. I ran over and righted the couch and then helped the dazed Brendan into it.

'Sit here and don't say a word,' I said.

Brendan's reply was a predictable, 'Owww.'

I approached my mother slowly. She was still in an attack stance and was breathing heavily.

'Someone should teach him not to do that.'

'I think you just did, Mom – and very impressively too, I might add. Let's all take a deep breath and calm down a little.'

Mom unclenched her fists. I took a seat and motioned for her to do the same. As she sat, she kept an eye on Brendan.

'Relax, Mom, I'm sure he won't try anything again. Will you, Brendan?'

'Owww,' Brendan repeated.

Mom finally turned to me. I smiled at her but she wasn't quite ready to return it. 'You still haven't told me what he is doing here.'

It's not like she had given me much of a chance but I decided to keep that comment to myself – enough feathers had been ruffled already. 'Brendan followed us through that portal you made.'

'That's impossible.'

'Why do you say that?'

'The portal was designed for the three of us and our horses – part of that spell was Truemagic, it should have killed someone from the Real World.'

'Well, I hate to disagree with you on a point of magic but there he is.'

'Strange things happen during Samhain,' Mom mumbled under her breath as she approached Brendan. 'Why did you incarcerate my son?'

Brendan didn't answer but the question succeeded in stopping him from saying, 'Oww, oww, oww,' over and over again.

'Mom, he was just doing his job.'

Mom gave me a sharp look and said, 'I am speaking to him.'

'He's right, ma'am,' Brendan said with a mixture of respect and fear. 'I was just doing my job.'

'And what job is that?'

'I'm a policeman,' he said but when he realised she didn't understand he sighed, 'I catch and punish evildoers.'

'And what evil could this sweet boy have done?'

'I thought he had killed his father.'

'And why would you have thought that?'

'Well, the house was trashed, his father was missing and he was spending his money.'

'Money?' Mom asked, turning to me.

'Like gold,' I said.

'I thought people in the Real World didn't use magic. What would they want with gold?'

I hadn't thought of that before but now wasn't the time to explain micro-economics to my mother. So I said, 'We just kinda like it 'cause it's shiny.'

'Did my son not explain to you about his father?'

'Yes, ma'am, he did but I didn't believe him.'

'Do you believe him now?'

Brendan paused for a moment and said, 'Yes, ma'am, I do. That is why I wanted to speak to you. I must return home.'

'How exactly did you get here?'

'I don't remember much, I was a bit out of it, but I remember grabbing onto a horse's tail and then I remember Conor clubbing me over the head. The next thing I know I was here.'

'You grabbed onto the horse?'

'Yes, ma'am.'

Mom walked back into the centre of the room, thinking. 'I see. Well, Mr …'

'Fallon, Brendan Fallon.'

'Well, Brendan, I see how you have arrived here but I still do not know how you survived the journey.'

'Well, I'm here and I need to return. The Fand woman said you could get me back.'

'I am sure I can, see me next Samhain.'

'And when is that?'

'In a wee bit less than a year.'

'A year!' Brendan was on his feet. 'I can't wait a year.'

'Why so long?' I asked.

'If I had known you were here earlier then things would be different but sending a mortal back now when the Real World and The Land are apart would be too dangerous – if it was two days ago, then maybe.'

'I've been trying to see you for a week!' Brendan said, raising his voice, which, by the look on my mother's face, wasn't appreciated.

I was about to intervene but then I saw my mother's countenance soften. 'I am sorry for your predicament but I only learned of your existence today. I have been quite preoccupied.'

'Is there no other way?' I asked.

'The only way to safely return him is to use the same piece of gold that I used to bring him here, but I no longer have it.'

'Where is it?' I asked.

'It's in your father's mouth.'

'Oh,' I said.

'What?' Brendan said.

'I placed the gold disc that I used to open the portal in Oisin's mouth so he would not suffocate while we encased him in Shadowmagic,' Mom said.

'So open him up and get the disc,' Brendan demanded.

'That would be far too dangerous,' Mom said. 'We were fortunate that the process worked the first time. I will not unnecessarily endanger the Lord of Duir a second time.'

'Unnecessarily,' Brendan shouted, 'you are going to maroon me in this god-forsaken place, while my loony-tune mother pollutes my daughter's brain with a caravan full of hippy tree-hugging crap?'

'If the girl's grandmother is teaching your daughter to hug trees, then I suspect she is in good hands.' Mom sat back at her desk and took up a pen. 'I'm sorry but that is my final word on the subject.'

I wouldn't say Brendan is a stupid man, but on occasion he is a slow learner. He grabbed Mom's hand and started to say, 'You don't—'

Because Mom was sitting this time she flipped him with her shoulder instead of her foot. On the plus side, Brendan didn't travel as fast or as far as before. On the minus side, he didn't make it to the couch. He took a long time getting up.

I put Brendan to bed with some poteen. I was pretty sure he wouldn't retangle with Mom. Still, for his own safety, I reposted Frick and Frack outside the door. Brendan didn't realise that those two judo throws were Mom's idea of restraint. If he tried something like that again, I wouldn't be surprised if she killed him.

I went back to my room and stared at the chipped wood panelling wishing Dahy was here so I could borrow a throwing knife. Actually I wished anybody was there. I had spent ages longing to return to The Land and now that I was here I was miserable and lonely. Dad was sealed in another world. Mom was preoccupied with castle duties and when she wasn't, she was sitting up all night with Fand in their Shadowmagic laboratory. Araf is a great friend on an adventure but for just hanging out, he can actually make me feel more alone than when I'm alone. And, of course, everything I saw in The Land reminded me of Fergal. Man, I missed him. And every time I was low and alone I would inevitably replay the moment Cialtie stuck a knife in his chest, and in every rerun I could do nothing to stop it.

And where the hell was Essa? No one could tell me where she was. Ah Essa – when I wasn't replaying Fergal's demise I was replaying my farewell with her. I may not have been able to save my cousin but I sure as hell could have handled my last moments with Essa better. I could have forgiven her – I should have forgiven her – I should have stayed with her. Instead I went back to Sally. I wonder if I could possibly have been more of an idiot. I went to sleep and dreamt of all of the stupid things I had done in my life. It was a very long night.

I had just gotten to about the age of twelve, where I broke my arm in a bouncy castle accident, when Mom woke me up very excited. I popped up quickly, holding my elbow. She had a wild-eyed look, like a student who had studied all night and drunk thirty cups of coffee. Over her shoulder hung a satchel.

'Conor, you must see this!' she said as she bounded off the bed and grabbed a book off the bookshelf. 'I think Fand and I have finally done it.'

'Done what?' I asked with a morning voice that made me sound as if I had been gargling with ground glass.

She opened the book, tore out half of a page from the middle and handed it to me. I was still dopey from sleep and stared at the piece of paper wondering what the hell she wanted me to do with it. Then she handed me a gold brooch with an amber stone set in.

'Clip it onto the piece of paper,' she said, bouncing on her toes like a kid showing off a new toy. 'Go on.'

I looked at the brooch. It was about the size of a half dollar with a spring in the back that allowed it to move like a bulldog clip. I pinched it open and clipped it onto the piece of paper. The paper started to glow with an amber light, then so did my hand where I was touching it. An all too familiar tingling sensation began in my fingers. It felt exactly like when I was under attack from a relative, and Mom's protective spell had just kicked in. I dropped the paper and clip and jumped straight up looking around my room for the source of the attack. There was none. When I realised I wasn't glowing any more I looked down on my bed and there attached to Mom's new brooch was a shining translucent book. I picked it up. It tingled in my hand but it felt real. On the cover I could faintly make out the title. It was the same as the book that Mom had just ripped the page from. In my hands it seemed to weigh the same as a regular book and when I opened it, the clear pages turned just like paper.

'What … what is it?' I asked.

'For want of a better word it is a Shadowbook. It's a hybrid of Truemagic and Shadowmagic. The paper, in a way, *remembers* the rest of the book.'

I turned the Shadowpages. It was strange still being able to see my fingers through what felt like a solid thing. As I moved the book around in the light I saw faint glimmerings on the pages but nothing legible.

'It's a shame you can't read it, though.'

'Ah ha!' Mom exclaimed. 'Here is the cold part.'

'The cold part?'

'Is not that what you say?'

I laughed, 'You mean the *cool* part.'

'Right, the cool part.' She opened her satchel and took out a clipboard-sized sheet of gold and laid it on the bed. When she placed the Shadowbook on top of it, the words appeared almost as if the book was real.

'Wow, Mom, that is very cold.'

It wasn't until her face lit up with pride that I realised that one of the things I missed most during this trip to The Land was my mother's smile.

She gave me a hug and then quickly picked up her things and hurried to the door. 'It shouldn't take too long for Fand and me to make a few more clips. I imagine we could leave the day after tomorrow.'

'Leave for where?'

'The Hazellands. We are going to find a cure for your father in the Hall of Knowledge.'

Chapter Seven
The Armoury

Ilistened for the sound of smashing furniture as I approached
Brendan's room. Frick (or was it Frack) said that he had been
eerily silent. I stuck my head around the door and found Brendan
in bed staring at the ceiling.

'Are you OK?'

'I'm still here, aren't I?'

'As far as I can tell, yes.'

'Then I'm not all right.'

'So you're just going to sulk?'

'What else is there to do?' he said. 'I'm stuck here for at least a
year. God knows what my life, my career and my little girl will be
like in a year's time. I'm under house arrest, followed around by
two dolts who keep staring at me like they expect horns to grow
out of my head. And I can't even read a book 'cause everything is
written in some ancient language that, although I can magically
speak it and understand it, I can't read it. And before you offer –
there is no way I'm going to let that aunt of yours do that molten
gold thing to my eyes.'

'I'm sorry, Brendan, but this isn't my fault and there is nothing
I can do.'

'Yeah, I know. I've been lying here thinking about it all morning – it's my fault.'

'Well, I wouldn't say that. How about we say it's nobody's fault?'

'No,' Brendan sighed. 'It's my fault. It started when I arrested an innocent man. Don't get me wrong, I had pretty good reason but, in the end, I arrested a man for a crime that not only had he not committed – it was a crime that never even happened. No good can ever come from something that starts like that. So as much as I would like to blame you – this is mostly my fault.'

'Well, if you insist,' I said, 'but don't beat yourself up too much – it could have happened to anyone.'

'Thanks,' he said, finally looking at me. 'So this is really … real then?'

'I'm afraid so.'

'And I have been acting like a serious jerk?'

'That too, I'm afraid, is true.'

Brendan placed his hand over his face in embarrassment. 'Oh my God, I rapped on your father's forehead like it was a door. Oh, I am so sorry, Conor.'

'Yeah, that was pretty bad.'

'Oh and the furniture and the … I really am sorry, Conor,' he said, sitting up. 'But in my defence, I did think I was going to wake up at any moment.'

'Fair enough, apology accepted.' I held out my hand. 'Shall we start over?'

'I'd like that,' he said, shaking it.

I had come in to tell him that I was leaving for a few days but instead I said, 'How about a road trip?'

That piqued his interest. 'To where?'

'The Hazellands.'

'Isn't that where the Leprechaun army is stationed?'

'Oh my gods, you were listening to me.'

'I'm a man of my word, Conor. I didn't believe or care about your story the first time you babbled it but the second time I promised I would listen and I did. Since Fand convinced me I wasn't dreaming, I've been going over your adventure in my head. Did all of that stuff really happen?'

'Yes,' I said, chuckling. 'Don't feel bad about not believing me. I sometimes have trouble believing it myself. But to answer your question, no, the Leprechaun army was disbanded and I don't know what's there now.'

'Who else is coming?' Brendan said, hopping up and dressing. 'Is that what's-her-name that trashed my police station and burned my ear coming?'

'You mean Aunt Nieve? I don't know.'

'How about the woman who throws me across the room with regularity?'

'Yes, I'm sure Mom is coming.'

'Who else?'

'Araf probably.'

'Who's he?'

'He's the guy who threw me the stick when I hit you on the head.'

'The first time you hit me or the second time?'

'The second time – gosh, you have been having a rough time lately, but The Land's like that in the beginning. It'll get better. Can I buy you some lunch?'

'You're getting to know me, Conor. My wife used to do the same thing. Whenever she saw me getting down she would only have to feed me and I was happy again.'

'Well then, let's get the chef to whip up something special. And if you like I'll teach you how to read Gaelic – since you can speak it, it shouldn't be too hard.'

After Dad regained the throne, in what is now called the Troid e Ewan Macha, or The Battle of the Twins of Macha, I had a lot of time on my hands and I spent most of it exploring Castle Duir. I even revisited the dungeon and issued my one and only executive order to have the cells cleaned out. I still feel sorry for whoever got that job. The only place that I never got to see was the armoury. After the battle, Dad still couldn't be sure if there were any of Cialtie's loyal followers still lurking around incognito, so he decided to seal off the weapons room until security could be normalised.

So that made this trip to the armoury my first one. Brendan and I hiked to the north wing, sailed past three sets of ten-hutting armed guards and found ourselves in front of a set of huge oak doors inlaid with a fine gold latticework.

Light flooded the hallway as we pushed our way in. Like Gerard's armoury, this was a glass-roofed gymnasium, but size-wise it made the winemaker's weapons room seem like a walk-in closet. Racks upon racks contained carefully stacked weapons: swords, axes, maces and rows and rows of banta sticks. Tournament practice areas were marked off on the floor and the entire far length of the room was an impossibly long archery range that could accommodate eight archers abreast, each with their own targets. At the far end there was a huge contraption that looked like it might be a catapult.

'Wow,' I said.

The sound of Brendan's and my footsteps echoed in the huge space. Surprisingly there was no one around.

Brendan whispered like he was in a church. 'Where is everyone?'

'Probably off pillaging.'

'Damn,' Brendan said, 'you mean it's pillaging season and no one told me?'

I smiled and shouted a tentative, 'Hello?'

'So,' Brendan said in a normal tone, now that it looked like we were alone in there, 'where do they keep the AK-47s?'

'I'm afraid if you want a long-range weapon, Brendan, it'll have to be one of those.'

Brendan turned to where I had pointed; the entire wall was covered with both long and short bows mounted neatly in rows. They were all unstrung with their strings hanging slack from the top notch. There were hundreds of them.

'Ah,' Brendan said, 'you may laugh, but I was a pretty good archer in my youth. My mother made me take lessons.' Brendan walked over to the wall and reached up to take down a medium-sized bow.

I never heard the twang of the bow that fired the arrow at him, I didn't even see it while it was in the air, I only heard the thwap of the arrow hitting its target and Brendan's yelp as he realised his arm was pinned to the wall.

The arrow had tacked Brendan's shirtsleeve to the wall, missing his skin by inches. I hit the ground, rolled to my left, upsetting a stand of bantas, and came up crouching with a stick in each hand. I poked my nose over the now-empty banta stick holder to see Brendan reaching to extract the arrow that stuck him to the wall. As his hand crossed his body another arrow pinned that sleeve as well. This time clothing wasn't the only thing it pierced – he howled in pain.

'I'm hit!'

Chapter Eight
Spideog

I ducked back down and reviewed my situation. The only thing I deduced was that I was in trouble and Brendan was screwed. What did Dahy tell me? 'When in doubt, stay still and listen.' So I did, but I couldn't hear anything except Brendan's heavy breathing.

'Brendan,' I said in a loud whisper, 'can you see anything?'

'Straight back at the other end of the room I saw a flash of something green.' He strained his neck for a better look. 'Nothing now.'

'Are you OK?'

'I think so.'

'Keep watching. I'm coming to get you.'

I peered around the corner of the weapons stand and was just about to make a dash for Brendan when I heard a footfall behind me. I whirled to see a hooded man in a bright green tunic and brown leather leggings. In one hand he held a bow and in the other an arrow. I instantly attacked with both sticks – one high and one low. Like he was reading my mind he twisted his body vertical and kicked his foot at my fingers where I was holding the low banta. The stick flew out of my hand. My other weapon he blocked with the string of his bow. No one had ever done that to me before. My stick sprang back so far I completely lost form. My whole left side was exposed and my opponent didn't hesitate in exploiting that fact. I'm not quite sure what he did next but I think it was a swipe to the kidneys with the bow and a kick to the back of the legs with his foot, maybe both feet. Whatever – I went down like a hippo on ice.

After bouncing my forehead off the deck I came to a stop with the green goblin kneeling on the backs of my arms and something very pointy sticking into the rear of my neck. My left cheek was pressed against the floor. Out of the corner of my right eye I could just make out an open-mouthed Brendan trying to escape his feathered clothespins. The sharp pain in my neck stopped and an arrow sizzled through the air, planting itself about two inches from Brendan's nose.

'Do not move, Druid,' greeny shouted.

Brendan may not have answered but he certainly obeyed.

The pain in my neck resumed, forcing me to the conclusion that he had a cocked arrow pointing at the back of my collar. Even though he didn't tell *me* not to move, I decided that not moving was a good idea.

'I've been waiting for you, Druid,' the green guy said as he pushed the point of the arrow hard into my neck.

'Hey, buddy,' I said, 'you got the wrong guys. We're not Druids.'

'Do not insult me. There are still people in The Land who can recognise a Fili and I am one of them.'

'The Fili have been exonerated. Haven't you heard?'

'The ones who own those bows will never be exonerated,' he said.

This guy definitely had the drop on me and I figured it was only a matter of time before he garrotted me so I made, what turned out to be, a futile attempt to buck him off my back. It only resulted in my head getting bounced off the floor one more time.

'Relax, Druid. I do not wish to hurt you before the Lord of Duir has a chance to question you.'

Up till then I figured, like I always do when somebody attacks me out of the blue, that this was probably some sort of assassin hired by Cialtie. Now I realised that this idiot worked here.

'The Lord of Duir is incapacitated. Does that mean you will now take commands from his prince?'

The pressure from the arrowhead slacked. 'Yes.'

'Then I, Conor of Duir, command you to – get your butt off of me!'

It's amazing what a royal title can do in the right situation. Greeny hopped directly off me. I groaned erect as fast as my not-quite broken limbs would allow.

My attacker's hood was back. I was a bit surprised to see wrinkles around the piercing green eyes. This guy had been around for longer than probably anyone I had yet met in The Land. He wore a waxed moustache and a meticulously trimmed goatee that pointed directly to the bow and arrow that he still had levelled at my chest.

'Lower your weapon,' I said, trying very hard to sound like my father.

'Yes, my lord,' he said as he released the tension on his bow.

'Who are you and why have you attacked my royal personage?'

As I have mentioned before, I'm not a big fan of all the regal bowing and curtseying people do around the castle but after a guy kicks you in the back of the legs, the sight of him grovelling is very satisfying.

'I am Spideog, Master-at-Arms of Castle Duir. I am sorry, Your Highness.'

Behind me I heard Brendan trying to extricate himself. Greeny pulled back his bowstring and fired another arrow that planted itself about an inch from the previous one. I think if this guy wanted to, he could shoot fleas off a dog at fifty paces.

'Conor, tell him to stop doing that,' Brendan shouted.

'Hey, stop doing that,' I said.

Spideog had already notched another arrow from the quiver on his back. 'Instruct the Druid to leave the yew bows alone.'

'OK, first of all, he's not a Druid and secondly we didn't know they were yew. Brendan!' I yelled over my shoulder. 'Don't touch the bows.'

'If he stops shooting at me I'll put my hands in my pockets and not touch another thing all day. Now will somebody unpin me? I feel like a wanted poster.'

'You heard the man,' I said to Spideog still using my dad voice. 'Put your weapon away and help him down.'

The arrows were embedded so far into the wood that we had to snap them to unpin the detective. Brendan rolled up his left sleeve and examined the cut that the second arrow had inflicted. It wasn't much more than a bad scratch but that didn't stop Brendan from being very mad.

'Why you son of a—' He took a swing at the archer's nose.

Without any seemingly quick movements, Spideog casually brought up his left hand, connecting the back of his palm with the side of Brendan's advancing fist, and pushed the punch off target. His hand sailed harmlessly past Spideog's ear and Brendan stumbled forward. Confused at what had just happened but still just as mad, Brendan took another swing to precisely the same effect.

'Lord Conor, instruct your companion to stop attacking me.'

'Stop attacking him, Brendan.'

He didn't listen. I once heard that the definition of insanity is when you do the same things over and over but expect different results. Well, Brendan did the same thing and he did get a different result. This time Spideog's hand parry was accompanied by a kick that dropped Brendan about as quickly as I had been earlier. It ended with Spideog kneeling on Brendan's back and holding his wrist in what looked like a very painful position. The archer gave me a pleading look.

'Brendan, are you going to knock it off?'

'Yes,' he groaned into the floor.

Spideog let go. I was expecting Brendan to get up furious, instead he came up wide-eyed and said, 'How did you do that?'

'Simple,' greeny said, bouncing on his toes, 'your attack was sloppy and I – well – I am very good.'

Brendan rubbed his sore shoulder and amazingly smiled. 'Can you teach me that?'

'Why, I would be delighted. First stand with your feet in a stance just wider than your shoulders, then—'

'Ah, excuse me. Remember me, Prince of Duir?'

'Oh yes, Your Highness. I will teach you as well,' Spideog said. 'You obviously need some combat training. Take today for instance. You were standing in an armoury with all manner of weapons and shields and when you came under attack from an arrow, you chose a stick. Who in The Land taught you defence?'

'My father and Master Dahy,' I announced defensively.

'Dahy, of course – sticks and elbows. I'm surprised any of you are still alive.'

'Now hold on a minute,' I said, straightening up. 'I'll not have you badmouthing Master Dahy. Why, I ought to—'

'Easy, Conor,' Brendan said, coming between us. 'You don't want to take a swing at him, I tried that, it doesn't work. Anyway didn't we come in here for a reason?'

'Yes,' I said, giving Spideog one last dirty look. 'Mom said the Sword of Duir is here.'

'It is, my lord,' the green man replied. 'The Lawnmower is right over there.'

'What did you call it?'

'The Lawnmower. Your father had it renamed when he returned it to the armoury.'

Sure enough there she was, in the middle of the weapon racks in a gold-flecked clear crystal case – the family blade. At the base was a silver plaque that read, 'Lawnmower – the Sword of Duir'. I couldn't help but laugh.

'Lawnmower?' Brendan asked, confused.

'It's a long story.'

'If I may ask, my lord, what is a lawnmower?'

'What did my father tell you?'

'Lord Oisin and I do not ... eh ... chat.'

'I can't imagine why not,' I said sarcastically, 'but to answer your question, it's a machine used to keep grass short.'

'What is wrong with sheep?'

Spideog removed an acorn-shaped gold medallion from around his neck and slid it into a slot at the base of the display. The gold embedded in the glass glowed, a seam appeared in the front panel and then it opened on invisible hinges like tiny church doors. I reached in and grabbed the Sword of Duir. It always surprises me how light and contoured to my hand the Lawnmower is. It felt like an extension of my arm. I once let Araf hold it and was amazed when he complained how uncomfortable the handle was. I mentioned what he said to Dad and he said, 'It's a Duir thing – the blade knows a Child of Oak.'

'OK, now that we are all pals,' Brendan said, 'how come you attacked me when I reached for the bow?'

'I did not attack you,' Spideog corrected, 'if I had attacked you, you would be dead. I merely stopped you.'

'OK, why did you *stop* me then?'

'He stopped you, Brendan,' I answered, 'because that bow is not yours.'

'I wasn't gonna steal it.'

'Yew wood is special around here,' I said. 'Only a master archer can use a yew bow and if you want one you have to get the wood yourself. Only a person who has been deemed worthy by the tree can use that bow.'

'Deemed worthy by a tree?'

'It's complicated, I'll explain later.'

'Oh, now I see,' Spideog exclaimed, 'you must be the voyager from the Real World.'

'I am,' Brendan replied.

'Ah. I pay little attention to the gossip of the castle but I now remember hearing of you.' Spideog turned to me. 'If I may, my lord, all that you say is true but that is not why I fired on the voyager. The reason I stopped him was because he looks uncannily like a Fili.'

'Why would you attack a Fili?' I asked.

'These bows belonged to Maeve's Druid archers from the Fili war.'

'Oh my gods,' I said, 'these are from the soldiers who were killed when Maeve's massive Shadowspell backfired.'

'That is correct.'

'But why were they not buried with the dead?'

'Who said they are dead?'

'Ah – everybody.'

'I was there, Prince, I saw no bodies.'

'What?'

'Everyone presumes the Fili died when Maeve performed her foul witchcraft but I saw no dead. I saw an amber wave, I saw the Fili scream and writhe in pain but then they vanished. Behind them they left their clothes and weapons, in fact all of their earthly possessions – but no bodies.'

'No body, no murder,' Brendan mumbled.

'Gosh,' I said, 'where have I heard that before?'

'Most think I'm mad,' said Spideog, 'but I live here in the armoury and guard against their return.'

'He *is* a bit mad,' Mom said later that night when I told her about my adventure in the armoury. (I left out the part where Spideog aimed an arrow at my neck. You know how Mom gets when somebody tries to hurt me.) 'But there is no better fighter in The Land. He has even bested Dahy. While Cialtie was on the Oak Throne he lived deep in the Yewlands and reportedly waged a pretty effective one-man resistance war against Cialtie's Banshee patrols.'

'Apparently Dad doesn't like him.'

'Oh, he drives your father crazy. To be honest, that's one of the things I like best about Spideog,' Mom said with a mischievous grin that quickly changed into the frown that she seemed to always be wearing these days.

'And he keeps that armoury so tidy.'

Chapter Nine
Mother Oak

I didn't see much of Brendan for the next couple of days. He spent almost all of his time in the armoury with Spideog and I spent most of that time sitting with Dad. Mom said maybe he could hear us, so I read him stories from books I found in the library. Even if he couldn't hear, it was good for me. Many of the tales were about Duir so it helped me bone up on family history and it also improved my ancient Gaelic reading skills. Mom said we were going to be doing a lot of research when we got to the Hazellands.

I read a chronicle of the Fili war. Fand's mother Maeve really did lose it. She not only decimated much of the Rowan forest but took out a lot of alder trees as well – another reason why the Brownies shun everybody in The Land. I read nursery rhymes about not killing animals because they might be Pookas, not sleeping under alders and a story about a bunch of guys who sailed away from The Land and got old. I even tried to decipher Elven poetry. I needed a dictionary for that.

As I sat by his bed conjugating a verb I started to laugh. 'Gosh, Pop,' I said aloud, 'I probably shouldn't do this in front of you. The shock of me doing language homework, on my own, could kill you.' I stared through the amber to see if I could detect the slightest of smiles. I thought I saw something move but maybe that was just the water welling up in my eyes.

When I wasn't with Dad I spent the rest of my time in my room throwing a knife I found in the armoury. If this knife had once had a gold tip it was now well worn off. Let me tell you, without Dahy's magic points, these suckers are hard to throw.

Aein came in while I was practising my knife-play. She gave me a dirty look and said, 'Like father like son,' then informed me that my mother and her entourage would leave at dawn. I went looking for Brendan to tell him. I found him in the armoury practising archery with Spideog. They already knew – Spideog was heading up the Queen's guard.

Every time I go on a trip in this place the person who plans it says, 'We leave at dawn.' What is it with that? Why doesn't someone say, 'Let's leave ten-ish,' or 'Whenever you get up will be fine.' No. Dawn it always is. And leaving at dawn means just that, so you have to get up at least an hour before dawn! I'm not very good before noon, so getting up before dawn means the majority of my day is useless.

Brendan was awake and ready when I got to his room.

'You're late,' he said.

'So shoot me. Oh wait, you already tried that.' I'm not only useless in the morning, I can also be a bit testy.

'I was going to make my way to the stables by myself but I didn't want your mother to ju-jitsu me into a wall when she saw me. What did she say when you told her I was coming?'

'Eh – I haven't quite told her yet.'

'Oh great.'

'You see, my motto is it's always easier to apologise than it is to ask permission.'

'That's a fine philosophy if it's not *you* flying butt over noggin in the air.'

'Fair point,' I said. 'I'll protect you – just don't touch her.'

'The thought of you protecting me fills me with *so* much confidence,' Brendan said sarcastically. 'Don't worry. My hands won't go near your momma.'

As is usual for these crack-of-dawn riding parties, everyone was pretty much saddled up and ready to go by the time I arrived. Being a royal personage means that most people don't give me any verbal grief for tardiness but that doesn't stop the dirty looks.

Mom of course is the exception to that rule. She was just about to chew my head off for being late when she saw Brendan.

'What is he doing here?'

'Chill, Mom, he's with me.'

'I most certainly will not chill, whatever that means – I will not have him coming with us.'

I took a deep breath and said, 'I am a prince of Duir and this man is under my protection. He travels with me.'

Mom and I stared into each other's eyes. I had never stood up to my mother and I was pretty sure pulling a royal card on her wasn't going to work. We glared at each other for about five seconds – the longest five seconds of my life – before she said, 'Very well. Hurry up, you have made us late.'

When I started breathing again and my heart rate dropped down to a manageable rhythm, I was addressed by a Leprechaun I remembered from the ruined stables in the Hall of Knowledge.

'Greetings, Lord Conor. It is good to see you again. When Lady Deirdre told me you needed your horse I was not sure which one she meant, so I saddled both.'

A stable-hand led out two sights for sore eyes. 'Acorn! Cloud!' I yelled. I didn't know which one to hug first and I certainly didn't want to insult one over the other. A woman scorned is trouble but

a jealous horse can pitch you into a ravine. I patted both s
simultaneously. Since Cloud is the easier ride, I suspected that she
was the less sensitive of the two – I gave her to Brendan.

We rode through the courtyard past a small throng of bowers
and wavers and up to the main oak gates of Duir. While reading
to Dad during the previous few days, I had read that Maeve had
promised to reduce them to kindling. That would have been a
hell of a trick. The two gates were over two storeys high and
almost as wide. When closed they displayed a huge carving of an
oak tree. On each leaf of the tree, inlaid in gold, were all the runes
of the lands comprising Tir na Nog. The largest rune was the
major Oak Rune; next to it was a carving of what was then hanging from my waist – the Lawnmower – the Sword of Duir. As the
team of horses pulled open the gates, the depth of these monsters
became apparent. The gates were as thick as I was tall. I promised
myself that after I woke Dad up I would ask him where they came
from.

A small battalion fronted by Spideog and Araf awaited us on
the other side of the gates. As we approached they saluted and
parted. Araf slipped in next to me.

'Hey, Imp buddy, I didn't know you were coming.'

'A prince of the House of Duir must always travel with a bodyguard. It was one of your father's first rules.'

'Do you mean every time I leave home I'm stuck with you?' I
said with a smile. Araf didn't answer me. He doesn't usually answer
straight questions. There's no hope he'd answer a rhetorical one.

I promised myself I wouldn't go on and on like I usually do
about how beautiful The Land is, but I just gotta say that fall in
The Land is awesome. I'm not using the word 'awesome' the
way a mall-rat would describe a slush drink; when I say awesome
I mean it. The scenery in the Forest of Duir actually inspired
awe and not just with Brendan and me. Most of our troop rode
with wide eyes and mouths open and the majority of them were

sand years old. I suspect you could never
ry no matter how many times you had seen

old your hands out in front of you palm up, like
one of these leaves would cover both of your
hands completely. The major colour of the foliage was 'inferno'
orange. The leaves were almost incandescent and gave off a glow
in the sunlight that made all our complexions look like we had
been caught in an explosion at a fake-tan factory. The reds and
yellows and greens were there to provide dazzling counterpoint.
Periodically you would see a bold tree that was solely in red or
another just in yellow. The colours were everywhere, even under-
foot, gently rustling under our horses' hooves.

The air, scented with the perfume of fallen leaves, was cool and
crisp – you felt like it could almost cut you – and it was crystal
clear, like the way the world looks after you clean a pair of dirty
sunglasses. I can honestly say I have never experienced a more
invigorating morning. Sorry about the gushing – I promise I won't
mention spring.

We rode in silence letting our eyes and sighs do all the talking.
About an hour before noon we entered Glen Duir and Mom
dropped back to talk to me.

'Oisin said Mother Oak was asking after you the last time he
spoke to her. Would you like to stop for a quick chat?'

'Yes please,' I said as an involuntary smile took over my face. I
kicked into a gallop with Araf close on my tail. I crested the hill
and saw the old lady dressed in her fall best. Her leaves were mostly
yellows and light browns like a comfortable patchwork quilt. I
dismounted before Acorn came to a stop, ran up to her and
wrapped my arms around her trunk.

'Oh my,' came that lovely voice in my head, 'who is this in such
a rush?'

'It's me, Mother Oak – Conor.'

'Oh my, my, the Prince of Hazel and Oak; I have been worried about you.'

'I'm fine.'

'Oh, but your father is not,' she said, reading my thoughts. 'Climb up higher and tell me all about it.'

I climbed a bit and she brought branches in behind me to rest against. I told her about what had happened to Dad, and what Mom and Fand had done.

'Oh, I had feared as much. I knew something was wrong with your father the last time he came to visit with me. But try not to worry yourself too much, my dear, your mother is a very clever witch. If anyone can find a cure it will be her.'

I knew that already but Mother Oak has a way of turning knowledge into belief. I hugged her again.

'I have to go,' I said, 'the others are waiting for me.'

'Take good care of yourself, Conor. Come and see me in the spring.'

'I will.' I started to leave and then added, 'By the way your foliage looks beautiful.'

'Do you really think so?' she asked. 'The fashion among the other trees these days just seems a bit gaudy to me.'

'Well, I think you look elegant.'

I hugged her one more time and I know it sounds impossible for a tree but I think she blushed.

I walked over the knoll. It always takes me some time to clear my head after talking to a tree. I saw a small group standing around someone on the ground. As I got closer I saw it was Brendan unconscious on his back.

'What happened?' I asked the throng.

'I don't know,' a guard said. 'Ask him.'

Spideog crested the knoll with a bucket of water in his hand. Ignoring my questions, he poured the whole thing onto Brendan's face. The detective popped up spluttering, tried to stand and then dropped back down holding his head.

'Has someone hit me with a stick again?' Brendan asked.

'Did you hit him with a stick?' I asked Spideog.

'No,' he said, 'a rock.'

'Why?'

'I would like to have a word with you in private, if I may.'

Spideog and I walked out of earshot and he said, 'Our friend Brendan was about to shoot a tree with an arrow. I was too far away to stop him so I threw a rock. It was either that or place an arrow in him.'

'Thank you, Spideog; he didn't know what he was doing.'

'I have spent many a year in the Real World, Prince Conor, and I know how mortals treat trees but there are others here who might not be so understanding. Remember he is under your protection. Make sure he does not do it again.'

We walked back. Brendan was on his feet.

'You have to stop your friends from hitting me in the head with sticks.'

'It was a rock.'

'OK,' he said. 'You have to stop your friends hitting me with sticks and rocks.'

'You promised you would keep your hands in your pockets. What were you doing when Spideog threw the rock at you?'

'Spideog hit me? What for?'

'What were you doing?'

'I got bored waiting for you so I notched an arrow and was about to do a bit of archery practice.'

'And what were you aiming at?'

Brendan pointed to a young oak. His misfired arrow was about ten yards behind it.

'Come with me,' I said, grabbing him by the arm and leading him to Mother Oak.

'Hug that tree,' I demanded.

'What?'

'Hug that tree.'

'I'm not going to hug a tree.'

'Hug that tree or I will have you dragged back to Castle Duir in chains and you can stare at Frick and Frack for the next year.'

He looked at me and then tilted his head. 'You mean it, don't you?'

'Yes.'

'If I didn't know better, I'd say my mother put you up to this.'

'Hug!'

Brendan approached the tree and with an *if it will make you happy* attitude, wrapped his arms around Mother Oak. His smirk disappeared in an instant. I wish I could have heard Mother Oak's side of the conversation 'cause all I heard from Brendan was 'Yes, ma'am' and 'No, ma'am.' His conversation finished with, 'It won't happen again, ma'am.' Then he let go of the tree and staggered.

I caught him by the arm. 'Steady, Detective.'

He tried looking me in the eyes but wasn't focusing well. 'I'm still concussed, aren't I?'

'I'm pretty sure you're not.'

'Yeah,' he said, regaining his balance, 'I was afraid of that.'

I waited for him to say something else but he just stood there. Finally I asked, 'So what did you think of Mother Oak?'

'That's a heck of a tree.'

I laughed. 'That's what I said when I first met her.'

A group of soldiers had galloped ahead and had started cooking so that dinner was ready to be served almost as soon as we made camp. Other soldiers pitched tents for Mom and me. As I have said I'm not a big fan of the royal treatment I get around here but after a hard day of riding – well, it would be rude of me to complain about a meal and a clean bed.

Brendan wolfed down his supper and then disappeared. I had a silent meal with Araf and then decided to hit the hay in the luxury of my own royal tent. As I approached it I heard a strange noise coming from inside. I unsheathed the Lawnmower and pushed open the flap only to find Brendan snoring in my bed. No amount of shaking and then kicking could get him to move so I grabbed a blanket and slept out under the stars on a lumpy piece of ground next to Araf. I fell asleep thinking of ways to strangle Brendan as he slept.

I was having a dream about Essa talking to an invisible man when I was awoken by a ruckus at the edge of the camp. I saw Mom heading towards the commotion. Araf and I followed. At the perimeter of the paddock we found Mom tending a wounded soldier. Next to him was a dead wolf with an arrow through its chest.

Mom stood up and walked over to the wolf. 'Who shot the beast?' she demanded.

'I did,' came a response from the shadows. It was Spideog.

'Explain yourself.'

'It was a last resort, Lady Deirdre. I arrived as the wolves were harassing the horses. The guards were shooing them away when they attacked. This man went down and lost his banta stick. I only fired when the wolf went for him on the ground. I had no choice.'

Mom looked at the wounded guard, who nodded in agreement. Mom placed her hand on the neck of the wolf and then began to run both her hands over the animal. She paused for what seemed to be the longest time, turning her head from one side to another, and then suddenly reached into her boot and pulled out a knife. She cut a long incision deep into the creature's abdomen and reached inside. When her bloody hand emerged she held a short wire necklace with a small flat gold disc attached. She held it up and displayed it to Spideog. The look on both of their faces made me feel very afraid.

Chapter Ten
The Athrú

Ididn't get a chance to talk to Mom until we were back on the road the next day. I slid Acorn up next to her and asked, 'What was that thing you pulled out of the wolf last night? It looked like it really spooked you.'

'Yes, I was certainly freaked up.'

'Out.'

'Damn, I thought I had that one right,' she said with a smile. 'No matter. The necklace I pulled out of the wolf was an *athrú*.'

'An athrú?'

'Do you remember the Pooka that died when you were first in the Fililands?'

'How could I forget.'

'Do you remember the piece of gold I placed in his mouth before he died?'

'I do, it scared the hell out of me. You put the disc in his mouth, then he changed into a wolf, howled, died and changed back.'

'Well, the disc I put in his mouth was his athrú – a Pooka amulet. The Pooka wear them around their necks, it helps them change. The wire it hangs from expands and contracts so it doesn't fall off during the metamorphosis.'

'Like Banshee blade wire?'

'Exactly,' Mom said. 'The wolf that Spideog killed had an athrú in its stomach.'

'That wolf was a Pooka?'

'No, if it had been a Pooka it would have changed into a man when it died.'

'So where did the wolf get the amulet?'

'I can only conclude that that animal ate a Pooka but that just does not make sense.'

'Why not?'

'The Pookas are very secretive with their lore but I know a small bit.'

'You once told me that one of your tutors in the Hazellands was a Pooka.'

'Well remembered, son; yes, she was. She told me some things she probably should not have. One thing she taught me was that each athrú has a marking for each creature. The athrú I found in the wolf was marked Gearr. It was worn by a Pooka that could change into a hare.'

'So a crazy wolf accidentally wolfs down a Pooka hare. That sounds plausible to me.'

'But it is not,' Mom said, looking perturbed. 'Pookas have an almost telepathic control over animals, and the Pookas that change into small creatures always change back when threatened.'

'So what's the answer?'

'I do not know, my son. I do know that no Pooka has come to Castle Duir since your father took the throne and you said you were attacked by boar in the summer.'

'So you think there is something wrong in Pookaville?'

Mom gave me her quizzical look, 'How do you come up with these words?'

The Land's fall colour spectacular continued throughout the day. Brendan, it turned out, was quite the equestrian. It made me regret letting him ride Cloud. Don't get me wrong, Acorn is a great horse and the best mount a man can have when the chips are down, but Cloud is a much easier ride, like having power steering in a car.

Our second night's camp was uneventful. I kept an eye on Brendan at dinner and followed him when he left early. As he approached my tent I said, 'That would be my tent.'

'Oh,' he said, 'I thought it was for guests.'

'Yeah, right. It's mine and if you steal it again, I'm going to tell my mother.'

'Oh,' Brendan said, 'I guess I'll find somewhere else.'

Sometimes it's handy having a warrior queen for a mother.

Acorn got jittery when we crossed the border into the Hazellands but it wasn't as bad as the last time. Mom rode up next to me and spoke into my horse's ear and settled him down. I think another reason why Acorn calmed down was because the Hazellands were starting to look a lot better. The first time I was here it seemed as if the life had been sucked out of it – now it felt as if the place was on the mend. Like fresh new skin growing on a bad wound. Fallen trees had been cut for wood and charred branches had been cleared away. As we climbed a small hill I remembered where we were. The top of the rise was the spot where Araf had first laid eyes on the destruction of the Field – the Imp garden where Araf had lost so many kinsmen. The last time he had seen the Field it had been trashed so badly he nearly fell out of his saddle. This time he crested the hill and said, 'Will you look at that.'

It is so rare for Araf to spontaneously make any noise that it always startles me when he does. I pulled up next to him and saw what he saw. What was once a scorched and blackened patch of land had been cleared and tilled. A team of Imps were planting trees and tending gardens. Araf looked on like a dog sighting a bird in a bush.

'Master Spideog!' I called.

Spideog rode next to us, taking in the wide-eyed Araf and the Field.

'Master Spideog,' I said, 'I wonder if Prince Araf might be able to be released from his bodyguard duties for a few hours.'

Araf looked at me like a boy getting permission from his mother to go swimming on a hot day.

'I think we can spare his stick for the rest of the afternoon,' Spideog said. 'Prince Araf, you are relieved.'

A rare ear-to-ear smile erupted on the Imp's face as he reached for the whistle hanging around his neck. He simultaneously kicked his mount into a gallop and blew. All of the Imps in the distance immediately stopped what they were doing and then began to cheer as they saw their prince speeding towards them. We watched as a mob of Imps practically dragged him from his horse. How anybody can get excited about spending an afternoon covered in dirt is beyond me but I knew Araf was now as happy as a pig in muck.

As we got closer to the outbuildings it became obvious how much work had been done. All of the rubble had been cleared away or stacked for later repair. Several of the smaller buildings had been rebuilt and then there was the landscaping. Those Imp guys sure can plant stuff. Hedges, young trees and flowerbeds were everywhere.

As we approached what looked like a guard house, Spideog kicked his horse and sped ahead. Just before he cleared the building, he notched an arrow in his bow and performed a magnificent full speed dismount. He hit the ground running using his horse for cover, then pulled his bow to full length and let his mount go on. He stood stock still, menacingly aiming a deadly arrow at something or someone that I couldn't see. I drew my sword and looked to Mom but she seemed more annoyed than concerned. She kicked her horse into a canter and I followed. Mom casually went behind Spideog – I on the other hand peeked around the building. Standing there with a crossbow pointed directly at Spideog's head was Master Dahy.

'*Boys*,' Mom said in a reproachful tone.

'Tell this old man to drop his weapon. His clumsy reconnaissance has been exposed,' Spideog said.

'First of all,' Dahy replied, 'I am younger than you.'

'In age maybe, but not in spirit.'

'Boys,' Mom said again. This time she sounded impatient.

'Secondly,' Dahy continued, ignoring the interruption, 'I have a Brownie crossbow aimed at your head. I'll drop you before you can even let go of that string.'

'Would you like to put that to the test, *Old Man*?'

Mom dismounted and walked between the two Masters. No matter how much they wanted to kill each other (and it sure looked like they did) their duty kicked in as soon as the Queen of Duir stepped into the line of fire. They immediately lowered their weapons.

'Now that is better,' Mom said in an overly calm tone. 'I'm going to return to my mount. I shall assume you two will not again raise your weapons to each other after I leave.' When she got no response, she said, 'Master Spideog?'

'Yes, my lady,' Spideog said, replacing his arrow in his quiver.

'Master Dahy?'

'Of course, Lady Deirdre,' Dahy replied, removing the bolt from his crossbow.

I don't know how many years those two had between them, probably thousands, but at that moment they sounded like eight-year-olds.

'Master Spideog, you are with me,' Mom commanded. 'Master Dahy, I have royal bodyguard duty for you. He is over there hiding behind that wall – I think you may have met.'

I stuck my nose around the building and waved.

'Conor!' Dahy said as he approached and placed his arms on my shoulders. 'When did you get back?'

'About a week ago; I would have thought someone would have told you.'

'News is slow around here. I don't have an emain slate. The Leprechaun who made them was killed when Cialtie blew out the east wing. The new ones don't work very well. I've had to rely on couriers. Tell me, how is your father?'

We mounted up and I told him what Mom and Fand had done to Dad and about Mom's magic Shadowbook paperclip. He took it all in without surprise like I was telling him the latest football scores. I guess if you're as old as Dahy and have lived all of that time with witches and oracles, it's easy to take news like this in your stride.

'So you are going to be with us for a while then?' Dahy asked.

'As long as it takes.'

'Good, I can use you.'

'Use me for what?' I asked suspiciously.

We passed one of the Hall's outbuildings; I recognised it as the one where Lorcan clothes-lined me so long ago. Just past that we rounded a bend and I saw a large group of soldiers standing around a pair of duelling banta fighters in full protective gear.

'You finally got your security force for the Hall of Knowledge,' I said.

'Yes,' Dahy replied, 'I imagine even your grandfather wouldn't have minded, given the circumstances. I wanted a more ecumenical group but they are mostly Imps, Leprechauns and Faeries.'

'Faeries?'

'Of course. There are a few Banshees but I couldn't get any Elves or Brownies to join and nobody has spotted a Pooka in ages. This lot are all very green. I could use your help to train them.'

I was just about to ask what a Faerie looked like when the banta stick duel captured my attention. The one guy wasn't doing very well. Every time he mounted an attack his opponent seemed to know in advance exactly where it was going to come from. His opponent's parries and counter-attacks were minimal and effective to the point of perfection. But what really caught my attention was the posture and footwork. There was only one person that moved like that and it made my heart race even before she took off her head protector and shook her wavy black hair over her shoulders like a model in a shampoo commercial. Essa turned and our eyes locked. She was definitely surprised to see me but, as usual with that girl, I wasn't sure if she was happy about it or not.

All eyes turned to Dahy and me as we approached. Essa's duelling partner took off his headpiece and for a moment I was hit with déjà vu. As he revealed his black hair with a white tuft in the front, I momentarily thought it was Fergal but then the Banshee's sharp facial lines and broad chin broke the illusion.

'Attention, Soldiers of the Red Hand,' Dahy shouted.

The group snapped to attention. I smiled. Dahy had held onto the same name as the army that last occupied the Hazellands.

'I give you Conor, Prince of Duir!'

Everybody dropped to one knee and bowed their heads, except, I noticed, Essa and her Banshee-duelling partner.

I dismounted. 'Hi, folks. Look, I'm gonna be around here for a while so you don't have to do that – OK?'

'As you were,' Dahy ordered and everybody relaxed as a buzz went through the crowd.

Essa gave a loud theatrical cough and thankfully the hundreds of eyes left me and turned to her. 'If our regal visitor doesn't mind, shall we continue with our training?'

Her troops straightened up and quieted down. She was more beautiful than I had even remembered. What kind of idiot was I, leaving a woman like this behind? She finished by staring at me with a question on her face and I realised she actually wanted *me* to answer her question.

'No, no,' I stammered, 'by all means continue.'

She seemed to smile at me but only from one side of her mouth. 'We have been working all day on banta fighting. Excellent for helping improve footwork and winning competitions, but in battle you are most likely to be attacked with a sword. What happens if you only have a banta stick to defend yourself with?'

I came very close to shouting out, 'You're screwed,' but two things stopped me: one was that I had seen Essa fight sword with stick and she was damn good at it; secondly, I instinctively felt that undermining Essa in front of her students would be a bad idea.

'Our new guest, Prince Conor,' Essa continued, 'fancies himself as quite the swordsman. Your Highness,' she said with just enough sarcasm that only I heard it, 'would you like to help me with this demonstration?'

'How about we nip off and spend a little alone time,' is what I really wanted to say. Instead I answered, 'Sure.'

I walked to the midst of about a hundred young eager eyes. Essa and I squared off in the centre and slowly circled each other. For the first time a proper smile crossed her face. Gods, she was stunning. I drew my sword and her smile vanished. She backed into the crowd and threw her banta stick to a soldier and took a training stick from another. She returned back to the centre.

'Conor is wielding a very good sword indeed. Does anyone recognise it?' A few hands went up. 'It is the Sword of Duir.'

A murmur shot through the group. Men and women strained to get a look at the Lawnmower as I held it aloft.

'The difficulty with fighting a sword, especially one as good as this one, is that you must not make direct contact. When wood meets steel head on – it is usually wood that loses.'

Essa was holding her stick straight out in a pre-duel position with her head turned to face her pupils. I swung the Lawnmower high and sliced about a foot off the top of her banta stick. It was like knife through butter. The crowd laughed. Essa turned and even though she had a smile on her face for the crowd, her eyes had a look I didn't like. She inspected the stick and then threw it into the audience. A replacement sailed back immediately. Dahy stepped into the circle holding a dulled training sword. I reluctantly swapped the Lawnmower for it.

'Thank you, Prince Conor, for that demonstration,' she said as she refaced her class. It was probably a good thing Dahy changed my sword 'cause I'm sure I would have done the same thing again. I think stuff like that a second time is even funnier than the first but some people don't agree and I knew Essa was definitely one of them. 'A sword is obviously the stronger weapon,' she continued, 'but it is inferior in length. You must use your superior reach to set the rhythm and tempo of the fight – directing the battle to your terms.'

She faced me directly and stood at attention, so I did too. We both bowed at the waist with our eyes locked. Our faces were inches away – I whispered, 'Miss me?'

She stood erect, assumed a fighting stance and said, '*En garde.*'

I raised my sword, adjusted my footing and asked, 'Is that a yes, or a no?'

Chapter Eleven
Essa

Essa and I circled to the right. This time, as she addressed her class, she never took her eyes off me.

'You will probably have almost double the reach of anyone wielding a sword. If your opponent sets up too close …' Essa nodded, inviting me closer, 'then give him a reminder that you are carrying a long stick.' With the quickest of clicks she tapped my blade out of its position and poked me hard in the chest with her stick.

'Hey!' I shouted, stepping back and rubbing my chest. 'You told me to step in.'

'And if your opponent is stupid enough to do what you tell him to do – make sure to take advantage of that.'

The crowd laughed. I forced a smile onto my face and stopped rubbing the place she had hit me – even though it still really hurt.

'Once you have set the proper fighting distance, your opponent will be forced to attack your stick, not you.'

I could see her point but I wasn't going to play her game and I certainly didn't want to stand there and swipe at a stick. I decided to make my first attack a deep body swipe – the kind of advance that would be dangerous to ignore. I bounced backwards and forwards on my toes, made a short backhand fake that brought her stick out of position and then lunged with a full cut to the body.

Without seeming to move her legs at all, Essa instantly backed out of reach. I had forgotten just how fast that girl moved. Her stick lightly engaged with the leading edge of my moving sword, circled around it and then pushed it away. By the time I got control my arm was way across my body and my weapon was nowhere near where it should have been. Essa slid one hand to the middle of her stick and swung the base of her banta into my kidney. It dropped me to one knee.

'Usually I would not have counter-attacked so soon in a match. As you all should know, the golden rule is to parry and retreat until you can ascertain your opponent's favourite attack. I have an advantage with the Prince – I already know his favourite attack.' Essa came over to where I was still on one knee. As she helped me to my feet she whispered, 'Miss me?'

I was still wondering if I would ever be able again to pass water with that kidney when she flowed back into her *en garde* position and asked, 'Ready?'

I held up my hand for a time-out and stepped in close to her. 'Do you think maybe I should have some protective clothing?'

'Aw come on, Conor, it's only a stick. You've got a great big sword.'

'You ... you could poke my eye out.'

'I promise I won't hit you in the head – even though it is such a large target.'

I tried to remember some old saying about a woman scorned but I didn't have time. She started circling again, this time to my left and she was doing that figure of eight spinning thing with her banta that I had seen Araf do – it made me feel a bit woozy. I decided that maybe Essa's students shouldn't be the only ones paying attention to her tutorial, so I attacked the stick. I just stuck my blade into the twirling thing and she flipped it into a counter-attack. Fortunately I was ready for it and brought my sword up into a high backhanded parry. When she saw the steel coming she checked her swing and bounced back in to her home position.

'Well done, Princess,' came a shout from one of the people in the crowd.

I took a couple more swipes at the stick and every time pretty much the same thing happened. She would make light contact and attempt to counter but would then pull back at the last second, to avoid her wood being damaged by my steel. Essa's bravado, the bruises on my chest and side, her cheering peanut gallery and the fact that she was the third best stick fighter I had ever seen had initially made me feel like I was the underdog but I was starting to remember that I had a sword. I had the better weapon.

I took another swipe at her banta but this time when she attempted her counter-attack I stepped in and took a full power cut at her weapon. My sword made hard contact with the top of her stick. If I had been using the Lawnmower I would have sliced that bit clean off – this dulled thing stuck halfway into the wood. As Essa pulled back I felt the tug and quickly twisted my pommel. I heard the crack as about ten inches of her stick spun into the air.

Essa backed and circled. The same voice from the crowd called out, 'Not to worry, Princess.' As Essa inspected her weapon I stole a quick glance to see who the cheerleader was. It was the Banshee she had been sparring with earlier.

While she was readjusting to the new length of her stick, I moved in a step and began my trademarked low sword attack. That's where I keep my blade low and then swipe upward using my natural agility to bob and weave my head out of the way. I should note that every fighting teacher has told me that this is a very bad idea but it usually unnerves an opponent the first time they see it and I'm pretty sure I never did it when Essa was around. It worked too. She backed up fast but before she ran out of room, she took a full baseball swing to my head that made me hit the ground with a roll.

'Hey,' I shouted as I jumped back to my feet, 'you promised not to hit me in the head.'

'If you're just going to hang your face out there, I can't resist taking a pop at it.'

'Good one, Essa,' the Banshee shouted.

The crowd was getting pretty worked up and from the sounds of it, I wasn't the hometown team. It's dangerous when emotions creep into a practice fight and at that moment I wanted to kill the girl of my dreams. From the look in her eyes *my love* wanted to do the same thing. I should have called it off right then and there – instead I modified my attack. While protecting my face, I succeeded in backing Essa into her cheering section. Just as she was about to run out of room – she did it. I knew she would. I knew she couldn't resist showing off for her pupils. She launched herself straight up and over my head and attempted to grind her banta into my shoulder as she pole-vaulted over me – but I was ready for it. When she was directly over my head, I dropped to the ground. Her stick made contact with nothing but air. The self-satisfied smile on her face vanished as she realised she didn't have enough leverage to complete her somersault. She instantly went from a graceful gymnast to a flailing circus clown and landed hard on her back.

I stood up and turned to the silenced audience. 'I know some of my opponent's favourite attacks too.' My line didn't do as well as when Essa used it. I think it was safe to say they didn't like me too much.

After rolling over onto all fours and taking a few quick breaths Essa stood and the look on her face made me realise I had gone too far. I lowered my sword and was about to call a stop when that damn Banshee shouted, 'You're not going to let him get away with that are you, Princess?'

Essa dropped right back into fighting mode and came at me with a series of short fast swings that got me back-pedalling. I didn't want this fight any more. I didn't mean to humiliate her in front of her students. I just wanted to sit with her and ask her how she was and tell her how much I had missed her but that stick just kept on coming. One swipe came so close to my nose I smelled the sap in the timber. I finally parried a cut hard and my sword once again stuck into the wood. As she tried to pull it free I stepped in. She was forced close. I don't think I had ever seen her this mad before – and I had seen Essa plenty mad.

'Come on, Princess – you can take this Faerie.'

'Who,' I asked Essa, her face inches from mine, 'is the Banshee with the big mouth?'

Essa grunted and with all of her strength threw me back, disengaging our weapons. 'That,' she said, while assuming a very menacing crouch, 'would be my fiancé.'

'What?' I stood straight up and dropped my guard. I looked directly into her eyes to see if she was serious. That's probably why I didn't spot the stick before it connected with my head.

In movies people wake up from a concussion and then feel their head like the pain comes as a surprise. That's not how it works. The pain comes way before you open your eyes and if you have had as much experience with involuntary unconsciousness as I have, you delay opening them for as long as possible, 'cause that's when the second wave of hurt arrives.

So as I lay there the first thing I noticed was the pain. Then I worked on the basics: who was I? – Conor O'Neil. Good, if you don't know that one you're in trouble. Where was I? – Scranton? No – Tir na Nog. How did I end up out cold and flat on my back? Essa. Essa hit me – she said she wouldn't but she did. I had been looking for Essa. Where did I find her? The Hazellands. And she wasn't as happy to see me as I thought she would be. In fact she seemed downright mad at me.

I felt a cold compress land on my forehead. The blessed cold ratcheted the pain level down a couple of notches.

Well, she couldn't be that mad at me, I thought, *if she was willing to nurse me. She must be feeling bad for hitting me in the head.*

I reached up and placed my hand on hers. So why did she hit me? It was an accident – I had dropped my guard. Why did I do that?

I shot straight up in bed and shouted, 'You're engaged!'

'No I am not,' said the startled and still blurry face in front of me.

Chapter Twelve
The Turlow

The aforementioned second wave of pain hit me like a well-swung mace. I closed my eyes and lay back down. The pain was lessened only by the revelation that Essa wasn't engaged. I squeezed her hand and she returned the gesture. This time I slowly opened my eyes but as the world became less fuzzy Essa got increasingly uglier. When I came properly to my senses I found myself holding hands with Araf.

'Who told you I was engaged?' the Imp demanded.

I quickly retrieved my hand. 'Essa?' I croaked.

'Essa told you I was engaged?'

'No, Essa is engaged,' I said.

'I know Essa is engaged but why is she going around telling people I am engaged? I'm a Prince of Ur. A rumour like that can cause a lot of trouble.'

My head hurt too much for this kind of confusion. 'No one said you were engaged.'

'You said I was engaged.'

'I didn't mean you, I thought you were Essa.'

'You think I look like Essa?' Araf looked concerned. 'I'll go get a healer.'

I dropped my head back on the pillow and covered my eyes. 'Maybe you should get a healer – I need something for my head.'

88

'There is something on your bedside table there.'

I sat up and knocked back the thimbleful of liquid from a silver shot-glass. I'm sure my face went as red as the inside of a thermometer and, as it returned to normal colour, my headache subsided. When I could breathe again I said, 'You knew that Essa was engaged?'

'Well yes, everyone knows that. Gerard announced it about three weeks ago. He sent all of the Runelords a cask of special wine – it was a lovely red. The bouquet had the slightest hint of—'

'Why didn't you tell me?' I interrupted.

'You didn't ask. I assumed, since you left, that you had no interest in Essa.'

'Well, you assumed wrong,' I said, as I slowly sat up and put my feet on the floor.

'But wasn't Essa interested in you by the end of your last visit?'

'She was.'

'And you left her?'

'Yes,' I said, feeling the pain in my head starting to return.

'That is not a good thing,' the Imp said in an ominous tone.

'Why?'

'I have known Essa a long time, my friend – she is not the forgiving type.'

Mom apparently had administered first aid and chewed out Essa for trying to take my head off. You know how she gets when someone attacks her little bear cub. She also had given me some sort of meds that knocked me out for the whole night – so I was surprised when sunshine blinded me as I opened the door. Morning in the Hazellands was a busy place. Imps and Leprechauns were clearing away rubble and rebuilding walls, while others were drilling or practising archery with Spideog.

I've started to realise that Araf only gets chatty when he is nervous or really happy. This morning he was still euphoric about his time with his fellow farmer Imps in the Field, so I pretended to be interested and asked him about his day digging in dirt. That kept him talking until we got our food and found a quiet table in the canteen.

'So who is he?'

'Who?'

'You know who, the Banshee who is engaged to Essa.'

'He is Turlow,' Araf said.

'So who is he then?'

'He's Turlow.'

'What does that mean?'

'He is The Turlow?'

'Araf, it doesn't matter how many different articles you use before saying Turlow, it doesn't explain anything.'

'Have you never heard the story about Ériu and her sisters?'

A spark flickered in my deep memory. Dad told me something about this when we were in the Rowan forest but there was so much going on and so much to remember. 'Remind me.'

Araf sighed like I was a schoolboy who hadn't done his home-work. 'Ériu was the first. She discovered The Land. She either found or created the first oak and maybe did the same for the Leprechauns. Then she sent for her two sisters Banbha and Fódla. Fódla,' Araf said as he touched his forehead in a semi-religious gesture, 'created or found the Imps and the Orchardlands.'

'What does this have to do with The Turlow?'

'Banbha was different from her sisters – darker. She created or, depending on what you believe, found the Yewlands. Then she travelled to the Otherworld, killed the Banshee King and convinced his son, Turlow, to come with her to defend Tir na Nog's shores. That is how the Banshees came to The Land.'

'Are you saying that this guy is *that* Turlow?'

'No, Turlow is the name passed down from father to son. This Turlow is said to be the direct descendant of the original Turlow. He is The Turlow. It is his name and his title.'

'So am I supposed to be impressed?'

'It is very impressive.'

'Did you hear him keep calling Essa "Princess"?'

'Essa is a princess,' Araf said, looking confused.

'Yeah, but it's the way he said it. And now that I think of it, he called me a Faerie.'

A little buzz started on the other side of the room which caused me to turn. Mom and Dahy had just entered and were making a beeline to our table.

Araf stood, so I did too. Mom gave me a hug and asked after my head.

'I'm fine thanks.'

'Are you sure?' She held my face in both of her hands and looked deep into my eyes.

'I'm sure, Mom.'

'Good, because we have work to do.'

The next couple of days were exhausting. The Land is a magnificent and beautiful place but it is seldom restful. I spent my time equally between rebuilding walls, training new recruits in sword-fighting and, most taxing of all, deciphering and filing old manuscripts, read with Mom's magic paperclip.

I tried to convince Mom that there were probably, hell definitely, a million people more qualified to sort through ancient Gaelic books than me but she said, 'If the gods will give us a way to cure your father, then I am betting on you finding it.'

There were only two of Mom's amber reader thingies, so ten of us rotated in twenty-four-hour shifts. It meant that I did four hours reading every twenty hours, resulting in my stint getting four hours later every day. My first couple of shifts were mostly spent trying to get my written Gaelic back up to speed. Dad had made me learn how to read, write and conjugate ancient Gaelic but it wasn't the language I read my comic books in and the stuff I was reading could hardly be called page-turners. My first thrilling manuscript was a contract and shipping manifest between the Elves and the Vinelands. It took me all of the four hours to figure out that it was a barter agreement where the Elves would provide wood for barrels and Fingal (who was Essa's grandfather) would pay in wine. From the amount of wine it seemed to me that the timber industry is a pretty lucrative business. I guess it's hard work when you have to ask permission from the trees if you want to cut them down. I had an image of an elf kneeling in front of a tree with an axe, saying, 'Please, I'm desperate for a drink?'

When I finally figured out that the piece of parchment I was studying didn't contain anything that would help us with Dad's condition I would place it in an envelope and label it so that in the future it could be transcribed into a new book. Not a job I will be volunteering for.

It wasn't just the grammar that was proving taxing but the actual reading of a manuscript required immense concentration. The paperclip thingy sensed the page you were looking at as long as you were focused, but if you were reading, say, a scintillating essay on seed germination and you happened to let your mind wander, the page you were reading would fade into all of the other pages in the book, producing thousands of words on one page. Since there was no way to find your way back to the page you were reading, you would have to go back to the beginning.

After my first session I staggered back to my tent and blissfully closed the eyes that I had been afraid to even blink for the last four hours. Not even the blinding headache could keep me from falling asleep, but I didn't nap long. Dahy woke me and, despite my protests, dragged me out to the training fields and put me in charge of teaching sword-fighting to a group of helpless recruits.

As soon as the old man was out of sight I told my charges to take the rest of the day off and I crawled back to bed. The next day Dahy warned me that if I did that again I would be cleaning latrines and I had a suspicion that he meant it.

My second reading session started promisingly enough when I found what I thought was going to be an interesting essay on banta stick manufacture. After I don't know how many pages, I figured out it could have easily been condensed to this one sentence without losing anything: 'Get some good wood and make a stick out of it.' By the end, my head hurt worse than when Essa hit me with one of those sticks.

I periodically saw Essa but we didn't speak to one another. I was desperate for some alone time with her but I was so busy, and when I wasn't busy, I was exhausted. When I did see her she was always with The Turlow. The closest I got was an uncomfortable lunch where the royal couple sat behind me at a table just within hearing distance. I couldn't make out much but every time I heard him say 'Princess' I felt like returning my lunch back onto my plate.

After about a week's worth of reading sessions I was starting to believe that 99 per cent of the books that were in the old library were about farming. I ploughed through endless manuscripts explaining crop rotation, plough manufacture, planting time-tables and even one about delineating soil types by taste. I filed that under the heading of 'Eating Dirt'. I got mildly excited when I found a scrap entitled 'Leprechaun Genealogy' but it was literally just a list of names. I filed that as 'A Short History of Short People'.

I started screening my reading material so as to keep my sanity. I'm sure Araf would find a paper on 'Planting Row Orientation According to Crop and Season' fascinating but it just made me want to hold my breath and bang my head against the floor. When no one was looking I scanned my new manuscripts for key terms.

I'd clip the reader on a sliver of paper and if I saw any words like: *seed*, or *soil*, or *yield*, I would slip the piece under the bottom of the pile. I prayed to the gods that I wouldn't still be doing this by the time we got down to that fragment again.

The reading eventually got easier, partly because I got better at it but mostly because Mom invented a Shadowbookmark that held your page if your mind wandered. But it was the sword-fight teaching that became the highlight of my day. In the beginning my students were pretty much in awe of me, even after seeing me get popped in the temple by Essa. They all wanted to know about the Battle of the Twins of Macha and how I chopped Cialtie's hand off and the Army of the Red Hand and what the Real World was like. I spent a lot of the first couple of days just talking to them, especially when Dahy wasn't around, but then I really started to get into teaching. A lot of these kids were just bad, so I had to reach back into my memories to the basics that Dad had taught me when I was a kid. Back when I thought it was really cool being taught sword-fighting, as opposed to when I was a teenager and I thought Dad was a borderline lunatic. I found that the nice thing about teaching is that it makes you realise that a lot of the stuff you think you do by instinct and without thinking, is actually a well-honed skill. Dishing out all of this stuff to eager students, who were improving, made me appreciate my father even more and it gave me strength when I had to go back to the reading sessions.

I was usually so tired at night that I didn't have the energy to kick Brendan out of my tent – so we became roommates. He spent most of his days under the tutelage of Spideog. When no one else but me could hear, he made fun of his master's *mystical ravings*, but he listened and adopted every drop of archery advice he was given. When he wasn't talking about arrows and trajectories or how sore his arms and fingers were, he quizzed me on our progress towards finding a cure for Oisin. He never talked about his daughter. I suspected that the reason he had thrown himself so fully into training was to give himself something else to think about.

Mom gently kicked me awake at four in the morning. It was my shift in the reading room. Since Mom had the stint before me we saw each other every day at changeover. We didn't say much. I didn't ask her if she found anything 'cause I knew if she did, she would tell me. She looked tired as she handed me an envelope that had my handwriting on it. Inside it was a fragment of a document I had read the morning before about the cross-pollination of grape plants. I had entitled it, 'Everything will be Vine in the Morning'.

'Is that a joke?' she asked.

'Well, it was supposed to be but obviously it didn't work on you.'

She gave me that patronising mother look.

'Sorry, Mom, I'm just trying to keep my sanity in there.'

'I know, son,' she said as she cupped my cheek in her palm. 'Just have a little thought of the poor people who are going to have to sort this paperwork out after us.'

'OK,' I said, kissing her on the cheek, 'get some rest, you look beat.'

It was still dark when Mom and I got outside. The November air stung my cheeks as I walked her back to her tent. She promised me she would sleep and not sit up all night working and worrying. Then I turned and took a deep cold breath and steeled myself for an early morning adventure in dull literature. It was as bad as being back at school – worse actually; I didn't have Sally's notes to borrow here. As I groped in the dark towards the always lit reading room, a flicker of light caught my eye. As I got closer I saw it was the unmistakable glow of *Lampróg* light. My heart skipped a beat as I saw the only girl I know that travels with a firefly. As she heard me approach she cupped the bug in her hand but when she recognised me, she opened her fingers and bathed her face in light. Wow, Essa is beautiful in any light but she really is made for firefly light.

'What are you doing up?' she said, breaking the magical moment that was obviously playing out only in my head.

'I'm off to do my shift in the reading room. What are you doing up? Is the Turd-low snoring?'

'It's Turlow,' she said, 'and you only have to call him The Turlow at official functions.'

'Like your wedding?'

'Well, yes.'

'So are you really going to spend a lifetime with a snorer? You would think with all of the magic healing stuff around here they could cure that and you wouldn't have to be roaming around all night.'

'I'm not awake because of him. I'm not sleeping with him *and he's not a snorer.*' She was getting more flustered with every word.

'Why not? Oh no, is he diseased? These royal weddings are so treacherous.'

Essa threw both of her hands into the air. 'Why did you have to come back?' she hissed and stormed off, leaving her firefly fluttering around confused. I whispered, '*Lampróg,*' and it tentatively came and sat in the palm of my hand as quietly, in the darkness, I answered Essa's question, 'I came back for you.'

I bounced into the reading room with the echo of Essa saying 'I'm not sleeping with him' rolling around in my head. It wasn't until I placed the first piece of parchment into the Shadowreader that my spirits dipped. The Shadowbook was a collection of Leprechaun poetry. I had to stick it back in the pile – there was no way I was going to sift through poetry at this hour of the morning. The next piece caught my eye 'cause it was short and it had two names I recognised on it. It was a letter from Spideog to Dahy describing the last battle of Maeve's army in the Fili war.

Apparently the forces of the House of Duir were seriously getting their butts kicked by Maeve and the Fili. The Shadowmagic stuff was completely unknown to them and they found it impossible to defend against. After Maeve issued an ultimatum to Finn, which he refused, the Fili regrouped into one giant battalion with Maeve in the centre. Using several barrels of tree sap, the Fili queen conjured up some sort of spell. Everyone watching could feel the power of it building in the air and then, with a large flash of light that seemed to implode without a sound, the Fili were gone.

I always thought the Fili were killed but they just vanished. They left behind their clothes, weapons and every other earthly possession, but the Fili themselves had just disappeared. Spideog finished by writing, 'It was a blessing for The Land, my friend, but a personal disappointment for me. I would have liked to have taken a few Fili down before I died in battle.'

I could see now why my grandfather Finn had forbidden Shadowmagic – it had caused much hardship. Now, ironically, it was the only thing keeping my father alive.

The next slip of paper grabbed my attention; it was a thesis on sword parries and counter-attacks. I knew I would find it interesting and possibly very useful for my students but it wasn't going to get Dad healthy so I just skimmed it and stuffed it into an envelope. I wondered when I would have the leisure time to come back later and read it properly. With a little over an hour to go I found something else. I was pretty sure it had nothing in it that would help Dad but there was no way I was going to skip it. It was entitled: 'Banbha and The Turlow'.

Chapter Thirteen
The Grey Ones

This manuscript was old and it certainly wasn't easy to decipher. I admit I started reading it just to get some dirt on Essa's Turd-low boy but I soon forgot all of that when I got into the meat of it. It was the story of the end of the first millennium, when the three sisters ruled The Land. The original Turlow went to Banbha and demanded to be allowed to return to the Otherworld. Banbha told him that leaving was impossible. She warned that the further any of them sailed from The Land, the faster they would age and die. The price of immortality, Banbha told Turlow, was that he and his kinsmen must remain in The Land.

Turlow refused to believe her and set sail for his long-lost homeland. But as he sailed away he and the members of his crew felt the effects of ageing in their bones. Their skin creased and when their hair began to grey, they turned back, daring to go no further. Turlow and his group, now called 'the Grey Ones', still did not give up searching for a way to leave Tir na Nog. A sorcerer atop Mount Cas told them of a creature called *tughe tine* whose blood could renew their youth and allow them to leave unharmed. Even though the sorcerer told them that getting this blood would be an extremely perilous undertaking, they swore that they would find it.

When Banbha heard of their quest she and her guard set out to stop them. Neither Banbha or her guard, nor Turlow and the Grey Ones were ever seen again.

I scoured my dictionaries and allowing for slight changes in spelling I translated *tughe tine* into 'red eel'.

I had been at this manuscript for well over my allotted time. Twice I told the Imp scholar who was scheduled for the slot after me to go away and have a cup of tea. When she came back a third time I could see she was just itching to get stuck into more gardening tips but I told her that I was keeping the Shadowreader and went in search of Mom.

I found her in the canteen sitting with Spideog. When she saw me holding a manuscript she stood. 'What have you found?'

I handed her the manuscript and gave them a brief summary of what I had discovered. It occurred to me that I might be telling a tale that everyone except me knew by heart but judging by the expressions on both of their faces, I was surprising them a bit.

When I had finished Mom said, 'I always suspected that my father had secret manuscripts that he only allowed certain people to see. I remember Banshees coming to the Hall and my father being very secretive with them. This story is amazing.'

'So you have never heard this before?'

'Well, I have heard of "the Grey Ones" of course but I assumed that that was just an old tale to warn us about going too far out in boats. I never heard that they were Banshees that wanted to leave. And there has never been an explanation as to why Banbha left.'

'How about this tughe tine?'

'I have never heard of it. Have you, Spideog?'

'No, my lady.'

'But if we could get some of this eel blood then it might reset Dad and the hand will stop killing him.'

'It's a very old manuscript and it doesn't even say if red eels exist. This is an exceptional find, my son, but I wouldn't get too excited.'

'What about this Mount Cas? We can at least check if this sorcerer guy is still there.'

'Conor, this was the first millennium, there will be no sorcerer there now.'

'Actually, my lady, that may not be entirely true.' Mom and I both snapped to attention as the old archer continued. 'The last time I saw Cialtie was not long after Oisin disappeared. I was travelling cross-country and at the base of Mount Cas I saw someone coming down from the mountain. I set camp and waited for the traveller, hoping to swap a meal for information about this mountain that I had never explored. As he approached I was very surprised indeed to find that it was Cialtie. The Prince accepted my hospitality but gave away little of what he was doing on the mountain except that he had been visiting a very old Oracle. A year later I travelled up Mount Cas in search of this man. About two thirds of the way up I found a house, made entirely out of yew wood, built into the mountainside. I knocked at the entrance but was told by a voice on the other side of the door that only those who are worthy receive an audience there. I left and never returned.'

'We should go,' I said, standing.

'Hold on, Conor,' Mom said. 'Let us stop and think about this.'

'What's to think about, Mom? We have been ploughing through these scraps of paper night and day for almost two weeks and what have we found – zip. This is our first good lead. Let me look into it. I'm going crazy around here. Please,' I said, sounding like a ten-year-old asking if he can go to the park by himself.

'It may be too late,' Spideog said.

'What do you mean?'

'Winter is close here but it may already have arrived on the mountain. The pass may be impassable.'

100

'Then we have to go now,' I said, getting to my feet. 'Mom, you said yourself that maybe the gods want me to find a cure for Dad, well maybe they wanted me to read this manuscript. Look, Mom, I don't want to defy you but I gotta talk to this Oracle guy.'

She stood and I braced myself. It's never a good idea to get into a conflict with my mother. She hugged me and said, 'Promise me you won't do anything foolish.'

'Who me?' I said, flashing a House of Duir smile.

'And dress warm.'

Araf, Brendan, Spideog and I set off at dawn. It was freezing out but I didn't complain. I was excited to be doing something other than just reading. Brendan and I spent all of the previous night trying to borrow warm clothes off my students. I felt sorry for a few who gave us wool underwear. Tomorrow they would find out from Dahy that I didn't have the authority to give them vacation. I may have looked like I got dressed in total darkness but I was toasty. I tried to dissuade Brendan from coming, on the count that it might be too dangerous, but he insisted. 'I'll be right by your side,' he said. I was a touched by his loyalty until he continued, 'I go where Master Spideog goes.'

Dahy saw us off. Before I mounted Acorn he whispered in my ear, 'If you get into trouble, trust Spideog. He is arrogant and annoying and he talks nonsense and I really do not like him – but he is a good man under pressure.' He gave me a leg-up. As he guided my foot into the stirrup he lifted my trouser cuff and strapped a leather sheath, containing one of his knives, to my leg. Then he pulled down the cuff, patted my leg and winked at me. I saluted the Master with a nod of the head.

Araf and I wanted to bring half a dozen soldiers to help pitch tents and cook and maybe set up a base camp but Spideog said we had to travel light and fast. 'If we beat the snows it will only be by days,' he said, 'and it will be a good thing for you two princes to go without your handservants for a while.' Dahy was right – he was annoying.

We travelled hard and while the sun was in the sky we took no breaks. On the morning of the third day we saw the peak of Mount Cas. It looked close but it took two more days to get to its foothills. On the fifth day we found a field and set up a base camp where we left the horses to graze. After that we went on foot. It took a day to reach the base of the main peak and then another day of circling the mountain to find the trail up. The days were cold and the nights freezing but there was no imminent threat of snow. The night before we started our ascent Spideog disappeared and came back with a couple of pheasants that he had convinced to give up breathing so we could eat. There was little talk over dinner. Araf and Brendan turned in early but something in the old archer's eyes made me think that he was troubled, so I just sat with him by the fire and matched his silence. Finally he blurted out, 'I want to know why.'

I waited for him to say more but when he didn't, I asked, 'Why what?'

He didn't look at me; he just kept staring into the fire. 'Why I was unworthy.'

'Who says you are unworthy?'

He pointed up the mountain. 'The Oracle. The last time I was here he told me that I was unworthy. I didn't ask him why, I just accepted it. This time I want to know.'

'Well, I think it's probably 'cause he's nuts and has been breathing thin air for too long. One thing you are not is unworthy. Even Dahy respects you.'

He looked at me. 'How do you know that?'

'He told me.'

That brought a crooked smile to Spideog's face. 'It must have pained him to tell you that.'

I laughed. 'I think it did.' I stirred the fire with a stick and felt the extra warmth on my face. 'I found a letter of yours in the library.'

'Oh yes?'

'Yeah, it was a letter you wrote to Dahy after the Fili war.'

'Really? Oh, I think I remember someone collating material for some sort of an archive. Good gods, that was so many years ago.'

'It seemed to me that you and Dahy were friends.'

After a sigh he said, 'We were. More than just friends, we were comrades in arms.'

'What happened?'

'What else? A girl. I thought he stole her from me. He thought I stole her from him. In the end we fought. She said that she loved each of us equally and it was tearing her apart. She left us both and I disappeared into the Real World. Dahy always said he wasn't mad about the girl, he claimed he was really mad about me leaving my duties but that is a false memory on his part. It was the girl. I needed to get away from him but more importantly I needed to find some peace of mind. I went to the Real World which was a pretty barbaric place back then. I didn't discover what I was look-ing for until I travelled east. In Asia I found that *the answer lies within*, and as a bonus I learned their way of fighting. It was excit-ing and it changed my life. Everyone thinks that fighting is about brawn but in the east I learned that success in a battle comes from thinking.'

'Dahy says that you know.'

'I'm not surprised; Master Dahy is the most natural fighter I have ever known. He didn't have to study to be as good as he is.'

'It sounds to me that you two still like each other.'

'Maybe.'

'What happened to the girl?'

'She found another, a man better than both of us.'

'Well, I think you are both great men,' I said, standing. It was time for bed. 'It sounds to me that this two-timing woman screwed up a great friendship.'

Spideog rose, his face grimaced in the firelight. 'You really shouldn't speak that way about your grandmother.'

Chapter Fourteen
The Yew House

Spideog would say no more that night. I went to bed trying to remember what Dad had told me about his mother. It wasn't much. He once told me that she left on a sorceress quest when he was still a baby and had never returned, but that was all I could recall. It was well into the next day, after the camp was packed and we were hiking up the trail, that I got a chance to speak to Spideog in private. It turned out that the love of his and Dahy's lives was indeed my grandmother, Macha the Sorceress Queen, the Horse Whisperer, Mother of the Twins of Macha – Dad and Cialtie.

'By the time I had come back from the Real World she had married Finn,' Spideog said.

'How did you deal with that?'

'I had found peace in Asia. She was my queen and Finn was my king – I re-entered into the service of the House of Duir.'

'But you never took a wife after her.'

'No,' he said. There was so much emotion in that one word I didn't have the heart to ask him any more.

The path up got steeper and narrower. By midday I was exhausted and ready to stop but Spideog was not a 'stopping for lunch' kind of guy. He was a 'one foot in front of the other' kind of guy. We walked into the night until we found a place where the trail widened enough to make camp. It was cold and windy but dry and we all went out like candles in a hurricane.

The trail got ledge-like on the morning of the second day. Around one bend a small stream had frozen where it crossed the path. It was nothing too dangerous but Spideog lashed us together with ropes. He said one can never be too careful and it would be disastrous if he lost one of the two princes, to which Brendan replied, 'What am I, chopped liver?' We camped well before dusk on the second day. I would like to think it was because Spideog's muscles were howling with the altitude and the cold as much as mine, but it was probably because we came onto a place that was wide enough for all of us to sleep safely.

It was not a comfortable night. The thin air meant that even though we had stopped climbing my legs still ached. We made a small fire to brew willow tea but we didn't have enough wood to build one for warmth. The wind whistled around so that we almost had to shout at each other.

I sat next to Brendan with my back against the mountain and said, 'Are you enjoying our vacation?'

He did a strange thing then, he turned completely away from me and presented his other ear and said, 'Say that again.'

So I did. 'Are you enjoying our vacation?'

He sat back down and asked me to say it again so I said it a third time.

'Well I'll be damned,' he said.

'What?'

'About five years ago I went to the rifle range to test some experimental ammunition. The officer in the firing stall next to me was a quick draw. I thought he was finished so I took off my ear protectors just as his gun misfired. I have only had about 20 per cent hearing in this ear ever since.'

'Sorry to hear that,' I said, wincing at my accidental pun.

'Don't be. The weird thing is, I can hear perfectly now. This place is astounding. If I wasn't so worried about my daughter and the junk my lunatic mother must be filling her head with, I'd think I was in paradise. I'm climbing a mountain without even breaking a sweat. Back home I could hardly walk up three flights of stairs without wheezing. And my accuracy with a bow and arrow is almost better than with a gun. This place is amazing.'

'As I recall, I told you that a long time ago.'

'Well, I'm starting to believe you, Conor.'

After half an hour of walking on the third day of the climb, we spotted the Yew House above us. Five hours later and after completing almost two circumnavigations, the sun was high in the sky and I was actually working up a good sweat despite the cold. We came to a sharp bend in the path that was covered by another one of those frozen fords and Spideog once again made us rope-up and don crampons and ice picks. I remembered laughing at the old guy when he made us pack all of this stuff, but not now. The wet ice in the noonday sun would have been impossibly treacherous to traverse without crampons.

Spideog, in the lead, had just rounded the corner when his rope went slack. Then Brendan, in front of me, disappeared around the bend, stopped and said, 'Oh my.' Rounding the bend myself I saw what had stopped my fellow mountaineers. Standing on the path just past the ice floe were two tall thin men dressed in tight woolly brown tunics and trousers – Brownies. They stood there with one fist on their hip. They would have looked just like an illustration in an old copy of *Peter Pan*, if it wasn't for the cocked crossbows in their other hands.

Spideog spoke first. 'Greetings. We come to speak with the Master of the Yew House.'

The Brownies just stood there and grinned. I didn't like it. Neither did Spideog. He raised his voice and repeated himself. Still we got nothing from the skinny guys in brown.

Spideog planted his pick into the ice and unslung his bow from his back. He didn't notch an arrow in it but I've seen the master archer load a bow and it doesn't take him but a second. Brendan planted his pick into the floe, mirroring his tutor. I guess I could have just stood there but the others were slamming their picks into the ice, so I did too.

The crack started immediately. It moved like lightning from the point where my pick pierced the ice, to where Brendan's was planted, to past Spideog's feet. Then the rumble began as the entire ice sheet began to slide. I thought the whole mountain was about to collapse. Brendan went straight down on his nose. I managed to keep one crampon on the ice but had to go down on one knee. Spideog kept his footing and yelled, 'Run.'

I dug in my spikes and passed Brendan as he was trying to stand up. Spideog ran straight towards the Brownies, whom I expected at any second to shoot us but instead they just stood there looking bemused. I reached hard ice-free ground not long after the old guy. We both grabbed the rope attached to Brendan and dragged him to safety. I was just about to switch grips to the rope that went from me to Araf when I was pulled sideways off my feet and back onto the ice. As my head smacked onto the cold floor I saw the terrifying image of the Imp prince sliding off the side of the mountain. Araf let out a squeal like a little girl while I dug all ten of my fingernails into the frozen water desperately trying to get any purchase on the sliding ice.

The rope around my waist pushed all of the air out of my lungs as it pulled tight. Brendan and Spideog were on the hard ground and had a good hold of my rope but the pull from Araf's weight was almost cutting me in half. The ice sheet slid past me and rained down on my poor bodyguard. I could feel the impact of every block of ice as it smashed into the Imp, who grunted with every blow. I just hoped his rope would hold.

When the frozen waterfall finished the only bit of ice left on the trail was below me. I rolled to my left and planted my heels into the hard stone.

'Araf,' I yelled, 'are you all right?'

There was no answer for two long seconds then I heard him say, 'I would appreciate it, Conor, if you could pull me up from here.'

Apparently Araf's mother had told him to always be polite even when he was hanging off a fatal precipice attached to a bit of string.

After getting him on solid ground, Araf gave me an uncharacteristic emotional hug that made us both fall over. The two Brownies stared down at us with strange grins.

'Thanks for the help, boys,' I said. 'We couldn't have done it without you.'

That seemed to bemuse them and I made a mental note to leave sarcasm out of any future Brownie communications.

'Now,' I said, getting to my feet, 'I'd like to see this Oracle of yours.'

'Yes,' the taller of the two said, 'but will he want to see you?'

The Yew House was the most un-Tir na Nogian thing I had seen in The Land. The all-wood façade and shuttered windows made it look like some Malibu beach house you would see on a TV show about the rich and famous. The Brownies wordlessly escorted us onto the porch then told us to wait. Unlike a Californian beach house the porch didn't have any furniture so we sat on the steps. Ages later the Brownies re-emerged and one announced that only 'the Son of Duir' might enter.

I was tired and I had recently almost fallen off a cliff and these guys were starting to tick me off, so I didn't even stand up. I just said, 'Nope.'

The Brownie looked beyond confused. 'I do not understand,' he said.

'Either we all go in or we leave,' I said, standing.

Poor Brownie guy, he looked so befuddled I had an image of his head popping off his shoulders and a bunch of spring works and cogs shooting out of his neck. 'Only the Son of Duir,' he repeated.

'So be it; let's go, guys.' I turned and started down the mountain. My companions just stared at me.

'Are we playing a bit of poker here?' Brendan asked, in English.

'Of course,' I replied in the same language, 'you think I'm gonna hump all the way up this hill and not get any answers? Let's just see how much he wants to see me.'

Brendan nodded and put his arm on Spideog's and Araf's shoulders and said, 'All right, let's go.' The boys started to object, there is obviously no Texas Hold-um in The Land. Brendan pushed them off the porch, 'You heard the boss, come on.'

'Wait,' came a squeaky sound out of the Brownie, 'wait here.'

He scurried into the Yew House. I sat on the bottom step suppressing the impulse of making them chase us down the trail.

Ten minutes later I was still trying to explain to Araf the subtleties of bluffing.

'You mean lying,' he said.

'It's not lying, it's saying an untruth in order to make your opponent give in to you,' I expounded.

'It still sounds like lying.'

'Well, I think we should try a little poker, Araf. I bet you would be quite good at it.'

'I don't lie.'

'It's not lying, it's bluffing!'

Our Brownie messenger came onto the porch, saving Araf and me from going around that circle again. Now that he had new instructions he looked much more composed. 'You may all enter but only the Son of Duir may speak.'

I felt like saying no deal again and sending him back inside but it was getting cold. 'Is that all right with you guys?'

Brendan spoke in English again. 'If I want to say something once I get in there – who's gonna stop me?'

'My thoughts exactly,' I said. 'Spideog, are you OK with this?'

The archer nodded but I could see he didn't like it.

'Araf, do you think you can manage not talking for a while?' I smiled at him but he gave nothing back. You can always count on Araf.

I nodded to the Brownie, who looked very relieved that he didn't have to face his master again with a problem. He motioned for us to follow and pushed open the double doors. Two other Brownies were waiting inside the entrance of a surprisingly long hallway. They fell into step on either side of us. The Yew House it seems was just a front; the dwelling was carved directly into the mountain. As we walked, our footsteps echoed in the lengthy and increasingly dark corridor.

Brendan leaned over my shoulder and said, 'Well, Dorothy, what are *you* going to ask the wizard for?'

A large carving of Eioho, the Yew Rune, marked the end of the stone hallway. To the right a couple of Brownies opened two wooden doors and gestured for us to enter; they didn't follow and closed the doors behind us. It took a minute for my eyes to adjust to the light. The high vaulted ceiling had glass discs inset into the stone which put out as much light as any electric fixture in the Real World. The light bounced dramatically off the black seamless polished marble floors that I assumed to be the stone the mountain was made of. The walls were panelled with yew wood. Mom had told me about how difficult it was for her to earn the tiny wand she received from a yew tree – it made me wonder what kind of power the builder of this house must have. As my eyes adjusted I saw the Oracle in the centre of the room. He was seated in a huge chair, or I guess I should call it a throne, made from the severed trunk of a yew tree – its roots spread out at the bottom like the appendages of a starfish. The discs from the ceiling spewed tight beams of light all around but not directly on him. He wore plain black robes that rippled in the cool breeze. His face was illuminated from the reflection off the black marble. It gave the same appearance as when a boy scout puts a flashlight under his chin to tell a spooky story around a campfire. The room went on for a distance that I could not make out. No one spoke for ages.

I'm not good with uncomfortable silences, so I broke it. 'Nice digs you got here.'

'The Son of the One-Handed Prince,' he said in a whispery voice that seemed as if it was unused to speaking. 'I have heard about you.'

'What did you hear?'

'I have heard that you are impertinent.'

'Yeah, I get that a lot. Have you heard anything good about me?' There was no reply so I continued. 'By the way, I'm no longer the Son of the One-Handed Prince.'

'Are you saying Ona was wrong?'

'No, Ona's prophecy was spot on but it wasn't about me. It was about Fergal of Ur – Cialtie's son.'

'Cialtie has no son.'

For the first time I saw a movement in the back of the room. It was hard to see in this light but it looked like there was a hooded figure towards the back of it.

'Well, if that's what he told you – he lied. I was there when Cialtie met his son, I was there when he killed him and I was definitely there when my uncle lost his hand.'

The Oracle leaned forward on his throne. The change in light allowed me to see him more clearly. He was old. Not decrepit old but at least young grandfather old, with lines on his face and silver hair that blew in the wind, like a singer in a Bollywood music video. For The Land this guy looked ancient. He also looked scarily crazy. He leaned back into the gloom and said, 'You came all of this way to bring me this news?'

'No,' I said. 'I know that you helped Cialtie retake his Choosing with my father's hand.'

This startled the old guy. 'He told you that?'

'No,' I said quickly, sensing that it was a bad idea to get this guy agitated. 'I did the math. Spideog saw Cialtie coming down from this mountain just before he retook his Choosing. Since no one in The Land knows how he did this, it stands to reason that you advised him.'

A smile came to his face that in the light sent a shiver down my spine. 'So you came to prove that you are clever as well as impertinent?'

'No, sir, I came to ask if you would help my father.'

'Why has he not come himself?'

'He's dying. His new hand and his body are in conflict. It is killing him.'

'Your trip is wasted then, Conor of Duir. I would have no idea how to save him from such a singular malady – no one in The Land would.'

'I'm not looking for a cure, sir, only directions.'

'Directions?' He looked confused but interested. 'Directions to where?'

'To where I can find the blood of a tughe tine.'

You would think that a wise old oracle would have a better poker face, but when he heard this he definitely twitched before he regained his composure. 'I'm sorry you wasted a trip but I know nothing of the place of which you speak.'

'I think you do.'

'You have charm, young prince, that has allowed me to forgive your impertinence but my patience is running thin.'

'The first Turlow came to you for the same advice. You told the Grey Ones how to find it.'

The Oracle threw his head back and laughed. As he did I noticed the hooded person, who had been lurking in the shadows the entire time, running out of the back of the room.

'You climbed all of this way to quote a nursery rhyme intended to keep children out of the sea? I am weary. Leave.'

'No,' came a voice from behind me. It was Brendan.

'You were instructed not to speak, Druid,' the Oracle hissed in a way that made me think that maybe we all should calm down.

'I'm not a Druid, I'm a policeman.'

'And what is a policeman?'

'I am – a seeker of truth and I don't believe you when you say you don't—'

It was just a flick of the Oracle's wrist but Brendan went over like he had been slugged by a heavyweight. Spideog pulled his bow off his shoulder and was just reaching for an arrow when his bowstring snapped and sliced a gash in his face. Then his bow exploded as he was thrown twenty yards into the air before back-sliding along the polished floor into the wall.

A loud gale of wind whipped around the room. Araf and I looked at each other and wordlessly decided to get the hell out of there. It's a good thing Araf doesn't speak often 'cause I had a gut feeling that the next guy that lipped off to the Oracle was going to have his head exploded.

The Imp hoisted the unconscious Brendan on his shoulder and we both backed out of the room. 'Sorry to bother you,' I shouted as complacently as I could, 'and thanks for your help. We gotta be going now.' When I got to Spideog, I unceremoniously grabbed him by the sleeve and dragged him out. We pushed through the exit expecting to be clobbered at any minute. As the doors slammed shut I could have sworn I heard laughter coming from within. The Oracle was definitely off my Christmas card list.

The Brownies on the other side of the doors were beside themselves with terror. They buzzed around, high stepping like little kids in need of a pee.

'What did you say to him?' one asked. I ignored him while I loosened Spideog's neckerchief.

Brendan croaked, 'What happened?' and Araf gently placed him back on his feet.

'I'll explain later. Right now I think we should get out of here.'

I held my ear against Spideog's mouth – he was still breathing. 'Araf, can we swap invalids?' I went over and steadied Brendan while Araf hoisted the old archer on his shoulder like he was a sack of ping-pong balls. Spideog grunted, which I took as a good sign.

The long corridor was longer on the way out. Brownies flitted around telling us to hurry while constantly looking over their shoulders, which was as annoying as it sounds. Brendan got steadier on his feet as we went and was almost walking under his own steam by the time we reached the doors to the outside. It had begun to snow. Araf gently placed Spideog on the porch and the Brownies freaked.

'No, no, you must go. Go now,' the tallest one of them shrieked at us and picked up one of the packs that we had left outside the doors and threw it down the steps. When he reached for my pack I kinda lost it and grabbed him by the throat and pinned him against the wall.

'We have an injured man here. We will go when we are ready.'

The other Brownies didn't come to their comrade's aid but huddled together shrieking. The guy I had by the neck didn't struggle; he just looked at me with puppy-dog eyes and said, 'Please go.'

It was then that I saw that all of their earlier bravado was just that. Talk about bluffing. These guys lived under the servitude of a nasty piece of work who they were terrified of. I let the Brownie go and said, 'Sorry, we'll be as quick as we can.

'Araf,' I said, 'these guys are annoying but they are also right. Can we move him?'

'He is still unconscious, but I agree. I think we should at least put a wee bit of this mountain between us and this place.'

Brendan tried to pick up a pack and almost fell over, so I assembled all four packs comically on my back while Araf rehoisted Spideog.

Halfway down the trail I looked back. About six Brownies were standing on the porch. They were a pathetic bunch. 'Come with us,' I mimed to them, not daring to shout. The five at the back rocked on their legs uncomfortably. The tall guy at the front just shook his head, no, and with a sad smile waved goodbye.

As I was turning back, I saw out of the corner of my eye an upstairs shutter open and the flash of a hooded black-robed figure throwing something. Even if I hadn't had four packs on my back, I don't think I could have stopped the knife from hitting Brendan square between the shoulder blades.

Chapter Fifteen
Broken Bow

Brendan went down from the force of the impact as the knife bounced off his back. The blade was still in its sheath. I jumped recklessly towards the edge of the cliff trying to catch it before it went over but the knife spun off into the void. The weight of the packs on my back meant that I almost followed it.

I slithered back from the edge and went to Brendan, who groaned, 'Son of a ...'

'Are you OK?'

'What the hell hit me?'

I didn't feel like explaining – I just wanted to get out of there, so I said, 'One of those Brownies must have thrown something.'

'Well, it hurt. Would I be overreacting if I shot one with an arrow?'

'Yes.'

'Even if it was just in the leg?'

'Yes. Come on, we have to get out of here.'

I tried to help him to his feet but with four packs on my back there wasn't that much I could do. We skirted around the corner and found Araf waiting for us with Spideog still out cold on his shoulder. Even though the ice sheet that had almost killed us earlier was mostly not there any more, Araf suggested we rope-up, and I agreed with him. As the snow started to come down harder and the wind picked up, I fantasised about starting a Real World/ Land smuggling operation. The first thing I would import was thermal underwear.

We made it all the way around the mountain. I called a halt just before we came to the part of the path where we could be seen by the Yew House above. Araf didn't argue with me. I was exhausted walking with the packs and Araf must have been shattered carrying a man on his shoulder. I got a fire going with some kindling I found in Spideog's bag, brewed up some willow tea and got some into the injured archer. It did the trick.

'Where is my bow?'

'Take it easy, Spideog. Don't try to talk.'

The old guy grabbed my shoulder and opened his eyes. 'My bow, where is it?'

'Rest,' I said.

'Tell him,' Brendan said.

'You tell him.'

'I was out cold. If you know what happened to his bow then tell him.'

'My bow,' Spideog said, trying to get to his feet, 'I must go back for it.'

'Wooh, big guy, you are in no fit shape to go anywhere. Your bow is gone. The Oracle trashed it.'

'What do you mean trashed it? You mean he took it.'

'No, sir, it's trashed, destroyed. He waved his hand and it exploded into splinters.'

'That is not possible,' he said, grabbing me by my coat. 'You lie.'

Araf reached over and gently took his hand from my lapel. 'It is true, Master. I saw it with my own eyes. This fell from your clothing when I first put you down.' Araf handed him a splintered piece of yew wood.

He took it and began to cry. 'It is true,' he moaned, 'I am not worthy.'

It was hard to watch a man so strong look so defeated. I rummaged through the bags until I found the flask of poteen that my mother had given me before we left and administered some to the unresisting archer. Brendan held him until he slipped back into unconsciousness.

Araf and I debated how long we should rest. I thought it would be a good idea to wait until dark before we entered the part of the path that exposed us to attack from the Yew House above, but Araf thought we should get going before the snow got so bad that we all just slipped off the side of the mountain. I agreed with him when I realised I could no longer feel my toes.

I didn't even bother to look up when we were in sight of the Yew House. I figured it wouldn't take much to take us out and if it came, I didn't really want to see it coming. Despite our fears, we passed unmolested. We donned crampons when we reached the ice ford we had crossed earlier. The snow on the other side was starting to drift so we tried keeping our crampons on but there wasn't enough snow for that. Crampons are great on ice and packed snow but on solid rock they just make your footing worse. Saying that, when we took them off we still slipped all over the place. After Brendan went down and almost slipped off the side, we all put a single crampon on one foot. We marched through the night limping like the winning team at a shin-kicking competition.

Three quarters of the way down the mountain the snow turned to rain. Wool and rain are not a good mix. It made me feel sorry for sheep. We found a wide and almost sheltered part of the path and camped for what remained of the night. The tea and stale rations did nothing to lift our mood. I had a feeling only a hot bath and a dry change of clothes could do that for me and I wasn't sure if Spideog would ever recover.

Spideog mumbled in his sleep at first but then like the rest of us settled down until awakened by a damp dawn. Brendan shook me awake from what was becoming a recurring dream of Essa holding hands with an invisible man. What did that dream mean? Was the invisible man supposed to be me?

The fog was so bad that dawn was almost unnoticeable; the view seemed as if we were looking at a white sheet. It was damp cold and the squelching noise my trousers made as I got up cemented my misery.

Spideog was up and on his feet. He walked like a man in a trance. Without a word he began to break camp so we followed suit and then trekked after him down the mountain.

'Has he said anything?' I whispered to Brendan.

'Not a word,' he replied behind his hand. 'He just got up and got going. Are you going to say anything to him?'

'I'm not going to talk to him – you talk to him.'

'I'm not talking to him.'

We both looked to Araf.

'I don't say anything to anybody,' the Imp mumbled. 'I am not starting now.'

We followed the silent archer down the mountain. For a guy who had just been pulverised by an evil warlock he set a pretty crisp pace.

You would think that going downhill would be easier than uphill and you would be right, but not by as much as you would think. My calf muscles screamed with the effort it took to stop me from becoming a runaway teen.

It was nightfall by the time we reached the base of the mountain. I suggested to Spideog that he should get some rest, but he looked at me like I had just stomped on his puppy and disappeared into the forest. By the time he had returned with wood and a rabbit, Araf had the beginnings of a fire going. Brendan and

I put up a very flimsy lean-to to keep off the rain. Together we ate in silence, none of us daring to speak for fear of being killed by the archer's evil eye. When he finished eating and started to set up a bedroll I bravely said, 'Thank you, Spideog, the meal was lovely.'

He didn't even acknowledge my presence.

Brendan, Araf and I sat around the fire staring at each other for a while. Each waited for the other to speak but none of us wanted to break the vow of silence that the old man seemed to have imposed on the group. We bedded down. Ah, there is nothing like sliding between two wet blankets, in your wet clothes, as the rain leaks onto your head.

Spideog seemed to be as broken as his bow. As the old song says, you don't know what you got till it's gone, and losing the courage and the sureness of our leader was unnerving – scary. I lay there and mixed all of my troubles together, letting them roll down the mountain of my mind like a giant snowball: I was cold and wet, my father was dying and this trip was a complete failure and then there was Essa. I had been trying to avoid thinking about her. I had been trying to cover over my hurt with bravado, but hurt I was. She didn't wait for me. She didn't wait for me.

'Why would she?' replied Araf, who was lying next to me.

'What?'

'You are talking about Essa, yes?'

'Oh, sorry, Araf, I didn't realise I was speaking out loud.'

'Oh dear, that's not a good sign.'

'Do you know him?' I asked.

'Who?'

'The Banshee she's marrying.'

'Of course,' the Imp replied, 'He is The Turlow.'

'Is he a good guy?'

'What is a "good guy", Conor? You are speaking in a Real World tongue – also not a good sign.'

'Sorry,' I said. 'Is he a good man?'

'The few dealings I have had with him have been favourable. Many like him. Some do not, but that is the price you pay when you are a leader.'

'Everybody likes you, Araf,' I said as I playfully kicked him in the back.

'Ah well, I *am* special.'

No matter how low I was I had to laugh at that. Araf cracks so few jokes that ignoring one would be a crime.

'Well, I don't like him.'

'And why do you think that is?' inquired Araf. 'Could it be you don't like him because Essa does?'

'No, that's not why. Well, it's not entirely why. I don't like the way he talks to her. It makes me want to throw up. And he called me a Faerie.'

'What is wrong with that?'

'Well, how would you like it if he called you a Faerie?'

'I would think it strange considering I am an Imp, but why would you object?'

'Are you calling me a Faerie?'

'Why wouldn't I?' Araf said, sounding a bit confused.

'Because I'm not a Faerie.'

'Yes you are, Conor. Surely you knew that? I am an Imp, Turlow is a Banshee and you, Essa, Gerard and Spideog are Faeries.'

'No.'

'Yes.'

'That's just great – a perfect ending to a perfect day.'

I dropped my head back onto my soggy pillow and thought, *well at least I couldn't get much lower* – but then I had another thought.

'Araf,' I called out into the damp dark, 'would I be correct in assuming that I am the Prince of All the Faeries?'

'Of course.'

'Great,' I said, as my head sloshed on my pillow, 'just great.'

Acorn woke me with a head butt and a snort just before dawn. The previous night I had asked Araf where the horses were and he said, 'They will be here.' He was so casual about it I believed him and, sure enough, there they were. I got up – there is no point in staying in a bed when it's cold and damp. Spideog was up too. He had rekindled the fire and was going through the packs.

'I am only taking the bare necessities,' he said without greeting me. 'You three will have plenty of supplies for the rest of the journey.'

'What do you mean you three?'

'I must face the yews,' Spideog said.

'You're leaving us?' I said, loud enough to disturb the others.

He ignored me and continued to pack.

'How will we get back?'

'Travel that way,' he said, pointing, 'and stop when you see oak trees.'

Brendan came up and crouched down next to Spideog. 'Master,' he said, 'I'll go with you.'

'No,' he said in a tone that made it clear that this was not up for discussion.

Still Brendan persisted. 'You can't go alone.'

'I said NO!' the old man shouted, then calmed himself. 'Your party needs an archer.'

Brendan stood and chuckled. 'These two? Araf and Conor will be fine on their own. You are the one I am worried about. You are still weak from your fight. I can help you.'

Spideog stood, turned and with the speed of a striking snake grabbed the detective by his lapels. He had a mad look in his eyes.

'I'm going to face the yews. Do you not understand? I'm going to be judged. I'm going to be judged – again. I'm going to tell the yews that I lost my bow. They are … they are going to kill me.' He let go of Brendan and turned his back on all of us, his head bowed.

'Do not go,' Araf said.

'That would be like asking you not to dig in the ground, Imp. I am an archer, I am Spideog the Archer. To be without a bow would be like being a bear without claws.'

He picked up his pack and set off without looking back.

I ran in front of him. 'Wait a second, you can't go to the Yewlands unarmed.' I reached into my sock and presented him with my knife.

He stared at it and said, 'Do you really think Dahy would want me to have his knife?'

'I know he would.'

As he took it Brendan shouted, 'Master Spideog!'

With a sigh he turned. Brendan was standing at attention. 'You, sir, are the most worthy man I have ever met. Let no man – or tree – tell you otherwise,' and then he saluted.

Spideog stood stock still like he had been slapped, then nodded and turned.

We watched as he faded into the morning mist. When at last he disappeared I said, 'Anybody know the way home?'

Chapter Sixteen
The Green Knife

After getting our butts handed to us good by Mr Yew House we had no other choice but to go home with our tails between our legs. We didn't talk much on the way back. The rain had given way to a wet fog. What my father would have called 'a little mist in the air'. If I had been driving a car I would have had to turn on the windscreen wipers every couple of minutes. We rode in silence while I fantasised about being in a limo with the heat turned up full.

We skirted around Mount Cas hoping to see a familiar landmark. Losing a guide is not a comforting thing. It's only after the guide is gone that you realise you should have paid more attention during the outbound journey. The other problem was how quickly winter had set in. During the trip out, The Land was still vibrant with the colours of fall, but in just the short time that we had been on the mountain everything seemed to have turned brown and grey. Araf remembered that we had approached the mountain perpendicular to a sheer cliff face. Brendan and I said we remembered that too but I think the cop was faking it – I know I was.

I did remember the cliffs when we got to them but I wasn't as confident as Araf when we turned right. I looked to Brendan for confirmation but he just shrugged. That made it official – Araf had become the new guide. I took one last glance behind me –

trying to calm the growing fear that I would soon be spending forty days and forty nights lost in a wet/frozen wilderness – when I saw a speck of green. I would have missed it if it had been summer but among the decomposing colours of winter something stood out. I walked Acorn back to the bottom of the cliff and dismounted. It was the sheathed knife that had hit Brendan in the back.

As soon as I picked it up I saw that it was a beautiful thing. The handle was made of green glass with a spiral of gold wire embedded in it. I untied the leather strap that attached the sheath to the hand-guard and studied the blade. It looked like one of Dahy's throwing blades complete with the golden tip. When I replaced the cover I noticed a piece of paper stuffed inside and fished it out. The message, written in haste on a crumpled piece of parchment, read, 'The changelings have the answers you seek.' It was not signed.

I stowed the dagger under my coat, remounted and hurried to catch up with Araf and Brendan. I tried to tell Araf about the knife but he was trying to concentrate on the path home and told me to shut up.

I said, 'If you are going to be like that, I'm not going to show you the neat thing I found.'

How he ignored me after that I don't know but he did. So Acorn and I fell in behind him and spent the rest of the day concentrating on being cold and wet.

That night I went for firewood. It's easy getting wood in the winter. In the summer the trees are chatty and want to know why you are in their forest and where you are going but in the winter they are groggy and just want you to leave them alone. They pretty much say the tree equivalent of, '*Yeah, yeah, just take some wood and stop bothering me.*'

When I mentioned this to Brendan he loped off into the dark and came back with a ton of logs. He heaped my modest little blaze into a full-blown bonfire. Then he made tepees out of lean branches and shocked Araf and me by stripping off.

The very naked Brendan placed all of his clothes and his bedding on the tepees to dry and shouted, 'I am sick and tired of being wet and cold,' then he started jumping up and down like a lunatic.

Araf and I watched – keeping our gaze as high as possible – as our companion enthusiastically lost his marbles. He danced and chanted, and before long Araf and I were mesmerised and laughing.

'You got to try this, it's great,' Brendan said as he dashed stark naked into the frozen night. Araf and I were just about to go and find him when he returned shivering and blue. He threw a stack of thin branches at us and recommenced his dance – dangerously close to the fire.

Araf stood up, made a tripod of branches and took off his overcoat.

'You're not gonna join him?' I said.

'I too am very tired of being wet,' the Imp replied.

I sat in terror as I watched a naked Brendan teach an equally naked Araf how to prance around a fire like a Native American chief. When I could watch no longer I decided to go to bed but when I stretched out my damp sleeping roll I thought, *aw, what the hell*. I wouldn't have believed it if I hadn't done it myself but I got to tell you – if you ever get a chance to dance naked around a bonfire in the middle of the winter with a cop and an Imp – don't knock it until you've tried it. Once you get started you just have to keep going. Spinning is important, 'cause one side is burning while the other side is freezing. After a while the whole world goes away and only the dance and the fire remain. We kept going late into the night and then collapsed into our sleeping rolls and slept like babies – like dry, warm babies.

The next day there was no mention of the night before, but we were certainly happier travellers. For years wise men have searched for the meaning of life; they should ask me because I found it – it's dry clothes. Now that I was unmiserable in the saddle, I was free to admire the stark beauty of The Land in winter. Many of the trees in Tir na Nog are so lush that seeing any distance is impossible but now only spooky skeletal frameworks of trees broke my view to the horizon. It was beautiful but also unsettling and made me wish all the more for a roof and a fire.

There was no fire dancing that night. If someone had suggested it I would have been up for it but I guess too much naked fire dancing is a bit weird. After a trout supper, I finally got to tell my companions about the knife.

'You are telling me those Brownies didn't throw a rock at me,' Brendan said. 'They threw a knife? You should have let me shoot them.'

'It was a sheathed knife and it wasn't the Brownies.'

'Then who threw it?' Araf asked.

'When we were in the room with the Oracle,' I said, 'do you remember a hooded figure in the shadows?'

'To be honest, Conor,' Brendan said, 'I don't remember much of my time in there. I got clocked pretty good.'

'I saw him,' Araf said.

'Well, I got a quick glance at the person who threw the knife and he was wearing a black hood. I think it was the same guy.'

'But why would someone throw a sheathed knife?' Araf asked.

'It was an envelope. I found this inside.' I took out the message and handed it around.

'What is a changeling?' Brendan asked.

'I don't know. Araf?'

'It's a very old term. When I was young and growing up in the Heatherlands my nanny Breithe used to use the name changeling when she told stories about the Pookas. They are beings that can change into animal form at will.'

'Yeah, I saw one do it once,' I said. 'OK then – where can I find a Pooka?'

'That might prove difficult,' Araf said. 'No one has seen a Pooka since before the Battle of the Twins of Macha. Your father was about to set up an expedition to the Pinelands just before he became ill.'

'Well, then it looks like I'll have to go there. Where is it?'

'I would have no idea how to get to the Pinelands,' Araf said.

'I bet my mother would know. She had a Pooka tutor.'

'She might. She is the only one ever to be schooled by a Pooka. They are a very secretive race. How your grandfather Liam persuaded the Pookas to provide a teacher for his daughter I have no idea.'

'Then let's get back to the Hall of Knowledge and ask her. Araf, are you certain we are going the right way?'

'Certain is a very strong word, Conor.'

'Well, that fills me with confidence,' Brendan said.

'Hey, look on the bright side,' I said, 'we may get so lost we find the Pinelands by accident.'

Araf was being unduly modest. Without one wrong step we reached the edge of the Hazellands two days later. It was just starting to get dark when we reached the outer structures of the Hall of Knowledge. Just past the first outbuilding, two Imp sentries jumped from out of nowhere with their crossbows cocked. I was tired and cold and hungry but, worst of all, I smelled really bad.

'The only way,' I said with a large outlet of air, 'you guys are going to stop me from getting a cup of willow tea is to shoot me.'

'Stand down, Imps,' is all Araf had to say and they lowered their weapons.

'Prince Araf and Prince Conor,' the sentry said, doing a bowing thing, 'Lady Deirdre and Lady Nieve have instructed us to keep a watch out for you.'

'Lady Nieve is here?'

'Yes, sirs; she arrived yesterday.'

'Go back to your posts.'

The soldiers snapped-to and double-timed it back to their hiding places.

We cantered into camp. I wanted to gallop – I really needed a bath.

The bath was obviously going to have to wait. Mom was waiting for us outside the library and she wasn't in a hospitable mood. She rudely dismissed Araf and Brendan in a very queen-like fashion. I was jealous – I would have loved to have been dismissed.

'Did you learn anything?' she asked even before I entered the room. 'Where is Spideog?'

'Hi, Mom, I'm fine, knackered but fine – oh yes I'd love a cup,' I said in one breath, as I kissed Mom.

'Hello, Auntie,' I said, planting a kiss on her cheek as I passed.

I collapsed on a sofa. The two of them stood in front of me like I was in trouble. I expected them to accuse me of nicking mead out of the pantry.

'What?'

'Oisin is getting worse,' Nieve said as Mom looked away.

I didn't jump up or shout – I just dropped my head in my hand and rubbed my eyes. Of course Dad was getting worse. Nothing, and I mean nothing, had gone right since I had gotten back to The Land – I should have expected this. I clamped my molars together to stop a flow of tears. 'Fand said he could stay like that for ever.'

'We thought he could. No one has ever frozen a person in Shadowmagic before.'

'How bad is he?'

Mom came over and hugged me. 'Not too bad,' she said. 'It is very slow. It took Fand this long to notice anything at all but it means that our time is not infinite. We need to find a cure.'

'Have you found anything in the *Shadowbooks* since I've been away?'

Mom shook her head, an exhausted *No*. 'What have you learned?'

I told Mom the whole story of our *welcome* at the Yew House, and the loss of Spideog. I left out the part about almost slipping off the edge of a cliff to our deaths so as not to unduly worry her. Finally I showed her the knife and the message that was within it.

Mom examined the knife in silence for a long time and then handed it to Nieve. Finally Mom straightened up and with the same queenly conviction that she had shown my companions earlier, said, 'You leave for the Pinelands tomorrow.'

I instantly changed from a son to a loyal subject. I stood, said, 'Yes, ma'am,' then hugged her.

On the way out the door Nieve pointed out that I could use a bath.

Chapter Seventeen
Pop-head

When I first came to The Land the dreams completely freaked me out, which was understandable. I never had a dream until I came to Tir na Nog. When I found out that dreams often gave me glimpses into the future I thought they were cool, but since I have discovered that a lot of dreams are just jumbled images of stuff that's rattling around in my noggin, they're starting to really annoy me. That night I dreamt about the usual stuff: Dad encased in amber, Essa walking with the invisible man, and of course the perennial favourite of Fergal with a Banshee blade sticking out of his chest. But then there were others that I couldn't begin to figure out. One was of a bear that then turned into a fox that then turned into an eagle. And then there was a rowboat that rowed itself to the shore where Cialtie was waiting for it. What the heck was that all about? The other problem is that sometimes the dreams get so intense that I wake up less rested than when I went to bed.

As if the dreams weren't exhausting enough, Mom woke me before dawn. 'Get up,' she said, shaking me, 'get up now if you want time for breakfast before you leave for the Pinelands.'

'Oh no,' I said, shaking the visions out of my head, 'I haven't had a bath yet.'

'There is no time for that,' she said, turning to go. 'Your party is preparing to leave now.'

I got up with only my blanket wrapped around me and ran to the bath house just in time to see Brendan leaving damp and happy. He was still steaming.

'Good morning, Conor,' he said, rubbing his hair with a towel. 'Man, I can't tell you how good a hot bath feels.'

I pushed past him. The Leprechaun that runs the bath house spotted me and said, 'Oh, I didn't know there was going to be anyone else this morning. I'll have some more hot water in an hour.'

I ran back to my tent and got dressed. I was going to have my breakfast and then a bath and there was no power in The Land that was going to stop me.

Brendan was the only person in the canteen that I recognised. I got some food and sat down next to him.

'How come you had a bath so early this morning?'

'Araf, your mother and molten gold lady—'

'Auntie Nieve.'

'Yeah her. They had a meeting last night. After the meeting Araf told me that you were going to the Pinelands this morning. So I got up early to be ready.'

'Why didn't you tell me?'

'You were asleep. What was I supposed to do, wake you up and tell you to have a bath?'

'YES.'

'OK,' the cop said, taking out an imaginary notepad and pen, 'let me just note that down for next time.'

'Do you know what is going on?'

'No, your mother still doesn't seem to like me that much. I tried to go to the meeting with Araf but she wouldn't let me in.'

Mom appeared just as I was finishing breakfast.

'Come, Conor.'

'Sorry, Mom, I'm off to a bath.'

133

'This is more important.'

'I beg to differ,' I said but followed her anyway.

Brendan fell into step next to me. When Mom gave him a dirty look I said, 'How many times do I have to tell you that he is with me?'

She backed down and I wondered if I had picked the wrong battle to win with my mother. I'd ditch Brendan in a second if it meant I could soak under some warm suds.

Araf and Nieve were mounted up when I got to the corral. 'Have you ever been on time?' Nieve asked.

'On time? On time for what?'

Brendan brought out Acorn and Cloud and handed me Acorn's reins. He was saddled and packed with full supplies.

Mom slid the strap of a full satchel on my shoulder.

'You looked so tired last night I had my men pack some warm clothes for you while I let you sleep.'

'Mom, it's not sleep I needed – it's a bath.'

'You should have thought of that earlier,' said a voice using a familiar tone. There behind me was Essa, dressed, mounted and ready to go. 'If you think we are going to wait while you lounge under hot water – you have another thought coming.'

I turned back to Mom. 'Essa?'

'Essa is your guide.'

'I thought you were coming.'

'I'm needed here. I'm still not convinced any good will come of this expedition. I'm staying and continuing the research. Also, I do not wish to stray too far from Castle Duir, in case … well, just in case.'

'OK, but Essa?'

'Essa has journeyed to the Pinelands before. She is one of the few people who ever has. You are lucky to have her.'

I looked at my party mounted up and waiting for me and nodded.

'Be careful, it is wild in the Pinelands at the best of times,' Mom said. 'No one has returned from that part of The Land in a long time – I have no idea what conditions are like.'

Mom handed me a muslin-wrapped parcel. 'Rhiannon is Queen of the Pookas – or at least she was the last time anyone was there. Give her this.'

'What is it?'

'It is the first of the hazelnuts from your new Tree of Knowledge. My father sent a regular supply of hazelnuts to the Pinelands. My Pooka tutor once told me that that was the reason Queen Rhiannon agreed to send her to teach me. Remember, son, never look at an amorphous Pooka in the eye – it can antagonise their animal self. And always look a Pooka directly in the eyes when they change back.'

'Why?'

'Because they will be naked.'

'Oh yeah.'

I hugged her.

'Go,' she said, pushing me away. 'You are losing sunlight.'

As I walked towards Acorn I felt a slap on my back. I turned to see Turlow dressed in shiny black leather. He put his arm around me.

'Ah, Faerie prince, I'm looking forward to getting acquainted with you on this adventure.'

'You're coming with us?'

'I travel with my betrothed,' he said.

'Great,' I said with as much enthusiasm as I could muster – which wasn't much.

Just before I mounted up, Turlow looked over his shoulder and placed his face close to mine. In a conspiratorial whisper he said, 'I don't want to embarrass you in front of the others, Conor. But from one royal to another, I'd like to give you a piece of advice.'

'What's that?'

'Well, my friend,' he said, 'you could really use a bath.'

People always complain about winter but not me. I like winter or, I should say, I used to. What I used to like about winter was the indoor stuff: the crackling warm fires, hearty soups and stews, and cosy quilts. This travelling around outside on horseback in the winter is for the birds. I take that back – even the birds have enough sense to fly someplace warm in the winter. Saying that, if I had to be outside this time of year it might as well have been on a day like this one. It was glorious – sharp, cold, with bright sunshine pouring from an indigo-blue sky. Mom had packed me a fox fur hat and mittens that kept my ears and fingers toasty warm. If only I had a pair of cool Rayban sunglasses I would have been perfectly contented to be out in the elements.

This was not a Sunday afternoon jaunt to visit Mother Oak – we had serious distance to cover. Essa set a near brutal pace that meant leisurely chats on horseback were out. Not that a private chat with Essa would have been possible anyway. The Turd-low stuck to her side like a duckling to its mother. Even during the infrequent short rests, he was attached to her like a burr. It made me think that she really must like him, 'cause if I crowded Essa that much I'd probably be bleeding before not very long.

On the first night I went to bed immediately after dinner. I said I was tired but the truth of it was that I just couldn't stand to watch the two of them snuggled up together in the firelight.

I awoke the next morning and thought I had gone blind over-night. Fog had crept in that was so thick I literally couldn't see my hand in front of my face. When The Land does weather, it doesn't do it in halves. It made me hope that we would avoid snow on this trip. At breakfast I spoke to Brendan and asked him to strike up a conversation with Turlow sometime during the day so I could have a chat with Essa. He said he would and added that he would also pass a note to her in the playground, if I wanted him to.

The morning ride was so slow that we might as well have been walking. It wasn't until an hour before noon that the fog lifted enough so that we could at least canter without braining ourselves on trees. Turlow dropped back and said that Essa wanted to talk to me. It looked like Brendan wouldn't have to make forced small talk after all.

When I pulled up next to Essa she said, 'So what do you want to talk to me about?'

'I thought you wanted to talk to me?'

'Turlow told me that you asked Brendan to distract him so you could talk to me in private.'

'Oh, he heard that, did he?'

'That is what he told me. So what is so important?'

'Nothing's important, I just wanted to … you know, talk.'

'About what?'

'I don't know; maybe about how come you got engaged in like three months?'

'That's what you wanted to talk about?'

It wasn't – well, it was, but it was stupid to use it as an opening conversational gambit but since I started, I just ploughed on. 'It's as good a topic as any.'

'And I have to justify my actions to you – why?' she said in a tone that made me realise that we were probably going down a conversational cul-de-sac.

'You don't have to justify anything. I just think it's strange that you went all bridal so soon after my departure.'

'Let me get this straight – you think that my getting engaged is because I couldn't have you?'

'Well, I wouldn't put it like that but …'

'Don't even think about finishing that sentence,' she hissed. 'You are the most arrogant, pop-headed imbecile I have ever met.'

'Pop-headed?'

'Do you have anything else to discuss?'

'Yeah, what does pop-headed mean?'

She made that exasperated Essa noise that she frequently makes just before she pummels you. 'You are dismissed,' she said.

Now I wasn't really into continuing this stupid argument, or getting pummelled for that matter, but I was not about to be sent away like a lackey. Thinking about it, I wouldn't even be that rude to a lackey – and I don't even know what a lackey is.

'Dismissed! You are dismissing me? Oh thank you, Your Royal Highness, for the privilege of your company. If there is anything else your Sire-ship requires don't hesitate to order your Turd-low to sneak in and overhear it.'

I pulled the reins on Acorn and let Her Ladyship pull ahead. Turlow passed me on the left and said, 'That did not sound very good.'

I spotted a glimpse of a smirk on his face as he caught up with his fiancée.

Araf came abreast. 'That didn't sound very good,' he said.

Araf it seemed had learned how to make unnecessary comments. I have only myself to blame 'cause I think he learned that from me. I let him go by and dropped into step with Brendan.

'That didn't sound very good,' Brendan said.

'That seems to be the consensus. Could you really hear us all the way back here?'

'Let's just say if you two ever get married, I don't want to live next door.'

'Don't worry, there is not much chance of that.'

'Conor, can I give you a piece of constructive advice?'

'Go ahead,' I sighed.

'Stop being such a jerk.'

'That's constructive advice?' I asked.

'Well maybe not – but it *is* advice.'

'So I'm the jerk? What about her? She was the one that tore my head off.'

'And you did nothing to provoke her?'

'No. Well, OK yes, but she overreacted and what about Turdlow creeping around in the dark listening in on our conversations.'

'It wasn't dark, it was in that pea-soup fog, remember? And he told me that he was just sitting next to us doing some Banshee meditation and *we* disturbed him.'

'And you believe him?'

'Conor, I can see why you don't like him but I hate to tell you this – he seems like a nice guy.'

'Well, you thought I was a murderer, so forgive me if I don't trust your judgement.'

Brendan just shrugged. He wasn't looking for a fight and it made me realise I didn't need another one either, so I changed the subject.

'Speaking of difficult women, where is my aunt?'

'She's a gone out a-huntin.'

'Hunting? My Aunt Nieve?'

'She thought it was strange that we weren't seeing any animals the closer we got to these Pinelands. So she nipped off to look for some. Ever since she mentioned it, I've noticed that I haven't seen a lot of living things around here for a while. Have you?'

'I haven't been looking,' I replied. 'I've been too busy wooing Essa.'

'Right, how's that going?'

'You know, Brendan, I liked you better when you were a mean cop. This sarcastic Brendan is annoying.'

'Nieve doesn't think I'm annoying. In fact this morning she said I was quite funny.'

'You had a conversation with Nieve? I thought you were scared of her?'

'Oh, I'm still plenty scared of her but you can't deny that she is quite beautiful.'

'Yes, I noticed that when I first saw her, but it went away.'

'When you found out she was your aunt?'

'No, when she tried to kill me. I find I lose that loving feeling with women that try to kill me.'

'Didn't Essa try to kill you?'

I didn't have a good answer for that, so I ignored it.

Chapter Eighteen
The Pinelands

The next couple of days were clear but icy cold. In the morning, frost covered our tents, which meant getting out of my cosy sleeping roll was almost impossible. Essa continued to set a pace bordering on the maniacal. In short, the entire trip was extremely not fun – but it seemed I was the only one who thought so. The princess and the Banshee lovebirds were as sickly as ever. Brendan and Nieve were getting along so well I could have sworn I heard my aunt actually giggle. That left me and Araf, and when he did talk, it was about the native flora or what a nice guy he thought Turlow was. I decided that my only course of action was to pout.

Either this group was a bunch of insensitive louts (which I am not discounting) or I wasn't doing it right. A proper pout should influence the mood of the entire group making them all almost as miserable as the poutee but my travelling companions seemed to be un-bring-down-able. If I complained about the cold they would say, 'Yes, but look at the blue skies.' If I sighed heavily and went to bed immediately after dinner they would just say, 'Good night.' I figured they would notice if I went off my food but as soon as chow was placed in front of me – I ate it. You have to be really committed to call a hunger-strike pout.

Actually one person noticed my sulk – Turlow. He slipped in next to me and said, 'You don't seem to be enjoying our little jaunt, Master Faerie.'

'I'm having a grand time,' I answered without looking at him.

'I don't believe you. How can you not be in high spirits when you are in the company of Essa of Muhn? Oh, but you're not really in her company that much, are you? Shame, I'm having a lovely time.'

'You done?' I asked.

'Funny,' he said as he kicked his horse and sped back to the front, 'I was going to ask you the same thing.'

A couple of days later the mood of the group turned, but I suspect that it had a lot less to do with my pouting than it had to do with us reaching the edge of the Pinelands.

Like many of the lands in Tir na Nog, you know you're in the Pinelands when you get there. It starts with rolling hills filled with – can you guess? – pine trees. Actually the trees are silver fir – *ailm* in the ancient language of Ogham. If you think that a hill filled with pine trees would give the place a nice Christmassy feel, you'd be wrong. These pines were scraggy and downright menacing. Like weird old men with long bedraggled beards who, if you talked to them, would probably say, 'We don't cotton onto strangers around here,' and when you got back to your car your girlfriend would be missing. These trees grew high and hunched over like they wanted to block out as much light as possible. The ground between the trees was a spongy carpet of brown pine needles in which nothing grew.

The trail grew steeper and the pace slower. It was tiring. You would think that since I was on horseback it wouldn't make any difference whether I was going uphill or down, but Acorn and I had a bond that made me feel some of his effort. All the good riders experienced the same thing, so I guess I was getting pretty good at this riding stuff. We also travelled slower 'cause none of us wanted to make too much noise in this place. If we could have gotten our horses to tiptoe, we would have.

After a couple of wordless hours inclining the Pinelands, Brendan rode up close to me and in a low voice said, 'This is going to sound very clichéd but I—'

'You feel like someone is watching you?' I interrupted.

He nodded.

'Yeah, me too. I thought something was shadowing us over to the left but maybe it's just these damn trees.' I said 'damn' wordlessly so the trees couldn't hear me.

We decided that we were better safe than sorry (or dead) so we kept watch. I looked right while Brendan tried to observe left. (Until our necks got sore and we traded sides.) The shapes that this forest made were so different than any nature we had seen before it really spooked us. We were like scared cub scouts by nightfall.

Essa built a tiny fire with the kindling from her pack. It was enough to make some tea and provided just enough light to pitch our tents by. No one complained because the person that did knew that they would have to be the one to ask one of the scary trees for wood. Brendan and I thought we should keep a watch and since we were the only ones that suggested it – we got to do it.

'I'm going to go out on a limb and say, I don't really like the Pinelands,' I said.

'I'm with you on that one, Mr O'Neil. Miserable, ain't it?' Brendan said, trying to warm his hands on the pathetic fire. 'For the first time in a long while I'm glad my daughter isn't with me.'

'You don't talk about her much.'

'I think about her all of the time, that's enough.'

'What's her name?'

'Ruby.'

'Ruby, that's a nice name.'

'You think? I like it now, I can't imagine her having any other name but when my wife suggested it I thought it sounded like the name of the local good-time girl.'

'It's also the name of a precious gem.'

Brendan smiled a sad smile of a homesick man. 'That's my pet name for her – Gem.'

I wanted to ask him more about his family but it was too cold and too dark.

'Screw this,' I said, standing. 'What is the point of keeping watch if it's so dark that you can't even see anything coming?' I turned to the woods. 'And I'm freezing my butt off.'

'You going to bed?' Brendan asked.

'No, I'm gonna get some firewood.'

'From where? You're not going to talk to those trees, are you?'

'What are they going to do, kill me?'

'Didn't you tell me that there are trees in The Land that can?'

He had a point, but I ignored him. If this stupid quest was going to force me to be out of doors in the middle of the winter I was going to have a roaring fire, damn it. I walked up to the nearest pine, which wasn't very close. We had chosen a campsite in one of the few clearings we had found. The closer I got to the trees the worse this idea got. My courage slipped out of me with every step. The faint light from our poor excuse for a campfire cast creepy shadows. I started to think, *do I really need to be any warmer? I'll just throw another blanket over me.* I stopped under the huge gnarled tree. A cold sweat ran down my armpit and then a shiver shook me from ear to knee. *What am I,* I asked myself, *am I a man or a mouse?* I knew I didn't have any cheese with me so I closed my eyes and touched my hand to the rough bark.

When you first touch most trees in The Land it's like a brain-scan. You don't tell them anything, they just zap into your cranium and take any information they need. I squeezed my eyes closed and waited. Nothing. I opened one eye and quietly said, 'Hello?'

'Are you a Pooka?'

That question shot into my head but instead of it sounding (or should I say feeling) like a nasty old hillbilly, I got the impression of a scared kid.

I tried to reply just by thinking – still nothing. *Hello*, I thought, then out loud I said, 'Anybody in there?'

'Are you a Pooka?' the tree asked again. His voice sounded frantic, laced with childish overexcitement.

'No, I'm …' I sighed and admitted, 'I'm a Faerie.'

'Do you know where the Pookas are?'

'No, we are looking for them ourselves.'

'Oh, when you see them could you tell them …'

I don't remember anything after that for a while. Brendan said I shot straight back about three feet and was out cold for about five minutes. At first he thought I was dead. When I came to I had a huge throbbing headache and couldn't really make sense of anything for a while. Brendan helped me over to the fire, gave me some willow tea and put me into my tent. In my dreams, I was a pinball going from pine tree to pine tree. Every time I was just ready to stop, a pine would whack me and I would bounce around the forest until I stopped at another, then I would get whacked again. I wouldn't call my night … refreshing.

I awoke to the smell and sound of a roaring fire. Everyone was up. Essa and Nieve were in the distance with their arms around trees. Brendan handed me a cup of tea.

'Where'd you get the firewood?' I asked.

'From the pines. They are very nice once you get to know them.'

'Or until they attack you with some sort of brain-exploding beam.'

'No one tried to explode your brain. It's just that M over there' – Brendan pointed to the tree I had chatted with last night – 'has been way behind on his emailing. He got overexcited.'

'M?'

'Well, I can't pronounce his name – I think it starts with an M so that's what I call him. He likes it. He never had a nickname before. Nice kid.'

'What are you talking about?'

'OK, here is what M and L over there' – he pointed to a big old tree – 'and Nieve have told me. Trees communicate with one another in The Land. Like when you told me not to talk around the beech trees because they gossip and I thought you were bonkers?'

'Yeah.'

'So when you enter a wood, the whole forest knows about it 'cause they talk to each other.'

'Brendan, you're not telling me anything I didn't know.'

'Yes, but that's the point. Pine trees can't talk to each other. And nobody knew it, except the Pookas.'

'So why did M attack me?'

'He didn't attack you – he just got carried away. The Pookas carry messages from one tree to another. L, that old tree over there, told me that they do it without even thinking. Apparently Pookas just walk through the forest touching trees, picking up and dropping messages as they go. They're like tree postal workers.'

'So where are they?'

'Well, L over there thinks he has seen a couple of Pookas in their animal forms but they haven't spoken to him and he hasn't seen one in human form since the middle of the summer. Poor M is just a kid. He hasn't been able to send a message to any of his gang in ages. When he talked to you he got excited and loaded about five months' worth of notes into your head. It was equivalent to having a hundred pound mailbag dropped on your noggin. He told me to tell you he was sorry.'

'So where are the Pookas?'

'That's what Nieve and Essa are trying to find out. It's slow going. Every time you talk to a tree they beg you to pass a message on for them. It's hard to say no.'

That day's journey was slow going. I had no intention of touching a pine again, but Essa, Araf, Brendan and Nieve had all promised a tree they would pass along a couple of messages. Turlow and I would go a couple of hundred yards and then wait while our companions zigzagged all over the forest. I got so bored with waiting, I actually struck up a conversation with the girlfriend-stealing Banshee.

'How come you're not playing Postman Plank?'

'I, Prince Faerie, am not an admirer of wood.'

'You don't like wood?'

'Oh, I like it fine in a chair or a fire but I don't like trees.'

'How can anybody not like trees?' I asked incredulously. 'Have you ever spoken to an oak or an apple?'

'I do not speak with trees.'

'Why not?'

'If you must know, I do not like the way their roots reach in to my thinking. My mind is my own.'

'Sounds like you have something to hide. A copy of *Naughty Elves Monthly* in the bottom of your sock drawer, maybe?' He gave me that Turd-low look that translates to 'I'll not dignify that with an answer.'

'Well, I wouldn't worry about talking to these guys,' I said. 'They're as thick as two planks. Get it? Planks – pine trees?' I waited. 'You wouldn't laugh at my jokes even if they were funny.'

'When it happens, Faerie, I will let you know.'

Not long after that Brendan rode up and said, 'That's it. I quit.'

'What, no more neighbourhood postman for you? You will have to hand back those snazzy Bermuda shorts.'

'Every tree wants me to send a message to ten others.' He scratched his head with both hands. 'It's just not possible. The sooner we find the Pookas the better these trees will be.'

'Poor guys, it sounds like they really miss the Pookas. They're *pining* for them.'

Brendan gave me a look not unlike the one Turlow had given me moments before and kicked ahead.

'Oh, come on,' I called after him, 'that was a good one.'

Chapter Nineteen
Hawathiee

That night most of the Tir-na-Nogian Postal Workers Union Local No.1 went to bed early – exhausted. Just Brendan and I were left to tend the roaring fire.

'Do you still think we need to keep watch?' Brendan asked. 'We have been prancing around these woods all day, I don't think there is anybody in here.'

'Me neither but I'm keeping watch just in case one of the postmen goes berserk and shoots us all.'

Brendan laughed. It was good that there was at least one person who got my Real World jokes, even if he didn't always laugh at them. He pulled out a couple of tin mugs then uncorked a bottle with his teeth and poured us both a drink.

'To your father,' Brendan said, holding his mug high. 'Long live the King.'

'Hear, hear,' I said and drank. 'Heeeeyooow,' I gasped as the firewater travelled down my throat, into my chest and then exploded out of my toes. 'Where did you get this stuff?'

'I was really in the mood for a drink so I kind-of found it … in Essa's bag.'

'A thieving policeman – you should be ashamed.'

'I am,' he said. 'Would you like some more?'

'Yes please. How did you know it was there?'

'Her father makes the stuff, so I just deduced.'

'You know, Brendan, when you are not charging me with murder, you are quite the detective.' I raised my glass. 'To your little Gem,' I toasted.

He nodded and stretched a pained smile across his face. 'To Ruby.'

We drank and he looked at his mug for a while.

'What's she like?'

'Ruby?' He laughed. 'She's seven going on thirty-five. Ever since her mom died she has taken it unto herself to be the grand bossy woman of the house. When she's home you'd hardly even know she's blind.'

'She's blind?'

'Yeah, she lost her sight in the same accident that killed my wife.'

'What happened?'

After a deep breath Brendan said, 'My wife liked to speed around on those back roads. Do you know Cobb Creek? It's not that far from your place.'

'I do. It's nice up there. Is that where you live?'

'Yes, my mother found the spot with her voodoo divining rods. She said there were lay-lines or some such thing there. My wife used to like my mother's craziness. I didn't care about energy lines; I just liked it because it is beautiful. Anyway, my wife was driving in her little red sports car with the top down, when, right outside our house, a horse ran in front of the car. We were having a conservatory built at the same time and the car slammed sideways into the truck carrying panes of glass. My wife was killed and Ruby lost her vision to flying shards.' He stopped and took another drink.

'My gods,' I said and put my hand on his shoulder. 'I'm so sorry.'

'Yeah, me too,' and then with a forced smile he said, 'More booze?'

'I think so,' I replied, offering my cup. 'How long ago was this?'

'About two and a half years.'

'Whose horse was it?'

'We never found out. It was injured pretty badly; my partner arrived about the same time as the ambulance and put it down. I was crazy mad and checked every farm and stable in a thirty-mile radius – no one said that they had lost a horse and I could never trace the markings on the saddle.'

'The horse was saddled?'

'Yes.'

'But there was no rider?'

'No,' Brendan shook his head. 'Well, if you ask Ruby about it she says otherwise.'

'What does she say?'

'You have to realise she was just five. She claims the horse had a rider dressed in black and that they appeared out of nowhere. She says it's the last thing she ever saw.'

The next day everybody gave up trying to carry messages for the trees. We just weren't up to it. The Pookas must have some special microchip in their heads 'cause we found the task impossible.

The path grew steeper but the mood was lighter. We no longer looked at each tree as a potential assassin. We saw them as they were, lost lonely souls who had been abandoned by their pastor. Oh, and I wasn't sulking any more.

The previous night's chat with Brendan rolled around in my noggin all morning and it sparked off memories that in turn ignited unanswered questions. As I watched my aunt riding in front of me I remembered the first time I had seen her. The memories were vivid and unsettling: Dad going berserk, throwing his axe at her head and knocking her guard off his saddle. The guard hitting the ground and instantly turning into a thousand-year-old swirl of dust. Nieve throwing a spear at me and then high-tailing it out of there and letting Cialtie's henchmen, all dressed in black, knock us out and chain us up in Dungeon Duir.

I cantered up alongside my aunt. 'Nieve, can I ask you a question?'

'I'm sure you can, Conor, because you just did.'

'Right,' I said a bit nervously. Nieve had an uncanny ability to instantly put me ill at ease. I wondered if she did it to everyone and I also wondered if she did it on purpose. 'Do you promise you won't get mad at me?'

'No,' came her immediate reply.

'OoooK, how about – do you promise you won't hurt me?'

She thought about that for a moment and said, 'No.'

'Oh well, never mind then.' I dropped back and waited for her curiosity to get the better of her.

And I waited – and waited.

About an hour later I pulled up next to her and said, 'OK, I know you are secretly dying to know – so here's my question: how come you helped Cialtie find me in the Real World?'

She quickly reached her left hand into her cloak and with her right hand she reached for the short knife on her belt.

I looked around to see if anyone else was watching us – they weren't. When I looked back Nieve had already cut the apple in her hand and handed half to me. There was a wicked twinkle in her eyes.

I took the apple half. 'You like messing with me, don't you?'

'If I understand the meaning of *messing with you*, then yes, but don't get too flattered.' She leaned towards me and in a conspiratorial whisper she said, 'I like *messing* with everybody.'

We rode and ate in silence for a little while. Nieve sported a little smile. I felt privileged that she shared that small secret with me. I felt like a nephew.

Finally she said, 'I didn't help Cialtie.'

'Well, you showed up at my doorstep and the next thing I knew I had chains for jewellery.'

'Do you not remember that I left when I heard Cialtie's men approach?'

'Yes. Why did you do that?'

'Because I was afraid of them. I did not wish to be unseated from my horse. I'm quite fond of my looks, Conor; I would rather not look my age.'

'So how did they find us?'

'They followed me. Remember the soldier that was with me?'

'The guy that fell off his horse and then dusted it?'

'*Dusted it* – that is an apt way of putting it. Yes, him; I found out later that he was one of Cialtie's spies.'

'I feel less sorry for him now,' I said.

'That is what I said when I found out.'

'So how did *you* find us?'

'I'm a very good sorceress you know,' she said without a smile. It was no brag – just fact. 'I found a war axe that was made at the same time as your father's axe was made. The gold inlay in the handle came from the same vein and gave off the same ...' she searched for the words, 'magic resonance. It was not easy to track but as I said, I am very good.'

'OK, now I see the how, but can I ask you one more question? Why? Why then? I mean, I was going to die in the Real World some day. What was your hurry?'

'I wanted to kill you before Cialtie did.'

That was an answer I wasn't expecting. 'Isn't that taking sibling rivalry a bit too far?'

'I was satisfied with your father's solution. I was happy to see you die in the Real World but when I learned that Cialtie was using the Hall of Spells to send forays into the Real World looking for you, I had to kill you first.'

'Why?'

'I was afraid that Cialtie would make a big spectacle of killing you. Maybe even a public execution. I couldn't have that. I wanted to kill you privately and cleanly.'

'Gee, thanks – I think.' I smiled at her but she did not return it.

'I took no joy in that task,' she said.

'I know,' I said. I put my hand on her arm, and then I changed the subject. 'So Cialtie sent riders to look for me and Dad even before last summer?'

'My information is that he was looking for years.'

'Where did you get your information from?'

Nieve smiled. 'Cialtie is not the only one with spies.'

That night I put it to Brendan that maybe his daughter really did see a rider dressed in black and that maybe they really did appear out of nowhere, but he got angry with me for even suggesting such nonsense and wouldn't speak about it.

Later I was awoken by rustling in the forest. Something *was* moving out there and it was something big. The fire was almost out so I walked up to a nearby tree to ask for wood.

An ancient voice appeared in my head. '*You are not Pooka.*'

'No, sir,' I said aloud. 'We seek the Pooka.'

'*There is Pooka in the forest tonight,*' he said.

'Have you spoken to them?'

'*The Pooka no longer speak to me – I am alone.*'

I felt so sorry for the old guy. I said, 'I can take a message to a tree for you. Just don't give me more than one – I can't handle it.' I shut my eyes expecting an onslaught of messages but none came.

'*What good is one message? The Pooka have renounced us, we are alone.*'

I heard the familiar creaking of the tree sucking the moisture out of some of its limbs. I said, 'Thank you, sir,' and backed off before he cracked off his branches and dropped them to the ground. I stoked the fire and kept watch. I continued to hear something moving in the gloomy dark but never saw anything.

That changed the next morning. Something was in the woods, on both sides of us, and whatever is was, it was tracking us. At noon Araf said he saw a wolf. About an hour later I saw one too. Like seeing a shark's dorsal fin in the water, seeing a wolf running low in a forest will make your heart go pitter-pat.

The higher we got in the Pinelands, the more the trees thinned and we got a better look at our escorts. It was a pack about ten strong. They shadowed us with military precision – four on each side and two slipping close in at our rear. If we turned in our saddles to look, the two that followed would slip back into the trees and wait patiently until our eyes turned ahead when they would slink back into position. It was unnerving. Essa said she thought the Pooka headquarters was over the rise. I bit my tongue before saying, 'You think?' This crowd was too tense for teasing and I knew from experience that annoying a stressed Essa was a dangerous thing.

The closer we got to the summit the bolder the wolves got. They moved in closer and no longer attempted to conceal themselves among the few remaining trees. These guys were big – Great-Dane sized – but they looked thin and just a little bit mangy. If you caught their eye it gave you a feeling that they were unpredictable – capable of anything.

Our mounts definitely didn't like them. Horses, I have learned, are travelling machines. They focus on the minutiae of the terrain ahead and because of that almost never put a foot wrong. What they don't do well is worry about what is behind them. It pulls their focus. Acorn periodically tried to look behind and every time he did I looked as well. A couple of times I almost fell off.

An explosion of gold light erupted behind me that nearly made me jump out of my skin. The wolves yelped and I saw one dart into the forest with his fur shooting straight out in all directions. Brendan notched an arrow.

'Put away your bow, archer. They are Pookas.'

'What did you do?' I asked my aunt.

'I didn't harm anyone but they were getting a bit too close for my horse's liking. Now they have a better idea of who they are dealing with.'

The wolves gave us a wider berth but it didn't last. They slipped in closer, zigzagging behind us, sometimes so close that our horses tried to kick them. Not the kind of thing you want your mount to do unexpectedly.

Essa pointed to a rock formation not too far off to the left. 'That is where I was greeted by Queen Rhiannon the last time I was here.'

Nieve blasted the Pineland wolves again. Any sane creatures would have scampered away with their tails between their legs but I wasn't too sure that these creatures were sane.

Now that we were closer to the rock wall I still couldn't decide if it was Pooka-made or natural. The wall looked like it could have been a long fault line that had collapsed in an earthquake. In the middle was an archway. Our plan of riding through the opening and fending off the wolves there was dashed when we saw that thick pine branches blocked the entrance from the other side.

'Nieve,' Essa shouted from horseback, 'can you move those trees?'

'That depends on the trees,' Nieve shouted back. 'I may need your help.'

'Everyone,' Essa shouted, trying to sound like a seasoned commander but there was a slight quiver in her voice that betrayed a fear that I think we all shared. 'Dismount quickly and protect the horses while Nieve and I clear the gateway.'

Turlow moved first, he performed a very impressive dismount while in full canter. In midair, even before his feet hit the ground, his Banshee blade rocketed out of his sleeve. It surprised the lead pack wolf to the point that he stumbled as he slowed. Acorn was barely walking when I dismounted, still I almost fell over. We fanned out and put our nervous snorting horses behind us. The wolves fanned too and paced sideways snarling – looking for a weakness in our defences. I couldn't help thinking that they were looking at me more than the others.

'Tell me again why I can't shoot one of them?' Brendan shouted.

'Because they are Hawathiee,' Araf said.

Now there was a word I hadn't heard before. 'Hawa what?' I asked, never taking my eyes off my junkyard dog.

'We are all Hawathiee: Faeries, Imps, Leprechauns, Fili, Elves, Brownies and Pooka. We are children of the trees. We do not kill each other.'

'You know I've read some of your history,' I said, 'and that's not exactly true.'

'Well,' Araf replied a bit sheepishly, 'we are not supposed to kill each other.'

'Notice he didn't mention Banshees in his little list,' Turlow said.

One of the wolves made a faint attack at Araf which it instantly abandoned. The rest of the pack quickly ran sideways and swopped positions.

'I do not think that *now* is the time to debate that, Turlow,' Araf said.

Turlow's reply was almost too soft to hear. 'That's what they always say.'

I really didn't like the look of the slobber that was drooling off the lips of one of the wolves in front of me. He had a look of desperation about him and his patience was growing thin.

'How's the tree pruning going back there, girls?' I shouted without turning around.

'The trees are alive but they will not speak to us,' Nieve called back. 'I do not wish to hurt them.'

'Well, something or someone is going to get hurt real soon,' Brendan said, 'and I would prefer it not to be me.'

Turlow broke the calm. With a well and proper Banshee scream, he lashed out at the two beasts that were facing him. They initially stood the charge with bared fangs but as he grew closer and louder they scampered away like poodles being reprimanded by a maid with a broom.

When I looked back to the wolves that were dogging me, I was surprised to see that they had crept in to almost a lunge-length away. I swung the Lawnmower and let loose a scream that sounded weedy compared to Turlow's. The wolves backed off and then, as one, they all turned and ran away.

I smiled at Araf. 'Well, I guess I showed them who's boss.'

Araf didn't look at me. He seemed to look above me. 'I can only guess at what *boss* means,' he said, 'but I am guessing that the boss is not you.'

I turned. That's when I saw the bears.

Chapter Twenty
Tuan

There were two of them. Kodiak-looking fellows about twenty feet high – or so it seemed at the time. To call them bears would be doing them an injustice, like calling a couple of sabre-toothed tigers kitty-cats. They were actually hairy mountains with teeth and claws. They loped towards us on all fours but as soon as they made eye contact, they stopped and reared up on their hind legs. I mentioned before that the sight of wolves in the forest made my heart skip a beat – well, the sight of these guys at full height produced a code-red cardiac arrest.

They dropped back to all fours and slowly came towards us. They didn't look menacing exactly – I think I could have coped with that – their expression was far more terrifying. They looked hungry.

I heard the creak of Brendan's bow as he pulled his weapon back to full tension. 'These guys I can shoot, right?'

'NO,' came a shout from Essa and Araf.

Brendan turned to Araf. 'Why not?'

'It will only make them mad,' the Imp replied.

'Girls,' I shouted behind me, 'you better hack through those trees.'

'No, Conor,' Essa hissed back.

'You either hack the trees or I have to hack a super bear and I have a suspicion that the bear is going to hack back.'

'We did not come here to kill trees and Pookas,' Essa said.

'Well, I didn't come here to get a good look at my lower intestines either. Make a decision or these bears are going to make one for us.'

A screech tore my wide and terrified eyes away from the approaching colossi. I looked up and saw what at first looked like a falcon, but as I watched the feathers on his wings began to be absorbed into what began to look like arms. The sharp beak disappeared into his widening face; talons extended and became long lean legs. He was fully human when he hit the ground. I'd like to say it was a stunning and graceful manoeuvre but that would be a lie. What I saw was a bird that, in midair, turned into a very naked man that then awkwardly slammed face down into the earth. I'm pretty sure even the bears thought it looked painful.

As he lay there moaning, one of us really should have asked him if he was all right, but, like the bears, we were frozen in shock. By the time he got up, the bears had seen enough and were moving again. He stood and shouted, 'BE GONE.'

Now, I don't know about you but if a naked man fell from the sky and then, in all of his dingly-dangly naked glory, stood in front of me and shouted, 'BE GONE,' then I would probably go. But these Pookas/bears, like the wolves, were not in their right minds – they kept coming. I didn't know what to do. Part of me wanted to step in front of this obviously deranged Pooka and save him from almost certain disembowelment. Of course the other part of me was delighted to have anything between me and the two mountains of slobber, fangs and claws that were heading my way.

'Hey,' I called to him. When he ignored me I tried again. 'Excuse me, naked Pooka guy. Can we help in any way?'

He turned to look at me; one side of his face was covered with dirt and grass stains. 'Stand back,' he commanded. Then he reached his hand to his neck, dropped his head to his chest and went down onto one knee. It looked like he was praying and I hoped it was a short prayer because the bears were almost on him. I heard Brendan's bow creak. I couldn't stand to watch. Just as I was about to turn away, he stood up – then he kept standing up. His feet thinned at the bottom, then his backside grew a tail and widened to the size of a downtown bus. His head grew a rack of flat antlers that must have been as wide as the bears were tall. He grew dark brown short hair all over his body. When the transformation was done, we all stood open-mouthed. It was one of the most impressive things I had seen to date. Standing between us and certain death was what I now know was a prehistoric Celtic deer. Imagine a moose the size of a large elephant and you've got the idea. He dropped his antler-adorned head, scratched in the earth with his hind legs and charged.

The bears didn't give it a second thought. They scrabbled out of there fast. Mr Moose gave a short chase then changed back into a naked man before collapsing onto the frozen earth.

Brendan and I ran up to him. 'Are you all right?' I asked.

He replied with moans that then became words. 'Aahh … leave … this … mountain.'

Araf ran up with a blanket and placed it over him. Without looking up he angrily pushed it off. 'Leave this mountain.'

I placed the blanket back over him. 'Really, you're going to freeze out here. Can we—'

He scrambled to his feet with a speed that surprised me. Apart from a gold disc that hung on a wire around his neck, and the mud and dirt, he was still very naked. He spotted Essa and Nieve still working on the trees that blocked the gateway. 'Get away from there!' he tried to scream but his voice was tired and thin. They looked but continued. He threw his head back, almost falling over. 'LEAVE THIS MOUNTAIN!' he shouted. He staggered as he brought his head down, his eyes still closed. I took a step forward to catch him if he fell. He opened his eyes. I think he expected us to be gone, instead of standing around staring at him. A look of mad anger took over his face. He dropped to his knees and grabbed the medallion around his neck. Brendan, Turlow, Araf and I all took an involuntary step back.

Black fur sprouted from every pore, his nose blackened and broadened. The teeth changed just before the snout formed, giving us a good look at the fangs. We took another step back. As his height increased he tried to stand. That's when the transformation stalled then stopped altogether. His eyes blinked rapidly and he shrank quickly into naked Pooka guy again as he fell face first unconscious into Araf's waiting arms.

Araf carried him over to the gate where Essa and Nieve had started a small fire and were brewing tea. Essa wrapped him in more blankets while Nieve placed her hands on his temples.

When she released his head she said, 'He is exhausted and starving.'

'Was he changing into a bear?' Essa asked.

'I think so,' Araf said.

'And he flew in as a bird,' Turlow said. 'Did you see that?'

'Very strange,' Essa said. Everyone, except Brendan and me, nodded in agreement.

'Look, everyone, changing into mooses,' Brendan said, 'is mighty strange for me but you people are talking like that's not strange enough.'

Essa answered him. 'Pookas spend decades, centuries, studying how to change into their chosen animal. I have never heard of a Pooka that could change into more than one. This must be some sort of master Pooka.'

'Have you had any joy with the trees?' Turlow asked.

'No, we cannot pass without hurting the trees,' Nieve said.

'Then we must hurt the trees,' Turlow said. 'I will do it.'

'Slow down, honey,' Essa said. 'We have a local here. When he wakes he may help us through.'

'Or he might turn into a wolverine and rip our throats out,' I said. 'And did I just hear you call him "honey"?' I said that last bit loudly. I shouldn't have but I was a bit stunned. The only thing I could ever imagine Essa calling honey is that yellow stuff that bees make.

'What is wrong with calling my fiancé "honey"?' Essa said with that customary fire in her eyes but also with, maybe, just a touch of embarrassment.

'Yes, Faerie, what is wrong with that?' her Banshee added.

I was racking my brains for a suitable quip that would stop me from getting clocked by Essa or stabbed by the Turd-low when I was saved by a moan from the Pooka. We all looked at him.

His head was resting on Nieve's lap. He had a mop of sandy blond hair sitting on top of an almost boyish face. As we watched, he opened his eyes; they were piercing blue. Usually it's the eyes here in The Land that give away how old a person is, but this Pooka's eyes confused me. I instantly thought he was very young but then I got a fleeting impression of very old age. After that his peepers were just unreadable. Nieve brushed a piece of grass off of his cheek and smiled at him. It was nice to see such tenderness from my aunt – I certainly hadn't seen that before.

The Pooka didn't get up and when he spoke he was hoarse and hard to hear. 'You must leave.' He closed his eyes again and I wondered if he had passed out, but then he opened them and looked at each of us. 'I can't protect you,' he said.

Nieve sat him up and Essa got some willow tea into him.

'I could have sworn I had some poteen with me,' Essa said. Brendan gave me a furtive guilty glance.

A little bit more of the spark of life returned to our shapeshifter with every sip of willow tea. Araf gave him some food and he gobbled it down. With a boyishly guilty look, Brendan produced the almost-finished bottle of poteen and handed it to Essa, who gave him such a dirty look I was sure glad I wasn't him. A shot of

Gerard's special moonshine brought all the colour back to our patient's cheeks and maybe a little extra. He sat with us around the fire wrapped in about four blankets.

'We do not seek your protection,' Essa said, breaking the silence. 'We seek Queen Rhiannon.'

Pooka guy made a snorting, laughing sound that I didn't like and said, 'Queen Rhiannon is indisposed.'

'None the less, we must see her.'

'You cannot.'

'We have come a long way and will see the Queen with or without your help,' Essa said.

He threw off his blankets and stood up. Our friendly fireside guest once again became very angry naked Pooka guy – which was disconcerting, 'cause we were pretty close and seated. 'You can't see her. YOU MUST LEAVE.' His face became repossessed – he reached for his neck.

'Woah, woah, woah, Pooka guy,' I said, as I grabbed his wrist before his hand made it to his medallion. 'I don't know you very well but I don't think you are up for one of your quick changes. And anyway, there are six of us and we are all pretty handy. You'd have to turn into a T-Rex to stop us.'

He stood there, unmoving. I wasn't sure if I was getting through to him.

'It's OK, really,' I said, 'we're like a royal honour guard here. Me and Araf are princes, those two are princesses and Turlow here is like a king.' Brendan coughed. 'Oh yeah, he's a cop.'

The Pooka placed his face in his hands. From behind his palms he said, 'You cannot see her. No one can see her.'

'I have even brought gifts, look.' I took out the muslin parcel, untied it and displayed the six hazelnuts.

The look on the Pooka's face was like that of a man lost in the desert for a week being offered a glass of ice water. 'Where did you get them?' he almost whispered.

'From the Tree of Knowledge.'

'You lie, the Tree was destroyed.'

'This is from the new tree. Essa and I planted it ourselves from my grandfather's hazel wood.'

The Pooka stared hard at my face. 'You are Liam's son?'

'I'm his grandson, Conor.'

'I will take them to her,' the Pooka said.

I pulled the hazelnuts out of his reach. 'No, this is a royal gift from Queen Deirdre of Duir to Queen Rhiannon of Ailm. I was instructed to present it to Her Highness in person or not at all.'

'Lady Deirdre has been found?'

'Ages ago,' I said.

'I sent a runner to find her. He never returned.'

'Was he a curly-haired guy who changed into a wolf?'

The Pooka nodded yes.

'He found her but I have bad news, he's dead.'

Sadness mixed with resignation crossed the Pooka's face.

'I'm sorry. Look, is there any way we can have this conversation while you wear clothes? You're making me cold just looking at you.'

He took the blanket I offered and wrapped it around himself. I filled him in on all the major news of The Land: Mom and Dad's and my return, Cialtie getting booted out of Castle Duir and the rebuilding of the Hazellands.

'So you are Deirdre's son. My sister was your mother's tutor – she was very fond of her.' He didn't have to say any more. The look on his face told me that she must have died when the Hall of Knowledge was attacked. 'My name is Tuan. I will take you, Prince Conor, to see Queen Rhiannon.'

He stood and placed his hands on the thick branches that blocked the stone portal, mumbled something in a language I didn't recognise and the trees creaked up and away. 'Quickly,' Tuan said, 'before the larger animals come back.'

We grabbed our horses and led them through. As the trees were bowing back down into position, I spotted the pack of wolves eyeing us from among some far trees. They didn't look happy.

Inside the wall, small animals, horses and sheep wandered freely. After I unsaddled Acorn I expected him to join the local horses for a frolic but he and the others grazed uneasily close by. Tuan said that the others in my party could make camp where they were and offered to take me alone to see Queen Rhiannon.

'I walk with Prince Conor,' Araf said.

'No.' Tuan was adamant. 'Conor alone may see the Queen.'

Turlow stood. 'What is to stop you as soon as you are out of our sight from changing into a bear and taking Conor's nuts?'

I hoped he was talking about hazelnuts but either way he had a point. 'Yeah, what assurance do I have that you won't go all hairy and fangy?'

'You have my word as a Child of Ailm, but if that is not enough then here.' He reached for the wire that held the medallion around his neck and it expanded at his touch. He slipped it over his head and dropped the gold disc into my hand.

I looked to my travelling companions, wordlessly asking them, 'Should I trust him?' Tuan stepped away and allowed us to confer.

Amazingly Araf spoke first. 'We have come a long way. I do not like leaving you on your own, and if you are hurt I shall have to hide from your mother for the rest of my days, but I think you should go.'

Nieve and Essa both agreed.

'I think he is exhausted and desperate which makes him unpredictable,' Brendan said, 'but I think he is one of the good guys.'

'You thought I was a murderer.'

'Yes, but if you remember I also said that you were not a bad man.'

Turlow was the sole dissenter. 'We have his changing medallion. We can force him to take us to the Queen without risk.' He looked around for support. 'Oh, don't look at me like that. This is a desperate place and we have been attacked three times today. Desperate times require desperate measures.'

I don't know what the others thought but I was glad of Turlow's opinion. It's good to have at least one person on the team that errs on the side of caution.

'Tuan,' I called, 'let's go meet the Queen.' Then I surprised everybody by handing him back his medallion. 'If you eat me, make sure you let Essa watch – she'd like that.'

I turned back to the group and said, 'If I'm not back in two days …' then realised I didn't know how to end that sentence. 'If I'm not back in two days – then I'm dead. You can do what you want.'

'We will be back tomorrow,' Tuan said. 'Do not eat any animals. They are not as they seem.'

Tuan and I walked along the wall until we reached a pile of clothes at the base of a tall pine. Tuan touched the tree and said, 'Thanks.' He put on a pair of very baggy brown trousers, a black shirt, a black sealskin coat, some leather boots and a rabbit-fur hat. For a guy that changed into animals, he didn't seem averse to wearing dead ones. We walked over a ridge until we could no longer see my companions.

'Now is a good a time to change into a wolf and eat me,' I said.

'I am not that kind of Pooka,' he replied.

'The ones on the other side of the wall were though – weren't they?'

'Those Pooka are … they are lost.'

'What do you mean "lost"?'

I could see he was struggling to come up with an answer. Finally he said, 'It is not in my power to tell you these things. What you may learn is up to the Queen.'

The hill levelled out into a broad plateau that led to a thick forest in the distance.

'Any chance of you changing into a horse and giving me a lift?' I asked, flashing my House of Duir smile. 'Or would that be too demeaning?'

Tuan laughed at that. 'Not demeaning, Prince Conor, just short.'

But when I asked him what he meant, I got the same stonewalling that I got before. I hoped the Queen was more forthcoming.

The sun was fully down by the time we entered the forest but a gibbous moon provided enough light for us to navigate. Not far in, the path became broad and ran parallel to a stream. A while later we came upon small bridges that spanned the stream and led to modest huts. I saw neither a person nor an animal. Finally we came to a series of ponds, each with a tasteful two-storey pine cottage with a porch that hung over the water. They reminded me of really nice country hunting lodges. We must have passed about a dozen pond/house combinations before we came to the last and most impressive house. We entered and Tuan lit several oil lamps. The large room was sparse but elegant. It had that minimalist feng shui chic – like it was inhabited by someone who didn't need earthly things. In the corner was an ornate high-backed chair made from polished white pine.

'Is that the Pine Throne?' I asked.

'It is. This is Queen Rhiannon's home.'

I looked around. 'Where is she?'

Tuan walked outside onto the porch. At intervals along the railings there were torches connected by a string of gold wire. The Pooka touched the gold and mumbled something that made a spark zoom around the wire, igniting the torches around the porch and then around the pond. I now got a good look at the outside of the house. It was nice, really nice but I still wouldn't have taken it to be a royal palace. The light glimmered, mirror-like, off the football-field-sized pond, reflecting the circle of flickering torches.

'There,' Tuan said, pointing to the pond.

I was about to say, 'Where?' when a large fish broke the surface of the pond and then vanished underneath the rippling water.

'There she is,' Tuan said, pointing, 'there is Queen Rhiannon.'

Chapter Twenty-One
Barush

'The Queen's a fish?' I blurted.

'In her fauna state Queen Rhiannon is *braden* – a salmon.'

'Can I speak to her?'

'May I have one of your hazelnuts?' Tuan tried to look calm but it was a look of calm desperation. I handed him a hazelnut and he cracked it with his teeth. 'Do you have a knife?'

I reached into my sock and handed him the green-handled blade I found at the bottom of Mount Cas. He stared at it for a moment then walked to the edge of the porch and shaved five tiny slivers off the nut, allowing them to drop in the water. The two of us stood shoulder to shoulder shielding our eyes from the bright torchlight. It probably only took a couple of minutes for Queen Fish to swim to the spot under the dock but it seemed like ages – I never was a very patient fisherman. Finally she tentatively swam up to the floating nut shavings. I thought she was going to ignore them but then she snatched at a sliver and swam away. Tuan sighed and returned my knife. In the middle of the pond, a salmon poked its head above the water. As I watched the large fish mouth pulled tight, the eyes drew closer together and then, as her feet touched the bottom, she rose. Queen Rhiannon did not possess the traditional beauty of, say, Essa or my mother but she was striking none the less. Her hair was long and shiny silver, it floated around her in the water just below her neck. The features on her face almost seemed chiselled but it was the eyes that drew your gaze – they were emerald green.

A set of stone steps rose out of the water. Queen Rhiannon walked out of her pond and up onto the porch. I'm so glad those eyes were that compelling – because I didn't want to get caught looking anywhere else. I didn't bow or say anything. I just looked her square in the peepers until Tuan presented her with a robe.

She started to speak and then stopped. It was almost as if she had forgotten how. She tried again. 'How long have I been lost?' she said in a whisper.

'We have a guest,' Tuan said, pointing to me with an open hand. 'This is Conor of Duir. He has brought us hazelnuts.'

I opened the parcel and displayed the five remaining nuts. 'A gift from my mother, Queen Deirdre.'

'Deirdre lives?' she asked, her voice a bit stronger.

'She does, Your Highness and she has been worried about your people.'

'What have you told him?' Rhiannon asked Tuan.

'I have told him nothing but if the choice was mine I would deem Conor *barush*.'

Rhiannon turned and walked back down the stairs into her pond and gently scooped up the four tiny slivers of hazelnut that were floating on the water and handed them to Tuan. 'Arouse the council while I talk to the Son of Hazel.'

Tuan turned and was almost out the door when the Queen called to him. 'Son, how long?'

'Two months. I have missed you, Mother.' Then he turned and left.

'Would you like a cup of tea, Prince Conor?'

'That would be lovely, ma'am.'

As she walked to a door on our left the Queen stumbled – she was unsure on her feet. I grabbed her arm to steady her. She stopped and shook me off, proudly straightening herself, but then she sighed in resignation and held my arm as we walked slowly to the kitchen.

'Deirdre's son,' she mused. 'That would make you Liam's grandson.'

'Yes, ma'am.'

In the kitchen there was a black kettle covered with a mesh of gold wire. Rhiannon lifted it to see if it contained enough water, then placed her index finger on a bit of the gold and hummed. Within seconds steam issued from the spout. She grabbed a handful of small white flower buds from a jar, distributed them between the two cups and poured in the hot water. I don't know what kind of tea it was but it was lovely and it seemed to revitalise the former fish.

We walked through the kitchen into a comfortable sitting room. The tabletops were dusty. Rhiannon apologised for the state of the place. 'I have been … away,' she said.

'Lost, was the word you used before,' I said as gently as I could.

Queen Rhiannon looked me directly in the eyes for one of those hour-long seconds and then looked vacantly into the distance. 'Lost … yes, lost is a better word.'

I waited for her to say something else. She was a queen after all, it wasn't like you could just drill her for information. After a while I feared she was getting lost again. I reached into my pocket and opened the parcel and presented her with the five remaining hazelnuts.

She broke the silence. 'Where did the hazel come from?'

I started to tell her how the new Tree of Knowledge came about and it turned into an autobiography. I told her about how I came to The Land, how Dahy gave me a hazel staff that was once owned by my grandfather and how I accidentally planted it at the site of the destroyed tree and it took root.

'And your mother gave you the hazelnuts to give to me?'

'Yes, ma'am.'

'Did she tell you why?'

'No, ma'am.'

'Can you guess?'

I took a deep breath and thought about this. 'I think you became a salmon, then forgot who you were and the hazelnut helped you remember your Pooka self.'

'You are a very good guesser, Prince Conor.'

I smiled like a schoolboy. 'I have not seen a Pooka since entering the Pinelands, except your son. Is that what happened to everyone?'

'Many were lost before me. I suspect that what you ask is what has happened. I confess I do not know – a sad admission for a queen. I must confer with my son and my council.' As if on cue, Tuan showed up with four confused Pookas in bathrobes. They bowed to their queen. 'If you will excuse us, Conor, we have pressing business.'

'Sure,' I said and then added, 'Hey, would anybody mind if I took a bath?'

It's such a drag to put on dirty clothes after a bath but I had no choice. After almost cooking myself in a bathtub that heated water with the same gold wire system that the kettle used, I re-donned my clothes and smelled pretty much the same as before.

When I arrived downstairs Tuan escorted me to a pair of doors that led to the Queen's council room. There were raised voices on the other side that I couldn't quite understand and then I heard the Queen's voice silence them all. Even if I couldn't hear the exact words the meaning was quite clear – the Queen had decided and *that was that*. Tuan gave me an embarrassed look.

'Don't worry about it,' I whispered, 'I've got a pretty tough mom too.'

His smile was interrupted by the opening of the doors. Inside the chamber there were a dozen or so people. Most looked *compos mentis* but a few still had that abandoned-puppy look. Tuan introduced me in that formal royal court manner that I dislike but have gotten used to: 'Queen Rhiannon, honourable council members, I give you Prince Conor of Duir.'

I did all the proper bowing and scraping and was then invited to sit.

'Prince Conor,' Queen Rhiannon spoke, 'we thank you for your gift.'

'Seeing your need, Your Highness, I can assure you that you and your people will have first priority to any fruit of the Tree of Knowledge.' I thought I was being magnanimous and princely but my statement was greeted by what I can only describe as grumbling. I racked my brains to think what I said wrong. 'Of course I can only speak until someone chooses the major Rune of Hazel but I will ensure that the new head of the House of Cull will know of your need.'

Well, if my first statement was a mistake, this was a blunder of Titanic proportions. The entire council was on their feet and shouting. The Queen raised a hand to silence them, to no avail. Their accents were so thick and they were speaking so fast, I couldn't figure out what they were shouting about.

Queen Rhiannon was forced to stand. 'Silence!' she hissed and the council did as they were told. 'Prince Tuan has recommended that Conor be deemed barush.'

'Prince Tuan is not a member of this council,' a robed woman in the front said.

'And you are not Queen,' Rhiannon said with a voice that almost made me drop to my knees and thank the gods that I was not that woman. The Queen regained a bit of her composure but when she spoke again her voice was still as sharp as a razor. 'While you splashed in your pool Tuan ensured you were not bear-food.'

'But tradition, Your Highness ...' the woman said, this time with much more contrition in her voice.

'If I had followed tradition – we would all be lost.'

One of the council members banged the arm of his chair with his fist in a signal of agreement. Others slowly joined him and soon the entire council was banging their chairs, even the chastised woman.

Queen Rhiannon gestured for Tuan to stand next to her. He looked confused.

'Prince Tuan, I, Rhiannon of Ailm, in recognition of your service to the Pinelands, salute you.' She stood and bowed the lowest bow I have ever seen a queen make. When she came back upright there were tears in her eyes. 'I am so very proud of you, my son.'

Tuan's eyes glistened as he embraced his mother and the entire council rose as one and bowed. They stayed that way until Tuan returned the salute.

'Take your place among the council, Prince Tuan.'

Tuan whipped his head towards his mother in disbelief. She nodded to him and the council resumed their chair banging again until the stunned Tuan took his seat.

Queen Rhiannon sat smiling for a while waiting for Tuan to get a grip on himself. For a moment she looked more like a mother than a queen. Finally she said, 'Councillor Tuan.' It took Tuan a micro-second to realise that she was addressing him. 'Earlier you proposed that Prince Conor should be anointed as barush. Do you still feel this way?'

'I do, Your Highness.'

'Do any council members object?' The lady in the front row that made the stink before had a furtive look around but said nothing. 'Very well, Tuan, would you please bring The Elements? It seems my clerk is still grazing somewhere.' I liked this queen. Anybody that can crack a joke at a time like this is my kind of monarch. 'Prince Conor, you have been chosen for the honour of barush. Do you know what this means?'

I hadn't the faintest idea. I assumed it was a good thing but at that moment it occurred to me that barush might mean lunch and they were all going to turn into lions and eat me. 'No, ma'am, I don't.'

'Barush means friend. It is the highest honour we bestow on a non-Pooka. There have been very few – but one was your grand-father Liam.'

Tuan entered pushing a rolling table that had three bowls on it. Queen Rhiannon stood and walked towards me. I began to rise but Rhiannon motioned for me to remain seated. She stood in front of me and asked to see my hands, which she took and turned palm up. 'Baruch like all friendship carries no rules or limits. Do you accept?'

'I would be honoured.'

'Then Conor, Son of Hazel and Oak, in the name of the Pookas of The Land' – she placed dirt from one of the bowls onto my hand – 'and of the rivers and lakes' – she splashed water from another bowl onto the dirt in my palm and smeared it into mud. 'And of the sky,' she said, bringing my hands up close to her face and blowing on them. Then she grabbed a handful of salt from the last remaining bowl and mixed it into the water. She stirred it with her hand then dribbled saltwater onto my palms, 'And in the memory of our sisters and brothers lost to the sea – I name you: barush.' She reached inside her robe and produced a coin-sized gold disc attached to a loop of gold wire no bigger than a bracelet. As she reached up the loop of gold wire expanded and she placed the medallion around my neck. Then she pushed my palms together as if in prayer and kissed me on both cheeks. In my ear she whispered, 'Lord Liam would have been very proud.'

With the pomp and circumstance done Queen Rhiannon announced, 'We have been asleep too long – there is work to do.' She instructed some councillors to house the rest of my party and ordered others to whip up some hazelnut potion to try to revive the herbivore Pookas that were inside the wall. The carnivores without, they wisely decided to leave until daylight.

Tuan led me to the guest wing. As we walked I patted him on the back. 'You are a Pooka hero.'

He blushed and looked embarrassed that anyone would even think such a thing. If he had been a cowboy he would have said, 'Aw shucks.'

'Really,' I said, 'you were the only one that didn't get lost and you're the only Pooka anybody has ever heard of that can change into more than one animal. You're like a super-Pooka. We should get you a tee-shirt with a big P painted on the front.'

'You are very kind …' Then Tuan's ears began to stretch and fur-up. He had to turn away and compose himself to stop from transforming into some creature. 'Sorry, Prince Conor, I sometimes change when I get emotional.'

'Don't worry about it and it's just Conor, OK.'

'You are very kind, Conor, but things are not as they seem.'

'Oh yeah, so what am I missing?'

Tuan paused and I thought he was about to tell me. It was obviously something important but then he looked over his shoulder and said, 'I am very busy. I must help round up some lost bunnies.'

'Of course, Councillor Tuan,' I said with a smile. He blushed again – this guy was cute.

'Just Tuan, OK?' he said.

Chapter Twenty-Two
Moran

I wandered around my chambers – they were pretty small for royal digs but the bed was soft and there was an en-suite bathroom. I walked out onto the balcony and let the cold air pink up my cheeks as I looked at the pond that a few hours earlier had been the Queen's swimming pool.

'I hope you do not mind this small room,' Queen Rhiannon said, startling me, 'but this room was a favourite of your grandfather's. I thought you might like it too.'

'I do,' I said, bowing my head. 'Thank you.'

Queen Rhiannon leaned against the banister next to me and looked out over her pond. 'I once asked Liam why he liked this room better than the regal rooms and he said it was because here he had a better chance to see me naked.' The Queen smiled. 'He was very cheeky, your grandfather. You have the same twinkle in your eyes.'

'That is very nice to hear, Your Highness.'

The cold and a clatter of teacups made us go back inside. A mousey little servant, that recently may have actually been a mouse, was twitchingly setting up tea, flatbread and dried fruits. When she spilled the Queen's tea, Rhiannon placed her hand on the servant's and said, with a reassuring smile, that she could go. My tea was served by a Queen.

'I thank you again for the hazelnuts, Conor, but since you did not know of our plight before you arrived, I wonder, is there another reason for your visit?'

'Oisin is dying.'

The Queen tilted her head like a confused puppy and said, 'Dying?'

That's when I realised that the concept of a slow death is quite alien to some of the people in The Land. People here either die fast, in battle or by falling out of a poplar tree – or they commit seafaring suicide by sailing out to sea in a boat – but since there is no sickness, a lingering illness followed by death just doesn't happen. So I told her the long tale about how Dad reattached his hand in the Chamber of Runes and how that seems to be killing him and how Mom and Fand encased him in Shadowmagic.

Queen Rhiannon took it all in, wide-eyed. 'For hundreds of years there is nothing new in The Land – I'm lost for a couple of months and all has changed. But I cannot imagine how I can help.'

'I was hoping you could tell me where I can get some tughe tine blood.'

I don't think I could have shocked her more if I had slapped her in the face. 'Who told you of tughe tine?'

I explained about the manuscript that contained the story of the Grey Ones and their search for the blood of the tughe tine and about our strange encounter with the mountaintop Oracle. Finally I told her of the knife and the message that told me that the changelings would have answers.

Queen Rhiannon just sat there with her hand over her mouth and shook her head for a time before she finally said, 'You certainly do not bring dull stories, Prince Conor. So Deirdre has developed a way to bring back lost manuscripts?'

'Yes, ma'am.'

'She is a very clever witch that mother of yours.' Queen Rhiannon thought again for a time then said, 'The answers to the questions you ask are … not easily given. There were members of the council today who wanted you and your party dead for what you have deduced already. We Pookas think like animals. So many animals live so much in fear that they hide their injuries. They think that if another animal sees their vulnerabilities that they will use it against them. But sometimes we think like animals too much. We forget that there are creatures that might want to help. If not for you, Conor, and the Faeries – we all would be lost. Your grandfather was the only non-Pooka to know of our dependence on the fruit of the hazel. If more had known then maybe the Tree of Knowledge would have been better defended.'

'Dahy is building a small regiment to protect it now.'

'Dahy lives? That is good news. I think it is time we ended our isolation. Do you think he would accept some Pooka recruits?'

'I know he would.'

'Good. Now to answer your question, Conor, I shall tell you of things that even many of my own people do not know. But in the light of recent events maybe more should learn of our history.' She dropped her head and took a deep breath collecting her thoughts.

'The Pooka were the first new race. We believe that only the Faeries, Leprechauns and Brownies are older. In the beginning we were not changelings but we had an affinity with animals. We tended herds for the House of Duir and learned magic from Ériu. Using gold we learned how to speak to the animals.'

'I've seen my mother do that by placing gold in her mouth.'

'Yes, I authorised my daughter to teach her that. As I said, she is a very clever witch. But we Pooka did not stop there. Soon we were using magic to completely empathise with the animals. Cults began – the most prominent were the Marcach and the Fia.'

'Horse and deer?' I said, remembering my father teaching me names of animals in ancient Gaelic when I was a kid.

'Yes. The cults submerged themselves completely in their chosen animals to the point where the first changes began. The

Marcach became half horse themselves and the Fia became half deer half Pooka.'

'Centaurs and Fauns,' I said aloud.

'Yes,' Queen Rhiannon said as if being roused out of a daydream, 'I have heard those words used by Pookas that came back from a Real World sojourn. But the half change was dangerous. Marcach and Fia began to lose themselves – they became horses and deer and no one could bring them back. A council was formed and the cults were banned, but they continued in secret.

'One of our kind was named Moran. He was reported to be the wisest of all the Pooka. He studied every creature that was known on the land and in the air, then he left for the sea. There he studied the fish and found the aquatic mind so different to our own that he could safely change into a half fish and not lose his Pooka identity.'

'Wait a minute. Are you talking about mermaids? Like topless girls with fish bottoms?'

It was only a matter of time before Queen Rhiannon gave me the dirty look that every other woman I had known had given me. 'Mertain is what he called them but yes, mermaid is the Real World name. At about the same time another of my ancestors travelled to the Hazellands. Before the Hall of Knowledge existed, wise men and women would gather at the great hazel tree and share ideas. My ancestor tried a hazelnut and it instilled him with such self-knowledge that he attempted a complete change into an animal and was able to return to his Pooka self. He arrived back at the Pinelands at almost the same time Moran did. Both of them drew supporters, each professing the virtues of their discoveries. Soon most were following my ancestor, changing into all manner of beasts using hazel. Moran warned that dependence on hazelnuts was dangerous but he was unheeded. I have not thought of him in a very long time but I must now admit that he may have been right.'

'What happened to Moran?'

'Finally he and his followers left to live permanently in the sea. The Pookas of the Pinelands never heard of them for centuries. Then a half woman/half fish washed up on the shore injured and the Banshees brought her to us. She told us that the Mertain live in the archipelago off the Fearn Peninsula. She named two of the islands – one was Faoilean Island and the other was Tughe Tine Isle.'

'What happened to her?'

'She was escorted to Fearn Point and she swam home. We have not heard from the Mertain since.'

'Do you have a guide that could take me there?'

'The Fearn Peninsula is in the Alderlands. Our peoples have had no contact in a long time but I may be able to help you, but not for several days. I would like to get my kindred unlost before I lose them again.'

'Of course. Thank you, Your Highness.'

She placed her hand on my cheek. 'It is so good to see Liam's seed in this room. Sleep well, Son of Hazel.' Before she left she stopped and turned to me. 'There is one more thing you should know, Conor. The Mertain that washed up on the shore …'

'Yes?'

'She was … old.'

I spent that night dreaming about a mermaid. I don't know if my dreams were a premonition or just the result of talking about them all day, but I can tell you one thing: the mermaid I dreamt about wasn't old.

I awoke in the morning to the sound of splashing. I had one of those surreal moments when I couldn't figure out whether the sound was coming from my dream or from the waking world. I sat up in bed and listened. Just because my grandfather was a peeping tom didn't mean I was going to cop a look at Queen Rhiannon swimming naked – as much as I'd like to. I dressed, walked downstairs and found Essa speaking to the wet-haired, robed Queen, at the entrance to the council room. They stopped when they saw me. The Queen and I swapped morning pleasantries and she left.

'Is everyone all right?' I asked.

'We're fine,' Essa said. 'Brendan has been complaining about not having any meat in a while. He asked a Pooka if he could change into something he called a New York porterhouse so he could eat him. I'm not sure if the poor Pooka was scared or just confused.' Then she smiled and I realised just how much I had missed that smile. 'The Queen seems to like you,' she said.

'Oh, yeah? What did she say about me?'

'She told me that I was with the wrong man.'

'Well, I have to agree with her there. I don't see how you can ignore such good advice from a queen and a prince. Come to think of it I'm sure I could get a king to join the focus group.'

'Turlow is a king,' she replied smugly.

'And here is me thinking that he was just a Turd-low.'

Essa's face got those lines in it that meant that our pleasant conversation was coming to an end. She turned to leave. I reached for her arm and thought better of it.

'Essa,' I called after her and she stopped. 'Seriously, even if we never get together again I still agree with the Queen. He is not the right man for you.'

She gave me that exasperated look, which was safer than her *I'm about to hit you* look. 'And why is that?'

'When you are around him – you … you just don't seem to be you.'

This looked like it threw her for a second. But then she bounced back, 'Maybe this is the real me and you are the one that brings out my worst.'

I shook my head. 'I don't think so.'

For a second I thought she was going to say something else but then she looked at her shoes and left.

Chapter Twenty-Three
Re-Pookalation

The Pinelands quickly became re-Pookalated. It must not take much hazelnut to help a Pooka remember how to stand on two legs 'cause everywhere I went I saw formerly fur-covered people being led back to their homes looking kinda dopey. I spoke to Tuan and he said that when Pookas are *lost* it takes them a while to start thinking like a person again. I saw one woman lick her hand and then wash her cheek like a cat.

Tuan hosted a dinner for us in his modest house. Believe it or not he cooked salmon.

'That's what I just don't get,' Brendan said between mouthfuls. 'You guys in The Land just go up to a bunny or a fish and say, "Could you please die for me?" and they do?'

'We are not as flippant as that,' Araf answered, 'asking for an animal's life is a skill that must be learned, but that is essentially what happens.'

'Why on earth would an animal agree to that?' Brendan asked.

'Because they know they will be born again,' Tuan said as if talking to a five-year-old.

'How do they know that?'

This question stumped Tuan, as if Brendan had asked him, 'How do you know the sun shines?'

'That is what they tell me,' the Pooka said. 'Why would I doubt them?'

It was nice having a boys' night. Tuan had invited the Turd-low but he said he would rather sit alone and wait for his beloved to return from the dinner she was having with Nieve and the Queen. Brendan, who usually sticks up for the Banshee, called him 'hen-pecked'. I, on the other hand, thought maybe Turlow had the right idea. Perhaps if I had paid more attention to Essa I would be doing something other than talking bull with guys and laying the groundwork for a hangover.

Saying that, it was a delightful evening. The food was good and Tuan produced a couple of bottles of some lovely Pooka mead-like stuff that had milk or cream in it. I almost asked if the milk came from regular cows or Pookas that were cows and then decided that I didn't want to know. It was stronger than it tasted and it loosened Tuan's tongue until I asked him how much hazel-nut it takes to make a Pooka remember that he has feet instead of paws.

Tuan clammed up and said that was not information that should be discussed outside of the clan.

'Don't worry, Pooka brother,' I told him. 'Remember I'm a barush and Brendan is my closest adviser. Any Pooka secret you tell him or me will go no further than this room.'

'I'm an adviser?' Brendan said. 'When did that happen?'

'And you can tell Araf anything 'cause he never speaks,' I said, patting the Imp on the back. 'Isn't that right, Prince Araf?'

The big guy gave me his hallmark blank stare.

'See.'

'Anyway what's the big secret?' Brendan asked. 'So you need hazelnuts. Pookas need hazelnuts and cops need donuts.'

'Do donuts come from *do* trees?' Tuan asked.

'Never mind,' I said, 'but Brendan has a point. Why keep it such a secret?'

'Because it is a weakness,' Tuan said, crouching down as if someone was overhearing him. 'If others were to realise our dependence on hazel then they could use it to exploit us.'

'It seems to me that someone already has,' Brendan said in such a matter-of-fact way that everyone looked at him a bit shocked.

'Explain,' Tuan demanded.

'Well, Conor told me that no one knows why the Hall of Knowledge was destroyed. It seems obvious to me that somebody wanted to take the Pookas out of the equation by destroying all the hazel trees. They almost succeeded.'

My gods, I thought, *it was so obvious. Why didn't I see it before?*

Tuan was unconvinced. 'But no one knew about our need for hazelnuts except Conor's grandfather.'

'Are you sure about that?' Brendan asked. 'The one thing I know about secrets is that there is no such thing. Somebody else always knows.'

'Who?' Tuan asked.

'Someone who is a master of ancient lore,' I said in a dreamy voice as I thought out loud. 'Someone who will do anything to get his own way.'

'Oh,' Araf said.

'Who?' Brendan and Tuan asked together.

I had to take a slug of Pooka-shine before I could even say the name. 'Cialtie.'

This kinda killed the happy party mood of the evening but it didn't stifle the discussion. We all eventually agreed that if the Hazellands were destroyed to stop the Pookas from getting hazel-nuts, then that meant that the Hall of Knowledge was once again in peril.

'We should inform Dahy,' Araf said.

'Inform him of what?' a woman's voice asked from the doorway. It was Aunt Nieve followed by Essa.

We filled the ladies in on our epiphany. At first they thought it was just drunken ramblings but then they asked more questions. Soon they thought it was a pretty good theory too.

'We should talk about this on our walk,' Nieve said.

'Good idea,' Brendan replied, jumping up to join her.

'You two have a walk planned?' I asked as I gave a questioning glance to Essa. The tilt of her head implied she knew something that I didn't. The walkers just smiled. Brendan came back into the room to pick up his jacket from the floor beside me. As he leaned down I whispered, 'And what's all this then?'

'It's a walk,' he replied with a smile. 'I have a choice between sitting here listening to you whine or a walk in the moonlight with a beautiful woman. Hmm, let me thin' on that for a second.' He grabbed his jacket and they left.

I turned to Essa. 'So I suppose you are off to join your snuggly Banshee?'

'Actually,' she said, plopping down on the cushion next to me, 'what I could really use is a drink.'

I jumped up and got her a glass. Tuan poured her a measure of Pooka-shine and she downed it in one.

Then she smiled at me and said, 'Can I have another?'

I took this to be a very good sign.

I really could have used a lie-in the next morning, but Tuan got me up to meet with the Queen so I could tell her about our theory of the night before. After that I had to give a briefing to the entire council. A few Pookas got a bit hot under the collar when they found out that Tuan and I were talking freely about hazelnut dependency in front of outsiders, but I told them that my companions had figured it out by themselves and if our theory was correct, then the cat was out of the bag anyway. Then I spent another twenty minutes trying to explain what an 'old expression' was and why a cat was in a bag in the first place.

In the end they came around and decided that there should be a Pooka presence with Dahy's army at the Hall of Knowledge. The Queen pledged a small detail comprising a handful of bear Pooka soldiers, a courier wolf and a Pooka hawk for reconnaissance. Aunt Nieve agreed to escort the Pooka recruits back to the Hazellands.

'I would really like it if you came with us,' I said to my aunt after the meeting, 'and I think Brendan would too,' I said, testing her reaction.

She didn't return my smile, she didn't really look very happy at all. 'I have a duty to your mother and to Duir. I have too long been too far away. Escorting the Pookas needs to be done and Castle Duir should not be left without one of the family.' Then she smiled, took my face in her hands and kissed me on the forehead. 'When I was young I worked on a spell that would allow me to be in two places at one time – I only ever succeeded in giving myself a headache. I wish now I had worked harder. Be careful, nephew. Find a cure for my brother and come back safe. Now I must tell Brendan.'

'Yeah,' I said, 'what's going on with you two?'

She smiled and gave me a very un-Nieve-like girly shrug then practically skipped away.

That night I was invited back into the Queen's sitting room for tea.

'My son Tuan has asked me if he could be your group's guide to the end of the Brownie Peninsula. Is this agreeable with you?'

'Yes, ma'am. I really like Tuan.'

'He is very fond of you, Prince Conor. May the gods take care of you both.'

'I'm sure we will be fine.'

'Well,' she said in a knowing motherly tone, 'just to be sure I am sending a bear with you.'

'If you insist.'

'I do,' she said in a voice that made it clear that I would have been an idiot to discuss the matter further. 'How you will reach Tughe Tine Isle I cannot counsel you on.'

'Don't worry about it. I'm a fly-by-the-seat-of-my-pants kind of guy – we'll figure it out.'

The next few minutes were spent in talking about what my pants had to do with anything.

'I would be happier if the Banshee were not with you,' the Queen said.

'What have you got against Turlow?'

'You suspect that the Banshees from the Reedlands destroyed the Hall of Knowledge, do you not?'

'I do.'

'Then how can you trust a member of that race?'

'A member of your race tried to eat me a couple of days ago. Should I distrust the Pooka? My father told me that Banshees were some of the most loyal guards he had ever known and one of the finest persons I have ever known was a Banshee.'

The Queen raised her hands and I stopped. 'Banshee loyalty is well known, Son of Duir, but in the past too many Banshees have been loyal to your uncle. Can you honestly say that Cialtie will bother Tir na Nog no more?'

I started to say something then shrugged – she had a point.

She reached across and touched my cheek. 'You remind me so much of your grandfather.'

'I didn't peek – honest.'

She smiled at that – a smile that charmed me as much as I'm sure it charmed my grandfather. 'Liam too voiced his opinions passionately but he was more stubborn than you. He refused to let

Dahy put soldiers in the Hazellands and that stubbornness eventually killed him. Make sure you do not allow pride to stop you from what you truly think should be.'

I wasn't sure what she was talking about and obviously it showed on my face.

'Let Essa know how you feel.'

'Oh,' I said, leaning back in my chair. 'Well, Essa is … Essa is a difficult woman.'

'The best ones always are. As a matter of fact, that is what your grandfather used to say.' She reached under her chair and produced a plain wooden box. 'Liam gave me this, years ago. I would like you to have it.'

She opened the box. Inside, on a bed of satin, was a throwing blade with a green glass handle inlaid with gold wire. It was identical to the one that contained the message and was thrown at Brendan on Mount Cas. I picked it up and admired it.

'As you can see I have never used it,' she said. 'The tip is still very golden.'

'Do you know where my grandfather got this?'

'Dahy,' she said. 'It was one of two that he made. Liam told me that Master Dahy gave one to him and the other to his true love.'

Chapter Twenty-Four
Yogi Bear

Uncharacteristically, I was the first to arrive for our crack-of-dawn departure. A small dusting of snow swirled in a bitter wind that stung my cheeks. It was flipping freezing. I wondered for a second why I wasn't snuggled up in a warm bed but then the image of my statue-like father pushed that thought away. Nieve's Pooka entourage mounted up. The five bears were on horseback while the wolf and hawk chose to travel in their animal shapes.

Nieve showed up with her arm locked onto Brendan's. She gave him a right proper thirty-second snog and then leapt on her horse. I was about to make a comment but the look on her face made me stop. She didn't need a joke.

The rest of my gang showed up and mounted up. We had all said our goodbyes the night before so the two groups saluted Queen Rhiannon and her council, then we waved to each other and went in separate directions. If I hadn't known better I could have sworn I saw tough-as-old-boots Aunt Nieve wipe a tear as she turned.

Tuan introduced me to our Pooka bear guard. His name was Yarrow.

'Yarrow the Bear?' I said with a laugh. 'Mind if I call you Yogi?'

I then had to explain what a nickname was. Yarrow liked the concept and he also liked the idea of being 'smarter than the average bear' so the name stuck and he became Yogi Bear.

The path to the Alderlands was on the opposite side of the mountain that we had come up. Tuan and Yogi casually touched trees as they passed, picking up messages that were then deposited on other trees. Pookas in animal form were in the forest as well, especially red squirrels jumping from tree to tree reinstating the pine tree telegraph that had been neglected for so long. Normal animals were also slowly repopulating the Pinelands. Queen Rhiannon had sent out a few envoys to persuade the normal animals that the Pookas were no longer bonkers. I didn't see any big creatures like boar or deer but the fast little guys, rabbits and foxes and squirrels, were back. Tuan said they seemed jumpier than normal but I couldn't tell.

We could have made it out of the Pinelands in one day but Tuan and Yogi decided to call an early halt. 'The less time sleeping under an alder tree the better,' Tuan said. I remembered the last time I slept under an alder – everything I owned, including my shoes, was stolen. I wasn't looking forward to spending time in a forest full of them.

'We are going to have to pay tribute to the King of the Brownies,' Tuan said that night around the campfire.

'Can't we avoid Brownie Castle and just get to the island?' I said. 'I hate all that royal bowing and scraping stuff. And I've met the King of the Brownies – I'm not a big fan.'

'As soon as we enter the Alderlands,' Tuan said, 'the trees will inform all of the Brownies that we are there. We cannot avoid Fearn Keep. Do you have anything to give the King for a tribute?'

'Yeah, Mom gave me some gold, mined by Leprechauns from Castle Duir.' I reached into my saddlebag and produced four slim pieces of gold imprinted with the Oak Rune. They were about the size of a candy bar. 'How many of them should I give him?'

Everyone's eyes nearly popped out of their heads. 'One will be more than ample,' Araf said. 'Put them away and don't let any of the alders see that gold or you won't have any to give.'

Admittedly I had never had a good experience with the Brownies but it kind of bothered me how people talked about them. 'You know, guys,' I said, 'I refuse to condemn an entire race just because the first one I met robbed me blind, but it seems to me that everyone hides their wallets when they come up against Brownies. What is it with those guys?'

'Brownies believe that the Faeries of Duir are pretenders to the Oak Throne,' Tuan said.

'Pretenders?'

'Yes, they believe that they are descendants of Banbha and therefore should be the custodians of the gold mines of Duir.'

'Banbha, she is one of the Three Sisters, right? Isn't she the one that sailed away and brought the Banshees to The Land?'

'That is the legend,' Tuan said. 'The Brownies believe that while she was away the other two sisters, Fódla and Ériu, forced a Brownie named Doran to take a Choosing against his will. He chose the Fearn Rune. Alder Island was created and the Brownies were banished to it. The Brownies believe that the reason the Alderlands are so swampy is because Doran's heart was not committed to the Choosing.'

'The Alderlands is an island?'

'It was,' Tuan answered. 'When the Pinelands were formed it was joined with the rest of The Land.'

'I still don't see why they have such a reputation as thieves?'

'Brownies do not like living by the rules of Duir,' Tuan said.

'What rules of Duir?'

'There really is no such thing,' Tuan said quickly as if I might take offence, 'but Duir was the first Land. It has an army and it has all of the gold. There are no official rules but if a throne displeases Duir then life for them could be difficult.'

I looked to Araf for confirmation. He shrugged and nodded yes. 'So Duir doesn't give the Brownies any gold?'

'Your grandfather Finn was very tolerant of the Brownies. After he disappeared Cialtie was very generous to them and since then they have grown bolder.'

'So let me see if I've got this right,' I said. 'They believe they should have all the gold, so they think it's OK to steal it whenever they feel like it.'

Tuan and Yogi looked at each other and nodded. 'That would be an appropriate summation,' Tuan said. 'Even a Brownie wouldn't mind being called a thief. They are taught thievery and stealth as part of their formal education.'

'Well, that would have spiced up high school.'

I had a quick face wash in a bowl of freezing cold water and stumbled in the dark back to my tent. Brendan was already in there. Now that Nieve was gone it seemed I had a roommate again.

'Don't you have a tent of your own?' I asked as I got into my sleeping roll.

'Why should I bother pitching my own tent when yours is so comfy?'

'I'm like a big important prince, you know?'

'Are you really?' Brendan said in the dark. 'I thought that was just a line you used to meet girls.'

'No, it's real. I got a castle, family sword, servants – the whole nine yards.'

'Gosh,' Brendan said, 'you would think with all that stuff that you wouldn't have to share a tent.'

'Yeah,' I said in resignation. 'Speaking of girls, that was quite a show you put on up there in the Pinelands.'

'What show would that be?'

'The thirty-second movie-star goodbye kiss you had with my aunt.'

'Oh, you saw that did you?'

'They saw it from the space shuttle. You realise, Brendan, that my aunt is probably like a thousand years old.'

'She doesn't look a thousand years old.'

'Well, I'm just saying, are you sure you want to get involved with a woman that you might have studied about in ancient history class?'

'Conor?'

'Yes?'

'Shut up.'

'I'm just saying ...'

'Good night, Mr O'Neil.'

'Yeah, good night, Detective Fallon.'

I had almost fallen to sleep when Brendan just had to get the last word in.

'Conor, no offence, but if I was going to ask for relationship advice – I wouldn't ask you.'

I didn't answer him. I just silently nodded in agreement.

The flaps of the tent cracked with the morning frost. Tuan and Yogi weren't happy with the dusting of snow. It made it difficult to choose the right path into the Alderlands. And being on the right path in the Alderlands is important, 'cause if you're not on the path – you're in a swamp.

After about an hour, the Pookas found what seemed to be a solid trail. The only swamps I had ever seen in Tir na Nog were the ones in Cialtie's Reedlands. I was not looking forward to going into another but once inside I was relieved to see that these swamps were much healthier than the foul and unnatural ones in my uncle's patch. Still, it was spooky. Leafless alder trees draped with long catkins lined our path or lived alone on bogie islands. Even though the ground was white with a light snow and the sky was cloudless, the place still seemed to be darker than it should, as if the light was mysteriously being sucked from the place. Small black birds darted through the trees but moved so fast I could never actually see one. Around the edges, the swamps were frozen but in the dark deeper water near the middle, unseen creatures submerged as we passed – their presence only given away by a tiny splash or an ominous plop.

The Pookas decided that someone should talk to a tree and let them know we were here. Araf was chosen, since nobody has any real beefs with the Imps. He placed his hands on a burly alder for a few moments, said, 'Thank you,' and walked back to us.

'She pretended to be surprised,' Araf said, 'but I got the impression that they already knew we were here. I told her we were coming to see the King and she wished us good luck.'

'Was that like an actual "good luck",' I asked, 'or a you're gonna need it "good luck"?'

As usual I didn't get an answer from Araf.

Essa pulled back and dropped in next to me later that day. I stifled the sarcastic comment about Turd-low. Call me genius but I was starting to realise that maybe one of the reasons Essa was so feisty was because I wound her up all the time.

'I have to say, Conor, this is not my favourite place.'

'First trip to the Alderlands then?'

She nodded yes. 'I'm not very happy about being here and neither is my father.'

'Your father? How does Gerard know you are here?'

'I have an emain slate with me.'

'You do? Why didn't you tell me? I could have used that to see how my father is.'

'I have been keeping track of Oisín's health. It is unchanged. I would have told you if it was otherwise.'

I relaxed a little. 'Mom said that he was getting worse.'

'That has not changed either but it seems the progression is still very slow.'

We rode in silence until finally I broke it. 'So your dad's not a big Brownie fan?'

'Some of my earliest memories are of Father complaining about the Brownies not paying their bills, but I think this is less about the Brownies and more about me being too far from home. He worries about me.'

'Well, I don't blame him. I worry about you too,' I said. 'I worry about you coming up behind me and clubbing me in the head.'

That one got a laugh out of Essa that was loud enough to make Turlow look around and wonder what we were talking about. I hoped he thought we were laughing at him.

'Maybe I should get back,' she said.

I almost replied, 'Oh, we wouldn't want to keep the Turd-low waiting.' But as she pulled ahead what I actually said was, 'Give your father my best.' Who says I *have* to be immature?

The cold air and the rhythm of Acorn beneath should have lulled me into that hypnotic state that makes travelling hours on horseback bearable, but I kept being disturbed by my companions flitting around me. Finally I broke my personal reverie, slid between Tuan and Yogi and asked what was going on.

'We are being tracked,' Tuan said. 'Can you not sense it?'

'Of course,' I lied, 'I was just asking you for confirmation.'

I had a look around. I neither saw nor felt anything. 'Brownies?' I asked.

'That would be a safe assumption.'

'Have you spotted them yet?'

'No, Brownies are very good at not being seen.'

'Why don't you, like, turn into a hawk and see if you can spot them from the air?'

An almost growling sound came from Yogi. The look on his face made me think that he was about to hit me. Tuan didn't look angry but I knew instantly that I had made a major social faux pas. He kept his eyes down as if embarrassed and said, 'That would not work.'

Even though I wasn't sure what for, I apologised and slunk back to Araf. I told him what I had just said and asked what mistake I had made. He didn't know but added how impressed he was that I could make blunders where no one had ever made blunders before.

Chapter Twenty-Five
The Alderlands

I didn't bother looking for our Brownie shadows. If expert trackers like Essa and Araf couldn't spot anything it was pointless for me to try. Also, from my experience of Brownies, it was unlikely we would get an arrow in the back – the real danger was getting robbed in the dark.

I made Brendan pitch the tent that night. I was drafted into begging wood from an alder. I found a not too menacingly sized tree and placed my hands on it.

'*You have slept under an alder before,*' came a strong and unpleasant voice in my head, '*but not in the Alderlands. You and … a Banshee slept under one of the lonely trees. Am I not correct?*'

'How do you know that?' I said. 'That alder was miles away from any other.'

There was almost a smirk in his voice when he replied, '*Perhaps we leave messages on the breeze. But where is that Banshee?*'

'Dead.'

'*Ah,*' his voiced echoed remorselessly in my head. '*He kicked my brother tree.*'

'And for that he deserved to die?'

'*Did he? I do not know what he deserved. I only know that he kicked a tree.*'

200

'The tree had just robbed him,' I said.

'*Robbed by a tree? How is that possible?*'

'The one who picks the lock on the door is as responsible as the thief that enters the room.'

'*A door made of wood perhaps?*' said the alder.

'Never mind, I refuse to talk in riddles to you.'

'*You started it, Faerie. What do I know of locks and rooms? If you are plain with me then so will I be with you.*'

He was starting to give me a headache so I just asked him for some firewood. The branches above creaked and fell around me. I thanked him, then just before I let go I said, 'Would you tell me if there are robbers watching us now?'

'*I would tell you, young prince,*' he said in a way that slightly reminded me of my Uncle Cialtie, '*but would what I tell you be true?*'

That night we set a watch again. Tuan took the first shift. I sat with him until everyone had gone to bed.

'Tuan, I want to apologise for what I said tod—'

Tuan grabbed my arm and placed his finger to his lips to shush me. He stared up into the tree canopy and then as I watched, his head sprouted feathers and shrank into his collar. I had to almost stand up to see that his head had turned into an owl's head. He leaned back and surveyed the treetops, then the feathers seemed to melt back into his face and his head popped up as before. He rubbed his eyes and said, 'I thought I saw something moving in those trees. Sorry, you were saying?'

When I could speak again I started with, 'That was pretty awesome.' Tuan shrugged. 'Right, what I was saying before you turned your nose into a beak is that I am sorry for breaking Pooka social protocol before when I asked you to turn into a bird. It would be helpful if you could explain what I did wrong so I could avoid that pitfall in the future.'

'You made no error, Conor.'

'Yogi looked like he was going to tear my head off.'

'Yarrow, or should I say Yogi as he is now known, helped raise me. He is very protective.'

'I still don't get it. What did I say to annoy him?'

'He thought you were teasing me.'

When I looked confused Tuan hung his head and collected his thoughts. Finally, without looking up, he said, 'You once called me … what was the word? A super-Pooka. That implies that I am the best of my race, does it not?'

'Well, even my Aunt Nieve said she'd never heard of a Pooka that could change into lots of different animals.'

Tuan shrugged again. 'I am not the best of my people – I am the least.'

'Why would you say that?'

He looked at his feet again, ashamed. 'I cannot hold to an animal form.'

'What do you mean?'

'Just that,' Tuan said. 'I have studied the disciplines of all the animals and I can change into each and every one but only for a few minutes, after that, my Pooka mind always comes to the fore and I lose the form. I change back.'

'But I saw you fly from a tree as a bird.'

'I climbed that tree when I heard the commotion on the other side of the wall. I almost never fly. To be honest, I am afraid of heights, but I needed to get to you and your party in a hurry. I thought I could make it to the ground before I changed back. As you saw, I didn't.'

'But you saved your people.'

'Not out of choice, Conor. I was saved from being lost because I am too stupid to hold onto a fauna form for more than a few moments. It is nothing to be proud of.'

'But who separated the carnivores from the herbivores?'

'That was me. I allowed the bigger animals to chase me through the gate and then locked them outside.' Tuan chuckled to himself. 'Several times it was a very close call.'

'I can't believe you saved an entire race and still call yourself "the least" of them. The council didn't think so – Councillor Tuan.'

'The council only instated me because of my mother. They think I am weak-minded and I do not disagree.'

This poor guy had been living with this shame for so long, his self-esteem was almost gone. I was tempted to give him a hug but instead I punched him on the arm.

'Ow. Why did you do that?'

'Because you're stupid.'

'Oh,' he said, looking at his feet, 'I know that.'

'No, you don't. Let me ask you something? How many creatures can you turn into?'

'I would guess two score.'

'And every time you failed you tried again and learned another animal?'

'Yes, I have been alive for a very long time.'

'A lesser man would have given up long ago. You have shown determination and fortitude beyond any of your people.'

He shrugged again – a habit I was determined to break him of.

'You have to admit it.'

'Well, I guess.'

'You must be the hardest-working member of a race that was saved from extinction because of you. If I ever hear you speak badly about yourself it won't be your arm I punch – it'll be your nose.'

The way he looked at me made me wonder if anyone in his hundreds of years had ever spoken to him this way. A smile started in the corners of his mouth and he whispered, 'OK.'

'OK?' I said louder.

'Yes,' he said, standing.

I started to stand up with him when he popped back down, grabbed my arm and shushed me again. Then he performed his owl head trick. When his head was normal-sized again he leaned in close and whispered, 'Get Yogi. We have company.'

I woke up the bear as casually as I could and then the three of us sat around the fire pretending we weren't being watched. Tuan passed around a bottle filled with water that we swigged as if it was moonshine. Tuan patted Yogi on the back and then dropped his head on his shoulder in what looked like a display of drunken camaraderie. In reality they were making a plan. Yogi got up and staggered to a nearby tree to relieve himself and Tuan laughingly told him to go further away. When he was under the right tree Tuan slapped me on the back and whispered in my ear, 'Are you armed?'

'I have one of Dahy's throwing blades in my sock.'

'Let us hope you have no need to use it.'

As he was speaking his head shrank down into his collar and those downy white feathers sprouted again. He leaned his whole body back (since his neck no longer tilted up and down), pointed to a space in the tree above Yogi and let loose a screech that made my blood run cold. It was like something out of a cheap horror movie. When I looked to see what Yogi was doing, he wasn't there. In his place was a pile of clothes. Yogi, now fully a bear, was climbing with lightning speed. Once in the tree there was a lot of screaming and growling combined with Tuan's screeching and pointing. I couldn't see much and didn't have a clue what was going on. Then I heard the unmistakable sound of a falling, screaming Brownie. Yogi climbed down so fast that I thought he was falling too. Tuan, now normal-headed, and I ran to the crumpled Brownie but just as we reached him, Yogi Bear came towards him roaring and we both backed off. The bear picked up the fallen Brownie and gripped him in what I can only describe as a bear hug.

'Come down,' Tuan shouted to the treetops, 'and I will try to convince my cousin not to eat your friend.'

We waited for a half a minute. 'Oh well,' Tuan said, gesturing to Yogi, 'enjoy your meal.'

The Brownie was comatose with fear; he didn't even whimper as Yogi opened his jaws wide enough to eat him whole.

'I have a crossbow aimed at you all!' a squeaky voice hollered from the dark. The second Brownie it seemed had jumped to another tree and was now shouting to us from the forest to our right.

Tuan stepped slowly away. 'And just how can you have one bolt aimed at all of us?' he shouted into the dark. 'If you shoot me it will not save your friend. If you shoot the bear then you will only succeed in making him angry.'

From the shadows a man, tall even for a Brownie, appeared. I find it so difficult to judge the age of Brownies, they all look like kids to me, but the way this guy carried himself, I suspected that he had been in sticky situations before. He stepped slowly towards us with his crossbow levelled at Tuan. 'Then I choose to shoot you.'

'You could try,' Tuan said with equal coolness, 'but that would not help your companion.'

Yogi roared again. I felt sorry for his poor captive as bear slobber dripped down the side of his face.

'Tell the bear to release him or I drop you,' the Brownie said.

'Put away your weapon and we can talk,' Tuan replied. 'There is no reason why anyone should be injured here.'

The Brownie in Yogi's arms tried to say something but the bear covered his face with his arm. All that came out were a couple of muffled yelps.

The one with the crossbow nervously glanced from Tuan to Yogi but never took his aim from the Pooka prince. 'The one that is soon to be injured is you, Pooka.'

'I really do not think that will be the case,' Tuan said at almost the exact moment that Essa materialised behind the armed Brownie. With an upward flick of her banta stick she hit underneath the crossbow, sending a singing bolt flying into the night sky. A micro-second later, the other end of the stick cracked him on the neck and he went down onto his knees. Araf appeared out of the darkness and hogtied the would-be assassin with a scarf. Brendan, relaxing his grip on his bow, and Turlow, sporting his Banshee blade, also stepped into the campfire light.

Yogi placed his captive in a one-armed headlock and slipped his athrú disc into his mouth. I'm not sure what scared the poor little guy more: being almost eaten by a bear or instantly discovering that he was in a wrestler's hold with a naked guy. Tuan relieved Yogi of his captive while he went back under the tree and put his clothes back on. The two night stalkers were plopped in front of the fire. Araf asked them if they were injured, but they weren't talking.

'Well,' I said, rubbing my hands together, 'it seems we have guests. Tea anyone?' I addressed the Brownies. 'I suspect you two would like willow, yes?'

The tall one glared at me then said, 'The alders will report that you have us captive. You will be surrounded by the King's men in hours.'

'Good,' Brendan said. 'It's about time we received an escort. This guy here, he's Prince Conor of Duir. Him and him are Princes Tuan and Araf of Pine and Heather?' Brendan looked to the princes to check if he got it right; they nodded and smiled. 'And the girl that clocked you in the head, she is Princess Essa from the boozy Vinelands and oh yeah – over there is The Turlow. I'm pretty sure he outranks everybody.'

'And who are you?' the increasingly worried-looking Brownie asked.

'I'm a cop and you, pal – are very busted. Personally I'm surprised that you want the trees to tell. If I had been rumbled in my own backyard by a bunch of royal hoity-toities and then laid out by a girl, I'd maybe not want my boss to know about it.'

The Brownie started to say something but Brendan interrupted him.

'On the other hand if you call your boss and tell him that you have met the royal entourage and are escorting them to Castle Alderland, then I suspect my fellow travellers would be delighted to have you along.'

Brendan looked around; everyone shrugged and nodded yes.

The tall Brownie was no dummy. It only took him about a second for the truth of what Detective Fallon was saying to sink in. Despite the panic in his eyes his voice was incredibly calm. 'May I speak with the alder, please?'

Araf untied him and he walked quickly over to the tree. Araf released the smaller one too and I handed him a cup of willow tea that he took with appreciation.

When he returned from speaking to the tree, the tall Brownie approached the fire and bowed. 'My name is Dell of the King's guard,' he said formally. 'Welcome to the Alderlands. It is my duty and pleasure to escort you to Fearn Keep.'

Chapter Twenty-Six
Dell and What's-His-Name

'So,' I asked, 'what about that army of Brownies that is supposed to be coming to your rescue?'

'It is not unusual for alder trees to misinterpret the actions of people in The Land,' the Brownie said. 'There is no approaching army.'

You couldn't deny that this guy was smooth.

Dell drank a cup of willow tea with us but wasn't interested in answering our questions. I offered them Brendan's tent. I even volunteered to pitch it for them but they chose to sleep in the trees. Although the chances of being robbed or attacked were slim, now that our stalkers had become our escorts, the thought of sleeping while Brownies looked down didn't fill us with enough security to abandon keeping watch. Tuan was knackered from his birdie-head trick so I offered to take the first shift.

I sat alone in front of the crackling fire and searched the trees to see if I could spot where Dell and his pal were sleeping. I couldn't see anything. I remembered the first time I had been alone at night in The Land, keeping watch by a fire. I remembered how awesome the strange star-filled night sky had been. Now I just stared up and shivered. The black silhouettes of the leafless branches made the starry sky look cracked and broken. On my first trip to The Land everything was new and wonderful but now everything was just cold and miserable. What had changed – me or The Land? The obvious answer was The Land. Fergal wasn't in it any more. Tir na Nog in my mind was the place where my cousin Fergal lived. His loss weighed on me like a stone yoke around my neck. Even if I was getting used to the weight of it, I always knew it was there.

And Dad wasn't here. I knew this was the time in my life where I wanted to figure stuff out by myself but the idea of him not being out there somewhere, just as a safety net, unnerved me. A world without Dad – any world without Dad – just didn't seem right. What if he doesn't make it? I pushed that thought out of my mind.

I was glad Brendan was here. Not just because he got my Real World jokes but because it felt like he belonged here. But he wasn't gonna stay long. As soon as Dad got better or come the next Samhain, he'd be out of here – back to his daughter and his crazy mother.

The most annoying thing was Turlow. I don't care if Brendan and Araf like him – I just don't *want* to like him. He gets in the way of me and Essa. There's no law that says I have to like him. Can't I just dislike someone regardless of whether they are likable or not?

'You look to be a man deep in the midst of a moral dilemma,' said a voice to my left. It was Turlow. 'Can I be of assistance?'

'Oh no,' I laughed, 'I don't think this moral dilemma is one you can help me with. What are you doing awake?'

'The thought of Brownies in the trees is not a restful one. Sleep eludes me.'

'That I can understand,' I agreed.

Considering that this particular Banshee was not my favourite person, one would be excused for thinking I was annoyed that he disturbed my solitude, but to be honest I was glad that someone broke my morose musings.

'Actually, Turlow, there is something I have been meaning to ask you about.'

'Yes?' Turlow took a seat and I offered him a cup of tea made from the stuff that Queen Rhiannon had given me. He took a sip and raised his eyebrows in approval. 'What would you like to know, Conor?'

'You are The Turlow?'

'You have been waiting to ask me that?'

'No, I mean you are like the King of the Banshees – right?'

He frowned at that and took a sip of his tea, collecting his thoughts. 'Actually, Conor, you were right the first time. I am not a king, I am The Turlow.'

'OK, but you're like the head Banshee?' I pressed.

Turlow smiled at this and said, 'I am tempted to repeat myself and say once again that I am The Turlow – for that title is all the definition that is needed by me or my clan – but yes, I suppose you could say I am the head Banshee.'

'And do all Banshees acknowledge this?'

There had been a light-heartedness to our conversation up till then but it disappeared with that question. 'Why do you ask?'

'I was wondering about the Banshees in the Reedlands. You may have heard from Essa that they attacked us and many suspect that they were responsible for the destruction of the Hall of Knowledge. Are they not your subjects?'

'I have no subjects, Conor. Being a Turlow is much more like being a father than a ruler. As it has been since the beginning of time, a father who pushes too hard one day finds that his son chooses to listen no longer. I do not rule, I just am.'

He continued. 'As for the Banshees in the Reedlands, I knew nothing about them or your attack until after your father regained Duir. This is very worrying for me. I have sent parties to find them – most have failed, while others have failed to return. The Reedlands is a treacherous place.'

'But you must know where they came from?'

'I have my suspicions.'

'And they are?'

He started to answer me but then stopped himself and thought for a bit. 'I have not been The Turlow long. During the time of my tenure my clan has been … uneasy. The cause of this uneasiness was your uncle.'

Now there was a surprise. 'Cialtie has been known to have that effect,' I said. 'What did he do?'

'Years ago he travelled to the Banshee shores. No dignitary of the House of Duir had been there in eons. My predecessor the Old Turlow greeted him as befitted a Prince of Oak. Cialtie stayed among us and befriended the younger members of the clan – including, I must admit, myself. He spoke of how lowly regarded the Banshee were in The Land and when no elders were around he spoke of a time when the Banshees would rule at his side.

'When the Old Turlow heard of this, he accused Cialtie of creating unrest. The Old Turlow ordered him to leave. Cialtie, appalled that a Son of Duir should be treated so, left, but with him he took a small group who openly defied the Old Turlow.

'When Cialtie attained the Oak Throne he came back to the Banshee shores. Although the Old Turlow did not like it, he welcomed him as one should the Head of the House of Duir, but when your uncle proclaimed that he wanted the new army of Duir to be made up entirely of Banshees, the Old Turlow said no. "Banshees defend the far shore, they are not mercenaries." Cialtie countered that all of the shores of The Land are the shores of Duir. The Old Turlow put his foot down, but the temptation was too great. Cialtie offered gold and a good life in Castle Duir. Many of my people joined him. The embarrassment of their desertion caused the Old Turlow to sail out to sea in shame. That is the sad truth of how my tenure as The Turlow began.'

'And what did you do?'

'I kept my word to the Old Turlow. I did not meet with Cialtie but I also did not forbid any of my clan from joining his army. After all he did hold the Oak Rune. If the Chamber of Runes deemed him worthy, who was I to disagree? Of course, now, it is easy to see that the Old Turlow had been right. Cialtie did not deserve the throne and too much Banshee blood was needlessly spilled in his name. If I had known then what I know now …' He shook his head. 'That thinking is the path to madness.'

'That still doesn't explain the Reedland Banshees.'

'The causes of war vary but the effects are almost always the same. One effect is that some men of war never tire of the fight. I suspect the Banshees who live in that unholy swamp are of that ilk. That is why I came to help Dahy. If I cannot find my renegades in the Reedlands, at least I can help defend the Hazellands from another attack.'

'So why are you here and not there?'

'Little did I suppose that when I came to the Hazellands that I would meet a royal woman as strong and fair as Princess Essa.'

'Yeah, lucky you,' I said, drinking the last of my now cold tea.

'I am very fortunate indeed. You said, Conor, that you wanted to ask me a question; now I have one that I have always wanted to ask you.'

'Shoot.'

'Once you had her, why in The Land would you have let Essa go?'

I toyed with the idea of grabbing a flaming log from the fire and clocking him with it. I even imagined the spectacular shower of sparks as he went down. Instead I answered his question with a question. 'Do you remember what you asked me at the beginning of this conversation?' When he looked confused I answered for him. 'You asked if you could help me with my moral dilemma. Would you like to know what my dilemma was?'

Turlow shrugged.

'I was debating whether it was OK to like you or not.'

'And what conclusion did you reach?'

'I'd gotten as far as deciding that I don't like you.'

'And you were wondering if that is OK?'

'Basically,' I said.

'I wouldn't worry about it too much, Conor, I don't like you very much either.'

'You don't?' I said enthusiastically. 'That's good to hear.'

Turlow smiled and shook his head. 'You are a strange man, Prince of Oak. Go to your tent, I will take your watch.'

'You don't have to do that.'

'There is no sleep in my near future – go.'

'OK,' I said, 'but don't think this will make me like you any better.'

'Good night, Conor,' Turlow said with that exasperated tone that I usually reserve for my friends and relatives. It didn't sound right coming from him.

I dreamt that night that the two Brownies climbed down from the tree wearing army uniforms. Then uniformed Brownies dropped from every tree, as far as the eye could see. They converged into ranks until a huge Brownie army marched towards me from all directions. Just as they were about to overwhelm me someone pointed to the sky and we all looked up.

I opened my eyes to see Brendan looming over me in the tent. It was still dark outside.

'What's up?' I croaked.

'Nothing,' he whispered. 'Go back to sleep.'

So I did.

Tuan and Yogi offered to share a horse and give Yogi's mount for the Brownies to ride. They declined the offer. I figured that since our guides were on foot that it would be a slow travel day – wrong. These guys were speedy. They moved so fast I felt like an old English fox hunter. It was actually hard to keep up. Mostly because the trails they chose were made for runners, not riders. I spent the whole day getting whipped in the face by alder branches that I suspected enjoyed it.

We broke for lunch and offered food to our guides. They might not be willing to share information with us but they had no problem packing away our food. I guess if you run as fast as a horse for four hours, you are entitled to eat like one. These guys each wolfed down what three of us would have had at a feast. I made sure I didn't reach for any food at the same time as one of them for fear of losing a finger.

I said this to Essa, who I noticed chose to sit next to me at lunch, and she laughed so hard she almost spat out what she was eating. I may not have the Turd-low's good looks or kingly crown but I can make that girl laugh. That's gotta count for something, right?

That afternoon the trail became wider and less whack-a-face but instead of going faster the Brownies slowed down to almost a jog. I couldn't figure out if these guys had burned themselves out on their morning sprint or if they had been running deliberately fast so that our faces were lacerated for the amusement of the alder trees. Araf, who is normally not the suspicious type, had a different take on it. He got the impression that the Brownies were deliberately slowing us down but he couldn't say why.

Late in the afternoon the Brownies halted for 'tea'. Essa forcefully pointed out that we do not halt for tea but even her menacing glare, a look that has withered many a determined man, could not dissuade Dell and his yet unnamed sidekick from plopping themselves down in the frozen dirt and demanding food.

'Don't they feed you in Brownieville?' Brendan asked.

Dell ignored him and the other one's mouth was too full to talk.

Brendan casually pulled me aside during our afternoon tea. 'You had a long chat with Turlow last night.'

'Are you spying on me? I'm surprised I didn't find you waiting up in the tent saying, "And what time do you call this?"'

'I don't have to spy on you, Conor. All I have to do is ask you a question – you're a crappy liar.'

'Thanks ... I think.'

'So what did you two talk about?'

'Well, if you must know, he talked about how my Uncle Cialtie had mucked up his life. I hate to say it but I'm starting to think that maybe Turlow isn't such a bad guy. I mean he's still a pompous jerk but maybe I should cut him a little slack.'

'Maybe,' Brendan said thoughtfully.

'What da ya mean maybe? You told me you liked the guy.'

'I did until he lied to me today.'

'What? Did he say he liked your shirt? Because you are right, that would be a lie.'

After an appropriately dirty look, Brendan said, 'I didn't sleep well last night. Those Brownies bother me.'

'Yeah, I wasn't too pleased with the thought of them up in the trees myself.'

'No, it wasn't that,' Brendan said. He flexed his fingers into and out of a fist. It was the thing he did when he was trying to figure something out. 'It's like when I'm in an interrogation room and there is something I am missing but I don't know what. That's what it's like when the Brownies are around.'

'Well, if you suspect them of stealing something you're probably right. But what's this got to do with Turd-low?'

'I got up last night to relieve myself and saw Turlow talking to that Brownie fellow. When they saw me the Brownie scooted back into the tree – fast – and Turlow looked mighty guilty when he walked back to the fire.'

'What do you think they were talking about?' I asked.

'I don't know. When I mentioned it to Turlow after lunch, he denied it. When I pointed out to him that I saw the two of them together, he suddenly remembered and said that Dell had just come down from the trees to relieve himself and he only passed a casual greeting with him.'

'It sounds like there were a lot of weak bladders roaming around last night. How do you know he's not telling you the truth?'

'I don't really,' he said with a sigh. 'It's just that … something isn't right here and I'm not going to sleep well until I figure it out.'

Chapter Twenty-Seven
King Bwika

After their afternoon tea, the Brownies resumed the lead – this time at a walk. Yogi once again offered them his mount but they declined and continued like it was a Sunday stroll in the park. At dusk they announced that it was time to break for dinner. Essa freaked out on them but they ignored her and started a fire. When Essa refused to give them any of our food they opened their packs and cooked their own. Everyone else resigned themselves to the Brownies' erratic schedule and dismounted. Finally Essa did too and we began to make camp while the Brownies ate their dinner – which they didn't share.

We were just ready to start cooking our food when Dell said, 'Let's go.'

'Now?' Essa shrieked.

'Of course,' the Brownie said. 'Fearn Keep is just a short way down this path.'

'Then why did we just break for dinner?' Essa asked in a tone that made me step out of her way.

'Because it was dinner time,' the Brownie said, not realising just how close to death he was.

We all walked on foot in pitch blackness for no more than fifteen minutes before we saw the first glimmer of light from Fearn Keep. I'd like to be able to describe what the Brownie castle looked like but I never really got a good look at it from the outside. There were lights in a dozen or so windows over what seemed like a vast structure but other than that nothing was visible. It was like a blackout street in London during the Blitz. As I got closer I saw that many windows were in fact blacked out with dark draperies that were only faintly outlined by the light within. Welcoming it was not.

Sentries popped out of the blackness like answers on a magic 8-ball. We were expected but I didn't get the feeling we were wanted.

Across an old-fashioned drawbridge over what I imagined to be an alligator-filled moat, we entered the castle. Dell and what's-his-name left us without as much as a 'Bye bye'. The sentries escorted us to four sparse rooms.

No one came to greet us that night. Turlow and Essa each took a separate room, forcing Brendan and me to share a bed. Yogi agreed to sleep in bear form on the floor in Tuan's room. I'm glad it wasn't in my room. I'd hate to think what would happen if I woke up in the night and stepped on his paw. We all met before we went to bed and tried to decide if something was amiss or if this was standard Brownie hospitality.

'Our Brownie guides deliberately slowed us down today,' Araf said. 'I believe they didn't want us to see Fearn Keep in the daylight.'

'OK, but why?'

'I didn't say I had all of the answers,' Araf replied.

'What do you think, Turlow?' Brendan asked.

'I too think this greeting is strange but apparently strange is the way of the Brownie. I say we sleep on it and see what the morrow brings.'

218

Back in the room I asked Brendan what his uber-cop senses deduced from Turlow's answer. 'Either he is a good liar,' he said, 'or he doesn't know anything.'

'So, nothing then.'

Brendan conceded my point with a nod.

I dreamt that night Cialtie was talking to the invisible man. I strained to hear what they were saying but, as in the way of dreams, I couldn't quite make it out. I awoke wondering what I had done to my ego to make myself the invisible man. I worried that my dream was a prediction and I would soon be face to face with my murdering uncle.

We found breakfast outside our doors – water and a couple of apples. Even though apples in The Land are practically my favourite things to eat, it wasn't like the Brownies knocked themselves out organising a menu.

After our hearty meal, Brendan suggested that we take a stroll outside to test Araf's theory. Sure enough an armed guard at the end of our corridor informed us that we had to wait in our rooms for information about an audience with the King. I said I understood but just wanted a quick nip of fresh air, but apparently nips or strolls were out of the question.

As we walked back to our room Brendan said, 'I'm feeling less like a guest and more like an inmate.'

About a half an hour later Essa came back fuming after an attempt to get past the guards. 'I am going to personally make sure that these people never get a drop of wine from the House of Muhn ever again.' That was a fate she hadn't even bestowed on me – and I'd dumped her.

After a lunch of, you guessed it, apples and water, a guard arrived and informed us that the King would grant us an audience in two hours. Essa was fit to burst. Actually, everybody was pretty peeved, including me. And you know me, I don't like all of the special royal treatment, but these guys were rude on any scale.

Brendan sidled up next to me and whispered in my ear. 'Do you notice that Turlow is taking this in his stride?'

I hadn't, but now that he mentioned it, Turlow didn't look put out at all. Now, I don't know The Turlow very well but he doesn't seem to me to be like the kind of royal who lets a snub slide, but there he was sitting with an 'oh well' look on his face.

Three hours later an honour guard showed up and informed us that the King would see us now. Araf respectfully asked if he could be excused from the audience due to a foot injury that he sustained the day before. It was the first I had heard about it.

'Are you OK, big guy? Why didn't you tell us before?'

'I did not wish to burden the group. It is nothing, Conor. It would simply be uncomfortable for me to stand for a long period. You go ahead.'

I was worried about my Imp buddy. He had never once complained about anything and I'd seen him get hit in the head with rocks. I was about to speak again, when he gave me a slight shake of the head that stopped the words in my throat. He was up to something and now was not the time to find out what.

'You take it easy, pal,' I said, patting him on his rock-like arms. 'Take a load off your feet.'

We were escorted through a series of damp hallways. Even though I wouldn't want to live here, I really liked the look of Fearn Keep. It was like a castle from an old black and white horror film. The walls were made of dark, rough stone built into long, not quite straight, corridors. Torchlight threw dancing shadows through periodic archways, making each corner feel like a place where a vampire might pop out.

We arrived at an open room and were instructed to wait at huge alder wood double doors. On the doors was carved a relief of an alder tree growing on top of a hill that seemed very much like the mound that Castle Duir was built on. A bulky Brownie informed us that we would have to be searched before entering the

Hall of the Fearn Throne. Essa by this time was livid and threatened to break any finger that touched her. I pleaded with her to calm down. I pointed out that the last time the Brownies came to Castle Duir I had their luggage searched and this was probably retaliation for that. It took me about five minutes but she finally allowed herself to be frisked. Watching that guy pat her down was one of the tensest moments of my life. Turlow produced and unhooked his Banshee blade and surrendered it without a word. The guard found my throwing blade in my sock. I really had forgotten it was there but the guard didn't look like he believed me. I handed it to him and asked for a receipt. I got a blank stare worthy of Araf.

King Bwika's throne room didn't disappoint. It was as spooky and as overblown as I expected it to be. There were huge tapestries, long rugs, ranks of soldiers in full armour standing at attention and a built-up platform on which the King sat, looking like a fat little kid, in a huge wooden throne. There were no other chairs. On either side of the King stood a dozen or so advisers.

We approached slowly on a long red carpet. Even though I am sure it was designed to be intimidating, I had a hard time not snickering. Long before we reached a comfortable conversational distance the King shouted, 'Prince of Duir.' I looked around to everybody, grimaced and stepped lively to the fore.

When I got to the bottom of the dais I bowed a low one and said, 'My lord, greeting in the name of the House of—'

'You think because you are of Duir you can sneak around my lands at will?'

'Uh, um,' was all I got out. I know it's rare for me but I was at a loss for words. What should I do? I was pretty sure that he shouldn't have been talking to me like that. I wondered if he would respect me if I stood up for myself, or maybe grovelling was the right way to go. I had no problem with grovelling; I really didn't want to be kicked out of the kingdom, or for that matter executed.

I really, really didn't want to be executed. I decided to go for a good bow and scrape.

'I meant no disrespect, Your Highness, and had no intention to trespass.' I produced the gold bar. 'See, I have brought you a tribute and have come on a matter of great import.'

The little flash of gold broke his concentration for a second. He motioned to someone on his right and a young man came down the steps to take the gold bar. As he got closer I saw it was the King's youngest son.

'Hi, Jesse,' I said with a smile.

Jesse frowned. He had never told his father about the time that he and his brother had snuck close to the Vinelands and robbed me and Fergal in the night. When I caught up with them and got my stuff back, I gave him and his brother the nicknames Frank and Jesse, in honour of the great American outlaws. He took the gold bar from me, all the while trying to avoid eye contact, and showed it to his father. King Bwika eyed the bar, and casually accepted my gift with a flick of the wrist. Jesse handed it to one of the dozen advisers that were standing in the shadows behind the throne and it disappeared inside his robes.

'That is the second time you have referred to my son as a "Jesse". What does it mean?'

Wow, this guy had a good memory, better than mine. I racked my brains for Jesse's real name and then it came to me – Codna. 'The first time I met your son was in the Hall of the Oak Throne, when my father bestowed on you the freedom of the Oaklands. I mistook Codna for someone I had known in the Real World and when we met socially afterwards I used the name as a small joke.'

'So because your father gave me permission to walk among the Oaklands, lands that I should rightfully own, and because you make idiot jokes with my idiot son, this gives you the right to spy on me?'

I shot a quick glance at Jesse. He looked like he had been slapped. 'I have no reason to spy on you, Your Highness, I come because my father is ill.'

'Ill?' he said in a tone that made me realise that illness was a concept he had never encountered.

'It's like a mortal wound that we cannot see, Your Highness. I need to find healing magic or he will die.'

This made the Brownie monarch think, which I suspected was something he didn't do very often. 'Is he cursed?'

'That may be the cause. We need to get to the Isle of the Tughe Tine that lies off the edge of your land.'

King Bwika threw his head back and laughed. 'What? Are you looking for help from the Grey Ones?'

'I don't know what I will find, Your Highness – I only want to save my father. For that I will do anything.'

The smile on the Brownie's face vanished in an instant. 'Your father,' he said, his voice filled with contempt. 'The last time your father was here … No, I lie – your father was never here. It was your father's father, Finn. Finn stood and called me "a supercilious toad" and then spat on the floor, there, before he left. I was a young king then, he was fortunate. If he had done that today he would have left with a bolt in his back.'

The more I hear about my grandfather the more I think we all would have benefited if he had taken a few anger-management classes. I stood and walked to the place where the King had pointed and dropped to one knee. 'Was it here that my grandfather spat?'

King Bwika stood and walked down the steps of his dais. Towering over me he pointed to a slab of marble floor directly in front of his feet. 'It was there.'

'Then let me spit on the same spot,' I said and I spat. Then I pulled my sleeve over my hand and used my shirt to clean up the spittle. 'So that I may wash away the memory of it. I, Conor of Duir, do humbly apologise for the rudeness of my ancestor.'

I didn't know what else to say, nor, I sensed, did the King. He looked up and scanned the faces in the room, then said, 'Go. My guards will escort you to the ends of the Keep grounds to the Peninsula Trail. There is but only one way to go from there and you must go alone – I cannot spare you a guide. Report to the alder trees daily.'

'Thank you, Your Highness, we shall leave at dawn,' I said, moaning silently to myself.

'You will leave now, before I change my mind, and you will not rest until you are off the Keep grounds.'

He gestured with his hand. The honour guard surrounded us and escorted us quickly from the room.

We found Araf resting on his bed.

'Is your foot up for a hike?'

'Why,' the Imp said, 'are we going on one?'

'The King says we can go, if we go now.'

We began to pack. It didn't take long. It's not like our welcome prompted us to put all of our underwear in drawers. I was almost ready to go when I answered a soft knock at the door.

Standing on the other side was the young prince with a cloth parcel in his hand.

'Jesse,' I said, extending my hand, 'or should I say Prince Codna. It's good to see you again.'

He looked confused and then shook my hand like he had never done it before. 'No, I like Jesse,' he said with a nervous smile. 'My brother and I still call each other Frank and Jesse when we are alone.'

'Are you going to be one of our escorts to the Peninsula Trail?'

'Oh no,' he said with a nervous laugh, like that was a ridiculous notion. 'No, I came because … Well, I stole this from Castle Duir and have been worried that it has been sorely missed by its owner. I would like for you to return it.'

I took the parcel and opened it. Inside was a round piece of brass. 'You stole a doorknob?'

Jesse shrugged. 'Frank got some better stuff but that Dahy man found it and took it back.'

'Well, thanks,' I said, rewrapping the parcel. 'I'm sure there is a door somewhere in my castle that someone is just dying to open. Speaking of Frank, where is he?'

'My brother prepares for war,' he said with a quiver in his voice that made me look at his face. He was almost at the brink of tears.

'Hey, guy,' I said, motioning him over to a set of chairs. 'What's the matter?'

'Demne,' he said, wiping his nose on his sleeve, 'you know – Frank. He's in the Torkc Guards.'

I searched my memory for the meaning of *torkc*. 'Pig Guards?'

Jesse laughed a little at this. 'Boar,' he corrected.

'So what's so bad about that?'

'I never get to see him any more and I'm worried about him. The Torkc are the first to attack in a war.'

'But the Brownies aren't at war with anyone.'

'They're not?' he said, beaming at me. 'Did you sue for peace?'

I didn't answer that right away, I didn't know what he was talking about. Just as I was about to ask, Tuan came to the door flanked by guards saying that the Brownies were insisting that we leave immediately. The guards made Jesse nervous. I told them to give us a sec.

'Thanks for returning the doorknob,' I said. 'Here, I have a present for you.' I reached into my pack and took out the green-handled knife that was thrown at Brendan on Mount Cas. 'Take this and give it to Frank; it's a throwing knife. The gold tip will make sure the blade hits its intended target. Maybe it will keep him safe.' I resheathed it and handed it to Jesse.

He smiled and then hugged me. That Jesse is a cute kid.

Chapter Twenty-Eight
Fearn Peninsula

It was dark outside but I could just make out two Brownies waiting for us at the end of the drawbridge.

'Hi, Dell, miss us?' He didn't answer; he and what's-his-name just turned and jogged into the night.

It was our turn to slow these guys down. There was no way we were going to go full pelt in pitch darkness. Yogi called a halt, dismounted, stripped off and handed his clothes to Tuan. He said he wanted to travel as a bear because his night vision was better. The Brownies came back to yell at us for stopping just as Yogi did his change thing. He towered over them and growled – they shut up. Yogi took the point behind our guides. He growled and snarled almost constantly so we could at least follow the sound. It was difficult going and the further we got from the castle the worse the trail became. Soon we had to take our branch-whipped faces off of our horses and power walk behind Dell and what's-his-name, who constantly told us to hurry up. I decided that when we finally got to where we didn't need the guides any more I would give Yogi permission to eat them.

It was about an hour before dawn when we reached the borders of Fearn Keep and the beginning of the Peninsula Trail. Dell asked Essa, 'What's for breakfast?' and she pulled her banta stick out of her pack. Bravely, I got between them and pointed out to Dell that

226

they might not want to hang out with a hungry bear and a much more dangerous princess.

Dell stared daggers into my eyes and said, 'We will meet again,' then the two of them ran off the way we had come. In the distance I heard Dell yell something that sounded like, 'In Duir.'

Tuan started up a fire while Yogi got dressed. We were all too tired to pitch tents so we just huddled up in front of the flames and napped in blankets for the short time left before dawn. I had one of those sleeps that, although it was probably a couple of hours, seemed like a blink.

The sun was well up at breakfast and nobody was what you could call chirpy. I had been trying to ask Araf about his hurt foot fib ever since we had come back from the throne room but any time I brought it up he would look over his shoulder and soundlessly say, 'Not now.' It wasn't until we were underway for about a half an hour and in a clearing large enough so we couldn't be overheard by the alders, that Araf called a stop.

'I had to be sure we were not being spied on,' the big guy said in a loud whisper. 'While you had an audience with the King, I snuck outside in daylight and saw what the Brownies did not want us to see.'

'And what was that?' The Turlow asked.

'An army,' the Imp replied. 'A large army and they looked to be preparing for war …'

'But who would the Brownies be at war with?' Essa asked.

'Me,' I said. 'Geez, I can be so stupid sometimes – now Jesse's conversation makes sense. Jesse, you know Codna, Brownie King's youngest son, thought I had come to make peace. The Brownies are going to attack Duir.'

'Or Cull,' Essa said, jumping off of her horse. 'Someone destroyed the Tree of Knowledge once before, maybe they are about to attack the Hazellands? We must warn Dahy.' She opened one saddlebag and looked inside. Then she opened the other and started frantically throwing things on the ground. Finally she unstrapped the bags and dumped the entire contents onto the frozen dirt.

'Damn it, damn it, damn them. They stole it. They stole it. Those little Brownie—'

'Stole what?' Araf said, getting down so he could help her.

'My emain slate.'

'You have an emain slate?' Tuan said incredulously.

'Not any more!' Essa shouted. 'Those little stinking—'

The rest of us just stood as still as possible while Essa kicked and used language that would have been inappropriate even in a Wild West saloon.

Essa really did need calming down but I had seen the Princess like this before and I wasn't going to go near her. It took someone that didn't know Essa very well to attempt such a foolhardy thing. Tuan walked towards her and pulled down the back of his trousers. I thought he was going to moon her. Then the hair on the back of his head grew *in*, then went coarse, curly and pepper grey in colour. His hands changed to paws as his back went horizontal and straight. His shoes, on what now were his back paws, fell off. Then I saw the reason for the mooning – a long tail, full flowing with long hair, sprouted out of the top of his trousers. Tuan had changed into a fully clothed Tuan-sized dog. An Irish wolfhound or something close to it and it was the funniest thing I had seen in a very long time.

Essa was shocked into silence, then smiled, then laughed, then dropped to one knee and gave doggie-Tuan a big hug around the neck. I would pay lots of money to find out how to do that. Tuan reformed back to his Pooka self during the hug and the two of them fell laughing on the ground.

'I used to do that for my mother when she was upset,' Tuan said, pulling up the back of his trousers.

'Did it always work?' Essa asked, still laughing.

'Never failed,' Tuan said, helping her up.

'Right,' Essa said, straightening her clothes, 'I'm going back to Fearn Keep.'

'Hold on, Princess.' Now that she was calm and it was safe, I dismounted. 'You can't go back there. We only just got out and I'm pretty sure accusing them of stealing and demanding your slate back isn't going to make them say, "Oops sorry, here you go."'

'I must get that slate back,' she said, her voice once again betraying her anxiety. 'Dahy must be warned about the army.'

'Which is probably why they took it,' Brendan said. 'I'm a cop, Essa, trust me, you won't get it back.'

'But I must. I send a message to my father every other day. He will be worried sick about me. And do you know how expensive those things are?'

'Princess, the others are right,' Tuan said. 'I agree that Master Dahy must be informed of what Araf has seen but we cannot go back. We are at the beginning of the Fearn Peninsula. Less than a mile back there is a trail that, if I remember correctly from my last journey in these woods, leads us to the beach. I propose we take it to the sea. From there we can send Yarrow to warn the Hazellands and then the rest of us can follow the coast to Alder Point.'

Everyone looked at Yogi, who said, 'I do not know the way.'

'I will guide you back to the Hall of Knowledge,' Essa said.

'You can't do that, Princess.' Turlow said 'Princess' in that lovey-dovey tone that was enough to make me vomit.

'And why not?' Essa shot back.

Turlow was foolishly about to start an argument with Essa when Araf piped up. And when Araf chooses to speak it's such a surprise that people tend to listen.

'This discussion is not for here. Tuan, will we make the coast before nightfall?'

'Easily, I should think.'

'Let us think on this as we travel and decide at the next camp. Until then, do not speak of this among the alders.'

Turlow looked like he had something to say, but none of us waited to hear it. We turned our horses and remounted.

The rest of the day was in silence not only because the trees were listening but also because the trail was narrow and forced us to ride in single file. By late afternoon the alders thinned out. In the distance the horizon widened and the slight sting of salt could be detected on the breeze. The trees disappeared altogether about a quarter mile from the coast. We trekked over rolling sand dunes covered with long grass until we reached a black sand beach. The warmth of the ocean changed the crisp dry air in to a cold misty one, but the relief from being out from under the spying eyes of the alders meant that no one complained.

'What happened to the trees?' I asked Tuan.

'The alders hate brackish water. They never live near the coast. That is why I proposed we come here. If Yarro – I mean Yogi and Princess Essa hug the coast, there is a chance that they can get out of the Alderlands without the alders knowing.'

'You think she should go with him then?'

'Yarrow is my friend and in a fight I would have no other at my side.' Then Tuan looked over his shoulder and leaned in. 'But he is not the smartest in the clan. Essa, I have learned, is a woman of substance and she is a natural guide. I think together they have a better chance of success.'

We set up camp while Yogi stripped off, bear-ed up and then had a dip in the freezing water. He came out holding a flat ray-like fish the size of a bicycle. I pitched tents while Tuan and Araf fried it up. Araf produced a bottle of Brownie-shine that he had stolen from the stores at Fearn Keep. Everybody knew it was a goodbye party for Essa and Yogi, but no one said it.

I tried to have a little alone time with Essa before I went to bed, but she was deep in conversation with her fiancé. I waved at her, mouthed, 'Good luck,' and promised myself that I would wake up early so as to have a chat with her before she left.

As it turned out she woke me. Long before the dawn she shook me awake to say goodbye.

'What kind of time do you call this?' I asked, rubbing sleep from my eyes.

'Yogi and I thought it might be a good idea to leave before it was light in case any alders could sense this far.'

I got out of bed and walked with her to what was left of the fire. I looked around expecting to see the Banshee.

'Where is Turd-low?' I said, and then mentally kicked myself for starting a fight. But Essa was calm.

'We have said our goodbyes.'

'Goodbyes? I thought he would insist on coming with you.'

'No,' she said dispassionately. I couldn't tell if she was trying to hide emotions or if she didn't really care. 'He tried to persuade me not to go, but when he realised I was not for turning he didn't volunteer to come.'

'If I could, I would go with you.'

She looked me straight in the eyes for one of those hour-long seconds, smiled – then changed the subject.

'Yogi has packed the boat onto Tuan's horse and has taught him how to assemble it. You be careful out there on the ocean.'

'Gosh, it almost sounds like you're worried about me.'

She started to scowl but then gave me a hug. 'I am,' she said.

Yogi appeared with the horses and Essa quickly turned to go, but before she could get away I caught her by the wrist. She tensed up and I instantly let go remembering what a foolish thing that is to do, but she didn't attack and I got to say what I wanted to say.

'Then we will both worry about each other. OK?'

She nodded and mounted up. I watched them disappear into the pre-dawn.

I went back to bed for another hour; when I awoke Brendan was already up. He had a good fire going and was cooking breakfast.

'Have you been up long?' I asked.

'I love the sunrise on a beach. I grew up near a beach,' Brendan said. 'Dawn is a magical time by the sea. That's what my mother always said. She also used to say, "Just because you can't see a skunk doesn't mean that things don't stink."'

'What does that mean?'

'I have no idea,' Brendan said, laughing. 'She used to say all sorts of crazy stuff. I've been thinking about her all morning. Once she woke me up and we trudged to the beach before the sun came up to hunt for driftwood. We built a fire and she told me stories until it was light enough to see. You know what she told me?'

I shook my head, no.

'She told me about a land where people never grow old – she even named it. I've been stretching my memory to remember and I'm pretty sure she called it Tir na Nog. She told me I came from a line of wise men, who were forced to leave.' He stopped and looked away.

'The Fili after the Fili war,' I said out loud as much to myself as to Brendan.

When he turned back his eyes were shining. 'See? That's why I thought this was all a dream at first. I loved those stories when I was young, but when I got older I stopped believing in them. Mom, though, never stopped believing. I started to think that she was stupid and later … crazy. Who's the stupid one now?'

He dropped his head and was silent for a while. I put my arm around his shoulders. Finally he wiped his eyes on his sleeve and stood – shaking off his heavy emotions. 'I'm glad my girl is with her now and I hope Mom is telling her those same stories. I have to get back, Conor. I have to tell them both that it's all true.'

Chapter Twenty-Nine
Fire Dancing

As we travelled along the coast, a foggy drizzle blew in from the sea. It was cold and damp and very unpleasant but it hid us from prying eyes, and we hoped it hid Essa and Yogi from the alders. Along with being moist and miserable it was also slow going. It was a beach, not a trail and we frequently had to dismount to negotiate boulders, large pieces of flotsam and jetsam or runoff streams. When we came to a good patch of sand we would break into a canter or even a gallop but I could tell Acorn didn't like the sand. It broke my heart to make him stay on the beach. I promised him I would get him some real snazzy oats when we got back to normality.

Dinner that night was what was left of Yogi's ray. Trust me, it was nicer twenty-four hours earlier. The loss of Essa and Yogi had left a hole in the group that no one tried to fill. It was early to bed and the next morning it was early to rise.

The previous day's drizzle whipped itself up into a full-blown storm. I guess I should have been grateful it wasn't snow, but at least then I would have been dry. The near-horizontal rain made me wet in places I didn't even know I had. Equestrianism is no longer fun when your trousers squelch with every bounce. We were all too miserable and frozen to talk. By lunchtime I was practically in a hypothermic coma and would have stayed that way if Brendan hadn't flipped.

We had stopped only long enough to decide to eat lunch on the hoof. Turlow dismounted and opened his saddlebag to get some grub. That's when Brendan lost it. He jumped from his horse and came down hard on poor Turlow's head. The Banshee didn't know what hit him. Turlow jumped to his feet and when he saw Brendan on the ground he assumed that Brendan had fallen on him after being shot by some unseen attacker. He popped out his Banshee blade and turned his back on the policeman, looking for the sniper. Brendan picked himself up and then tackled Turlow from behind like a linebacker in full blown 'roid-rage.

Turlow went face down hard into a sand dune. Brendan jumped on his back and tried to pull his arms, like he was handcuffing him, but by this time Turlow was no longer confused. He wrenched his wrists free and then, like a rodeo bull, he arched his back and pushed his body up on all fours. Brendan sailed three feet into the air. He came down face first with his body at an angle that made me worry he had broken his neck. Turlow was on him in a second. To the Banshee's credit he didn't run him through. Brendan obviously was still not thinking properly; he reached for the Banshee blade with his hand. Turlow pulled the razor-sharp edge out of the way and gave Brendan a swift kick in the side that doubled him up.

'I have been restrained with you, Real Worlder,' Turlow said, pushing his blade at Brendan's side, 'but my restraint is not infinite. Tell me why you attacked me or die.'

I dismounted, ran between them and managed to back Turlow off a bit. 'Brendan, what's gotten into you?'

'He's in league with Cialtie,' Brendan said.

I spun around and my heart jumped into my throat. Turlow stood there with his sword drawn and for a second I thought he was going to attack us both. I reached for the Lawnmower but it wasn't there – it was strapped to Acorn. 'Brendan, what are you talking about? How do you know this?'

Brendan took a step towards Turlow. The Banshee raised his blade menacingly and Brendan stopped.

'Turlow,' I asked, 'what is he talking about?'

'I do not know; your friend has gone mad.'

'All right,' I said, 'let's everybody calm down a bit.' I turned to Brendan. He took a deep breath, dropped his shoulders and nodded. Turlow backed off and reluctantly flicked his Banshee blade back up his sleeve. 'Right, Brendan, explain yourself.'

Brendan composed himself. He straightened his clothes and put on the kind of face I imagine he uses when testifying in court. 'Conor, you told me that you were attacked in the Real World by black riders that were sent by Cialtie.'

'Yes.'

'And your aunt told you that Cialtie had been looking for you for years.'

'That's what she said.'

'My mother bought the farmhouse I live on in the Real World because she thought it was close to lay-lines and portals to an Otherworld. Two years ago my wife was killed in a car accident when she hit a black horse. A couple of days ago, Conor suggested that that horse had a rider and that that rider was sent by Cialtie.'

'If I recall, Brendan, you told me that I was crazy for suggesting that.'

'Well, I have been thinking about it, Conor. It's amazing how living in Faerieland can make one reassess one's opinions.'

'What has this to do with me?' Turlow asked.

'Open his bag,' Brendan said.

'If you think I am going to stand here and let you search my possessions then think again,' Turlow said. I saw his fingers twitch but the Banshee blade didn't reappear.

'Just lift the flap on his saddlebag and look at the marking underneath.'

I slowly backed to Turlow's horse. Man, it was tense. I had a feeling that if I took my eyes off the two of them that they would be at each other's throats in a second. I lifted the flap on the bag and saw what Brendan was talking about. Burned into the leather was a symbol not unlike an Ogham rune but more swirly and stylised. I couldn't read it.

'That is the same marking that was on the saddle of the horse that caused my wife's accident.'

'And from that you have deduced that I am a spy for Conor's lunatic uncle?' Turlow turned from Brendan and walked over to Tuan, who was still on horseback, and unlatched his saddlebag. He flipped open the flap and sure enough the same symbol was there. 'You idiot,' Turlow said. 'That is the mark of Master Bothy, probably the finest saddler in The Land. That mark may be on a quarter of the saddles in Tir na Nog.'

I looked to Araf; he nodded in agreement. I turned to Brendan and said, 'Oops.'

Turlow was still steamed. He walked right up to Brendan and said, 'To lose a wife must be an awful thing. That has obviously clouded your judgement so I will let this event go unpunished – but touch me again, Real Worlder, and you will see your own blood.'

Brendan didn't waver in his gaze; he looked the Banshee straight in the eyes and said, 'I am sorry.'

Turlow nodded, indicating that he had heard but not necessarily forgiven, and went over to his saddlebag, took out some dried meat and passed it around to everyone, including Brendan.

'And here's me thinking that lunch was going to be dull,' I said, saddling up. 'Come on, let's get out of here.'

We all mounted up except for Brendan who just stood there, staring into space, the rain dripping off of his face. Finally I said, 'Druid, are you coming?'

That broke his reverie and produced a sad smile on his face. 'No, not a Druid, just a cop who should have known better. I'm sorry, everyone.'

That afternoon's journey was silent and tense. I got the feeling that Brendan was kicking himself and that Turlow wanted to join in. The rest of us didn't dare say anything lest we jump-start a bust-up. The ice-cold rain had stopped but a frigid sea breeze made sure we remembered how damp we were. Our tongues tasted the salt air and our eyes felt the sting as the sky stayed solid grey as if to match our mood.

I missed Essa. I bet we all did. Hell, we were only without her for one morning before we were at each other's throats. Periodically, I unconsciously looked for her in our group only to be reminded that she was gone. It made me realise that I had spent the entire journey staring at her as we rode. I hoped she was all right.

An hour or so before dusk, as a thick fog crept in from the sea, Tuan announced that we were here.

'Where here?' I asked.

'Here, here,' Tuan replied. 'This is Fearn Point and out there is Red Eel Isle.'

I looked in the direction that the Pooka was pointing. I had trouble seeing the end of his finger let alone an island out to sea.

'Yeah, it looks lovely,' I said. 'I just wish somebody had built a motel here.'

Tuan unpacked the boat that Yogi had brought from the Pinelands. I knew that the Pookas were not known for their nautical skills but this boat was ridiculous. It looked more like a kite than a boat. I knew that it had to be portable but as I examined the skin, which would eventually be stretched over the toothpick frame, I wondered if it would float. I tried to remember if a fortune teller ever predicted that I would end up in a watery grave.

I walked the shore and found a tiny bay on the windward side where the currents had beached tons of driftwood. We were all cold and damp and tempers were frayed. I decided that we didn't need a fire – we needed a bonfire. Brendan pitched tents and Araf and Turlow threw nets into the sea. After chatting to the fish and letting the ones that wanted to live go free, we ended up with a sea bass each.

Araf produced yet another bottle of nicked Brownie-shine. When I asked him how much he stole, Araf said, 'The Brownies were well looked after the last time they came to Ur. I took less than what the Brownie King drank his first night. I don't feel guilty, if that is what you are getting at.'

'Hey, don't look at me – I'm all in favour of shoplifting from Brownies.'

After dinner we felt well fed and watered. Brendan and Turlow sat at opposite sides of my inferno. The flames were so high they couldn't see each other – probably a good thing.

Brendan was in a non-verbal sulk, Tuan was trying to put together a boat in the dark and you know how chatty Araf is, so I was pretty much forced to talk to Turlow or climb into my nice damp sleeping roll.

'You once asked me how I could have let Essa go,' I said, sitting next to him. 'I could now ask you the same thing.'

Turlow didn't look at me, he kept staring into the fire and said, 'Not that it is any of your concern, Faerie, but she did not want me to come with her.'

Well, that was the end of that chat. If I wanted to have friendly banter around this campfire, I really needed to work on my ventriloquist act. I stood up and resigned myself to an early night. It was a shame really. I had hoped to have a little fun the night before I turned myself into fish food.

Before I left him I said, 'Thanks for not stabbing my friend today; he was well out of line.'

'Brendan was lucky,' Turlow said. 'You saved his life today.'

'I saved his life? You stopped yourself before I even got there.'

'I was in a rage, Conor, but I stopped when I spotted you out of the corner of my eye. In that, your friend was lucky.'

'Gosh, I had no idea I had such a calming effect on you.'

Turlow laughed in a way that made me realise I was missing something. 'Do you know about the Banshee affinity with death?'

I did. My cousin Fergal had once told me that Banshees could sense imminent death. 'A little,' I said.

'I was enraged today. Never in my life have I been treated like that. I was fully prepared kill your countryman but then I saw you and I knew that if I killed him – I would have had to kill you too. I was not prepared to do that.'

'Oh,' I said, not really knowing how to reply to a statement like that. 'Well … ah … thanks.'

I walked back to my tent spooked with the knowledge that I had recently come so close to being killed. I stuck my nose into my tent and smelled the dampness of everything. When I touched my cold wet blankets, I said out loud, 'Screw this.'

I stumbled back down to the pile of wood by the sea and came back to the fire with an armful of thin branches. I built a little drying frame near the blaze and draped my sleeping roll over it and then I built another for the clothes on my back. Araf spotted me and didn't wait for an invitation. He built his drying rack and joined me stark naked, howling and dancing around the fire like a Red Indian in a Hollywood Western. Turlow looked on in amazement, while Brendan held fast to his funk and refused to join us. I didn't care. I had apparently almost died today and I would probably drown tomorrow, so I was dancing and I wasn't gonna stop. Tuan came back to the fire to ask what all the commotion was about. As I bobbed and weaved I explained the principle of naked dancing/clothes drying. Being a Pooka he had no problem with nudity and was gyrating with us in no time.

The two party-poopers were making it difficult for me to reach that uninhibited mindless state that makes naked fire dancing so much fun. Every time I passed by the moping Brendan or the stern but shocked Turlow, I pleaded with them to join us. It wasn't until Tuan turned into his shaggy wolfhound and barked at Brendan that he finally smiled and before long the only one wearing any threads was the Banshee. I even stopped and risked freezing my thingy off long enough to build a drying rack for Turlow. Finally he broke when we ganged up on him. When you think about it, four naked men jumping up and down in front of someone, while he is sitting, makes for pretty heavy peer pressure. Turlow was unenthusiastic to begin with but then really got into it. He started spinning like a top and then began screaming like … well, like a Banshee.

I still had trouble getting trance-like. Something was tugging on my brain cells that kept pulling my consciousness back to reality. Finally I stopped and checked my laundry. My blankets were still wet but my clothes were dry, so I got dressed and decided to take a walk to clear my head. The others were so lost in dance that they didn't even notice I was gone. I had to walk quite far away before Turlow's howling was distant enough to allow me to think. Something was weighing on me and I wasn't sure what it was. Then it hit me. Essa had said that Turlow hadn't wanted to come with her, but then Turlow told me that Essa didn't want him with her. One of them was lying to me. There were lots of reasons why neither of them would tell me the truth. As Turlow had rightly pointed out it was none of my business. It might mean that their relationship wasn't going as well as it seemed, which from my point of view was good news, but then again maybe it was something else. I had no way of knowing but at least I had figured out what was bothering me. Now that my mental conflict was solved,

I turned back to my frolicking companions and decided to give the dangly-dance one more try. As I got closer I saw them bopping in silhouette and I knew something was wrong. I stood stock still, surveyed the area and listened. I couldn't see or hear whatever it was that was making the hair stand up on the back of my neck but something was wrong, something was very wrong. What was it? That's when I saw it; I saw it and my heart jumped in my chest. As I watched my four companions dance around my bonfire, I counted them: one, two, three, four – *five*.

Chapter Thirty
Red

The four of them were so lost in the fire dance that they didn't notice that there was a strange man bopping along with them. Twice today I hadn't had the Lawnmower on my hip when I wanted it, so I had made sure I brought it with me on this walk. I drew it and advanced slowly. As I got closer I could plainly see that the interloper was without a stitch of clothes, which, on the plus side, meant he was definitely unarmed. I lowered my guard a bit and jogged the last stretch of beach until I stood just outside the moat the dancers had made in the sand. Still none of them noticed me. The stranger was as absorbed in the dancing as the rest of them. His straight red hair flew around like a sixties go-go dancer. If I had seen him clothed and from the back I might have said he was a woman, but in the firelight there was no avoiding his gender. He was dancing behind Tuan and I was struck at how similarly they were built except for the stranger's arms – they would have put a post-spinach Popeye to shame.

I waited until Araf came by and grabbed his arm to pull him out of the circle. Instead he pulled me in. I had forgotten just how solid that guy is and I almost fell into the fire. Anyway, I got his attention. He stood and looked at me confused, like a sleepwalker that just found himself in the hallway of a hotel.

'Look,' I said to him, pointing to the other dancers.

Araf was still out of it and tilted his head like a dog being taught algebra.

'Intruder alert!' I shouted, pointing to the new member of our dance troupe.

He saw him and snapped into action. He leapt over the edge of the fire (something I would never do without clothes on) and grabbed his banta stick. This startled Turlow enough for him to notice that we were not alone. Turlow had the good sense to throw his clothes on. I grabbed a blanket and wrapped it around Brendan. Turlow came up next to us holding his Banshee blade. Tuan was still completely oblivious.

'Who is he?' Turlow asked.

'I don't know. You were dancing with him – you tell me.'

We watched as the stranger and Tuan spun and danced around the dwindling fire. Tuan sailed past us in his own little world, then the stranger, right behind him, turned and gave us a little chest-high wave. On the next pass we grabbed Tuan and made him see who his dance partner was. At first he looked shocked and then he dropped onto all fours and turned into his wolfhound. The stranger kept dancing and spinning like he owned the place. When he came by again wolfhound-Tuan stuck his nose in for a sniff and our visitor stopped and gave him a little pat on the head, like he was casually walking in the park.

'Excuse me,' I started, but the naked stranger just danced away. We all looked at each other. On his next pass I tried again and was again ignored. On the third pass I stepped in front of him. My sword wasn't pointed at him but then again it wasn't in its scabbard – he had to stop and he did.

'Excuse me,' I repeated. 'This is our fire.'

He looked at me. I still couldn't see his eyes in the light and he tilted his head just like Araf had done minutes before and said, 'You own fire. How does that work?'

Now it was my turn to be confused. 'Well … we made the fire.'

'So you think if you make something, then you own it?' He smiled a toothy grin and shook his head. 'I have known many a parent that thought that. They were usually disappointed.' Then he turned and danced around in the other direction.

Tuan returned to Pooka form and the dancer came around again.

'A Pooka that would rather shiver in his skin than stay in his fur.' He pushed past me and we waited for his next lap. 'A Banshee in the company of Hawathiee?' He then put his hand on Araf's head as if to measure him. 'I see an Imp' – he grabbed Araf's hand and looked at it – 'with no dirt under his fingernails?'

He spun off again. This guy was really starting to annoy me. I tried to speak to him when he came around again but he put his hand in front of my face to stop me. I wanted to chop that hand off. I wanted to tell him that I had chopped a hand off before.

He stood inches in front of Brendan and looked him up and down. 'I don't think I have ever seen a Druid look so confused.'

'Who are you?' I demanded.

He finally then gave me the once-over. 'A Faerie. Is it hard for you, Faerie, being so far away from your mountain of gold?'

'Who – are – you?'

'Who am I?' he said indignantly. 'A Banshee and an Imp and a Druid and a Pooka and a Faerie are dancing naked in the Alderlands without a Brownie in sight and you ask – who I am? Whoooo arrrrrre youuuuuuu?'

'I am Conor of …'

He dashed into the night and came back roughly dragging the boat that Tuan had almost finished assembling. 'Sailors are we?' Tuan grabbed the boat from him and half of the flimsy frame popped out from the oiled leather skin. 'And where are the sailors sailing to?'

I didn't think that telling him our plans was a good idea but Brendan answered him. 'We are going to Red Eel Isle.'

'And where is that?'

Brendan pointed out to sea.

'Red Eel Isle – is that what you call it?'

'What do you call it?' I asked.

'Why would I call an island? Do you think it would come?'

He cackled and walked over to where our bags were piled together and started looking through them. Turlow ran over and stuck his Banshee blade in his face. 'Leave our possessions alone,' he demanded.

The stranger simply ignored him and continued to look through our stuff. 'Why? If you plan on sailing to Red Eel Island in that boat, you won't be needing your things and it will be easier for me to scavenge them here, than when they are on the bottom of the ocean.'

'Leave our bags alone,' Turlow repeated, poking the scavenger with his Banshee blade.

The stranger stopped. 'No matter, I'll come back and take what I want when you are dead. I'm off home now; I know when I am not welcome. Thank you for the dance.' He stopped with a faraway look and said, 'It has been a long time since I have danced.'

'Where is home?' Araf asked. As I have said, when Araf speaks people listen. Even though our stranger had only just met the taciturn Imp it worked on him too.

He turned and said, 'Red Eel Island. If you had been nicer I would have given you all a trip in my boat.' Then he ran naked into the black night.

I turned to the others. They all had their mouths open. I pointed to the spot in the darkness that our visitor had disappeared into. 'My agent, ladies and gentlemen.' That got a chuckle from Brendan. As I have said, it was good to have him around.

'Who was that?' Brendan asked the night.

'What was that?' Tuan replied.

'Whoever it was, I think we should keep watch tonight,' Turlow said. 'I will take first shift.'

I didn't argue. I got my stuff off my drying rack and within minutes I was inside my warm dry sleeping roll. Brendan followed me. As he got into bed I asked him, 'What did you think of insane guy?'

'Oh,' he said, 'I think he was crazy all right but I wouldn't say he was insane.'

I laughed. 'You said that about me once if I recall.'

'And I was right,' Brendan said. 'I got a feeling that our dancer tonight tried a little too hard to be crazy. Saying that, he did say one thing that I agreed with.'

'What was that?'

'We really are going to drown in that dinghy.'

I was last up the next morning. Tuan was still working on the boat. Every time he got the skin stretched over part of the frame on one side, the other side would pop out. Araf was off scavenging for driftwood, Brendan was cooking breakfast and Turlow was tending to the horses. I felt a bit guilty doing nothing so I grabbed a brush and joined the Banshee. Since Turlow was brushing Acorn I started working on his horse.

'You know,' I said, 'I don't know your horse's name.'

'Banshees do not name their horses.'

'Why not?'

'It makes it easier in case you have to eat them.'

'Oh, don't listen to him,' I said, covering the mount's ears. 'I won't let him eat you and I'm going to give you a name. I dub thee – Fluffy. There, no one will eat a horse called Fluffy.'

'You are a strange man, Conor of Duir.'

'But loveable, don't ya think?'

Brendan called us to breakfast. Araf was sitting by the fire examining a piece of wood. He didn't seem to notice me when I said good morning.

'You OK, big guy?'

'You,' he said.

'Me? What me?'

He still didn't look up. 'No, you.'

'Who you? Me? Who's on first?'

He finally looked at me with an exasperated face that I usually reserve for my closer relatives. 'The wood,' he said, holding up the branch in his hand. 'It's yew wood.'

'Oh, yew who.' I shrugged. 'So?'

'Most of the wood in that driftwood pile is yew.' Araf handed me the piece that was in his hand. 'And look.'

I saw it right away. I didn't need to be a forensics expert to see that plainly there were axe marks in the bark. 'This ain't wood from the Yewlands I've been in,' I said. 'There is no way you could chop down one of those babies. You'd be dead by the end of the backswing.'

Araf nodded in agreement.

'Could they have come from another island?'

'Conor, today I am going to leave the shores of The Land in a boat. It will be the first time in my life.'

'It will probably be your last – have you seen the boat?'

I got that look again. 'What I mean to say is, I have no idea what is beyond the beaches of Tir na Nog.'

'It is ready,' Tuan said, trudging back to the fire. 'And I am ready for one last meal and then we can go.'

'One *last* meal?' I said. 'I don't like the sound of that.'

'No, no, not one last meal. One meal before we—'

'Drown?'

'Faerie,' Turlow said, addressing me, 'has anyone ever told you that your attempts at humour are often annoying?'

'Yes, often.'

We ate in silence. Fish for breakfast isn't my idea of a perfect last meal but I couldn't see a waffle house anywhere nearby. The morning mist was clearing with a not too chilling offshore breeze. As we ate, a dark shape became visible out to sea – Red Eel Isle. It didn't look too far but I'd had a little experience sailing. Once Dad and I went to the New Jersey shore with a school friend, Dad refused to step into a boat, but I loved it. I remembered that on the water things were usually further away than they looked.

We decided that the less weight we carried on the boat the better. Araf dug a hole in the sand and we wrapped what we weren't going to bring in blankets and buried them in the dune. Tuan placed the athrú that was hanging around his neck into his mouth and whispered to the horses.

'What did you tell them?' I asked.

'I told them to wait here for as long as they could forage and if we don't return then to make their way back to the Pinelands.'

I gave Acorn a rough rub on the nose the way he likes and said, 'You take good care of yourself, ya hear.' I swear he glanced over my shoulder to the boat and then stared at me with eyes that said, 'I'm not the one you should be worried about.'

Araf threw a disc into the fire and it went out fast, like somebody had just put a glass dome over it. Then he reached into the ash and charred wood and dug the fire coin out. I missed the heat of the fire instantly. I looked at the surf rolling onto the beach, the island far out at sea, I felt the cold salty breeze on my face and a shiver ran down my back. I whispered to myself, 'Dad, you'd better appreciate this.'

I'm sure that everyone realised it was a bad idea as soon as we tried to get into the boat. This thing was made for a calm lake – it was not an ocean-going vessel. Tuan kept telling us to make sure we stepped on the big pieces of wood that made up the frame and to, under no circumstances, step on the skin or we'd put our feet through it. If that wasn't unreassuring enough, the boat was as stable as a beach ball – Tuan tipped it trying to get in. We finally figured out that the only way to board the damn thing was in pairs, one on each side to balance out the weight. But when we did that the framework bent so badly that we were sure we were going to break it. Turlow and I were the last in and we had to wade into freezing-cold waist-deep water to get the thing off the sandy bottom. We were only seconds onboard when the first wave hit us. I wasn't ready for it. I bounced around and hit the skin of the boat hard with my fist, but luckily I didn't puncture it. The others grabbed oars and paddled. The 'ship' came with two oars and Araf this morning had fashioned another two out of driftwood.

We survived the next two breakers The surf hadn't looked this rough from shore but now that we were on the water we were really getting tossed around. The fourth wave did us in. The bow raised like it had for the other waves but then it just kept going. It went straight up and tossed us out the stern. I had the tent on my back and when I hit the water it dragged me straight down. The water was so cold it only took a nanosecond to become numb all over – it was like a full body shot of novocaine. I untangled my backpack from my shoulders and then forced my way to the surface. I got my head above water just in time to get creamed by another wave that spun me underwater like I was in a washing machine. Then next time I reached the surface I spotted Brendan and Araf spluttering off to my left.

'Are you OK?' I shouted over to them.

Brendan shouted back, 'I think so.' Araf looked a bit panicky. I had never seen him panicky. I looked around – the boat was upright and seemed to be doing just fine sailing out to the island without us. I couldn't see anybody else.

'Where's Turlow and Tuan?' Just as I said that Turlow surfaced gasping for dear life.

'I lost my saddlebag,' he gulped. He dived down again only to pop up seconds later in even more of a panic. 'I can't see anything. I have to—' A wave came and knocked him over – he resurfaced coughing. Turlow was not a natural swimmer.

Just then a sealion wearing the remains of Tuan's shirt came up underneath Turlow and pushed him towards the shore. I started swimming and it wasn't long before there was sand under my feet. I turned back and saw Brendan was using a lifeguard hold on Araf, dragging him to safety. I waded back in and helped them. Turlow and the now half-naked Tuan were in front of us. The five of us limped back and collapsed shivering on the edge of the surf.

'You just can't beat a day at the beach,' I said while spitting out a mouthful of sand. 'Is everybody all right?'

I didn't hear their reply; what I did hear was a familiar voice shouting, 'Yoo hoo, could you boys use a nice warm fire?'

I looked up. I almost didn't recognise him with his clothes on. There, straight ahead, standing next to our campfire, which was now fully ablaze, was the strange red-headed man from the night before. I can't honestly say I was happy to see him but that fire looked like the nicest thing I had ever seen in my life.

We all dragged ourselves off the sand. My frozen joints moved like door hinges that had been without grease for twenty years. We crouched by the fire trying desperately to get some circulation back into our extremities.

'Thank you for rebuilding our fire,' I said through clattering teeth.

'I knew that you would need it if any of you survived drowning,' he said. 'I wasn't expecting all of you to make it though – I guess I'll have to give your stuff back.' He walked over to the other side of the fire and came back with the blankets and extra clothes that we had buried in the dunes. All of us were too grateful at seeing a dry set of clothes to yell at him. We stripped, dried off and changed clothes while our thief/saviour brewed up some tea.

'What is your name?' Brendan asked.

'Call me Red,' Red said, shaking his hair madly with both hands. 'That is what my friends called me … back when I had friends. Or maybe you should call me The Red Eel,' he said, doing a snakelike dance.

That perked my interest. 'You're Red Eel?'

'That is the name you gave this island, is it not? I never have heard it called that but since I am the only person that lives out there – I must be Red Eel.'

I should have known better than to get excited by anything that madman said.

'Have you ever seen a red eel?' Araf asked as Red handed him a cup of tea.

'There are eels in the lake but I don't like 'em. Slimy things they are. I cannot say if I ever saw a red one. Why?'

'That's a long story,' I said.

'Well then, why don't you tell me on the way over to the island in my boat?'

'Thanks,' I said, 'but no thanks.'

'Hold on a minute, O'Neil,' Brendan said, holding up his hand to me like a traffic cop. 'You have a boat?'

'It would be pretty strange of me to offer you a ride in my boat if I didn't have one. Do you not think?'

'Everything you do is strange,' I said. 'And one thing's for certain, I'm not getting into a boat with you.'

Chapter Thirty-One
The Digs

I sat in the back of Red's boat with my arms crossed and refused to speak to anyone all the way to the island. I had fostered a fantasy that I was the leader of this group but when everyone ignored me by waltzing into the strange man's boat, I realised that my leadership qualities only applied to my horse and then probably not even to him. Left with the option of sitting by myself on a cold damp beach or getting a free ride in a sturdy seaworthy vessel, to a destination I had been labouring for weeks to get to, I decided to go but I wasn't going to do it without getting into a really good pout.

The boat was big enough for us and maybe a couple more. There were two large oars set in iron oarlocks. Red ordered Araf and Tuan to man an oar each and the two of them stepped lively to their stations faster than they ever did anything for me. Obviously Red was now the captain. *Well, they'll be sorry*, I thought, *when he makes them row off the end of the world.* The boat cut through the surf like we were sailing on a millpond. When we got out into deeper waters Red ordered the rowers to stop and climbed up to the edge of the bow. From the floor of the boat he picked up two metal rings that were attached to thick ropes. He clanged the rings together, they vibrated in his hands producing an eerie ringing sound, and then he threw them into the water.

'Ooh that tickles,' he said, flexing his fingers and then rubbing his hands together. Then he sat and smiled at us.

None of us spoke. When you are in the middle of the ocean with a leering madman at the helm, silence is definitely the best policy. You literally do not want to rock the boat. Saying that, I was in a bad mood and I'm not very good with uncomfortable silences. I was just about to demand to know what was going on when the ropes in the water went taut, the boat lurched and we started speeding towards the island like we were being pulled by a nuclear submarine.

'How is this happening?' I shouted to Red, but he was oblivious, facing out to sea with his arms spread like he was flying or re-enacting a scene from a movie about a doomed cruise liner.

Tughe Tine Isle loomed before us. It looked like your typical volcanic deserted island. There was a lot of vegetation but no trees. I assumed that the lake Red spoke about was up on the island's plateau.

The ocean air felt warmer the further we got from the shore. About a half an hour out Red turned around and said, 'Can you feel it?'

'Feel what?' Turlow said.

'Can you feel yourself getting older?'

Turlow was on his feet. Araf grabbed onto the side as the boat shook. 'Stop the boat,' Turlow said.

'Why would I do that? We are almost there.'

Turlow flicked his wrist and his Banshee blade flew into his hand with frightening speed. 'Stop the boat now,' he demanded.

'Turlow,' Brendan said, 'what has gotten into you?'

'He is trying to kill us. He is going to turn us into Grey Ones. He is going to take us out to sea and we will all grow old and die.' Turlow took a step towards Red. 'Turn us around.'

'Banshees think that pointy things up their sleeves are the answer to everything,' Red said in his light-hearted manner. Then he turned stone-cold serious. 'Take one more step towards me with that sharp edge, Banshee, and you *will* go back – swimming.'

Turlow and Red stared at each other for a minute, then Turlow flicked his blade back up his sleeve and sat down.

'Good,' Red said, regaining his jovial tone. 'My island will not kill you, Banshee, nor will it turn you grey. Have any of you been to the Real World?'

Brendan and I sheepishly raised our hands.

'You will have to go further than my island to wither and die. The island will age you as fast as you aged in the Real World. Stay for eighty seasons and you will notice the difference.' Red looked out to sea and then quickly turned back to us with concerned eyes. 'You're not going to stay for eighty seasons, are you?'

A wooden dock loomed up ahead as our magical underwater motor died. Red fished the rings out of the water and reordered Araf and Tuan back to rowing duty.

'What was pulling us?' I asked.

Araf gave me a sideways look like he does when I make a Tir na Nogian social faux pas. It's apparently bad manners to ask how someone's magic works. Red didn't seem to mind but that didn't mean he was going to give me a straight answer.

'You were pulled by the past – into the future,' he said.

We followed Red on a narrow path through head-high vegetation. The trail didn't seem to be used much. Periodically it was so overgrown with gorse bushes that they caught and scratched at our clothing and faces.

'Red,' I called out from the back of the parade, 'where is the eel lake?'

He ignored me or maybe he was just lost in his own little world – both were possible. I passed my question up the line to Brendan, who only succeeded in getting Red's attention by tapping him on the shoulder. The message was relayed back to me like we were in a schoolyard playing a game of Chinese whispers.

Over his shoulder Araf said, 'He says we cannot go there today.'

'Why not?' I asked – then shouted to Brendan, 'Ask him why not.'

'Why don't you ask me yourself?' Red shouted back.

I waited then hollered, 'OK, why can't we go there today?'

'Because it is too late and you are almost at The Digs.'

'The whats?' I shouted and got no reply. Red had gone back into his hard-of-hearing mode.

The gorse thinned out and we came to a clearing. In the middle stood a wooden guest house not unlike the ones in the Pinelands.

'Welcome to The Digs. You can stay here the night.'

As we got closer it became obvious that no one had stayed in this place for a long, long time. Vines grew across the porch and there was so much dirt on the windows that Brendan had to wipe the glass with his sleeve to look in. Red opened the door and invited us to enter before him. Inside the only good light was from the window that Brendan had just cleaned. On the floor we left footprints in the quarter inch of dust that reminded me of astronauts on the moon.

'I see your housekeeper is on vacation,' I said, but Red wasn't behind me. I went outside and he wasn't there either. I walked the entire perimeter of the clearing but there was no Red. I went back inside.

'He's gone.'

'Who's gone?' Brendan asked.

'Red's gone, vanished into thin air.'

'Don't be silly,' Brendan said and went outside with everyone else to look for him. They all came back wearing my confused countenance. 'He's gone.'

'Gosh,' I said, 'is he?'

It was dark by the time we got the digs habitable. I just hoped that none of us had dust allergies 'cause if he did, he was going to keep all of us up all night. The stack of wood outside was mostly rotten but there was enough to get a decent fire going. Brendan found a dusty bottle of something. He uncorked it, had a sniff, thought better of it and put it back. The Digs may have been a bit neglected and forlorn but it was good to be inside with a roaring fire for a change.

We spoke into the night mostly about the strangeness of our host, but came to no conclusion except that our host was strange. After a light meal made from our dwindling rations Brendan decided to take a walk and I went with him.

'Are you OK?' I asked him as my breath fogged in the starlit night.

'You sound like I shouldn't be.'

'Well, you did seem pretty mad at yourself yesterday when you wrongly accused Turlow.'

'Oh that. I flew off the handle, for that I am mad at myself. But I'm not wrong about Turlow.'

'I beg your pardon?'

'It took a while but my cop radar tells me he is not to be trusted. I'm sure I was right about him, I just don't have any proof.'

'Your radar once thought I was a murderer.'

'No, it told me that there was something wrong with you, Conor, and I sure wasn't wrong there.'

'So what should I do, tie up Turlow 'cause your bunion is throbbing?'

'I'll figure it out, Conor, I always do. Just … don't turn your back on him.'

That night when I put my head on what I laughingly called my pillow I thought about my chat with the local cop. Part of me wanted to distrust Turlow. If Brendan had dissed King Banshee earlier in our trip I would have joined in but as much as I hated to admit it, I was begrudgingly starting to like the guy. I know I shouldn't put much stock in my nocturnal soothsaying but I had a feeling that if he really was betraying us, I would have dreamt about it. I put those thoughts aside and tried for the first time ever to direct my dreams. I closed my eyes and said to myself over and over again, 'Where are the red eels? Where are the red eels?' I fell asleep with that mantra in my head but it didn't work. The stupid image of Red grinning at me annoyed me not only during the day but in dreamland as well.

The next morning I awoke to see that same grinning face sitting next to a roaring fire inside The Digs. How Red could sneak in and rekindle our fire without waking us worried me. He was wearing a ridiculous outfit made from what looked like snake skin. Imagine a pair of crocodile lederhosen and you get the idea. He had fish cooking between a wire mesh. I expected him to say, 'Guten morgen,' but he just waved when he saw me.

'More fish for breakfast,' I said. 'Yum.'

He offered me a cup of tea and I accepted.

'When can we leave for Eel Lake?'

Apparently his hearing was fine this morning. 'I am waiting for you. I expected everyone to be up and ready to go. It is not an easy hike you know.'

I roused everyone and after a quick brekkie of mackerel and moss tea that surprisingly wasn't as bad as it sounds, we were out the door and heading towards the highlands in the middle of the island.

The trail to Eel Lake was worse than the one to The Digs. The gorse bushes often encroached on the path to a point where it was impossible to pass. Instead of hacking our way through, like I would have done in the Real World, we had to plead with the bushes to back off. It was slow going.

I tapped Red on the shoulder as we walked. I had made sure I was directly behind him so he couldn't ignore me. 'I thought you said you came up here a lot.'

'I do.'

'This doesn't look like a well-used path to me.'

'It's not.'

I waited but Red wasn't in an extrapolating mood. Sometimes it was easier when he ignored me. 'So how do you get up there?' I finally asked.

'I go an easier way.'

'So why aren't we going that way?'

'My way would not be easier for you.'

'Why not?' I asked a couple of times along with some shoulder taps, but Red was just as good at ignoring me when I was directly behind him as he was when I was at the end of the parade.

As the morning progressed the trail became much steeper. Whoever originally designed this route didn't bother with any of that zigzagging to make climbing easier stuff – when the mountain got steep, so did the path. Getting down on all fours became common. Eventually I wouldn't say we were hiking as much as rock climbing. An hour after missing my lunch, we finally took a break on a level shelf about two thirds of the way up. We were all, including Red, uncharacteristically exhausted. I wondered if our lack of stamina was due to being so far away from the immortality mojo of the mainland. It was a thought I kept to myself. We drank from a sparkling clear stream that fed into a small pond. Next to Gerard's wine it was the nicest thing I have ever drunk.

'So tell me, Son of Duir,' Red said, 'what are you going to do with these red eels when you find them?'

'I'm going to use them to cure my father.'

'Cure him? Of what?'

I didn't really want to tell him, but I didn't have the strength to lie so I explained about Dad reattaching his hand and how that same hand was killing him. Red's reaction surprised me. For the first time since I met him he looked truly interested.

'And what makes you think red eels will help?'

'Have you ever heard of the Grey Ones?'

'Oh,' Red said, 'I remember the Grey Ones.'

'I found an old manuscript that told of the Grey Ones' search for the blood of the red eels.'

Red was agitated and on his feet. 'This manuscript said red eels?'

'No, that's the translation into the common tongue. The scroll said they were searching for the blood of tughe tine. We came here 'cause a Pooka once called this place Tughe Tine Isle.'

Red placed both of his hands over his mouth to cover his surprise then threw his head back and began to laugh. If anyone else had done this it would have looked like they were losing it but with Red it strangely made him, for the first time, look sane.

'I should have known.' He stood and began to walk down the mountain.

'Wait a minute,' I said, grabbing him by the arm. Still laughing, he spun around like a rag doll. 'What should you have known?'

'I cannot believe I walked halfway up this mountain just so I could find out what you wanted with eels. Thank you for reminding me why I live alone.' He laughed again but then became angry. 'For the love of the gods – has The Land gotten so stupid that the Prince of Duir cannot even translate two simple words?' He grabbed my head with both hands and pulled my face close to his. '*Tine*, my feeble-minded gold miner, does not mean *red* it means *fire* and *tughe* does not mean *eel*. Do you not have scholars in Duir? Have you never heard of the Hall of Knowledge?'

'The Hall of Knowledge is gone.'

'Gone? What do you mean gone?'

'It was destroyed.'

Red grabbed me by my shirt and spun me to the left. I lost my footing and he fell on top of me still pulling my shirt with both fists. 'What have you done?' he said with fire in his eyes.

'I didn't do anything. I lost my grandfather there.'

Red let me go, stood and started back down the path. 'I cannot help you,' he said without turning around.

I chased after him. 'What does it mean? What does *tughe* mean?' I placed my hand on his shoulder. He stopped but didn't face me.

'It means … *worm*. Now leave my island.' He strode down the path with his arms outstretched, brushing the gorse bushes. As he did, they closed behind him. We couldn't have followed even if we wanted to.

The rest of the gang, mouths open, were on their feet.

'Does anyone know what just happened?' I asked.

Chapter Thirty-Two
The Invisible Man

It took a while before the gorse bushes let us pass. There was little talking on the way back. For the most part we concentrated on not plummeting.

Back at The Digs I volunteered to hike down to the beach and scrounge for driftwood. Tuan agreed to come with me and help persuade some fish to be our main course.

'What do we do now?' Tuan asked as we weaved our way through the gorse. 'Should we start digging for smoking worms?'

'I have no idea what to do.'

'Oh, that's not good. Conor, you are our ideas man.'

I made a guttural sound. It was meant to be a laugh but by the time it made it out of my mouth it was a pitiful grunt of a broken spirit. 'Well, start thinking up your own ideas, 'cause I'm fresh out.'

Tuan wisely didn't say anything else during our walk. I didn't blame him, even I wasn't happy with my own company. What the hell was I doing here? What if Red never comes back? What if this whole thing was a giant goose chase? What if Dad dies while I'm shipwrecked out here and I don't even get a chance to say good-bye?

My mood was no better back at The Digs in front of a roaring fire. When Brendan sat down next to me he had that look on his face, like he was going to bestow a pearl of wisdom.

Before he could open his mouth I said, 'Shut up.'

'Well, it looks like someone forgot to put on his feathered underwear today.'

'I got them on, Brendan, they're just damp – like everything else in my life. Leave me alone will you.'

'OK, maybe I'll just have a game of checkers with my good buddy Turlow. Where is he anyway?'

It wasn't until the food was ready that we all started asking the same question. We scouted as much of the perimeter as we dared in darkness but The Turlow was gone.

An hour of discussion over a cold dinner couldn't solve the mystery of what had happened to the Banshee. The only constructive product of the conversation was a plan to search for him at first light.

As I stood from the table I said, 'Maybe he's the only one of us with enough sense to abandon this stupid quest.' No one was disappointed when I went to bed.

Later Brendan sat on the edge of my bunk. 'Conor, I know about things being so bleak that it seems easier to give up. I've been there – but now is not the time.'

'I know and you're right,' I said without opening my eyes. It was exactly what I had been lying there thinking for the last hour. 'I'm sorry for my foul mood. Do me a favour, apologise to Tuan for me.'

Brendan nodded.

I made the effort and propped myself up on my elbows. 'I'm not giving up, Brendan. I'm just tired and scratched to hell and cold and … and too tired to even finish this sentence. We've been at this for a long time. I'm going to rest tonight – tomorrow I'll figure out how to save The Land.' I attempted a smile. 'I've done it before you know.'

I dropped my head back on my pillow with that thought on my mind. Sure I saved The Land once before but I had my dad with me then – without him I just didn't have a clue.

'Tomorrow,' I said, not even knowing if Brendan was still there. 'Things will all become clear tomorrow.'

Little did I know how prophetic that sentence would be.

That night was full of fits and starts punctuated by vivid and cryptic dreams. It seemed that the more experienced I became with dreaming the less understandable they were. I had almost given up trying to decipher any meaning in them. That night I dreamt I was in a mayonnaise jar filled with little smoking red-faced worms. I stabbed a tiny red earthworm and he slid away with the Lawnmower. In another dream the invisible man was back. During a phase of amateur psychoanalysis I had decided that the invisible man was me, but in this vision I dreamt that the invisible man was skulking around stealing stuff and I thought maybe it was Red. Red did have a creepy habit of sneaking up on us. I woke in the darkness and listened – nothing. I reached under my bed and strapped on the Sword of Duir then fell back into a fitful sleep. The last dream I had that night would have, under normal circumstances, shot me right out of bed. The invisible man pulled up a chair next to my bunk and stuck something into my shoulder. Then he reached to his collar and removed an amulet from around his neck – instantly he became visible.

When I opened my eyes I knew exactly what had been done to me – I didn't have to wonder. Once you have had one of my Aunt Nieve's paralysing pins stuck in your neck, you don't forget the sensation. This pin wasn't actually in my neck; it was in the top of my shoulder. Otherwise I wouldn't have been able to turn my head when I heard Turlow's voice.

'How do you spell butcher?'

Just like in my dream, Turlow was sitting in a chair next to my bed with his legs crossed as he casually wrote onto an emain slate.

'You're the invisible man.'

He looked up from the slate. 'I'm who?'

'You are the invisible man – I dreamt about you.'

'That, Conor, is not possible.'

'No, I did. I dreamt about you but I didn't know it was you. You were invisible. I saw you walking with Essa and talking to Cialtie, but I thought it was me. I didn't see that it was you until you took that amulet off your neck.'

Turlow stopped writing and poked the amulet that was now hanging around the emain slate. 'You and your uncle's dream vision is truly remarkable. You are the only ones that have ever seen even the tiniest bit past my *seithe* amulet.'

Seithe, I thought, searching the language database in my head. *Seithe means hide*.

'I suspect all of the dreamers in The Land will spot me now, but I had to use the amulet on the slate 'cause I don't want a reply to come through and erase this message before Red can read it.'

'That's Essa's slate I take it?'

He tilted his head in a gesture of false guilt. 'I always take the opportunity to steal something when I am in the Alderlands. The next time you are there, you should try it. Everyone always suspects a Brownie. But I don't imagine you will be visiting in the Alderlands any time soon – or ever.'

'So Brendan was right, you *are* Cialtie's lackey.'

He stopped his writing and looked sharply up. 'There are no lackeys here. Cialtie rightfully wants back his Oak Throne and I want the Banshees to finally hold the position they deserve in The Land.'

'Yeah, as Cialtie's lackeys.'

I thought for a second that he was going to hit me, but then he laughed. 'I find it very hard to be provoked by a person who can't move from the neck down.'

He had a point. I would have shrugged in agreement if I could have moved my shoulders. It was amazing how calm I was about all of this. Maybe 'cause last night I had already decided that I had failed, this was just the icing on the cake.

'How did you get one of my aunt's paralysing pins?'

'I have a bag full of them. Cialtie stole Nieve's recipe book and he still has a couple of Leprechaun goldsmiths under his protection – so to speak. I've been aching to use one of these on you for ages – if only to shut you up. I didn't know what I was going to do when I lost them and Essa's slate on the bottom of the sea. It took me all night to convince Red to get them for me.'

'How did Red get them?'

'Your uncle is right about you – you're not very clever. You know so little about Red *he* might as well be your invisible man. Now quiet, I have to finish this before he comes back.' Turlow bent back down to the slate and asked, 'How do you spell mortals?'

'What did you tell Red?'

'I just pointed out how you and that traitor Pooka over there destroyed the Tree of Knowledge, marooning all of the Pookas in their fur and then I told Red how you were planning to butcher him, so you could use his blood to bring an army of mortals over from the Real World to take over The Land.'

'Red's blood?'

'Like I said, Conor – there is a lot you don't know about our host.'

'And did he believe you?'

'Well, he hasn't talked to many people in a long time and I do lie particularly well, so yes, he did. And when I show him this letter here that *you* wrote – then I'm fairly sure he'll kill you. It would be better if Red kills you. That way I don't have to lie to Essa when she asks me if I did it – in case she uses that Owith glass she has. I'll tell you what, if she doesn't use that pesky truth crystal, I'll tell her that you died saving my life. Don't say I never did you any favours.'

'I wouldn't want to be you when she finds out.'

'She'll be dead before she finds out – along with everyone else in the Hall of Knowledge. The army of the Banshees and the Brownies will see to that.'

He finished forging the message and said, 'Time to meet Moran.'

'Who's Moran?'

Turlow let out an overly dramatic sigh as he stood up. 'Red is Moran.'

Moran, where had I heard that name? Yes, I remembered, he was the Pooka that left to start the colony of mermaids – the *Mertain*. Queen Rhiannon had said he was maybe the smartest Pooka that ever lived and that he could change into any animal.

'So what – does Red change into a worm?'

'Well well,' Turlow said as he grabbed me by the hair. 'The Faerie can be taught.'

Aunt Nieve's paralysing pin only meant that I couldn't move – it didn't mean that I couldn't feel pain. Turlow dragged me out of bed by my hair and then bumped me like an ironing board over empty bunks. My heels hit the floor hard as I was dragged backwards at a forty-degree angle through The Digs. Just inside the front door I saw Araf, Brendan and Tuan all vertical and propped against the wall. Araf was still curled up like he was asleep. Brendan had his arm outstretched as if to stop an attacker and Tuan looked like a toy soldier who had fallen backwards against the wall while at attention. As I was dragged past, their eyes frantically dashed back and forth in their sockets, but they couldn't speak. Turlow must have pinned them very high on their necks.

'Red is Moran,' I shouted over to Tuan. I saw his eyes widen just before the sunlight blinded me.

My heels slammed painfully into each of the steps that led down from the porch. It hurt like hell but I refused to let the Banshee hear me yelp. He finally propped me precariously up against a tall stump. When he let me go I slid and fell nose first into the hard ground. He didn't even try to catch me. When he propped me up again I spat in his face.

'Ooh,' he said, wiping his cheek with his sleeve, 'I was wondering when you would get a little fight in you.'

'Wouldn't you really like to fight me yourself – man to man? Take this pin out of my shoulder and grab a sword. Only lackeys use lackeys to do their dirty work for them.'

'Conor, I am The Turlow, I do not need to prove my manhood to anyone. I have long ago discovered that it is not the way of winning that matters, just the winning.'

'The ends justify the means.'

'Yes, well put.'

'I can see why you get along with my uncle so well. Tell me, Turlow. Where were you when I cut Cialtie's hand off? Were you in Castle Duir?'

'No, I was in the Reedlands.'

'You're welcome,' I said with a snort.

'For what?'

'I saved your life.'

Turlow shook his head. 'Cialtie told me that you would say something like that.'

'Yeah, 'cause he knew it was true. He tried to kill you.'

Turlow wasn't listening any more. He looked past me – I couldn't turn my head far enough to see what he was looking at. He walked towards me and stuck another one of Aunt Nieve's pins in me. This time in my neck, then he removed the one in my shoulder. I could no longer turn my head and when I tried to speak I found that I no longer could do that either. All I could do was look straight ahead as a strong gust of wind from behind whisked my hair into my face.

'Good morning, Moran,' Turlow said as Red appeared in my peripheral vision.

Red walked around me. All of the previous frippery in his demeanour was now gone. He eyeballed me like a general inspecting his troops.

'What do you have to say for yourself?' Red asked me. When I said nothing he asked, 'Can he speak?'

'He could speak if he chose,' Turlow lied, 'but he knows he is caught. I found him writing this letter to his father – the father that is *supposed* to be encased in glass.' Turlow showed Red the message on the face of the emain slate.

'I am sorry for bringing these troubles to your island,' Turlow said, 'but I must go. I must make the tide and I must warn my people of what I have just learned.'

'Of course, Banshee,' Red said, 'and thank you for bringing them to me. I have been away from the treachery of The Land for too long. Where is the Pooka traitor and the others?'

'They are in The Digs – dead. They put up quite a struggle when I found them out. It is a mess in there, I wouldn't go inside.'

'Thank you, Banshee. It is about time I had new digs.'

Red bowed and Turlow returned it, then with the tiniest of smiles to me he turned and jogged to the beach path.

Red crouched down and covered his face with his clenched fists – then he stopped and stood up. 'Have you nothing to say for yourself, tree killer, before I send you and your cohorts to the pyre?'

From Red's point of view I must have looked like the coldest of criminals. I just stood and stared – inside I was screaming.

Red walked up to me. 'Do you not even want another lesson in translation? I told you that *tughe* means worm but worm is an old word. Do you not want to know what worm means in the common tongue? No? Well I'll tell you anyway – no wait, better yet, I'll show you.'

He took off his shirt and then the kilt-like thing he had around his waist. Even though no one could hear it and I couldn't even say it, a wisecrack sprang into my mind along the lines of 'What worm are you talking about?' He dropped down on to one knee and once again placed his balled fists in front of his face in a gesture of intense concentration. I had seen Pooka changes before and it is always impressive but I had never seen anything like this. Not only did it look impressive but it sounded impressive. First he went red – not redhead red but cooked lobster red. Then fist-sized scales clinked into place as he got big. First he got bull big, then elephant big and finally dinosaur big. He raised his head at the same time that his wings fully extended. Of course, I said to myself, worm means – *dragon*.

I think this would have been one of the most magnificent moments in my life if it hadn't been ruined by the realisation that momentarily I would be dead. I could hardly blame Dragon Red, in his eyes all he saw was a cold-hearted expressionless killer. He didn't see my knees knocking 'cause I couldn't move them and he didn't even see me open my mouth in wonder 'cause I was frozen solid. I must have looked like a man prepared to die for his sins.

Dragon Red rocked his huge spiny head back and forth then placed his snout inches from mine. Smoke seeped out from between his fangs, my eyes watered and my nose burned from the smell of brimstone. Then he cocked his head back like a snake getting ready to strike. I saw the hair that was hanging in front of my eyes curl and burn as he sent a fireball the size of a car past me. It was aimed directly at The Digs.

Chapter Thirty-Three
Graysea

I didn't see the fireball hit but I sure as hell felt it. It felt like I had been clubbed with a refrigerator. The fire passed and surrounded me as I flew through the air like a test dummy at ground zero during an atomic bomb test. The first thing I did was to pat my head to make sure my hair wasn't on fire and then I realised that I could. The blast must have knocked Nieve's pin out of my neck. I turned to see The Digs completely engulfed in flames.

I was instantly on my feet. 'ARAF, BRENDAN,' I screamed. I started running around to the far side of The Digs hoping that the fire was not so fierce on that side. Hoping I could get them out of there.

'TUAN!'

I looked around to get help from Red, to tell him that they were alive in there, but he was nowhere to be seen. At the rear of The Digs, flames were pouring out the back door. I took one step towards it and that's the last thing I remember.

The pain was excruciating. I suspected from the way it was hanging from my hip, that I had broken my left leg. My head was bleeding like a stuck pig and there was intense pain in my shoulders where the talons pierced my flesh. But the worst agony came from the sight, hundreds of feet below me, of The Digs completely and totally engulfed in flames. There was no way that Araf, Brendan and Tuan made it out. My friends had been burned alive. I retched and then watched as the contents of my stomach sailed down between my legs, then were dispersed by the wind until they landed in the sea below.

I looked up, a painful and difficult thing to do when you are hung from your shoulders.

'YOU IDIOT!' I shouted at Red. 'YOU KILLED THEM.' I'm sure that with the sound of the rushing wind and considering the substantial distance I was from the huge dragon's head, that Red wasn't ignoring me – he simply couldn't hear – but the memory of Red's games on the island came to mind and made my blood boil. I kicked and screamed some more.

'YOU KILLED THEM AND I'M GOING TO KILL YOU. YOU MURDERER.'

I instinctively reached for the Lawnmower and was shocked to find it hanging at my side. I drew it and slashed at his talon. That got his attention. He screeched and let go of my right shoulder, swinging me to the left. Then he banked sharply right – this swung me up, under his underbelly. The scales there were thinner and a pale yellow-green. I knew I would never get a better chance – I jabbed the Lawnmower as I was propelled up towards Red's belly. The sword found a spot between two scales and it sank almost half its length into the body of the huge beast. Blood spurted out of the wound. Red let go of me and I lost my grip on the Lawnmower. As I fell I saw the huge red dragon flapping away with the Sword of Duir sticking out of his belly.

As I have mentioned before, time usually slows down for me when I'm in mortal peril but I didn't need it in this situation. I was so far up in the air I had a lot of time to assess my dire circumstances. I was plummeting to earth at terminal velocity without the aid of a parachute or even a comedy umbrella. If the fall didn't kill me, I was going to land in the sea about half the way between Red's island and another island behind it. It didn't look like a distance I could swim, even without a broken leg. The major irony was that I was covered with dragon's blood – the blood of the tughe tine. The stuff that I had spent so long searching for, the thing that I had travelled so far for and had lost so many friends because of – the blood was all over me, in my hair, on my face, soaked in my clothes and I was about to plunge in the ocean where I would have the privilege of watching it wash away as I drowned.

I stretched my hands out to my sides and used the air current to slowly spin me around. I took in my last look of the beautiful islands on the edge of The Land. Then I shouted, 'I'm sorry, Dad!' and slammed into the water.

'Who is Brendan?'

She was blurry but I could see that she had long blonde hair and was dressed all in white. I know it's corny and clichéd but trust me, if you see someone that looks like that immediately after having an almost certain death experience, you too will think it's an angel and like me – it'll freak you out.

'He is friend,' I croaked. 'There was … fire. Is he here?'

As she came into focus I saw that she was certainly pretty enough to be an angel. Disappointingly she had no wings but I had a faint image of her floating in the air – or was it … water. Then two things happened that dispelled my illusion of being in heaven. First I tried to get up and was racked with the most enormous wave of pain and secondly my angel giggled. Maybe I could deal with an afterlife that had pain in it but under no circumstances should angels be allowed to giggle.

She lifted my head and put a small glass of liquid to my lips. 'You say the funniest things,' she said as I drank. The liquid was very pleasant, which made me think that it wasn't medicine, but when I tried to speak I realised just how wrong I was. Like with one of Aunt Nieve's paralysing pins, I couldn't move or speak, but unlike my aunt's pins, this was quite pleasant. I drifted off into a dream of heaven filled with giggling angels.

The next time I came to I was mentally in better shape. I was in a cave – a very nice cave. Bottles filled with brightly coloured liquids, as well as unusual scientific instruments and perfectly folded linens, sat on shelves that were carved directly out of sparkling stone walls. Light came from coral-looking glowing things that sat on almost every surface. I touched the one that was on the table next to my bed and I heard it (or felt it in my head) ask me if I wanted it brighter or darker. I asked it to tell me where I was but 'brighter or darker', was about the extent of its vocabulary. I braced myself for the coming pain as I tried to sit up and was delighted to find that I didn't hurt that much, but then I made the mistake of looking under the bed for my clothes – all of the blood rushed to my head and my vision began to darken. Maybe I wasn't in as good a shape as I thought. I pulled myself back, laid my head on the pillow and closed my eyes until the dizziness passed.

I was in this position when my angel zoomed into the room. She was beyond me by the time I opened my eyes. I sat up to watch her golden hair bounce as she knelt down and placed a stack of towels on a low shelf. I was going to say something but instead I just watched her. When she stood she kept her back straight; the way she moved reminded me of a dancer. Finally she turned – and to my forever shame, as she turned – I screamed. She was old – really old. Now don't get me wrong, I don't go around screaming at old people and she wasn't hideous or anything, as a matter of fact she was a very attractive old person. It's just that you get out of the habit of seeing older people in The Land and, also, I wasn't expecting it.

She placed her hands on her hips and said, 'Do I look that scary?'

I started to answer her but I couldn't figure out how to explain why I screamed when I saw her face, so I just said, 'Sorry.' She walked behind me and roughly took my head in her hands. 'What are you …?'

'Shush,' she said and I did. Then she said 'Hmmm,' in a knowing sort of a way that made me want to ask her what was wrong with me but before I could say anything, she left.

I lay there for a long while listening and then dozed off until I heard the old woman saying, 'Faerie, oh Faerie man.'

I opened my eyes and saw the old nurse and her twin – except maybe eighty years younger – my giggling angel.

'I imagine this is the one you were expecting,' the senior nurse said. 'I am sure you will find that she is not as scary as me.'

I looked up with an apologetic gesture but still failed to say anything other than 'Sorry.'

'Pathetic,' she said, shaking her head as she left.

'She *is* a little scary,' giggling angel said and then giggled. 'I do not think she likes you very much, Faerie man.'

'Conor,' I said.

She looked confused and turned her head like a baffled puppy. 'What does Conor mean?'

'It's my name. I am Conor.'

'Oh,' she said, placing her hand up over her face, laughing. 'Oh, I'm very pleased to meet you, Conor,' she said and then did a little curtsey.

'And yours?'

'And my what?' she said, again with that head tilt.

'Your name? What's your name?'

'Oh' – giggle – 'my name is Graysea.'

'It is a pleasure to meet you, Graysea.'

'And it's a pleasure to meet you, Conor.'

'You already said that.'

'Did I? Oops.'

'So tell me, Graysea, where am I and how long have I been here?'

'Oh, so many questions. Which answer do you want first?'

'I don't mind, either.'

'OK,' she said. 'Um … what were the questions again?'

'Let's start with where am I?'

'You're in the Grotto of Health.'

'And where is that?'

That question stymied her for a minute before she came up with, 'In the Grotto of Health.'

'OK, how long have I been here?'

'Ever since I brought you here.'

That was not quite an answer to my question but it was a nugget of information. 'You brought me here?'

'Uh huh.'

'And where did you find me?'

'In the water.'

'And what were you doing in the water?'

'Flying.'

'Don't you mean swimming?'

'I don't think so.'

I took a deep breath and started again. 'So you were *flying* in the water when you just came across me drowning?'

'Oh no, I saw Tughe Tine drop you. That's why I came.'

'You saw the dragon drop me?'

'Oh, everyone did. We don't see Moran very often – usually only once every twenty years at the blood fete.'

'What happens at the blood fete?'

'That's when Moran gives dragon blood to the King so he won't grow old. Don't you know about that?'

'I've heard something about it.'

This seemed to please her. I sat up higher in bed and as I did I winced where my side hurt. Graysea unabashedly pulled back my sheet and asked me where it hurt. I pointed to my side and she told me to 'Scoot over.' Then she sat next to me in the bed, placed her hand on my rib, put her feet up on the bed and crossed her ankles. With her free hand she placed into her mouth a silvery shell that was hanging around her neck by a string of tiny pearls. I watched as her neck thickened, then three slits appeared that began to open and close like a beached fish gasping for air. When I looked down I wasn't that surprised to see that her feet had changed into one fin. Her fingers, now webbed, pressed hard against my rib. That caused a sharp stab of pain that instantly disappeared as Graysea made a deep gasping noise. She reached up and removed the shell from her mouth and by the time I looked at her fin, it was feet again.

'Oh, that one was broken,' she said, getting up and rubbing her own side. 'I'm sorry we missed that.'

I covered myself up and then flexed the rib. It didn't hurt at all. 'How did you do that?'

'I took your hurt and then lost it during The Change. That's what we do here. It took quite a few of us a long time to heal you. What happened?'

'Have you ever seen a hawk swoop down and catch a rabbit?'

Graysea nodded yes, but wrinkled her nose to show that she didn't like it.

'Well, that's what happened to me.'

'You said lots of funny things in your sleep.'

'Like what?'

'Mostly you said "Brendan, Araf and Tuan".'

I wasn't expecting that and her words stabbed me with a pain worse than my broken rib. I tried to push the thought of them being burned alive out of my mind. I knew I would have to deal with the emotions of that loss – but later – I didn't have the strength now. I turned my face away from Graysea and slammed my eyelids closed, willing them not to leak. When I looked back, Graysea was upset.

'Oh, oh what have I done?'

'No, it's OK. They are friends that I have lost. It's not your fault.'

'Oh, no, I'm not supposed to upset patients. Oh, I have to get matron.' She turned and ran out of the room. There was no way to stop her.

A couple of minutes later the older nurse came in and stood at the foot of my bed with her arms crossed. 'Graysea says that you are upset.'

'I think she is more upset than me.'

'What happened? What did you do to her?'

'I didn't do anything. She just mentioned the names I have been speaking in my sleep for the last ... How long have I been here?'

'Nine days.'

'Wow, I've been here for nine days?'

'What did you say to her?'

'Oh, nothing, she just said the names of my companions that ... they were killed during my ... adventure. She took me by surprise and I turned away for a second. Honest, I told her it was OK but she bolted out of the room.'

The matron uncrossed her arms and her countenance softened. 'She is a sensitive little fishy.' She pushed the sheet away from my feet, held both ankles and closed her eyes performing what I presumed was some sort of examination. 'So how did you like your chat with our Graysea?'

'It was … interesting.'

'I bet. I should have warned you about the rule of having a successful conversation with her.'

'And what would that be?'

'Don't ask her any questions.'

We both laughed. 'Hey, sorry about screaming when I first saw you. I really—'

She waved her hand and cut me off. 'Don't give it a second thought. If I had seen me when I expected her – I would have screamed too.' She came behind me and held my head with both hands; when I started to talk she shushed me again. 'Actually there are some mornings I want to scream when I look in the mirror.'

'Can I ask you a couple of questions?'

'You can ask.'

'You are mermaids – right?'

'Oh my, that is word I haven't heard in a long while, but yes – I am Mertain.' She pulled my sheet away. 'OK, Faerie, let's see if you can walk.'

'You wouldn't have my clothes around, would you?'

'It's nothing that I have never seen before.'

'Still,' I said, standing with my hands in front of my dangly bits, 'I think you have seen enough for today.'

She said she didn't know where my clothes were, so she gave me a white robe, the same as she and Graysea were wearing. I put some weight on my leg and it felt good. 'It's a little stiff but no pain. It was broken wasn't it?'

'Actually it was dislocated at the hip. What in the sea happened to you?'

'I got pounced on by a dragon.'

'Moran pounced on you?'

I nodded yes.

'Ouch.'

I walked around the room and everything seemed to be OK. I had a twinge in my knee and the matron had me sit while she did her fish trick and then it felt fine.

'Would you mind if I ask you how old you are?'

'Yes.'

'Sorry, I don't want to upset you. I'm just trying to sort some stuff out in my head.'

'And what does my age have to do with your head?'

'Well, I think I'm on one of the islands off Fearn Point.'

'You're under one actually.'

'Under?'

'You're in an underwater cave about half a league under Mertain Isle.'

'That's sounds deep.'

'It is. Healing is faster this far down.'

'How did I get here?'

'You will see when you go back up.'

'Which will be when?'

'Soon,' she said. 'I think you are ready to travel and I'll tell them that – once you stop asking me questions. So what does this have to do with my age?'

'Well, I figure you must grow old out here, except for the King …'

'How do you know that?'

'Graysea told me.'

'You got information like that out of our Graysea – I am impressed.' She folded her arms again. 'Go on.'

'I guess I just want to know how fast people age out here. Is it as fast as in the Real World?'

'I do not think so,' the matron said, 'if you must know I am under a thousand.'

'OK, so no then. And let me say you don't look a day over five hundred.'

That got my usual dirty look. 'You are obviously well enough to answer the King's questions. I imagine his school will be here shortly for your ascent.'

'School?'

'Yes, the King's guard.'

'Oh, mermaids, fish – schools. I get it.'

The matron shook her head and left.

Chapter Thirty-Four
The Mertain King

It took a half an hour before the school came to escort me to the King. I tried to rest but every time I put my head down I saw an image of Araf, Tuan and Brendan with wide terrified eyes, being burned alive. I just didn't have the strength to think about it. I tried using a Fili mind mantra but eventually I just had to get up. I spent most of the time before the guards came peeping into all of the nooks and crannies, searching for my clothes. I didn't find them so I guess I was doomed to go to see the King in my nightgown, which I suppose was better than my recurring nightmare of going naked.

Matron and Graysea walked me to a larger cave containing a beach and an underground lake. Waiting for me were six humourless macho thugs – the school. A couple of days previously I would have cracked a few jokes about them being a bit old for school, but it seemed that Moran killed my sense of humour along with my friends. In the centre of the lake was the top of a car-sized submerged brass dome.

'Get in,' the senior guard said.

'How do I get in there?'

'You swim, Faerie,' the matron said. 'Follow Graysea; she will show you the way.'

'Aren't you coming with us?'

'It is very close quarters in the pressure chamber and I am certain that you would rather have Graysea scrunched in with you than me.'

'I don't know, after the initial shock you're not so bad.'

She scowled at me but it had a smile in it. 'Good luck, Faerie.'

Graysea took my arm and walked into the water. I stuck one toe in and then popped it right back out again. 'It's freezing.'

Graysea giggled, grabbed me by the wrist and said, 'Come on.' That girl was stronger than she looked. I hit the water and my body exploded with cold. I screamed so loud I was sure that the walls of the cave above the water must have collapsed and crashed down on matron like a bad guy's lair in a British super-spy movie. Swimming was out of the question. I struggled to get back to the surface but then Graysea, equipped with her flipper bottom half, zoomed me through the water into the underside of the pressure dome. She placed my shivering hands onto the railings before she was finally forced to push me up the stairs with her shoulder. I was beyond cold and just shy of being cryogenically preserved. I flopped down on a metal deck, dripping wet and rattling my teeth so hard I was sure I was going to crack a molar.

Graysea knelt next to me, looking like she had just stepped out of a garden on a summer's day. 'Dry off,' she said.

'I cccccaaaaan't mmmoove.'

She placed her hand on my robe and it instantly dried itself and me. Then it lengthened and heated up. She tucked the material around my feet and slowly I started to thaw out.

'How did you do that?'

'You can do it too. Your robe is made of kelp. If you are nice to it, it will do what you ask.'

Just as my core temperature was reaching the point where I could talk without sounding like I was riding over cobblestones on a bicycle, the chamber began to move. I looked over the side of the metal platform we were lying on and saw the ocean floor moving horizontally. Periodically a mermaid would zoom past the hole in the floor.

'Aren't they going to close a hatch or something?'

'Why?' Graysea said as we lurched upward.

I looked over the railing and saw the ocean floor disappear at an alarming rate.

'Because I really don't want to—'

I didn't get to finish that quip 'cause that's when the first pressure change hit me. Pain exploded in my ears and Graysea, looking uncomfortably worried, told me to swallow to equalise the pressure. I wanted to tell her that I wasn't an idiot and I had been doing that, but the pain was too intense to allow me to speak. Graysea cuddled up beside me as a spark of pain hit me in the ears, which was so bad I thought I was going to pass out. When I pulled my hand from my head it was covered with blood. Graysea placed her hands on both sides of my head and I felt her flipper flap against my leg. The pain subsided and when I turned to look she was changing back from a fish already. We didn't have much time to talk – the ascent must have happened at a phenomenal speed. In the process I punctured both eardrums – my right one twice. Closer to the surface I started to get pains like I had never experienced before. Tiny strange twinges in my joints grew to the point where I started praying that I would soon die.

'What is happening?'

'I am stopping your blood from boiling – shush,' she said as she hugged me from behind. Her legs changed from fish to feet with increasing speed – each change brought blessed relief.

By the time we felt the chamber bob to the surface, the two of us were physically spent. Graysea was crying and I held her.

'Are you all right?'

Sobbing, she didn't say anything but nodded her head yes.

'Thank you,' I said, holding her until her crying turned to sniffles.

I wiped the tears from her eyes. She was remarkably beautiful, my giggling angel, and it pained me to see her cry. When she finally had the strength to return my smile, I couldn't resist it – I kissed her.

That, of course, is the position that the captain of the King's school found us in. Graysea got up so fast she banged her head and it rang in the chamber like a bell. My body felt like I had tripped at the opening gun of a marathon and had been trampled by the subsequent five hundred runners. Graysea didn't look like she was moving all that well either until she hit the water and then she … she flew. I doggie paddled underwater until I broke the surface and saw that we were like a mile from an island. I wasn't sure I was going to make it but my choice was either swimming or drowning, so I started kicking. Graysea saw me struggling and swam up under me. She turned her back and gestured for me to place my hands on her shoulders. I did and she reached up, grabbed both my wrists and dived straight down underwater. We went so fast the water scrunched my face like an astronaut during a rocket launch. After travelling to what felt like forty thousand leagues under the sea, she turned and we broke the surface, clearing the water by at least ten feet. If Graysea was giggling, I couldn't hear it over my screaming. We were on the beach in no time.

As I crawled to the shore I said, 'Warn me next time you do that.'

She tilted her head. 'Do what?'

Standing shivering on solid ground I willed my robe to dry. It did, but also shrank to the size of a halter top. Graysea ran over quickly and made it become a full-sized, dry, warm robe again.

'You shouldn't do that here,' she said with a disapproving look.

'Thanks, I'll remember that.'

The walk to the royal residence was a quick march along the sand. Not that I could feel the sand, my feet were like blocks of ice. None of the Mertain, I noticed, wore shoes. I found out later that if their feet were cold or sore all they had to do was a quick change and everything was back to warm baby softness again. It was a trick the Pookas of the Pinelands hadn't learned. When their animal selves are injured they carried their injuries through the change.

The King had a cool beach house that had a wide porch-like jetty that stuck out over the water. Graysea had told me that the King was old – when I asked how old, she said, 'Old old.'

Me and my frozen feet were escorted to the royal porch where I stood and waited for about a quarter of an hour. Finally I sat on the decking and tried to instruct my robe to cover my feet, but I only succeeded in making it turn pale blue – the same colour as my toes. Talking to this robe was like trying to communicate with a blind Chinese guy. I decided to give up 'cause I didn't want to be left in a miniskirt when the King arrived.

A huge whoosh startled me to my feet as the King vaulted out of the water and landed dry as bone, on his feet, on his porch. It was a very ostentatious entrance but I must admit – impressive. I'm sure if I could do it, I would do it all the time too.

I shouldn't have worried about showing off my legs 'cause this guy's kelp robe looked like a very short Roman toga. He seemed youngish, late twenties or early thirties, but the weird thing about him was that he had absolutely no hair. Not on his head, not on his legs and, disconcertingly, no eyebrows. He paced back and forth, never once actually looking at me.

'Why were you dropped by Tughe Tine?' he asked the sea.

'Your Highness, that is a long story – that I am happy to tell you but right now I think I'm going to either faint or go into hypothermic shock. Can we have this chat inside over a cup of tea?'

He finally looked me straight in the eyes. He was as humourless as his bodyguards. I tried desperately not to stare at the space where his eyebrows should have been.

'Tell me, what are your dealings with the dragon?'

As he spoke my teeth started chattering again. My cold brain started to slip into that state where I just didn't care what happened to me any more – I got lippy. 'Do you know who I am?'

In response the King snarled – I was beyond caring.

'I'm the friggin' Prince of Duir and I deserve better than this. Now, I'm happy to answer any of your questions but only over a cup of tea and with a blanket over my feet.'

The only good thing about the Mertain dungeon was that it was warm. I got a cup of water and a leathery piece of dried fish. The fish smelled like sulphur but then so did the rest of the place. I'm sure that if I lived in that cell on a diet of baked beans, no one would notice.

At that moment in my life, a dungeon was not a good place for me to be. It wasn't just that it was damp and dark and dingy. The main problem was that there was nothing for me to do, so I was forced to live with my thoughts – and they were far from comforting. War was coming to the Hazellands. I needed to get off this rock to warn everybody about Turlow, but even if I could get out of this cell, I had no idea how to get back to the Tir na Nog mainland.

I had no idea how Dad was. The last thing I had heard was that he was slowly getting worse. Was that still the case, or was his condition rapidly worsening? Or was he dead?

I didn't have to wonder if my travelling companions were dead. I hoped that somehow their end was swift but in my heart I knew it wasn't and it was all my fault. I should have insisted that Brendan stay in Duir and I should have listened to him when he told me not to trust Turlow. If I ever got out of here, I knew I would have to go back to the Real World and try to explain to his mother and daughter about how he had died trying to help me. I dreaded that moment almost as much as having to tell Queen Rhiannon what had happened to her Tuan. The last thing she had said to me was, 'Look after my son.' If there was one thing I didn't do on this trip, that was look after anybody. And I lost Araf – first Fergal and now Araf – there is just so much a heart can take. Not hearing Araf not speaking was deafening in its silence.

I tried not to think about how they died. I tried to push it out of my mind but with nothing else to distract me in my prison's gloom, the imagined images of their agonising death overwhelmed me until I was curled up into a foetal ball, openly weeping on the dungeon floor.

That was the position that the King of the Mertain found me in. I heard the sound of a throat clearing and looked up to see his face in the barred window of the door. 'This is how a Prince of Oak acts.'

I didn't stand but I did sit up. I wiped my cheeks with my knees. 'You don't know what I have lost.'

'No loss would make me act like that,' he said.

'No,' I said, looking fully at him for the first time. 'No, this would never happen to you 'cause you have lost it all anyway. You may have followed Moran out of the Pinelands and escaped the dependency of hazel but you have lost what it means to be human – no, you have lost what it means to be Pooka.'

The King's eyes grew wide in surprise. 'How do you know of Moran and the hazel?'

I stood, reached into my collar and pulled out my athrú medallion. 'I know these things 'cause I am barush.'

Well, what a difference one little word and a necklace can make. Guards were called and I was taken to a royal guest suite where I was fed and bathed. I even had my back scrubbed and my face shaved by mermaids. It's not often you can say that and yes, it's as nice as it sounds. After a short nap I was escorted *inside* the King's abode and sure enough, there was a blanket and a cup of tea waiting.

'My apologies, Prince Conor, for my previous abrupt manner; I am unaccustomed to visitors and your arrival, it must be said, was troubling.'

I came real close to saying, 'Just don't do it again,' but instead I apologised for my own behaviour.

'So, Son of Duir, you have a cup of tea and a blanket, will you now tell me what your relationship with my brother is?'

'Your brother?'

'Yes, Moran is my brother.'

I squinted my eyes and tilted my head a bit, then in my mind's eye I used an orange crayon to draw hair and eyebrows on the King. Sure enough he was Red's hairless twin. 'I see it now,' I said. 'Has your brother always been that strange?'

'I believe I have waited long enough for my answers,' he said but then a tiny smile crossed his lips, 'but I shall answer one last question of yours. Yes.'

So I spewed out the whole tale again. It seemed that on this trip to The Land I was doomed to constantly meet people and tell them my entire life story. I was getting pretty good at it. The last bit was hard to tell but I got through it without choking up – just. I finished by saying, 'So as you can see I must get back to the mainland as soon as possible. Can you help me?'

The King sat and stared for a while. I took that as a testament to my superior story-telling ability – he was stunned into silence. Finally he said, 'I can and I will.' For the first time in a long while my spirits rose only to have them dashed by his next sentence. 'As soon as Moran arrives to verify your story.'

'When is Red due?'

'My brother comes and goes as he pleases but he will definitely be here for the blood fete.'

'And when is that?'

'In three years.'

Chapter Thirty-Five
The Stream

When he finally let me out of his dungeon again, the King explained that he *had to* lock me up 'cause I insulted him in front of his guards. I was surprised that he knew what a 'trumped-up spineless guppy' meant but I guess the tone was pretty clear. He only made me sit in his sulphur pit for a day.

When I was released I was shown to a little beach shack and was told I had the freedom of the island. I went back to the King's royal beach house but the guards there wouldn't let me enter and finally told me that the King was elsewhere. I doggedly sat in front of the house for three days waiting for his return. I waited and thought. Thoughts filled with dead friends, a dying father and a disappointed family and clan. If I had owned a neurology textbook I would have performed a self-lobotomy. I had to get out of there.

There was always food outside my shack in the mornings and in the evenings but I never saw anyone put it there. No one came near me. After two stints in the King's dungeon, not many of the Mertain had the courage to talk to me. There was obviously no ex-con chic culture going on in Mermaid Island.

My only contact was with two kids. They had obviously been told to stay away from the dangerous Faerie. So obviously they didn't. They would hide in bushes until I passed and then dare each other to touch the back of my robe. I remembered being a kid myself and throwing snowballs at cars. The fun wasn't in the throwing – the fun was when the driver got out and chased us. I usually saw the kids hiding but pretended not to until after they touched me, then I would roar and chase after them. I mean, what's the point of being a monster if you can't scare kids?

On this particular day, I just couldn't stare at the King's beach house any more. I went for a walk to clear my mind. It seemed all of my injuries from being swooped on by a dragon had healed. I tested my legs with a jog and it felt pretty good. In the distance I saw the two pint-sized Mertains hiding so I quickly changed direction, doubled back and came up behind them as they were craning their heads out of the bushes trying to see where I had gotten to. I rushed them screaming, 'I want filet-o-fish!' I think one of them wet himself, but you can't really tell with those quick-drying robes of theirs. As I vaulted after them through a bush, I practically ran into Graysea.

'What in the sea are you doing?' she said, crossing her arms.

'I'm scaring the crap out of little kids. What does it look like I'm doing?' I then explained that tormenting these guys was pretty much the only contact I had with any of the Mertain since the King had thrown me into his dungeon – twice.

Graysea took me by the arm and we found the kids. She made us apologise to each other and shake hands. A shame really – I'm sure they were going to miss their dangerous game.

She told me that she had gone back to work at the Grotto of Health and this was the first time she could convince the matron to get some time off.

'I think one of the guards told her that we were kissing.'

'Oh,' I said, 'sorry about that.'

'Are you?' she replied with a shy smile. 'I'm not.'

I spent a lovely day walking the beaches with Graysea. As much as I tried to convince myself that I was fine with my own company, just talking to her made me realise how lonely I had been. She gave me lessons in the care and feeding of my robe. I had mentioned that it had recently been ignoring me and she told me that that was 'cause it hadn't been in the ocean for a long time. We took a swim that wasn't so bad after Graysea taught me how to regulate my robe's warmth and then she coached me in the subtler ways of making it lengthen and even change colour.

Once again I blurted out my life story (conspicuously leaving out any mention of Essa). Graysea was particularly interested in my father's illness and thought the King was being unreasonable by not helping. The day ended with a campfire on the beach before she swam back to work the midnight shift, which matron insisted she be on time for. If I said there was no kissing involved, I'd probably be lying.

The next day the war between me and the mini-Mertains was back with a vengeance. The little twerps obviously realised that détente was dull and began tormenting me by throwing pebbles. I ignored them, even when the pebbles got bigger, until one of them hit me in the head with a rock. Now I was chasing them for real. If I caught them I was going to kill the little dirt-bags. Fortunately for all of us Graysea appeared right before I caught the littler one.

'He started it,' I said to Graysea when she had once again got the three of us around a peace table.

'I did not,' the bigger one said.

'You did too – you threw a rock at my head.'

He put on the most angelic of smiles and turned to Graysea. 'We were just quietly playing and he tried to attack us. We feared for our lives.'

'You little—' I said as Graysea stopped me from grabbing the smiling liar by his neck. 'I hope you find a jellyfish in your trousers the next time you go swimming.'

Graysea patted the little future politician on the head, promising that 'the mean old Faerie' would never bother him again.

'You really shouldn't scare them so,' she said after the boys skipped off cackling to themselves.

I started to protest but instead just said, 'Sorry,' vowing to myself that the next time I saw the brats they'd really be in fear of their lives.

'Come with me,' my dizzy mer-friend said, 'I have a surprise for you – actually two surprises.'

She took me by the hand and led me across the island. It was so good to see Graysea again. You may find this hard to believe but walking hand in hand with a beautiful mermaid is preferable to being hit in the head with rocks.

After about an hour of walking, during which Graysea infuriatingly refused to tell me what her surprises were, we climbed over a bluff of rocks and then down onto a small beach. At the edge of the sand sat a conspicuous pile of branches. Graysea, looking and acting like a magician's lovely assistant, pushed away the brush to reveal Tuan's portable boat.

'Surprise!' she said, jumping up and down.

'That's our boat,' I said as I gave it a closer look. 'Where did you find it?'

'I saw it ages ago drifting all by itself on the far side of Inis Tughe Tine. So I went back to see if it was still there – and it was.'

'Did you find oars?'

'You don't need oars.' She reached into the bow of the boat and took out two metal rings attached to a rope. They were exactly like the ones that Red had on his boat. 'I'll pull you back to the mainland.'

'Are you strong enough?'

'It will be easy – I'll take The Stream.'

'The Stream?'

'There is a sea current that travels around Tir na Nog. I can find The Stream and then it will be easy to fly through the water. I can do it in my sleep.'

'You can swim and sleep?'

'Not my whole brain, silly,' she said, playfully slapping my chest, 'I can only sleep one side of my brain while I swim.'

'You can sleep one side of your brain at a time?'

She leaned in and spoke as if it was a secret. 'Some people think half my brain is asleep most of the time – and they'd be right.'

'So I can get off this island,' I said as the realisation dawned on me. 'I can warn my friends.'

'Yes,' she said, and I joined her jumping up and down.

'When can we go?'

'Now.'

'Thank you, Graysea, they are wonderful surprises.'

Graysea stopped jumping. 'No, that's only one surprise.'

'Really? What's the other?'

She reached into a pocket and handed me a small glass vial that was set into a gold mesh sleeve. Inside was a dark liquid.

'What's this?'

'It is dragon's blood.'

I hadn't realised until that moment just how much hope I had lost. Deep down I had all but given up on saving my father; now this wonderful girl had just handed me the ways and the means of curing him. I lifted her off the ground, spun her in my arms and then kissed her. But as soon as my lips met hers a question flashed in my mind. I pushed her away and held her at arm's length.

'What's the matter?' she asked.

'Where did you get this?'

A coy smile crossed her face. 'I sort of borrowed it.'

'Borrowed it – with permission?'

'Well,' she said, pivoting on one toe, 'not really.'

'You stole it?'

'You could say that.'

'From the King?'

'Well yes; who else?'

'I can't take it.'

This produced a pout that made her look like a ten-year-old. 'Why not?'

'Because you will get into too much trouble.'

'No I won't,' she said casually.

'Oh I think you will.'

'No,' she said, 'I never really get into too much trouble – you see, people think I'm really dumb. So they never stay mad at me.'

'But you have never been in as much trouble as this will get you into.'

'Maybe. But believe it or not, I have thought about this. Moran is due within three years, the King is not going to die of old age before then and your father is sick. I am a healer, remember – he needs this. I may get into trouble, but what I am doing is not wrong.' She placed her hands on her hips in a defiant *so there* type of pose.

I stepped forward and kissed her on the cheek. 'If anybody calls you dumb, tell me and I'll punch him in the nose.'

She placed her hand on my robe and a pocket appeared. She dropped the dragon blood in the pocket and then sealed the vial within the fabric.

We decided to swim the surf, towing the boat, as opposed to risking me being tossed out by the breakers. This was the third time I had swum with Graysea and I still couldn't get used to the way those gills opened up on her neck. To be honest it creeped me out a bit. But boy oh boy, once those gills appeared and her feet finned that chick could swim. I held on to the rings that were attached to the boat and then she grabbed me around the waist from behind and zoom, like being strapped to a jet-ski, we were off. She dived down at a speed I thought was impossible in water and then we soared out of the ocean like dolphins at a SeaWorld show. This happened over and over again. I wasn't sure if we were diving through the air so I could breathe or if she was repeatedly trying to kill me. Once past the surf I had to pry her hands from my waist to make her stop. I floated on the surface – my kelp robe providing buoyancy when I asked for it.

'Did I get carried away?' she asked after she had broken the surface and healed the gills in her neck so she could speak.

'No,' I said, 'my sinuses needed a good flushing.'

'Maybe you should travel in your boat.'

'You think?'

She nodded yes, missing the sarcasm.

'Are you sure you are up to this?'

'It will be easy, honestly. Look, The Stream is just over there.'

I looked to where she was pointing but saw nothing but water. 'I don't see anything.'

'You will when it gets darker. Now would you like me to help you get into your boat?'

I said, 'Yes,' expecting her to hold on to the other side so I could climb in without tipping it, but she had another idea. She gave me a quick kiss then once again grabbed me from behind. The next thing I knew I was plummeting to the bottom of the sea before changing direction and diving straight out of the water. As we were directly over the boat Graysea dropped me and I landed flat on my side on the bottom of the boat. I was very lucky to have not put my foot through the canvas. Then the boat lurched, as my own personal mermaid escort broke the water before me, holding the rings in both hands. She gave a hoot, which was the only sound she could make with a neck-full of gills and then did a lovely flip while blowing me an upside-down kiss. Then we were off.

It was not a smooth ride, being towed from the front means that you bounce on every wave and swell. The afternoon sun was setting and I hunkered down trying to think about anything other than the breakdancing my stomach was doing.

As the sun began to set The Stream came into view. It was a watery road filled with luminous algae that, as the night grew darker, became more incandescent. I could see that we were travelling in the opposite direction to the current and that made me wonder if Graysea was lying about this not being difficult for her, but those fears disappeared when I peeped over the bow. Graysea was just below the surface and completely outlined with the glowing algae. Her arms were outstretched like an Olympic gymnast performing the iron cross. Her tail wasn't even moving. She looked like an angel. Graysea had told me that the Mertain gain power from The Stream and I had just thought she meant it made ocean swimming easier, but here I saw The Stream provided real power, like gold in Truemagic or tree sap in Shadowmagic. Graysea was truly 'flying'.

But just 'cause my mermaid outboard motor was sailing smoothly, that didn't mean I was. I had to tear my eyes away from my miraculous escort and lie down in the boat to make sure I didn't blow chunks.

It was just before dawn when Graysea woke me up by tipping me out of the boat. As soon as her gills disappeared she started to giggle and my anger at my damp awakening evaporated. She was still covered with whatever luminous microorganisms that lived in The Stream and it transformed her into the most beautiful creature I had ever seen.

'You are glowing.'

'I know,' she said, spinning around. 'Do you like it?'

'You are radiant,' I replied, 'in every way.'

She pointed over my shoulder, 'From what you have told me I think this beach is close to your home. I will miss you, Conor.'

'You're not coming ashore?'

'No, matron needs me back at the grotto.'

'You're gonna be in a whole mess of trouble back there. Are you sure you don't want to come with me?'

'No one can stay mad at me, Conor – I am too dumb.'

'Maybe,' I said, 'they can't stay mad at you 'cause you're so wonderful.'

She kissed me and as she did we dropped below the surface. If you're looking to add things to your list of top ten, all-time best experiences I highly recommend kissing a mermaid underwater. She pulled back from me and those (getting less creepy) gills appeared and even though she was underwater I could have sworn there was also a tear in her eye. She turned and disappeared into the gloom of the sea.

Chapter Thirty-Six
Ona's Book

I swam to the shore, almost drowning when my robe dragged me under. (I was sure I told it to float.) I thought about Graysea. I think she would have come if I pushed her but, to be honest, I really didn't want her with me. I was going into such uncertainty – I didn't want to subject my innocent glowing angel to that kind of danger and chaos. I could almost imagine her standing in the middle of a battlefield saying, 'Why is everyone being so mean to each other?' It was better that she was with matron back in her grotto. I just hoped she didn't catch too much grief for helping me escape and giving me the dragon's blood. I was also glad I didn't have to explain her to Essa.

Of course I couldn't be sure that Essa and Yogi got out of the Alderlands alive. For that matter, I couldn't be sure that any of my loved ones were safe. I started to fret over all the time that I had lost and swam harder. My robe increased its buoyancy and I body-boarded the surf right onto the shore. The sun was newly up as I stood on the beach and rubbed the stinging saltwater out of my eyes with the sleeve of my warm insta-dry robe. I looked around and what I saw almost made my already queasy stomach bring up everything I had ever eaten. I was in the Reedlands.

There was no mistaking the foul vegetation. This was the land that had been created when Cialtie had first taken his Choosing.

John Lenahan

The last time I had been here Fergal had almost been drawn and quartered by living vines and a band of feral Banshees (the same ones who had destroyed the Heatherlands) had used me and my friends for archery practice.

A shout to my left made me scamper into a mangle of trees, the like I had only ever seen in B-grade horror movies with names like *The Re-return of the Swamp Creature*. The trees didn't provide much cover but I might not have been spotted if I hadn't then instructed my robe to darken so as to blend in with the vegetation. As the troop of soldiers came towards me, my annoyingly disobedient robe went practically fluorescent orange. Then, when I tried to run, I found that some vines had wrapped around my ankles – I couldn't have gotten away even if there had been anywhere to go. As they came closer I noticed that they were Brownies and the one at the front was an old acquaintance of mine. He stepped right up to me wearing a smug smile that only a Brownie mother could love.

'Hi, Frank,' I said. 'Did you get the knife I sent you?'

The soldier's uniform did nothing to make the Brownie prince look any older than the kid I had reprimanded for stealing my shoes so many months before. He pointed to his ankle where a sheath held the green-handled throwing knife to his leg.

'Yeah, I did,' he said and as a thank you, he clocked me in the head with his banta stick.

There are many times when little situations remind me of how much I miss Fergal. I must say that waking from a concussion tied to a post was much more fun with my cousin bound to the one next to me.

At least this place was a cut above my usual stinky dungeon. I was tied to the centre pole of a pretty opulent tent. This was no

301

travelling structure, or if it was, then somebody was doing some serious heavy lifting. There was a full oak-framed bed in the corner, a complete eight-seat dining table set, and an office desk adorned with a collection of peacock quill pens. When the occupant of these posh digs came into the tent I wasn't surprised. I was expecting him. He stood in front of me with his right wrist tucked into his shirt like Napoleon. On his face he wore a smirk that made me want to slap him, but then, all of his expressions make me want to do that.

'Hello, Uncle, I was so worried that we weren't going to get to meet this trip. You know how difficult it is finding time to see *all* of one's relatives.'

I had been practising that line for the entire time I had been waiting for Cialtie to arrive. I hoped that the bravado of it would hide the bowel-clenching fear that was ripping through my body.

'Why are you here and how did you get here?'

'I was hoping to borrow some money for university. You know Dad, he's such a skinflint. Why he won't even pay for—'

A backhand across my face shut me up. While I fought to remain conscious I said, 'I could have sworn uncles are supposed to give you hugs and kisses when they see you.'

'I don't want to hurt you.'

'I don't believe you,' I said. The time for jokes was over. 'In fact I think that is exactly what you want to do. I think that this interrogation is an annoyance. I think what you really want to do is kill the nephew that made you a lefty. Am I right?'

Cialtie took his wrist from his shirt and with his remaining hand scratched the stump that I had created. Then he dragged a chair from across the room and sat down in front of me. 'You think me a monster.'

'No, monsters have no choice, that's just the way they are. I think you are a demon.'

This brought a look of incredulity to my uncle's face. 'You think I have *choice*? You think any of us has choice? You of all people should know that we are all just pawns of Ona's prophecies.'

'Oh don't make me sick. You killed your son, my cousin, my friend. *You*. You did that. Don't you dare try to pass off that responsibility to some old fortune teller.'

'Old fortune teller?' Cialtie laughed. 'You have no idea, have you?' He stood and walked over to his desk. From his pocket he took a key and opened a golden box, from which he took a leather-bound manuscript. He sat down again and placed the book at my feet. 'These are Ona's predictions. She was truly omniscient – we have no choice but to do what she knew must be done.'

'Is that why you killed her, to get that book?'

'No. I had the book before I killed her.'

'You sound proud of yourself.'

'No, not proud, only … resigned. When I had seen only twenty summers, I stole into Ona's room and found this book. As if guided by fate I opened it to the page that foretold my ultimate destiny. When I looked up Ona was standing beside me. She told me that if she were to be allowed to leave that she would tell my father what I had done and he would banish me. Then she took the book and opened it to the page that foretold *her* death. She handed the book to me and lay down on the bed. As I stood over her she handed me a pillow and I smothered her – just as she had written. There was none of your precious *choice*.'

'You could have chosen not to kill her.'

'You can think that if it helps you sleep – I know better.'

'So did Ona tell you to destroy the whole land with your golden circle?'

'No, that was my idea. I thought if I wiped clean the slate of The Land, that finally Tir na Nog would be free of the cage that Ona has put us in.'

I laughed at that. 'So you wanted to free The Land by destroying it? I think if you asked, a few of us would have objected to that.'

'Your precious free will is an illusion. You too are doomed to follow Ona's puppet play whether you know it or not.'

'So you're back in The Land-destroying business again.'

'No, I have learned my lesson. Ona's will is not to be denied. I now only seek to regain the Oak Throne. As long as I am the King of Castle Duir, I will be safe. That is why I must do this.' He reached into a pouch on his belt and took out the gold-rimmed glass vial. I looked down to where Graysea had sealed the vial of dragon's blood into my robe. There was a slit cut into the living fabric. Cialtie undid the stopper and began to tilt.

'No, please,' I begged.

He stopped. 'Turlow told me that you sought dragon's blood, but he told me you failed. Where did you get this?'

'I stole it,' I lied. I didn't want Graysea to be dragged into all of this.

'From where?'

'Duh – from a dragon.'

He looked as though he was going to hit me again but then just said, 'No matter, my spies in Castle Duir have told me that Oisin is much worse. It will not be long.' Then he lifted the corner of the carpet and poured the blood into the dirt below.

I tried to scream, I tried to tell him that I was going to kill him but nothing would come. As if I had been punched in the solar plexus, I had no breath. When finally I could speak, I found I had no strength to do it. You can only lose hope so many times before life is no longer worth fighting for. I dropped my head to my chest and waited for the sword that I knew was going to come, not even caring.

I think I actually dozed off then. I had a vision that I was dead – riding a dragon off into a heavenly sunset filled with red and gold clouds and beams of light like you see in the paintings on the walls of Italian churches. I sputtered awake as hot liquid slipped down my throat and exploded my senses. I opened my eyes to see Cialtie holding a bottle of poteen.

'I thought you had killed me already,' I said with the husky voice of an alcohol-burned throat.

'I have not decided what to do with you yet,' he said, sitting back into his chair. 'I've won you know. The Brownies and the Banshees are loyal to me. The Faeries, without your father, will splinter back into a squabbling mess. The Pookas will all turn again into dogs once I destroy the Tree of Knowledge. That only leaves the Imps and the Elves. The Elves, as usual, will scamper up their trees and wait to see what will happen – and the Imps … well, the Imps fight like farmers.'

'We'll stop you.'

'Or you could help me. You know I'm right, you know I will win. You don't have to like me but you can see that if you stand by my side we can avoid this war. You can save your friends and The Land much heartache.'

'What do you know about heartache? You have to have a heart for that.'

Cialtie stood and returned Ona's book to its box. Without looking around he said, 'When one's entire lifetime is presented to you in an afternoon then one experiences a lifetime of pain – in a day. Oh, nephew, I know heartache.' He turned back to me. 'Think about what I have said,' and then he left.

As much as I wanted not to do as he commanded, thinking is pretty much the only thing you can do when left tied to a pole. I didn't believe it was possible but I felt a little sorry for my uncle. I tried to imagine what life would be like if I knew everything that was going to happen to me and I had to admit it would be a nightmare – especially if my life was like Cialtie's. I also had to admit that he had a point about my family and friends being in trouble – things didn't look good. I wanted to laugh at the clichéd 'Join me and together we can rule the universe' speech but I'd be lying if I wasn't tempted. Don't get me wrong, the idea of spending any time with Cialtie made my stomach churn but the thought of all my loved ones getting massacred in the Hazellands made it churn more. I had seen the young troops that Dahy had put together, I had trained with them and if I was brutally honest – they weren't up to much. They were no match for a well-trained army of Banshees and Brownies. If I was certain my friends were going to be killed, wasn't it my duty to save them? But then I imagined Essa and Dahy's faces as I rode in at Cialtie's side. It wouldn't make any difference – they would never give up. The only difference would be that before they died they would hate me and I was pretty sure that Essa would find a way to haunt me for the rest of my life.

Cialtie knew what he was doing; he had left me alone to think and that was the cruellest cut of all. In the end I came to the conclusion that, preordained or not, Cialtie was a monster I could never join with. I had failed my father, my friends were almost certainly doomed and I would soon die. Cialtie didn't need to torture me – I was doing it to myself. I would like to be able to say that at that moment I welcomed death but the truth is I was afraid. I decided that when my uncle returned that I would accept his offer just so I could survive the day and maybe find a chance to escape later.

'You were not thinking of accepting his offer were you?' I heard a familiar voice say from behind me and then I felt the ropes being cut from my wrists.

'Not me,' I said, as a spark of hope returned to my soul and blood returned to my hands. I silently groaned as I stood and turned to see a very welcome face covered with camouflaging dirt.

'I myself would have accepted,' he said, his white teeth shining in his dark face, 'and then looked for a chance to escape.'

I started to say, 'Actually that's what I was going to do,' but then just decided to say, 'That's why they call you *Master* Spideog.' I bowed and then hugged him.

'I think we should get out of here,' he said, crossing the tent and opening Cialtie's wardrobe.

'What are you looking for?'

'You need to wear something that is a bit darker than that bathrobe.'

'Hold on, let me try something.' I concentrated. This time the robe cooperated and turned a dark bark brown.

'Impressive,' the old archer said while throwing me a pair of my uncle's shoes.

I was still putting on the left shoe when he grabbed me by the collar and I hopped out of the slit he had cut in the back of the tent. There was more moon than we would have liked as we tried to keep the vegetation between us and the roving soldiers. Spideog held a staff but no bow. Seeing him without a bow was like seeing a zebra without stripes. It made me want to ask what had happened to him in the Yewlands but this was no place for a chat.

He led me through the spooky vegetation and then pointed into the gloom. In the distance I made out a horse corral with two guards. We snuck in closer, then Spideog offered me a knife and pointed to the guard on the left. I looked at the deadly weapon.

'Can't I have your stick?' I whispered.

His face showed his displeasure at the breach of silence, then he surprised me by saying, 'No.'

'I can't just stab a man in the back.'

'Conor, we are at war.'

'Why won't you let me use the stick?'

'Because it is mine. Now do you want to get out of here or not?'

I knew by the tone that this was the end of the conversation. I took the knife and as I crept up on the guard I repeated to myself, 'We are at war … we are at war.' But the closer I got, the less my resolve became. While I was still in the open, the clueless soldier bent down, picked up a rock and batted it into the night with his staff. This was just a kid and then when I got closer still I realised it was a kid I knew. What were the odds? Like he was the only Brownie in all of the Reedlands – it was Frank. I came up behind him and placed the knife onto the front of his neck but I couldn't kill.

'Make a sound, Frank, and I'll slit your throat from ear to ear.'

Frank let loose a tiny childish squeal.

'That would be a sound. Would you like to try me again?'

I took his silence for a 'no'. I instructed him to plant his staff in the ground and take a step forward. I held the knife to his back and picked up his staff.

'You should have said "thank you",' I whispered as I clocked him in the side of his head. He went down with a slow wobble of the knees. I took back the green-handled knife but then had an image in my mind's eye of poor worried Jesse and replaced it in his sock. 'Stay out of trouble, Frank.'

Chapter Thirty-Seven
War

We rode out on two mares. I wanted to stampede the herd but Spideog thought getting out of there unnoticed was more important than making them round up horses for a couple of hours. We galloped into the night.

Since we couldn't find any saddles, we rode bareback. And since all I was wearing was my stupid kelp robe thing, I really was riding bareback. Last summer Mom had taught me the basic techniques of riding without a saddle but on that occasion I didn't have to hoik up a robe exposing my bare bottom to horsehair and the rest of my lower parts to a winter breeze. Spideog rode in front of me and to be honest, I couldn't blame him. I wouldn't want to be confronted with that view for a prolonged period of time either.

Kidding aside, it was a profoundly uncomfortable ride. Riding bareback is twice the work than in a saddle. I was already exhausted from being knocked out and trussed up, and my legs (as well as my nether regions) were going numb with the cold. Spideog was determined to get far away from Cialtie's camp before I was discovered missing and he wanted to reach the Hazellands as soon as possible to warn of the imminent attack. So we travelled fast and only stopped to rest the horses. I couldn't disagree with his logic but I would have loved to curl up in a pile of leaves for an hour or twenty.

The sky was dark and overcast during our entire escape. A couple of snow squalls made it almost impossible to see our way but then again, it made us also impossible to spot. All the while I practised the Fili mind-calming chant that Fand had once tried to teach me. I decided on and repeated a mantra 'Would you like fries with that burger?' over and over again until my mind and body were almost separate. Spideog said it took a full twenty hours to get out of the Reedlands but I hardly remember anything except the cold.

There were two Banshee guards at the border path leading into the Hazellands. Spideog spotted them before they spotted us. I waited while he snuck up and dispatched them. All that could be heard were two quiet thumps.

In the Hazellands we found our first clean stream. The horses drank greedily and I fell into it face down. My robe had been getting lighter and colder the longer it had been away from water; after the bath it dried and warmed itself and me. I noticed that the slit that Cialtie had cut in the fabric had healed so I decided to give something a try. I slit the robe down the middle from my crotch to the floor and wrapped the dangling pieces of fabric around my legs and then willed the fabric to join together like trousers. It worked – my butt still hung out of the back but I was much warmer for the rest of the trip.

A day into the Hazellands I could go on no longer. Spideog decided we were not being followed. He caught a rabbit and risked a small fire.

'Do you have enough energy to tell me what has happened to you since we parted?'

I had dreaded that question. The Fili chanting had not only helped me endure the cold, it had also stopped me from remembering how badly I had failed and how many friends I had lost.

'Brendan is dead,' I blurted, hoping that if I said it fast it wouldn't hurt so much.

The archer gave a deep sigh that was the only grieving he allowed himself. 'And the rest?' he asked.

'Araf is dead too, along with a Pooka prince who was our guide. Essa left for the Hazellands, I don't know if she made it or not. Turlow betrayed us.'

'I gathered that from what Cialtie said.'

'You heard our whole conversation?'

'Most of it,' he said. 'I had already cut a slit in the back of the tent when your uncle came in. If I had had a bow, he would be dead now.'

'So the yews didn't give you a bow?'

'The yews do not give bows, Conor, the yews give wood for a bow – if they find you worthy.' To answer my question he held out the staff he was holding – it was of course yew wood.

'So the yews told you that you were worthy, eh? I could have told you that.'

'They also told me something else. They say that someone has killed one of them.'

'But I always thought a yew could kill anybody before they could chop one down.'

'That is how it has always been.'

'Then who did it?'

'I do not know, nor do I know what this means, but I do know that it does not bode well.'

I asked Spideog if I could have his knife to cut some roast rabbit and he asked, 'Did I not see you take a knife from that Brownie in the corral?'

'I did but then I gave it back to him,' I replied.

'Why in The Land would you do that?'

So I told him the story about how I had first met Frank and how I had given the worried Jesse the knife that had been thrown at us on Mount Cas.

That sat the old guy up. 'What did you say?'

'You know – the knife with the message that was thrown at Brendan when we were up at the mountain.'

He shook his head. He looked confused and very concerned.

'Oh yeah, I forgot, you were a bit out of it when it happened and you were gone when I found the knife.' So I told him the whole story about finding the message in the sheath of the knife, which then led us to the Pinelands. I wanted to get some rest but he insisted I tell him everything in detail, especially describing the knife.

'It was a gold-tipped throwing knife with a green glass handle with a spiral of gold embedded in it. It was almost identical to the one that Queen Rhiannon gave me.'

Spideog was on his feet now. 'Where did Rhiannon get her knife?'

'Ah …' I said, not knowing what could possibly have gotten the old guy so worked up. 'She said my grandfather Liam gave it to her.'

'We must go now,' Spideog said, kicking out the fire and knocking my half-eaten rabbit into the dirt.

'What? I thought you said we are safe for a bit.'

'You have had your *bit* – we leave now.' He picked up his yew staff and jumped on his horse before I even stood up.

I struggled onto my horse. It took some hard riding but I finally caught up with him. That didn't mean he was answering any questions. Whatever I had said that was making him ride at that breakneck speed was not up for discussion. I mumbled back in to my McMantra, clamped my thighs to my poor frightened, overworked mount and zoomed into the remainder of the afternoon.

As the sun got low in the sky I started recognising landmarks – we were at the outskirts of the Hall of Knowledge. Every bone in my body screamed for rest and every cell of my skin yelled for a bath, but I also dreaded arriving and having to tell the Imps that their prince was dead. I thought about how Essa would take it and then it hit me that I wasn't sure if she had even made it out of the Alderlands. I kicked my poor horse and bent my back into the wind.

At dusk, Spideog dropped in next to me, grabbed my horse's mane and gestured for me not to speak. We dismounted but were spotted by a group of riders in the distance. Spideog looked around for options, cursed under his breath and braced himself for what was to come. We were definitely under-armed. The old guy handed me a throwing blade and held his yew staff in readiness for a fight. I knew that the knife wasn't going to save me from being killed but at least I would be able to take one down with me.

As they drew closer Spideog sighed with relief and then waved. I recognised one of them, a Leprechaun from a training session in the Hall of Knowledge. Fortunately they recognised us as well.

'Did Essa return safely?' I asked, waving away all of the saluting and bowing. This question confused the senior officer.

'I do not think so,' he said.

'She never returned from the Alderlands?'

'Oh yes, ages ago. I thought you meant now.'

'Where is she now?'

'She should be a league east of here.'

'Is Turlow with her?'

Confusion once again crossed the Leprechaun's face. 'We are seeking The Turlow.'

'Explain,' Spideog commanded.

'A pair of Brownie swiftriders arrived this morning, waited outside our embattlements and demanded a parley with The Turlow. Turlow wanted to go alone but Dahy insisted he bring a guard. When they met the swiftriders at the bottom of the windward knoll, the guard was killed and The Turlow was taken.'

Spideog and I exchanged knowing looks. 'Are you in contact with Essa?'

'I have a whistle but it is only to be used in an emergency.'

'This is that emergency, soldier,' Spideog said. 'Blow it.'

Ten minutes later we heard the thundering hooves of a company in full gallop. Essa saw me and dismounted without even slowing her horse. She hugged me while still at a run and almost knocked me over.

'I thought you were dead.'

I allowed myself a momentary return hug before I told her my grim news.

Essa spoke before I could say anything. 'The Brownies have taken Turlow.'

'No, Essa, they haven't.'

'What do you mean they haven't? I saw them.' She looked around. 'Where is Araf?'

Which question should I answer first? Neither was good news. 'Turlow hasn't been taken – he has escaped. The Brownies knew that I was coming and they rode here to warn him.'

Essa threw her shoulders back. 'Warn him of what? Where is Araf? Where are Brendan and Tuan?'

'Dead,' I said bluntly, there was no other way. 'Turlow betrayed us.'

'You lie.' Her eyes blazed.

'No, I don't. Turlow is working with Cialtie. Because of his treachery Araf, Brendan and Tuan are dead. I barely escaped with my life.'

'That's not true.'

'It is true, Princess,' Spideog said.

Essa turned to the archer as if she had only just noticed he was there. 'What do you know, you crazy old hermit! You've spent the last hundred years dusting banta sticks.' Then she turned on me. 'You never liked him. You're jealous, you're making this up.'

'I'm not, Essa. Use your Owith glass if you don't believe me.'

She looked like I had just slapped her in the face. She pressed her hand to her chest on top of the place where her truth-seeking glass hung from a gold chain. 'I will not go about interrogating people with the Owith glass.'

Spideog stepped up to her and took her by the shoulders; for a moment I thought she was going to squirm away and for another second I thought he was going to slap her. 'Use the glass, Princess. We are at war – we must be certain. Use the glass on us, as you should have used it on him.'

She looked at me. For a nanosecond she was just a girl with pleading eyes wishing me to say it wasn't so. She bowed her head and removed the finger-sized crystal from around her neck. As tears welled up in her eyes she asked, 'Did Turlow betray ... me?'

'He did, Princess,' Spideog replied.

'He betrayed us all,' I said.

The crystal remained clear. Essa turned and secretly wiped her eyes as she placed the crystal back around her neck. Then she got back on her horse, raised her chin high and shouted to her company, 'Mount up! We must return to the Hall of Knowledge. Prince Conor and Master Spideog bring news and it means – war.'

Chapter Thirty-Eight
Ribbons of Gold

My return to the Hall of Knowledge was not the triumphant one I had imagined when I left. News of Araf's death swept through the camp. The usually taciturn Imps jabbered among themselves and often broke down into mournful cries. Yogi ran up to me and asked about Tuan. When I shook my head, he threw his own back and turned into the bear. His cry transformed into a roar. It was frightening and heartbreaking. I reached to comfort him but he growled and swung at me. Even so I tried again and this time he let me hug him. He shrank in my arms and I was left with this strongest of men crying on my shoulder.

'Where's Mom?' I asked Nieve, who was the only one in the headquarters tent.

'She has returned to Castle Duir.'

'How is my father?'

'Oisin lives but I fear not for long.'

Nieve waited for me to say more; when I didn't, she asked a one word question, 'Brendan?'

Oh gods, I thought, *I had forgotten that there was something going on between those two*. 'I'm sorry,' I said.

She dropped her chin and allowed herself one deep sigh then said, 'Dahy has called for a war council in half an hour. You should freshen up.' Before she left she held my face in her hands and then kissed my forehead. 'I am very glad you are safe,' she said.

There was hot water, so I washed up a bit and found some clothes. By the time I got to the meeting everyone was there. Dahy looked up and said, 'I'm glad you could make it, Prince Conor.' I couldn't figure out if he was being sarcastic or not so I just bowed and found a place to sit.

'I believe the attack will come as soon as Cialtie's forces arrive. This is good. It means that tomorrow's battle will only be half of the day.'

'Cialtie's attacking tomorrow?' I blurted.

'If we are lucky tomorrow's attack will not be until the afternoon or late morning at the worst.'

'When did we find that out?'

'We, meaning everyone here, found out fifteen minutes ago when they arrived at the war council – on time,' Dahy said, laying to rest my doubt over whether his greeting had been sarcastic or not. 'We must assume the attack is imminent. With your escape, Cialtie knows that surprise is no longer on his side. He will attack swiftly before we can call for reinforcements. Our Pooka hawk scout has just confirmed my suspicion. The Brownie and Banshee army is less than a day's march away.'

A day, I said to myself, *I was hoping to join the contingent that rode to Castle Duir for reinforcements*. I was hoping to see Dad before it was too late. Now, looking around the faces in the room, I knew I couldn't leave. Tomorrow we make a stand and the only thing that I could hope for was to survive the day.

'As you all must have heard by now The Turlow has betrayed us,' Dahy said without emotion. I looked to Essa. Other than her jaw clenching, she too showed nothing. 'That means the enemy knows our strengths and our weaknesses. We can put this to good use. We have erected stone ramparts on three sides of the Hall but the western ridge above the valley, as you know, is undefended.

This is where the main attack will come. Turlow will be certain that there is no way to defend the hill from a frontal assault – tonight we will prove him wrong.'

I turned to Yogi, who was next to me. 'What is he talking about?' I asked but the Pooka shushed me.

'Archers, go with Master Spideog to the battlements – the rest of you grab a shovel and come with me.'

Any thought of spending my last night resting and reminiscing about the shortness of my life were dashed when I got to the hill. This was going to be a big job. Using swords, long strips of turf were carefully cut from the ground and then five shallow trenches were dug the length of the entire hill.

Five impromptu gold forges were set up on the summit. Leprechaun goldsmiths minted and hammered long strips of thick gold ribbons that were then laid into the trenches. Essa, Nieve and a handful of Imp and Leprechaun sorceresses spent most of the night kneeling and incanting their mumbo-jumbo over the gold. Then the turf was carefully replaced.

It was only a couple of hours before dawn by the time we were finished. I saw Essa almost swoon when she placed a spell over the last of the strips of gold. I ran to her and placed her arm around my neck and walked her back to her tent. She was almost unconscious when I laid her down, but before I could go she said, 'Stay.' I held her as she instantly dropped off into a heavy sleep. I was glad she asked me to stay; if I was to die tomorrow she was the one with whom I wanted to spend my last hours.

As I held Essa I slid seamlessly into a dream. Her tent faded away and we were lying in front of the fireplace back in my house in the Real World. I knew at once that this was just a dream and not a prediction. I never had the courage to ask Essa how old she was but I wouldn't be surprised to find that she had like fifty years on her. Although that makes you a youngster around here, I'm sure she wouldn't appreciate a couple of decades worth of wrinkles just for a tour of my old high school in Scranton, Pennsylvania. Shame, I'd love to show her around where I grew up. I have no idea what she would make of the Real World – it would be fun to find out.

Saying that, as I watched the fire dance in the fireplace of my old living room, I realised that I would never in reality see that sight again. I would never go back to my home. I lived in The Land now and if I made it through tomorrow's battle, I knew I would only be taking one last trip to the Real World. That would be to tell Brendan's mother and daughter how he had died. They probably wouldn't believe me but it's the least I could do.

Still in my dream, I was grabbed from above by the talons of a dragon. He zoomed me into the sky as the sun was setting and flew me to Castle Duir. Ah, the more accustomed I became with dreaming, the more my dreams became just like everyone else's. There in my subconscious I acted out my heart's desire. The dragon dropped me into my father's room where he was sitting up, drinking a cup of tea (there seemed to be no ceilings in my dreams), and standing next to his bed were Tuan and Brendan, all fit and smiling. I reached for my fallen companions ...

I awoke with the euphoria that for a microsecond follows a dream into wakefulness – before the realities of life crush it. My father and my friends were gone, and soon I would engage in a hopeless battle. I turned to Essa but she too was gone. It took all of my will to get out of that bed.

I expected everyone to be a hive of busyness but they weren't – they were just sitting around waiting. Some were writing letters, others were polishing their swords or fussing with their bows. Morale was definitely not good.

Spideog spotted me having breakfast in the canteen. 'You must speak to them.'

'Speak to who?'

'Your troops.'

'There not my troops, they're Dahy's troops.'

'Dahy is their general,' the old archer said, 'but you are their prince.'

'Look, I told you before I don't feel very comfortable with all of this royal stuff.'

Spideog scoffed, 'Since when is *your* comfort an issue? You are what you are – and what you are is the royal heir to the Throne of Duir. These men and women need to know what they are fighting for and you must tell them.'

'I don't even know what we are fighting for.'

'Well, you had better figure it out fast, Conor. Dahy is massing the troops now.'

Dahy was finishing up explaining the battle plan when I finally emerged from the canteen. It had occurred to me that none of these guys knew anything about the Real World and I thought about stealing a choice speech from history.

The first thing that came to mind was, 'We have nothing to fear but fear itself.' That might have been appropriate for Americans safe in their homes during the Great Depression but these guys did have something to fear – screaming Banshees.

I toyed with 'We shall fight them on the beaches,' but the beaches were miles away. And 'Ich bin ein Tir na Nogier,' would most certainly go way over their heads.

So as I walked to the front of the eager faces of the troops … my troops, I still didn't know what I was going to say.

'Friends, Tir na Nogians, countrymen, lend me your ears.' I instinctively looked around for someone to get the joke but the only two who could, Brendan and Dad, were not there. I paused and looked at the eager faces waiting for me to orate some great wisdom but all I could think of were the people that weren't there.

'I have only been here a short while,' I said quietly.

Someone shouted, 'Speak up.'

I cleared my throat. 'I have only been here a short while but during that time I have lost much: my cousin, my friends, and as I speak my father lies dying in Castle Duir.' I looked at the soldiers, they were all silently nodding. 'I know I'm not the only one. You Imps and Pookas have lost your princes and we all know of the hardships that you Leprechauns suffered when Cialtie held the Oak Throne. It would be easy to say this battle was about revenge.' A few cheers popped up in the crowd but I waved them quiet. 'But my father once told me that revenge was a poisonous emotion. He said, if we must fight, we must fight because it is right.

'This battle didn't start today. Decades ago the same people who attack us now trashed the Hazellands. They wrecked the Hall of Knowledge and they destroyed everything in it. You know, I once had a teacher in high school – he was a real jerk but he did say one thing that has always stayed with me. He said, "History is not about what we did, it is about who we are." By destroying the Hall of Knowledge, Cialtie and Turlow are not only trying to kill us, they are also trying to kill what we are as people. My mother, using Shadowmagic, has invented a way to get much of our history back from this place. We must hold the Hall of Knowledge. By holding the Hazellands long enough for reinforcements to come, we will not only be giving ourselves a chance to live tomorrow but we will be saving what we were – and *are* – we give ourselves a chance to be remembered. That is what immortality truly is.

'We stand together at the brains of Tir na Nog. Let's kick some Banshee tail!'

A cheer rose up that was so loud and fast, it shocked me.

Spideog walked up to me and did something he had never done before. He bowed and said, 'My Prince.'

'I did good?' I asked.

He smiled – a rare smile. 'You did good.'

I spent the rest of the day visiting with the troops – basically acting like a prince. I walked around faking being brave and I actually think it helped calm people. Maybe that's what bravery is – pretending not to be scared. Many soldiers told me stories of their homes and their families that made me realise just how little I truly knew of Tir na Nog. It made me determined to save as much of it as I could.

Essa was doing pretty much the same thing. I was watching Essa help a man write a letter when Spideog caught me staring at her. 'Can I ask you a personal question, Conor?'

'Sure,' I said.

'I thought you and her …' the old archer nodded his head towards Essa, 'I thought you two were … you know … wooing.'

'Oh Master, that was a long time ago.'

Spideog looked confused and said, 'I thought you only first arrived in The Land last summer?'

'I did,' I said and laughed. 'I guess you and I have a different definition of "a long time ago".'

'So what happened between you two – *so long ago?*'

'Well, she tried to kill me.'

He turned and took a long look at Essa, then looked me in the eyes and said, 'If I were you, I wouldn't let a little thing like that put me off.'

It was well into the afternoon when I found myself with Dahy standing on the makeshift battlements.

'Have you ever fought against Banshees before?' I asked the old warrior.

The question made him look older. 'I have fought with them – never against them.'

'So what about that Banshee sixth sense? If they can tell when they are going to win a battle, doesn't that mean we have already lost?'

Dahy gave me a look like I had just cursed in church. 'I spoke with the troops about this before you came out this morning. The Banshees have a very good sense of how a battle is going but they cannot predict the future. Just because they are good at knowing which way the wind blows doesn't mean that winds cannot change. They are not the mystics they think they are. They drop their trousers to crap just like the rest of us.'

'But if they attack, doesn't that mean the wind is blowing their way?'

Dahy laughed. 'There is a tornado blowing our way, son. Any fool can see that. I have sent wolves to Castle Duir and to the Pinelands. I wanted to send the bird but I needed her for reconnaissance.' He looked to the sky but it was empty. 'Our only hope is to hold out until we get reinforcements. When we do, the Banshees will turn tail. That sense of theirs also tells them when they are going to lose.'

A screech above us forced our eyes to the sky as a streak of black came towards us. I stepped instinctively back but Dahy just reached into his satchel and took out a silk robe. The hawk landed between us and as it raised its head it continued to grow into a black-haired woman. Dahy handed her the robe.

She looked at me and then, like a bird, sharply turned her head to the general. 'They are here,' she said.

Chapter Thirty-Nine
There Will Be Blood

Just as Dahy had predicted, Cialtie's army, using Turlow's intelligence, ignored the stone ramparts, swept wide behind the Hall and prepared to attack what yesterday had been the unprotected hill. Cialtie's forces took their time setting up. If their sixth sense was warning them about the buried gold barrier, then they weren't showing it. We stood in a row, two deep, banta sticks in hand, waiting for the attack.

The previous night there had been a pretty heated debate about whether we should be defending with swords or sticks. Spideog said we were at war and should be using swords like warriors, but I said no. These people were not monsters or robots – they were men and women whose only crime was to have their minds corrupted by evil men. Spideog pointed out that they would not give us the same courtesy. Before I could reply Essa said something that finished the argument.

'What would we win,' she asked, 'if after we defeat our enemy, we then become just like them?'

At that moment I wanted to kiss Essa square on the mouth – but then again I could say that about most moments.

The battle began with a mortar attack. The enemy cheered as they sent conch shells sailing overhead. Except for the one that Essa batted back like a major league baseball player, half a dozen shells landed on the ground with smoke rising out of them. We backed away expecting the worst but they did nothing. Finally brave souls picked them up and threw them back. Our enemy's cheering stopped and for a while they looked confused. Orders barked from the back of their ranks refocused the troops and they strapped short shields to their arms, drew their swords and waited for the order to charge.

The silence, as the old expression goes, was deafening. I looked to my left and saw Yogi morph into a bear and growl. I looked to my right; Essa nodded and spun her banta stick. There wasn't a smiling face to be seen. How I wished Fergal was there with me.

I didn't hear the order to charge but I sure saw the results. A couple of hundred screaming Banshees and howling Brownies charged up the hill under the shadow of a flock of arrows launched from the rear. The attackers must have seen the arrows explode into flame as they crossed the gold barrier. They probably expected it. What they didn't expect was what came next. As the first line of Banshees crossed the point where we had buried the ribbons of gold, their swords and shields vanished in a puff of smoke. Their forward momentum carried them straight into our waiting sticks. It was like hunting in a zoo. Baffled and surprised Banshees ran straight at us as we mercilessly clubbed them and then dropped back so as to let the next line step up and have a full swing. Banshees, then Brownies, dropped like bowling pins and piled up on one another. Others collided and tripped over confused retreating soldiers who were running in every direction. It was horrible. The sound of it was sickening and the look on their faces just before we hit them was pathetic. I thank the gods we weren't using swords. I don't think even the hardest of us could have withstood that guilt.

When they finally retreated, what remained was a long pile of moaning Banshee and Brownie bodies lying twisted in a heap three deep.

Since we had no provisions to take prisoners, a detail of soldiers was chosen to untangle and roll the unconscious aggressors back down the hill. Among them were Nieve and her little cabal of sorceresses. They stuck most of the enemy in the leg with one of my aunt's special paralysing pins – when they woke up, they found it difficult to use that leg for a day or so. It would make a little bit of a difference but not much. Cialtie's forces were still substantially larger than ours.

It was too late for my uncle to mount another attack. Since he knew he had the upper hand and we had little chance for reinforcements by tomorrow, they simply backed out of archery range and made camp.

'Well, it looks like we won round one,' I said to Spideog.

'War is scored with the dead, Conor,' the old warrior said. 'This battle has yet to begin.'

I continued with my morale-man job, dispensing pep talks as deemed necessary for a while, and then went to headquarters to check if I was needed or maybe get a little nap in. I caught my Aunt Nieve by surprise and she quickly turned away and wiped her eyes.

'Are you OK?' I asked.

She tried to put on a brave face but at the last second she told the truth. Her voice wobbled as she said, 'No,' and sat down.

That was an answer I wasn't ready for. Of all people Nieve was the last person I would have expected to crack under pressure. I sat on the arm of her chair and put my hand on her shoulder.

'How did he die?' she asked, not looking at me.

That question hit me like a slap. How should I answer that? How did Brendan die? If I was truthful I would have told her that one of her spells made him powerless to move while he was burned alive, but instead I said, 'It was instant, and painless, he wouldn't have even known what hit him.'

That seemed to do the job. She wiped her face, stood up and said, 'Right, we have a battle to prepare for, yes?'

'Actually I was hoping to have a kip. Do you think that's OK?'

'Of course,' she said as we gave each other a proper hug. 'You may be our Prince but you're still just a Faerie.'

I nodded and left for my tent. I understood what she meant but it still didn't sound right.

I willed myself to not dream but that didn't work. Once again in dreamland I zoomed to my father's side. I have to admit that even though I would never abandon my comrades, I'd be lying if at that moment flying away to Castle Duir wasn't what I truly wished I could do.

It was well after midnight when I awoke. I walked to the battlements and found Spideog with a very short Imp sorceress. The sorceress mumbled over an arrow and then handed it to the old archer, who notched it into the biggest bow I had ever seen. He let it fly and I lost it in the night sky. I started to look away but Spideog said, 'Keep watching.'

As the lost arrow began to descend, it started to glow then it exploded on top of a tent, showering it in flames. Screaming and cursing could be heard wafting up from the enemy camp.

'You havin' fun?' I asked.

'We are not sleeping tonight,' Spideog said. 'There is no reason why they should.'

We spent the rest of the night lobbing arrows into Cialtie's camp. By morning Essa, Yogi, Dahy and Nieve had all joined us and we giggled like schoolchildren every time Spideog let an arrow fly. Some of Spideog's archery students tried their hand with the big bow but none of them was as good as the Master. It was amazing how many tents he hit even though he couldn't see them until they went up in flames.

With the troops assembled at the ramparts, Dahy asked me if I wanted to address them again. I told him I had already done my bit and maybe he should do it. He didn't disagree.

'Today will be different from yesterday,' Dahy said, raising his gruff voice. 'Today, we use swords – today, there will be blood. But the first victim of your sword should not be your enemy, it should be the little voice inside you that is saying that this battle is already lost. You must find that voice and kill it – because all is not lost. I would not have us here if it was. I have trained you and I know what you can do – and this – together – we can do. Today there will be swords – today there will be blood – let us make sure that the blood that runs is not ours. Let us make sure that those who would take away who we are will pay for their arrogance. Today there will be blood and today we shall endure.'

The crowd went wild. I patted my old master on the back and said, 'Awesome, dude.'

Spideog turned to Dahy and said, 'I thought it was a bit flowery,' then he smiled and the two old rivals shook each other's hand.

'Are you ready to go into battle with me again – old friend?' Dahy said.

'Who are you calling old,' Spideog replied. 'By the by, remind me that I have to tell you something when this is all over.'

Dahy was just about to ask what, when someone cried, 'Incoming!' and the battle began.

The sky blackened with arrows. We all ducked behind the battlements and watched in horror as soldiers who were caught out in the open scrambled for cover. Then I saw a conch shell hit the ground about twenty-five feet behind me. This one, unlike the ones yesterday, wasn't smoking. I peeped over the battlements and seeing that there were no arrows on the way, I dashed over intending to throw it back. I was no more than an arm's length away when I heard an ear-piercing sound and was instantly doubled up in pain. All around me men dropped to the ground pulling their knees up to their chest. I'm sure that like me they were howling in pain but nothing could be heard other than the screaming sound that was coming from the shell. I knew we had to get rid of it but every time I tried to straighten my legs, the pain, which was already unbearable, doubled. I had started dragging myself forward with my fingers in the dirt when I saw Essa, obviously in pain but on her feet, stagger over to the shell and then smash it with her banta stick. The sound and pain went as suddenly as they had come. Essa poked through the rubble of the shell and picked up a small gold amulet that was buzzing with a tinny sound. Then using her teeth and fingers she bit and twisted it until it stopped.

Dahy, who I am embarrassed to say was on his feet much faster than me, walked over and took the amulet from Essa. 'It's a *gleem*,' he said.

Gleem, where had I heard that before? That was the thing that Cialtie had used on Dad to win the boat race. It inflicted the pain of childbirth.

'Well, that settles it,' I said. 'I'm not *ever* getting pregnant.'

Someone shouted, 'INCOMING!' and we ran back to the ramparts for cover. Spideog kept his nose over the wall and then popped up to shoot a second shell out of the air like a Kentucky skeet shooter.

Essa ducked next to me. 'Didn't that gleem thing hurt?' I asked her.

'Of course it hurt but it was nothing I couldn't take.' She rolled her eyes and shook her head. 'Men.'

Cialtie's first attack was small – designed to force us to show our strengths and weaknesses – it was also designed to fail. On strictly a tactical standpoint I guess it was sensible but using any other yardstick, especially a moral one, it was despicable. It was a suicide mission – that is if the attackers in the first wave volunteered. If they were ordered to go, then it was a death sentence and we were the executioners. About seventy Brownies dashed directly at the ramparts. The first thing they discovered was that Dahy and the Leprechauns had, for months, been hammering every flat rock or piece of shale that they could find into the ground in front of the stone defences. Running on it at any speed was almost impossible – it was a minefield for ankle twisting.

Many Brownies tripped and many more were mowed down by Spideog and his archers. Only four Brownies reached the wall and when they did they seemed not to know what to do. Several of their attacking comrades had been carrying siege ladders but they had been stopped by arrows. As our archers bore down on the four, Dahy ordered them not to fire.

'Brownies,' Dahy called down to them, 'you have fought bravely but you have no chance to scale these walls. I offer you safe passage if you go back now.'

As I watched, I prayed that they would take his offer. They looked like lost cold orphans shivering in a big city alley. If they defiantly started to climb we would have no choice but to kill them. I can't tell you how quickly I was getting tired of this war stuff. They huddled up and then accepted. With their heads held high, they marched back over the ankle-twisting stone field. About halfway across, a huge volley of arrows from Cialtie's camp dropped all of them as one. It was my uncle's way of showing the rest of his army how he felt about surrender.

Dahy made no comment, nor showed any emotion in regards to the slaughter, he just nodded like this was business as usual.

'Cialtie and Turlow have learned all that they need to know,' the general said. 'The next attack will be all of them.'

I stepped off my post in hopes of getting to the wash tent so I could splash some water on my face and maybe wash away some of the horror that I had just seen – some of the horror that I had just been part of. I used a shortcut that brought me around the back of the tent and there I found Spideog sitting with his back to a low ruined wall, his knees up and his face in his hands. I hesitated before I disturbed him. I hoped that when he removed his hands that his eyes were not awash with tears. If Spideog broke under this pressure, what chance had the rest of us for surviving unscathed? But surviving unscathed was probably impossible anyway.

'Are you OK?' I asked, crouching down to his level.

He looked up. His eyes were clear but filled with a millennium's worth of sadness. 'May the gods damn your uncle.'

'Yeah,' I agreed, 'and they will have to get in line. There are a few of us around here who would like to damn him and do a bit more.'

'Those Brownies …' Spideog paused – on his face he wore the sorrow of a man searching through old, painful memories. 'Those Brownies fought like the Fili. During that war, Maeve threw her Fili at us like they were toy soldiers that could later just be glued back together.' He shook his head and looked down. 'How do they do it? How do these madmen get their people to follow them with such suicidal abandon?'

'I don't know, Master,' I said. 'I don't think we will ever know but isn't that what makes us better than them?'

He looked up, smiled at me, then stood, instantly regaining his innate heroic stance. 'You have your grandmother's eyes, you know.'

'You must tell me about her sometime.'

'I will, when this is all over.' He laughed to himself as he turned. 'I might even do better than that.'

He jogged back to his post without giving me a chance to ask him what he meant.

Back on the battlements the sun rose to its zenith in a crystal-clear blue winter sky. The heat was welcome as it allowed us to believe that the sweat that was dripping down our backs was caused by the sun and not our jangling nerves.

In Cialtie's camp there could be heard orders being barked and bugle-sounding things being played as the army of Banshees and Brownies readied for their main offensive. Essa dropped in next to me.

'Dahy thinks that the attack will be soon,' she said. 'Are you ready?'

'Born ready,' I said automatically. As I scanned the horizon I felt Essa reach down and entwine her fingers in mine. I looked at her, she was fierce and scared and oh so achingly beautiful – all at the same time. She leaned in and kissed me. I placed my hands gently on her shoulders and pushed her back.

'We are not going to die,' I said.

She turned away, looking out over the field and then I felt her tense up like the strings of a tennis racket. She pointed to the edge of the rise. I followed the line of her finger and saw hundreds of screaming soldiers charge into view.

'Tell that to them,' she said as she drew her sword.

Chapter Forty
The Isles

What must have been a thousand Brownies and Banshees swarmed onto the stone plain. They looked like those red army ants that you see in old Tarzan movies. I was half expecting the fallen to end up as stone-white skeletons.

As soon as they got into range, our arrows flew. The fallen were not even considered by their comrades – if the arrows didn't kill them then the trampling surely must have. The same fate awaited those that tripped on the stone field. Just behind the first wave were a line of siege ladders carried by teams of three. The ladders had shields strapped to the front so as to protect the carriers from all but the sharpest archers who aimed for their heads and legs. Spideog assigned his best bowmen for that task and they had a reasonably high measure of success. Still, any ladder bearer that was hit was instantly replaced by another. The ladders clambered closer.

All the while volleys of arrows came at us from the back of the enemy's advance. Dahy's ramparts were designed well, giving cover as well as enough gaps for the archers to continue shooting even while arrows were flying in. One gleem arrived during the first part of the attack but was swiftly taken care of by the special gleem-team that Nieve had equipped with gold earplugs.

The enemy soldiers that reached the ramparts huddled together under their shields in an arrow-proof phalanx. The ones that did this too close to the walls had boulders thrown at them by teams of very brawny Leprechaun miners. The huge rocks smashed into the shields then the archers finished them off.

I'd like to be able to say that I was appalled by all of this bloodshed but as those ladders drew closer and with the realisation that this screaming horde was hell bent on killing me, it caused a bloodlust to explode in my brain. Some men never get over this experience and sell themselves as mercenaries for the rest of their lives in order to feel that savage passion again. As for me I have no want to repeat the experience but I would be lying if I said it was unpleasant. In fact it was damn exciting. Never have I felt so alive. It was kill or be killed and every fallen enemy soldier was one that I knew I wouldn't have to face with my sword and I cheered with the rest of my comrades as each went down.

When the ladders reached the ramparts I finally got to use my sword. It was a good blade but heavier and nowhere near as finely balanced as the Sword of Duir. I missed the Lawnmower. I had a fleeting image of the last time I saw it, sticking out of the underbelly of Dragon Red. A ladder hit below my gap in the wall. I tried to reach down and push it but it was just out of reach. Leprechaun boulder tossers were engaged elsewhere so I waited for the first of the Brownies to climb the ladder. He reached the top in no time and we engaged in a pointless just out-of-reach sword-fight where we clinked sword tips but were too far away from each other to make serious contact. My father's sword-fighting instructions sprang into my head. 'When an attack ceases to make sense,' he once said to me, right before he tripped me over a low wire he had earlier set up in the garden, 'look around – something else might be happening.' I continued to swing but looked under the ladder and saw another Brownie with a crossbow taking aim at my nose. I ducked back just in time to avoid a bolt in the brain.

A gleem came over the wall far to my right. The gleem-team got to it quickly but not in time to prevent a couple of Banshees from clearing the ramparts. They fought and another five were allowed to reach the top before they were thrown back over. Ladders had now reached almost every part of the rampart wall. All of the ladders seemed to me to be too low. It made them difficult for us to repel by pushing them over but it also made it extremely difficult for the enemy to breach the top of the walls. It didn't make sense. I used my father's advice again and scanned the length of the battlements. That's when I noticed that under every ladder was a team of two soldiers crouched down fiddling with something at the base of the wall.

I shouted to Dahy, 'SOMETHING IS HAPPENING UNDER THE LADDERS.'

As he looked, a horn was blown and all the attackers dropped from their ladders and ran away from the wall.

'RETREAT!' Dahy shouted. 'EVERYONE OFF THE BATTLEMENTS!'

Having been a student of the Master I didn't have to hear a Dahy order twice. I flew off my post and into the midst of the Hall of Knowledge. A few of my comrades were not so lucky. The explosions blew a dozen holes in our defences. The Leprechauns and Imps who were on the wall were thrown twenty feet in the air.

'BACK TO THE AISLES,' Dahy ordered. 'BACK TO THE AISLES.'

Our secondary defence was what Dahy had called 'The Aisles'. We had knocked down some of what was left of the Hall's walls and reinforced others. The idea was to force any advancing army into narrow channels – aisles, allowing us to battle one or two abreast as opposed to a huge wave of marauders. Archers were positioned so as to shoot anyone that tried to come over the top.

The air hadn't even cleared when the Banshees, covered with the white dust of the explosions, came screaming out of the smoke. Dahy had said that there would be blood; well, this was the time he was talking about. I don't know how many I killed. All I know is that they weren't very well trained. They had strength and the energy that adrenalin brings but they all swung madly and allowed me to parry their wild swings to the outside and stab them in the chest, or the shoulder if they were wearing a breast protector. May the gods forgive me but what else could I do?

Even though I was killing many, I gave ground with almost every clash and I was getting tired. An Imp finally grabbed me from behind, pulled me back into the Hall and took my place at the front of the aisle.

I found Dahy barking orders outside of the library. On my left a bunch of Banshees broke through and Yogi, as a bear, roared into them, throwing two into the air and shocking the others into a retreat, while Dahy ordered swordsmen back into that aisle. This battle was not going well and it was just about to get a whole lot worse.

A troop of Banshees had snuck around to the site of the first attack. They guessed that if they each carried a bough of a tree that the gold strips might not register the branches as weapons and would let them through. They guessed right. Because of our small numbers we had only defended the hill with a handful of soldiers. The Banshees attacked with the branches and at the same time catapulted a bag of swords over a wall from the side. The Banshees quickly overpowered the guards on the hill and armed themselves. Our defences were dangerously thinned as soldiers were ordered to defend the Tree of Knowledge on two fronts.

I think at this point Dahy would have surrendered but no one was offering. This was it – it was a fight to the death and the realisation hit me that the death would be ours.

That's when time began to slow for me, not a good sign. My gift is only a help when I am personally in a fight. Here, watching this failing battle, my gift was a curse, just as it was when I watched Fergal die. I saw my comrades fall in slow motion. I saw every wound, every spurt of blood as if I was watching some bad war movie. It also gave me time to assess the entire battlefield and what I saw told me it was all over. We were moments away from being overrun.

The aisle on the left broke. Banshees and Brownies poured out. Dahy called forward the soldiers that had been guarding the Tree of Knowledge. A mêlée of hand-to-hand combat opened in the yard.

I looked for Essa. If this was to be the end I wanted to be at her side. In the confusion I couldn't see her but I heard her when she yelled, 'THE SKY!'

I looked up as the entire firmament turned into flame. A huge fireball rolled over and through the holes in the shattered battlements. Fire leapt in and set alight the attackers at the entrances of the aisles. Flames rolled over the top of the defences forcing us to hit the ground as hairs curled on the top of our heads. Then, swooping through the smoke flew a huge green dragon. It circled and came in to land almost exactly where I was standing. As I dived for cover I saw that the dragon had a rider. I got to my feet just in time to see him jump off as the dragon skidded into a stone wall. The dragon rider hit the ground in a graceful roll and popped up on his feet, banta stick in hand. It was – Araf!

I didn't question how or why. I just got to my feet and shouted, 'IMPS AND LEPRECHAUNS, TO ME. THE DRAGON IS ON OUR SIDE. EVERYONE, TO ME.' Araf blew his whistle. To their credit our force spent no time in dazed wonder when they saw their prince arrive miraculously from the grave astride a dragon, they went right into battle mode and cheered as they went back on the offensive.

The attackers that were still standing retreated as fast as their legs would carry them. If that Banshee sixth sense is true then it pretty quickly told them to *get the hell out of there.*

Another explosion of fire lit up the southern end of the battlefield as a crimson-coloured dragon – one that I recognised as Red

– swooped over our position. Its rider, with that unmistakable American accent, shouted, 'YEE HA.'

Dragon Red landed on the top of the headquarters building just long enough for Brendan to slide off.

'Hey, O'Neil,' the policeman/dragon-rider shouted over the sound of Red launching himself back in to the sky, 'it's good to see you're not dead.'

'Same to you, Copper,' I shouted. I was just about to ask Araf what the heck was going on when we heard a sound of a battle horn coming from the courtyard.

Someone shouted, 'THEY ARE ATTACKING THE TREE!'

By the time I got to the entranceway it was almost over. A dozen Brownies were lying dead on the ground with arrows sticking out of the centres of their chests. Spideog was still firing even though he had a crossbow bolt in his thigh and another in his shoulder. There were four remaining Brownies; two of them had axes and were trying to get to the Tree of Knowledge. Spideog went for the axe bearers when he should have gone for the one in the back. I saw that Brownie cock his arm and then I saw the dagger leave his hand. A split second later two arrows hit the knife thrower – one in the throat from Spideog and another in the chest from Brendan on the roof – but they weren't in time to stop the throw. The knife was well off the mark but as I watched, it curved in midair and honed in on the ancient archer's heart. It hit him square in the chest. He dropped his bow, then crumpled first onto his knees and then onto his back.

Brendan dispatched the other attackers from the roof and then out of habit shouted, 'OFFICER DOWN.' He slid down a buttress and arrived at Spideog's side almost as quickly as I did. I lifted the archer's head; he coughed and blood poured from his mouth.

'Is the Tree safe?' he asked.

'Yes, Master.'

'Good.' He coughed again, closing his eyes in pain. 'Conor, don't let Essa go. If you don't tell her how you feel, you will regret it for the rest of your life – trust me, I know.' He coughed again and wiped his mouth with the back of his hand. When he saw the blood on his fingers he said, 'Oh dear, could you find Dahy for me?'

Brendan took the archer's head. I turned, there were several soldiers watching dumbfounded. 'Get Dahy,' I ordered and they scattered in several directions.

Brendan was weeping openly. Spideog smiled and said to him, 'If the yews allow it, I want you to have my bow.'

Brendan tried to speak but nothing came out.

Dahy crashed to his knees next to us. He took Spideog's hand and said, 'Hey, old man.'

'Who are you calling old?' Spideog smiled, his eyes still closed.

Dahy looked up and barked, 'Someone get a healer.'

Dahy's old comrade in arms shook his head. The meaning was obvious – a healer would do no good. Then he opened his eyes and said, 'She lives, Dahy.'

'Who lives, old friend?' Dahy asked.

Pain and coughing racked Spideog's body, blood poured freely from the side of his mouth. I didn't think he would open his eyes again but then he reached up and grabbed Dahy on the side of the arm. 'Macha ... Macha lives.' Then his hand dropped and he breathed his last.

The folds of his tunic had obscured the knife in Spideog's chest. As Brendan laid him down the material fell away and the green knife handle came into view. Dahy pulled it from the torso and examined it closely. 'Where did this come from?'

A sinking feeling like a punch in the stomach almost made me retch. I walked over to the dead Brownie that had thrown the knife. I knelt down and rolled his body over – it was Demne, the eldest son of the Brownie King. It was Frank.

By the time I looked up Essa, Araf and Tuan were in the court-yard. My head was spinning. Overwhelmingly conflicting emotions mixed with confusion made me almost catatonic. I had just won a battle but had been partly responsible for the death of Master Spideog. But then – here were my friends brought back from the dead.

The sound of flapping and screaming in the sky snapped me back to full attention. High, high above us flew a dragon; below him hung a writhing, screaming man. When Red was directly above our heads he opened his talons and let the man go. The screaming ended when the freefalling body hit the side of the headquarters roof. The snapping of his neck was plain to hear. He bounced and landed on the ground face down, not far away from Essa. The Princess used her foot to flip him over. It was Turlow. Essa stared at him with a clenched jaw as her eyes watered up.

'I wanted to do that,' she said.

Chapter Forty-One
The Green Dragon

I looked back up and saw Dragon Red flying away and remembered. I remembered what the last months had all been about. I started shouting, 'NO, RED, RED COME BACK.'

I looked to Brendan. 'Where is he going?'

I didn't wait for an answer, I was getting frantic. 'RE-E-E-ED!' Then I spun on Araf. 'You were riding a green dragon – where is the green dragon? Where?'

Araf grabbed me by the shoulders, he was uncharacteristically smiling. I looked to Brendan and Tuan; despite the recent tragedies, they were smiling too.

'I need dragon's blood!'

'Calm down, Conor,' Araf said. 'The green dragon is here.'

I spun around, searching the courtyard for any sign of a dragon. They were all still smiling like idiots. I was just about to slap them when Tuan placed his hands together into a two-handed fist, then crouched down like a man about to drop to his knees in prayer. When he began to straighten up he didn't just stop at his own height. His clothes tore away as palm-sized green scales loudly clinked into place on his chest and back. He continued to grow as his face extended and spines grew out of his receding hair. As he reached full size he blocked the sun and extended his wings, sending a cloud of dust and leaves swirling around the courtyard, forcing us to shield our eyes.

'*No*,' I said incredulously.

'Oh yes,' Brendan said, patting me on the back.

I stepped up to Dragon Tuan and he lowered his head. I looked into his eyes, thinking that I would recognise my old travelling companion but his eyes were green and yellow with slits for pupils.

'Is that you in there, Councillor Tuan?'

He threw his head violently back and blew a massive plume of fire into the air. Brendan grabbed me by the arm and pulled me back. 'Don't make him laugh, he's having trouble controlling the fire-breathing stuff.'

Tuan folded back his wings and lowered his body to the ground. Brendan took a running start and hopped on his back like a cowboy in a movie. Then he held out his hand and said, 'You comin'?'

'Where?'

'To Castle Duir. Tuan wants to donate some blood.'

I took a running start. I was so excited that I almost sailed straight over the back of Tuan.

Then Nieve ran into the courtyard and shouted, 'Brendan, you are alive.'

'I am indeed, gorgeous,' the cop replied from dragonback. 'I'm off to Castle Duir to save your brother. Come with us.'

Honest to the gods she hopped up and down like a schoolgirl at a boy-band concert and ran two steps towards us before she stopped and dropped her head.

'I cannot. I must tend the wounded.'

Brendan turned to me and said, 'Can you give me a minute?'

I nodded and he slid off Tuan's back and gave my aunt a right proper, back-dipping, snog.

Dahy approached me holding the knife. He looked shell-shocked. 'Where did you get this?' he asked quietly. It was almost as if he was afraid to hear the answer.

'It was thrown out of the window from the house of the Oracle, on Mount Cas. Araf was there, he can tell you all about it.' He nodded thoughtfully and backed off as Brendan dramatically remounted.

Tuan extended his school-bus-sized wings and began to flap. The muscles in his back tightened and rocked me up and down as I searched for something to hold on to. I grabbed Brendan around the waist. He didn't seem to mind.

Detective Fallon turned to me wearing a huge ear-to-ear grin. 'Have you ever been on the rollercoaster at that amusement park in Elysburg, Pennsylvania?'

'Yeah,' I screamed back as the wind roared around us. 'It was very scary.'

'Well, hold on, O'Neil, 'cause this is a whole lot worse.'

As I held on for dear life, Brendan filled me in on what had happened.

'That damn paralysing pin that the *late* Turlow stuck in Araf, Tuan and me was apparently placed high enough on our necks so that we couldn't speak but our eyes and ears still worked. Tuan managed to do that Pooka transforming thing with the unparalysed part of his head. The top of his head changed into like a dozen different animals. Every time he grew feathers or fur or even scales, he managed to push out the pin just a little bit further, until it popped out completely. He saved us.' Tuan, who had been listening, shook his head up and down.

'Nice one, Councillor,' I shouted.

'We were just outside the back door of The Digs,' continued Brendan, 'when the fireball hit. We dived into the swampy bit behind the house to protect ourselves from the heat and by the time we popped out again, you were already being carried off into the wild blue yonder. Tuan used hawk eyes and said he saw you fall into the ocean. How'd you survive that one?'

'Mermaids,' I shouted over the sound of the swirling wind and laughed out loud at the ridiculousness of it.

Brendan laughed with me. 'A couple of months ago I'd have locked you up in the loony bin for saying stuff like that.'

'And now?'

'Now' – the cop thought for a second – 'now my response is – yeah, that sounds about right.'

'So what happened when Red came back?'

'Well, he was surprised to see us alive, 'cause Turlow had told him we were dead. Also he had a problem.'

'What was that?'

'You stuck your sword in him in a spot that he couldn't reach and he was afraid to change back to Red with it sticking out of him. Oh, that reminds me, I've got your sword.' He patted the sword hanging on his belt. I peeped down and instantly recognised the Lawnmower's pommel.

'I hope it hurt him like hell,' I said.

'I think it did. Tuan agreed to pull it out if he consented to listen to us before he tried to kill us again. It didn't take us long to convince him that The Turlow had duped us all. He was livid and zoomed off to try to find him, but he came back a week later having had no success.

'While he was gone we found his house – or I guess I should call it his lair – and waited for him there. Tuan discovered all of these manuscripts in Pooka lingo and sat in the corner and read them the whole time – he hardly talked to us. When Red returned, Tuan and Red got talking shop. I tried to get Red to give me some blood and a lift off the island, but they were so into talking about changeling stuff that they acted like Araf and I weren't even there. When I got mad at them for ignoring us, Red switched to dragon, grabbed Tuan and flew away. The two of them disappeared for another week. When Red came back there was a green dragon with him.

'Apparently in order to become a dragon you have to study how to change into every animal there is and Tuan had done that already. Oh, and that problem that he had about not being able to hold a form – well, that's gone.' Brendan patted the dragon's neck and looked over the side. 'I hope.'

I shivered in the cold air as the sun began to set in an explosion of reds and golds. 'You know I had a dream about this. But I never …' I chuckled to myself. 'I never dreamt it would happen. I only hope we are in time.'

The guards on the ramparts of Castle Duir shot arrows at us as we approached so we had to fly away and land in the field in front of the castle. By the time a whole battalion of soldiers came at us on horseback, Tuan was Tuan again. The captain recognised me – and recognised Brendan as that madman from the Real World – and once we convinced them that there was no dragon attack, he gave us horses and we galloped to the main gates.

The three of us burst into Dad's candlelit room. Mom and Fand and a handful of sorceresses were there. Dad, still encased in amber, looked like he was dead.

Mom flew into my arms and hugged her head to my chest.

'Is he gone?' I asked. 'Am I too late?'

She held my face in her hands; her eyes were swimming in tears. 'It's not long now – I'm glad you are here.'

'He's not dead?' I said excitedly. I looked to Fand. 'He's not dead?'

'No,' the Fili answered.

I grabbed my mother by the shoulders. 'Mom it's not eel's blood. It's not red eel blood.'

She looked at me confused. It had been so long since Mom and I had discovered that old manuscript that she had almost forgotten about it. She had given up hope.

'Tughe tine – we thought it meant *red eel*; it doesn't, it means *fire worm*. Fire worm,' I said again louder, trying to make it sink in. '*Dragon!*'

I turned to Tuan and motioned for him to change.

'Here?' he said, looking around. 'Will I fit?'

'We'll find out. You better stick your nose out of the window.'

He did as he was told and clasped his hands together and crouched down facing the window.

OK, maybe it wasn't a good idea to have him change in Dad's room, especially without warning anybody. Dragon Tuan was a lot bigger than I realised. His back pushed up against the ceiling as plaster cracked and rolled down his sides. Sorceresses were pushed into corners and furniture splintered against the walls. Dad's bed was pushed at a forty-five-degree angle but remained unharmed. Deirdre and Fand, backs pressed against the wall, stared open-mouthed. I had to shake Mom to get her attention.

'Dragon's blood, Mom. The mermaids use it to become young again. It will reset Dad. It should save his life.'

Finally Mom said, 'How do we do it?'

'Red told me that just a couple of drops in the mouth should do the trick,' Brendan said.

Mom found a crystal glass as I drew the Sword of Duir and cut a nick into Tuan's wing. We were lucky that his head was out the window 'cause the pain caused him to cough a small fireball that, if it was in here, would have been enough to fricassee us all.

Fand placed her hands on the sides of Dad's head and incanted. The hard amber shell softened and then dripped like honey off of his face and head. She reached into his mouth and removed the gold disc. Brendan quickly held out his hand and the Fili gave it to him. Dad looked bad and he didn't look like he was breathing.

Fand placed her ear to his mouth and nose. When she came up she held her thumb and index finger just a quarter of an inch apart indicating that he was still breathing if only a tiny bit. Mom took her yew wand, dipped it into the dragon's blood and then dripped three drops into Oisin's mouth.

The effects took hold almost immediately. First it was just the colour of his lips but then the wrinkles on his face vanished like someone under the bed was pulling his skin from behind. As Tuan changed back, giving everyone in the chamber some elbow room, Fand moved quickly and incanted over the rest of Dad's shell and it dripped away. We watched as life and vigour radiated down his neck and all over his body. By the time the shell exposed his right arm there was no difference between his wrist and his runehand. Mom picked up his hand, looked at it from both sides and then gasped as Dad's fingers entwined with her own. Dad opened his eyes and then amazingly propped himself up on his elbows. He looked like he could have been my fraternal twin.

'Was I dreaming,' he said, his voice betraying no hint of illness, 'or was there just a dragon in my room?'

Chapter Forty-Two
Friends and Enemies

'Did I wake you?'

'Oh my, no,' she replied faster than I had anticipated. 'Your father did that two days ago. I would have preferred to sleep for at least another moon. I am an old woman you know.'

I had no idea what she looked like two days previously, but by this conversation new shoots and small, almost fluorescent leaves covered all of her boughs. She may be the oldest thing in The Land but to me, she looked brand new.

'I'm sorry, Mother Oak,' I said.

'Oh now, don't listen to me, with all of the excitement in Duir I probably would have scolded you if you had not awoken me. But my, my, your father was a rude awakening. I have never seen a man with such energy. It was hard to keep up with his so many thoughts.'

'Yeah, I'm sorry about him too. He's been pretty embarrassing lately.'

'From what I can tell, it seems that it is a father's responsibility to embarrass his offspring.'

'Maybe so but he is taking it to a whole new level.'

Dad had jumped out of his deathbed with the energy of a five-year-old who had just eaten an entire bag of Halloween candy. What really spooked me was that he looked my age –

some said he even looked younger. After lots of hugging and kissing and jumping and staring into mirrors – and way too much loud whooping – he insisted I tell him everything that had happened since he had been paperweight-ed. When I finally finished the whole adventure, he ordered new clothes (he had been listening to my story wrapped only in a sheet, like some Roman emperor) and horses. We eventually convinced him that travelling in the pitch dark would be a bad idea, so he ordered a crack-of-dawn departure for the Hall of Knowledge. I really could have used a lie-in and a day off but Dad had lost the meaning of 'lie-in' along with his grey hair. I tried to convince Tuan to give me a lift but he made it clear that he was not an air taxi service.

We rode to the Hazellands in record time. (There was none of that stopping and resting stuff.) We were greeted by Dahy and Queen Rhiannon. The Pookas had arrived with reinforcements only a day after I had left. Red/Moran had made peace with the Queen and had flown around long enough to make sure that Cialtie and his army had really retreated back into the Reed and Alderlands. Then he flew back to his island.

Dad, despite his newly imposed adolescence, acted mostly kingly. He visited the wounded and held meetings about future defences and the allocation of the kingdom's resources, but at other times he acted annoyingly juvenile, usually by challenging me to arm wrestles or grabbing Mom and dragging her kissing and giggling into any nearby tent.

'I am sure he will calm down soon,' Mother Oak said, reading my thoughts. 'I have never grown young, but I have certainly grown old – it must be an exciting thing for him.'

'I know. It's just a bit – freaky.'

'But enough about your father, Prince of Hazel and Oak, how went your winter?'

How went my winter? Gods, now there was a question.

'Busy,' I said with a sarcastic laugh. 'You know, the first time I came to The Land I was just trying to stay alive. This time I spent the whole time trying to keep my father alive. For once I would love to spend some time here having … fun.'

'Oh my my,' Mother Oak said and I could feel her sad smile. 'Oh, I have heard that grumble before. *Responsibility* is what you complain about. As far as I can tell, as you get older, *responsibility* is what replaces fun.'

'That sounds like a bad deal to me.'

'To me as well, but I can tell you this. The ones that do not shoulder their responsibilities may stay young but – they never stay happy.'

'So what,' I said, 'I should grow up, do my duty, and stop cracking jokes.'

'I am not here to tell you any such thing,' she said forcefully. 'Who am I to give advice? I do nothing but stick in the ground and bathe in the sunlight all day. If you are looking for advice there are countless better than me. But it seems to me that you do not need advice. You did what *needed* to be done. You saved your father from death and the Pookas from extinction. You reunited Moran and Rhiannon, and were victorious against Cialtie and Turlow's forces in the face of overwhelming odds. I have known men centuries older than you who have grown less. No one need counsel you on responsibility.'

'You know, Mother Oak, I think if I burned down a house you would probably compliment me on what nice ashes I made.'

'As long as the house was not made of oak,' she said and in my mind I felt her wooden smile.

Maybe it wasn't just hollow praise, maybe I had grown up a bit. I wasn't sure I liked it. What had been bothering me most lately was the pain of Spideog's loss. Not that it hurt too much but that it hurt too little. I knew war and death had become too commonplace for me, but even after all I had been through, I should have had tears for Spideog.

'Do not worry that you have yet to grieve for the archer,' Mother Oak said, interrupting my thoughts. 'The tears will come soon, or perhaps not for a year, but they *will* come. Grief makes its own appointments.'

I hugged her and hoped that she was right.

'Conor,' she said before I left, 'although I never understand them, I think it would be a shame if you no longer told your jokes.'

I whistled for my horse, gave Mother Oak one last hug and dropped directly into the saddle.

I rode quickly back to Castle Duir. All this talk of responsibility made me realise I had one more thing to do.

The cold thin air bounced off the warm woollen cap that Mom insisted I wear. At first she forbade me to go on this trip. Like almost everyone, she was dead set against me making this journey. When I put my foot down she actually threatened to have me locked in the dungeon. When I finally convinced her and every-one else that I would probably be OK, considering my travelling companion was a fire-breathing dragon, she insisted that at least I wear long underwear and the woollen cap. The cap I must admit was nice and toasty – the underwear itched a bit.

I patted Dragon Tuan on his green scaly back and shouted, 'You sure you're not lost?'

In reply he banked sharply to the left and bucked. I grabbed tight onto the makeshift dragon reins that the stable master and I had quickly invented earlier that day.

'OK, OK,' I shouted. 'You lose all sense of humour when you're in reptilian form.'

I looked down at the passing Tir na Nogian topography below. Winter was in its last clutches. Every once in a while brave crocuses or a tree defiantly popped a dab of colour into the dying season's grey and brown landscape. It wouldn't be long before it was shorts and tee-shirt weather. I was looking forward to that.

I breathed deeply and collected my thoughts. It was good to be alone for a moment – without Dad around. Since his re-adolescence, every time he saw me he challenged me to a sword-fight or, worse, a wrestling match. A couple of days ago, as he was pinning me with my arm twisted up my back, I asked him if we could talk without violence. I finally impressed on him that I would like it if he acted more like my father and less like an annoying younger brother. He promised he would be more fatherly and then punched me hard in the arm – this was going to take time.

Dahy vehemently didn't want me to go. The old master wasn't big on giving succour to enemies. He also thought this trip was a waste of resources. Dahy was gung ho about putting together an attack force to storm the Oracle on Mount Cas but Dad ordered him to calm down. Dahy insisted that Macha, Dad's mother, was alive, but Dad said finding an old knife didn't prove anything – no matter what some crazy old archer said. (Dad and Spideog had never seen eye to eye.) Dahy didn't like it but he accepted the orders from the teenage-looking King. In fact everyone seemed to think that a king that looked like he wasn't even old enough to drink was just fine.

Essa and I started getting on very well indeed. I took Spideog's dying advice and told her how I felt. I said if she promised not to try to kill me again that I would like to have a go at a relationship. She didn't say yes but then again she didn't say no either and we had been pretty snuggly ever since. She even said that she wanted to take a trip to see the Real World with me when we send Brendan back home.

I looked up to the heavens and said a silent thanks to Spideog. If anybody saw my eyes at that point I would have told them they were watering because of the cold air, but the truth was the tears Mother Oak had promised would someday come – came. I finally felt the loss of that strange but sweet old archer.

I took out my white flag when I saw alder trees below. Our first pass over Fearn Keep was high, out of crossbow range. As we circled lower the Brownies showed uncharacteristic restraint and didn't fire at us. Tuan banked sharply to the right and dropped altitude.

'Hey,' I shouted at him, 'I almost fell off back there.'

Tuan wasn't the best flyer in the sky but I wasn't going to tell him that. He was still a bit touchy about the ribbing he had been getting after he accidentally landed on two Leprechauns, breaking one of their arms.

We landed far enough away from the main entrance so as to not freak everybody out and so that if Tuan landed on his face, people wouldn't see. There have been smoother landings. I jumped off when we started tipping and Tuan hit the ground rolling.

When he finally righted himself, I patted his side and said, 'How are the ballet lessons going?'

He turned and gave me the dragon equivalent of a dirty look – and when you are stared at by someone who can breathe fire, that's pretty scary. Tuan stayed in his dragon form until a Brownie battalion arrived. Once they knew we were here on a diplomatic mission and not to eat ice cream and Brownies, Tuan became Tuan again.

'There's a saying that pilots use in the Real World that goes, "Any landing you walk away from is a good landing."'

Tuan delivered another dirty look – this one, less scary. 'You want to walk home?'

Tuan transformed into bodyguard bear and in his arms he carried the reason we had come. At the main gate I declared who I was to the sergeant at arms and asked for an audience with King Bwika. When he told us that we would have to wait in the guest wing, I informed him that we were to see the Brownie King now or we were going home. He came back ten minutes later and informed us that we were, 'in luck', and the King would see us immediately.

We were still made to wait a short time outside the throne room but were then escorted on a long walk between two rows of hastily dressed Brownie honour guard. They did not look kindly on me or my bear. I am sure they had all heard by now that he was one of the dragons that incinerated many of their comrades. I felt like an away-team supporter in a crowd of home-team football fans. King Bwika sat on a dais in his Alder Throne. I approached and bowed my low bow.

Before I could start my practised royal protocol speech, the King said, 'You have a cheek coming here.'

'This visit is neither diplomatic nor is it some sort of victory lap; I come on a sorry task.' I threw back the blanket that covered Tuan's burden and then carefully took the shrouded body into my own arms. 'I have come to return to you the body of your son.' I stepped up on the dais and laid Frank at his father's feet.

Bwika was speechless as I backed away down the steps.

'Did you kill him, Faerie?' came an angry voice from behind the throne that made me and the King jump. I hadn't recognised the voice but when he stepped into the light I of course knew the face.

'No, Jesse,' I replied.

'My name is Codna.'

'Of course, Prince Codna,' I said, bowing. 'I did not kill him. If I had arrived earlier and had recognised your brother I would have done all that I could to prevent it. But I was too late.'

'Who did kill him?' the King asked.

'If it is vengeance you seek, Your Highness, then you should know that the one that killed your son was also killed by him.'

'Who?'

'Spideog, Your Highness.'

'My son killed Spideog – the warrior archer?'

'He did.'

King Bwika sat higher in his seat. 'Then he did indeed die a noble death.'

'He certainly was brave,' I said, 'but I don't think I can call anything about this war *noble*. I knew your son, Your Highness, and even though we had our differences, I liked him. I am very sorry for your loss and I am here to try to make sure that no other fathers lose their sons. What can I do to persuade you to stop this aggression against Cull and Duir?'

The Brownie King sat back in his chair and said, 'Give us what is our due. Give us Castle Duir and the mines beneath.'

'You know I can't do that.'

'Your audience is ended, Son of Duir. Returning my son to me has saved your life today but in the future you will no longer be welcome in the Alderlands.'

I had also rehearsed a royal-style exit speech but since he was no longer being nice I just said, 'I want my horses.'

'What?'

'I left my horses at Fearn Point. I assume that you now have them.'

The King came as close to standing as his hulking frame would allow. 'Are you accusing …'

'The horses are in our corral,' Jesse said, 'I will take you to them.'

The King turned to his son. 'You most certainly will not.'

'Prince Conor has been good to me in the past, Father. He brought Demne back to us and now I am going to give him his horses.'

I don't think I ever really knew the definition of flabbergasted until I saw the look on King Bwika's face. Jesse turned and walked out between the honour guard gauntlet and we followed. I'm sure that all three of us expected a crossbow bolt in our backs at any time. I know I did.

Jesse didn't say anything until we reached the gates of the corral. When he turned, his face and collar were drenched with silent tears. As soon as we looked at each other he flew in to my arms and buried his face into my chest.

'I'm so sorry, Codna,' I said while stroking his hair. I know it was silly and he was probably older than me but he felt like the little brother I never had.

His crying jag didn't last long and when he finally straightened up and wiped his eyes he said, 'You can still call me Jesse if you want.'

I smiled at him and he tried hard to return it. 'I wish things were different,' he said.

'Yeah, Jesse, me too.'

Cloud, Acorn and Araf and Turlow's horses had, by this time, made it over to where we were standing. Jesse ordered the stable boy to fetch two saddles but Tuan said, 'Just one,' and then changed himself into a horse.

'You keep The Turlow's mount,' I said to Jesse. 'His name is Fluffy. He's a good horse and he deserves a better master than his last one.'

'Will I ever see you again, Conor?'

'I hope so,' I said.

'And if I do, will we still be friends?'

'Ah, Jesse, wouldn't this place be so much better if it was run by smart people like us?' I said, flashing a Fergal-esque smile. 'Others can make us enemies, Jesse, but no one can unmake us friends.' I patted him on the shoulder. 'Be safe, my Brownie friend.'

John Lenahan

As I rode away I felt worse with every step. Poor Jesse, stuck alone in that castle without his brother and with a stupid misguided father. I toyed with the idea of turning around and taking him with me but I was certain that that would only end in more tears.

Chapter Forty-Three
Get a Room

'Why don't you two get a room?'

'We have a room,' Dad said while coming up for air after kissing Mom. 'As a matter of fact, we have a whole castle.'

'Well, why didn't you do all of this *in* your room?' I asked.

'We did,' Mom replied with a smile I wasn't all that comfortable with. 'Sorry if we embarrass you, I'm sure your father will calm down in a couple of years.'

I looked over to Brendan for support, but he and Nieve were lip-locked as well.

'Oh for crying out loud,' I protested.

'Conor,' my aunt said, 'I do not know when I will see Brendan again.'

'You've decided to stay in the Real World?' I asked.

Brendan shook his head. 'I still don't know, Conor.'

'So what, you're going to go back to being a cop?'

'I was a good cop.'

'Oh yeah?' I sneered. 'The last bit of detective-ing you did was to accuse me of killing him,' I said, pointing to Dad.

'Well, I knew there was something squirrely about your family and I was right about that.'

Dad untangled himself from Mom and walked over to Brendan.

'You are forever welcome in Duir. The job of armoury master is vacant at the moment.'

'Brendan, Master-at-Arms of Duir,' Nieve said, 'I like the sound of that.'

'I do too,' Brendan replied, looking at his feet, 'but my first responsibility is to my daughter. Until I see her, I have no idea what to do.'

We all turned when we heard horse's hooves coming from the corridor. Essa and Fand appeared at the archway followed by Tuan leading Essa's horse.

'I thought you were going to be my horse on this expedition,' I said to Tuan.

'Your mother did not think that was a good idea,' the Pooka said.

'Well then come as a dragon – we can be on television and freak the whole world out.'

'I don't think so,' Tuan said but he smiled and his ears fuzzed up for a moment as if he liked the idea. 'Be careful in the Real World, my friend.'

Fand walked up to Brendan and said, 'I am very pleased to have met you, pool-eece-man. It does my heart good to see that at least one of the exiled ones is so well. May the blessings of the Fili live with you – Druid.' Brendan bowed and Fand placed her hands on his head. 'And give my regards to your tree-hugging mother.'

Brendan smiled. 'I will, Your Highness. I can't wait to tell her that I know the Queen of the Druids.'

'Are you sure you are up to this?' my mother asked Essa.

Essa nodded. She had volunteered to act as our sorceress for this journey to return Brendan to the Real World. I was going too.

'So how old are you anyway?' I asked Essa. 'Just in case you fall off your horse, will you dust-it?'

'It will not kill me, is all you need to know and Tuan has volunteered some dragon blood in case I do.'

'Thanks, Tuan. I really don't want to date a wrinkly old grey one.' Essa actually laughed at that – I was loosening that girl up.

There was one last round of smooching. Essa mounted up and asked if everyone was ready to go, but before we could reply I heard someone in the corridor screeching my name. We all looked as Graysea came bounding around the corner. She spotted me, shrieked and ran directly into my arms.

'Oh Conor, I have missed you so!'

I tried to say something but couldn't as she planted her lips onto mine. When I finally was able to remove myself from that kiss of life she said, 'Did you miss me?'

I didn't answer; I didn't get the chance. The last thing I saw was Essa's banta stick heading towards my right temple – after that everything went black.

Acknowledgements

It's hard writing a novel but these people made it a lot easier.

Yvonne Light, the uber-hyphenator.

Evo, Chris & Tee at the fabulous Podiobooks.com.

Scott and all at The Friday Project.

The amusing and inspiring commenters on the Hazel & Oak bulletin board at podiobooks (especially those that spotted my mistakes).

And everyone that emailed me at john@shadowmagic.co.uk – thank you so much. The kind words I have received about *Shadowmagic* make it a lot easier to sit down and put my fingers on the keyboard every day.

Shadowmagic

and

Shadowmagic:
Prince of Hazel and Oak

are both available as free podcasts from
iTunes and www.podiobooks.com

and are read by the author